"DEMON!"

. . .

A man clad in armor decorated intricately enough to designate him as the commander of the expedition pushed aside the rest and strode toward the shadow steed. He carried no sword, but something in his right hand emanated so much stored energy that Darkhorse grew uneasy.

"Listen to me, you fools! Talak—"

"—will not suffer your masters' reign of tyranny ever again!" The commander held up a small black cube.

"My masters? I am no thrall of Drag—"

Darkhorse got no further. The tent interior melted into a surreal, fog-shrouded picture. The shadow steed tried to argue, but his words were muted by whatever trap he had been caught in.

"Would that I could command you to tear your masters apart, but such is not within the power of this object! I can only command it to perform its original function—and send you back to whatever hellhole spawned such as you! Begone now!"

"Foooolsssss!" was all Darkhorse had time to cry. Then he was kicking uselessly at the empty space around him . . .

ALSO BY RICHARD A. KNAAK

FIREDRAKE
ICE DRAGON
WOLFHELM

PUBLISHED BY
POPULAR LIBRARY

RICHARD A. KNAAK

SHADOWSTEED

POPULAR LIBRARY

An Imprint of Warner Books, Inc.

A Time Warner Company

POPULAR LIBRARY EDITION

Popular Library ®, the fanciful P design, and Questar ® are registered trademarks
of Warner Books, Inc.

Cover illustration by Larry Elmore
Cover design by Don Puckey

Popular Library books are published by
Warner Books, Inc.
666 Fifth Avenue
New York, N.Y. 10103

 A Time Warner Company

Printed in the United States of America

First Printing: December, 1990

10 9 8 7 6 5 4 3 2 1

SHADOW STEED

I

You will raise me a demon.

The words were seared into Drayfitt's mind. The chilling
visage of his monarch haunted him still. There had never been
any doubt that the king had been serious. He was a humorless,
bitter man who had, over the last nine years since his horrible
disfigurement, become everything that he had at one time
despised. The palace reflected that change; where once it had
been a bright, proud structure, it was now a dark, seemingly
unoccupied shell.

Yet, this was Drayfitt's ruler, the man who represented what
he had sworn his loyalty to more than a century before. Thus,
the gaunt, elderly man had simply bowed and said, "Yes, King
Melicard."

Ahh, Ishmir, Ishmir, he brooded. *Why could you not have
waited until my training was complete before you flew off to die
with the other Dragon Masters? Better yet, why did you have to
train me at all?*

The chamber he occupied was one of the deepest beneath the
palace and the only one suited to the task at hand. The seal on
the door had been that of Rennek II, Melicard's great-great
grandfather and a man known for dark tastes. The chamber had
been cleaned so that Drayfitt could make his marks, etch the
lines of the barrier into the floor. The cage, a thing of
enchantment, not iron, filled much of the room. He was
uncertain as to what dimensions a demon might possess, and

much of what he did was guesswork, even with the aid of the book Quorin had located for the king. Still, Drayfitt had not outlived most of his contemporaries by leaping blindly into things.

The room was dark, save for a single torch and two dim candles, the latter necessary for reading the pages of the tome. The flickering torch raised demons of its own, dancing shadows that celebrated the coming spell with gleeful movements. Drayfitt would have preferred the place brilliantly lit, if only for his own nerves, but Melicard had decided to watch, and darkness preceded and followed the king wherever he stalked. Shifting, the ancient sorcerer could feel the strength of Melicard's presence behind him. His lord and master was obsessed—obsessed with the destruction of the Dragon Kings and their ilk.

"How much longer?" Melicard's voice throbbed with anticipation, like a child about to receive a favorite candy.

Drayfitt glanced up. He did not turn to his ruler, but rather studied the design in the floor. "I am ready to begin, your majesty."

The voice of Quorin, the king's counselor, abruptly cut through the sorcerer's thoughts like a well-honed knife. Mal Quorin was the closest thing Talak had to a prime minister since the demise of old Hazar Aran, the last man to hold the position, two years ago. The king had never replaced him, though Quorin did nearly everything the prime minister was supposed to do. Drayfitt hated the counselor; it was the short, catlike man who had first reported to Melicard that there a spellcaster in the city—and one sworn to the king. If there was any justice, any demon he succeeded in summoning up would demand the counselor as a sacrifice—if a demon could stomach such a foul morsel.

"One was beginning to wonder, Drayfitt, if your heart was in this. Your loyalty has been . . . cool."

"If you would like to take my place, Counselor Quorin, I will be happy to let you. I certainly would not want to stand in the way of someone obviously more well-versed in sorcery than myself."

Quorin would have replied, always seeking the last word, but Melicard cut him off. "Leave Drayfitt to his task. Successful results are all that matter."

The king supported Drayfitt—for now. The old man wondered how long that support would last if he failed to produce the creature his liege desired. He would be lucky to keep his head much less his quiet, simple position as Master of Appointments. Now, the latter was probably lost to Drayfitt, success or not; why waste a man of his power on a minor political post even if it was all Drayfitt had ever wanted?

Enough dreaming of things lost! he reprimanded himself. The time had come to summon the demon, if only to tweak the well-groomed mustache of Quorin.

Neither the king nor his counselor understood how simple the summoning itself actually was. There had been times when he had been tempted to tell them, to see the disbelief on their faces, but his brother had at least taught him that the secrets of sorcery were the most precious things a mage owned. To maintain his position and to counterbalance those like Quorin, Drayfitt had to build himself up as much as possible. It would have been laughable if it had not been so tragic. There was a chance that success might get them all killed. The barrier might *not* hold whatever it was, if anything, he summoned.

Raising one hand in a theatrical manner he had practiced long and hard to perfect, Drayfitt touched the fields of power with his mind's eye.

The summoning was simplicity itself; surviving the encounter with whatever happened to be snared was another matter.

"Drazeree's ghost!" Quorin blurted in growing fear.

Drayfitt would have smiled, had he heard the outburst, but his mind was on the link he had created. There was only the link—no chamber, no king, not even his own body. He was invisible—no—formless. It was an experience that he had never before achieved and the wonder of it almost proved fatal, for in maintaining his link with the spell, he nearly broke the one binding him to his mortal form. When the sorcerer realized his error, he immediately corrected it. A lesson learned, Drayfitt realized . . . almost too late.

Before him, the stream of light that was the mental representation of his bond disappeared into a gleaming tear in reality. He knew that the tear was visible to the king and Counselor Quorin, a sign of success for them to mull over while he moved up. If failure greeted him at any point onward, he hoped that Melicard would realize that he had tried his best, that he had proved his loyalty.

A cold presence with a feel of great age grazed the outer boundaries of his seeking mind. Ancient was not a satisfactory description for such a creature. A desire to abandon the summoning washed over Drayfitt, but he fought it, understanding that it was a ploy by the creature he had snared. The analogy of a fisherman who has caught the grandfather of all sea monsters did not escape him. What he had snared was powerful—and very reluctant to the notion of being forcibly brought to Drayfitt's world. It was ready to fight him with all weapons available to it.

Some would have fought the demon here, in this place with no name, but Drayfitt knew that he could only bind his catch if he battled it from the physical as well as the spiritual planes. The earth, whose existence was interwoven with both the fields of power and his own life, was his anchor.

As he retreated toward his body, the sorcerer was amazed at the ease with which he drew the demon after him. The struggle was far less than he expected, almost as if the demon had some strong bond of its own with his world, a bond it could not deny. That a thing spawned out *there* could have any tie with the mortal plane disturbed him. The thought of a trap occurred to him, but it was a brief notion. Such a trap was too daring; the closer they moved back to Drayfitt's domain, the more difficult it would be for the demon to free itself.

The sorcerer felt the creature's growing frustration. It *was* fighting him—constantly—but like someone forced to do battle on a number of fronts. Had they met on equal terms, both with their respective abilities intact, the elderly sorcerer knew that he would have been no more than a breath to his adversary. Here, the battle was in Drayfitt's favor.

The return seemed endless, far longer than when he had departed his body. As he finally neared his goal, he was struck by a great wave of panic emanating from the demon. The link stretched as he had not known it could and, for a moment, it felt as if part of the demon had *broken away*.

Nonetheless, his prey was with him. Body and mind began to meld. Other things—sounds, pressures, odors—demanded a measure of his attention.

"He's *stirring* again!"

"You see, Quorin? I told you he had not failed. Drayfitt is loyal to me."

"Forgive me, my liege. Three hours we've stood here, waiting. You said he'd dare not die and, as usual, you were correct."

The voices echoed from a vast distance, as if the spellcaster were hearing them through a long, hollow tube ... yet, both men surely stood nearby. Drayfitt allowed his senses time to recover and then, still facing the magical cage he had created, opened his eyes.

At first glance he was disappointed. The rip in the middle of empty space still remained and nothing stood within the confines of the barrier. Around him, the shadows still danced merrily, among them the two distended forms of his companions. The shadows of the king and the counselor loomed over his head while his own seemed to crawl across the floor and up a good piece of the far wall. Most of the pattern that he had drawn on the floor was smothered in darkness as well.

"Well?" Quorin asked testily.

The link still remained, but it no longer extended beyond the tear, instead twisting uselessly back into the shadowy regions within the boundaries of the magical cage. The rip was already closing. Drayfitt, confused, stared at the empty scene for several seconds. He *had* succeeded—at least all indications pointed to that. Why, then, did he have *nothing* to show for his efforts?

It was then he noticed the difference between the flickering dancers on the walls and the stillness of the inky darkness within the barrier. The shadows did not move when they should and even appeared to have depth. Drayfitt had the unnerving sensation that to stare too long was to fall into those shadows—and never stop falling.

"Drayfitt?" The king's confidence was turning to uncertainty tinged with burgeoning anger. He had not yet noticed the difference in the shadows.

The gaunt sorcerer slowly rose, a wave of his hand indicating that silence was needed. With one negligible thought, he broke the link. If he was mistaken and there was no demon, Melicard would soon have his hide.

Stepping nearer—though not so near that he was in danger of accidently crossing the barrier—Drayfitt examined the magical cage with a thoroughness that left the king and counselor fidgeting. When Drayfitt saw the shadows twist away, he knew he had succeeded.

There *was* something in his trap.

"Do not try to play me for a fool," he whispered defiantly. "I know you are there. Show yourself—but beware of trying any tricks! This cage has *surprises* designed just for your kind, demon!''

''What's that you're doing?'' Quorin demanded, starting to step forward. It was clear he still assumed that Drayfitt had failed and that the sorcerer was now stalling in the hopes of saving his neck.

''*Stay where you are!*'' Drayfitt commanded without looking.

The counselor froze, stunned by the sheer intensity of the spellcaster's tone.

Turning his attention back to the barrier, the elderly man repeated his earlier command, this time for the other two to hear. ''I said show yourself! You will obey!''

He waved a hand in the air, using it to guide the lines of power to the results he wanted. He was not disappointed.

It *howled*! The noise was so horrifying that Drayfitt's concentration all but broke. Behind him, Quorin swore and stumbled back. Whether Melicard was also shaken, the sorcerer could not say. Even the king had his limits. As the ringing in his ears died down, Drayfitt wondered if everyone in the palace—everyone in *Talak*—had hear the demon's howl of pain. He almost regretted what he had done . . . but he had to show the creature who was master. So it had always been written.

At first, he did not notice the darkness draw inward, thicken even, if such a thing was possible. Only when the first limbs became recognizable—and then the fact that there were *four* of them, all legs—did he fully appreciate his success. The demon had finally, completely, bowed to his will.

The three men stood mesmerized by the transformation occurring before them. Forgetting their uncertainty, the king and counselor joined Drayfitt near the outer edge of the barrier and watched as a trunk joined the legs, and a long, thick neck stretched forth from one end, while a sleek, black tail sprouted from the other.

A steed! Some sort of ghostly steed! The head coalesced into a distinct shape, and Drayfitt amended his opinion. It was more like the *shadow* of some great horse. The body and limbs were distended, changing as the demon moved, and the torso . . . The spellcaster had the uneasy feeling that if he stared too long he would fall *into* the demon and keep falling forever and ever. Anxious to rid himself of the idea, he turned his head, only to find the face of the king.

Unaware of the sorcerer's nervous gaze, the disfigured king giggled at the sight of his new prize. "You have done me a *wondrous* service, Drayfitt! This is all I asked for and more! I have my demon!"

With a smooth, swift motion, the huge head of the dark steed turned to face the trio. For the first time, the ice-blue eyes became noticeable. Drayfitt returned his gaze to his prisoner. He shivered, but not nearly so much as he did when the demon arrogantly shouted, "You mortal fools! You *children!* How *dare* you pull me back into this world! Don't you realize the havoc you've brought forth?"

Drayfitt heard a sharp intake of breath from beside him and knew immediately that Melicard was mere moments from one of his fits of rage. Not wanting the king to do something foolish—something that might release the demon in the process— the spellcaster shouted back, "Silence, monster! You have no rights here! By the spells I have performed, you are my servant and will do my bidding!"

The black horse roared with mocking laughter. "I am not quite the demon you originally sought, little mortal! I am more and I am less! You caught me because my link to this world is stronger than that of any creature of the Void!" The steed's head pressed against the unseen walls of his cage, eyes seeking to burn through Drayfitt's own. "I am the one called *Darkhorse*, mage! Think hard, for it is a name you surely must know!"

"What is he talking about?" Quorin dared to mutter. He had one hand pressed against his chest, as if his heart were seeking escape.

In the dim torchlight, neither of his companions could see Drayfitt's face grow ash white. He knew of Darkhorse and suspected the king did as well. There were legends, some only a decade old, about the demon steed, a creature whose former companions included the warlock Cabe Bedlam, the legendary Gryphon, and, most frightening of all, the enigmatic, cursed immortal who called himself Shade.

"*Darkhorse!*" the sorcerer finally succeeded in uttering, as a whisper.

Darkhorse reared high, seemingly ready to burst through the ceiling. In a mixture of regret and anger, the demon steed retorted, "Aye! Darkhorse! Exiled by choice to the Void in the hopes of saving this mortal plane from the horror of a friend who is also my worst enemy! This world's worst nightmare!"

"Silence him, Drayfitt! I want no more of this babbling!"
Melicard's voice had a dangerous edge to it that the spellcaster
had come to recognize. He feared it almost as much as he
feared what now struggled within the barrier.

"Babbling? If only it were so! Darkhorse shifted so that it
was now the king who faced his inhuman glare. "Don't you
listen? Can't you understand? In summoning me back, you've
pulled him along, for I was *his* prison! Now he roams free to
do whatever ill he so desires!"

"Who?" Drayfitt dared to ask, despite the growing rage
of his liege at the lack of obedience. "Who is it that I have
accidently released?" It was the thing he had feared all during
the preparations, that he would accidently loose some demon
on the Dragonrealm.

Darkhorse turned his massive head back to the sorcerer and,
oddly, there was a sadness inherent in both the chilling eyes
and the unholy stentorian voice. "The most tragic being I have
ever known! A friend who would give his life and a fiend who
would take yours without a second's care! A demon and a hero,
yet both are the same man!" The spectral horse hesitated and
quietly concluded, "*The warlock Shade!*"

II

So different from Gordag-Ai. So big!

Erini Suun-Ai peered through the curtain of her coach
window, ignoring the worried looks of her two ladies-in-
waiting. A light wind sent her long, blond tresses fluttering.
The breeze was pleasantly cool against her pale, soft skin and
she leaned into it, directing the delicate, perfect features of her
oval face so that the wind stroked every inch. Her dress, wide,
colorful, and flowing, made it impossible to sit directly next to
the window, and Erini would have preferred to take it off,
hating it the way it ballooned her slim figure.

Her ladies-in-waiting whispered to one another, making disparaging remarks. They did not care to see their new home, the huge, overwhelming city-state of Talak. Only duty to their mistress made them come. A princess, especially one destined to be a queen, did not travel alone. The driver and the cavalry unit escorting her did not count; they were men. A woman of substance travelled with companions or, at the very least, servants. Such was the way of things in Gordag-Ai, in the lands once ruled by the Bronze Dragon.

Erini's mind was unconcerned with things of her former homeland. Talak, with its massive ziggurats and countless proud banners flying in the wind, was her new home, her kingdom. Here, after a suitable courtship, she would marry King Melicard I and assume her duties as wife and co-monarch. The future held infinite possibilities and Erini wondered which ones awaited her. Not all of them would be pleasant.

The coach hit a bump, sending the princess back against her seat, her companions squealing with ladylike distaste at the rough road. Erini grimaced at their actions. They represented her father, who had made the marriage pact with the late, unfortunate King Rennek IV almost eighteen years ago. Melicard had been a young boy just growing into manhood and she a newborn babe. Erini had met Melicard only once, when she had been perhaps five, so she doubted his impression of her had been very favorable.

What made all three of them nervous were the rumors that floated about the Dragonrealm as to the nature of Melicard. There were those who called him a fanatical tyrant, though none of his own people ever talked that way. There were rumors that he trafficked with necromancers, and that he was a cold, lifeless master. Most widespread of all were the horrible tales of his appearance.

"He has only one true arm," Galea, the stouter of the two companions, had whispered at one point. "They say that he cut it off himself, so as to wear that elfwood one he now sports."

"He has a lust for the worst aspects of sorcery," Magda, plain but domineering, uttered sagely at another time. "A demon it was that is said to have stolen his face so that the king must always hide in shadow!"

After such horrible statements as these, the two ladies would eye one another with their perfectly matching *Poor Princess Erini!* expressions. At times, they somehow succeeded in looking like twins.

The princess did not know how to take the rumors. She knew it was true that Melicard sported an arm carved of rare elfwood, a magical wood, but not why. Erini also knew that Melicard had suffered some catastrophe almost a decade before that had left him bereft of that original arm and disfigured as well. Even magical healing had its limits at times, and something involved with the incident made it impossible to repair the damage to any great extent. Erini knew she was marrying a crippled and possibly horrifying man, but her brief memories of gazing up fondly at the tall, handsome boy had combined with her sense of duty to her parents to form a determination matched by few.

That did not mean she did not wonder—and worry.

Returning her gaze to the spectacle outside, she studied the great walls. They were gigantic, though the arrogant ziggurats within thrust higher. Against any normal invader, these walls would be unbreachable. Talak, however, had always been in the shadow of the Tyber Mountains, lair of the true master of the city, the late and unlamented Gold Dragon, Emperor of the Dragon Kings. Drakes had little problem with walls, whether in their birthforms or the humanoid ones they wore more often.

Things have altered so much. She had, as a child, understood that, as queen, she would rule beside Melicard but that, at any time, the Gold Dragon might come and make demands of the city. Now, the Dragon Kings were in a disarray; with no heir to take the place of the Dragon Emperor—though there were rumors about something in the Dagora Forest far to the south—Talak was, for the first time, independent.

An army of majestic trumpets sounded, giving Erini a start. The coach made no move to slow, which meant the gates had been opened and they would proceed straight through. The sides of the road began to fill with the locals, the farmers and villagers, some clad in their holiday best, others looking as if they had just come from the fields. They were cheering, but she expected that. Melicard's advisors would have arranged such a showing. Yet, Erini was somewhat skilled at reading faces and emotions, and in the dirty, worn features of the people cheering her she did see honest hope, honest acceptance. They *wanted* a queen, welcomed the change.

The rumors about Melicard whispered mockingly in the back of her mind. She forced herself to ignore them and waved to the people.

At that moment, the coach passed through the gates of Talak and the rumors were once again buried as Erini devoured the wonders of the inner city with her eyes.

This was the market district. Bright, clashing tents and wagons competed with decorated buildings, many of them tiny, multileveled ziggurats, exact copies of the titans looming over all else. The more permanent structures appeared to be inns and taverns, a cunning move to snare the unwary traveler who might, merely because it was so convenient, end up buying a few extra things from the bazaar. Even *more* banners flew within the walls, most bearing the patriotic symbol of Talak these past nine years: a sword crossing a stylized drake head. Melicard's warning to the remaining drake clans, including the Silver Dragon's, to whose domain the city was now geographically annexed.

Galea and Madga were oohing and aahing over everything, having finally given in to growing curiosity and forgetting that they did not want to be here. Erini smiled slightly at that and returned her attention to her new kingdom.

Clothing styles differed little here, she noted abstractly, though they tended to be even brighter, yet more comfortable in appearance than the bedsheet she was wearing. There was also a propensity toward military uniforms, a confirmation of one rumor that Melicard was still expanding his army. A troop of footsoldiers saluted smartly as she passed, as alike as a row of eggs—with shells of iron. The precision pleased her, though she hoped that there would be no need for all this training. *The best armies are those that never have to fight,* her father had once said.

The coach continued on its way through the city. The market district gave way to more stately structures, obviously the homes of an upper class, either merchants or low-level functionaries. There was a market here as well, but this district was subdued in comparison to that of the more common folk. Erini found this section pleasant to view, but rather lacking in true life. Here, the shadowy masks of politics were first worn. She knew that from this point on reality would be slightly askew. Without hardly being aware of it, her posture stiffened and her smile grew empty. It was time to play the part she had been trained for, even though she had not yet met her betrothed. For the lowest courtiers on up, the princess had to wear a mask of strength. Their loyalty to her depended on their belief in her power.

Power. Her fingers twitched, but she forced them still. In the excitement and then the uneasiness of finally arriving in Talak, she had almost dropped her guard. Erini glanced at her ladies. Magda and Galea were staring at the palace, awed by what was the greatest edifice in the city, and had not noticed the involuntary movements. The princess took a deep breath and tried to steady herself. She dared not trust them with her problem.

What would she do about Melicard, though?

By the time the coach reached the outskirts of the royal palace, she felt she was ready. The turbulence of her tired mind had been forced down again. Now, her only concern was making the proper impression when Melicard came to meet her at the bottom of the palace steps, as was custom.

"Don't these people know anything about protocol?" Magda sniffed imperilously. "The royal steps are all but bare of the members of the court. The entire aristocracy should be here to meet their new queen."

Erini, who had been straightening her clothing out of nervousness, looked up. Pulling aside the curtain of her window, the princess saw what, in her anxiety, she had not noticed before. It was true; there were no more than a handful of people awaiting her arrival and even at a distance the princess could see that none of them matched Melicard's description in the slightest.

The coachman reined the horses to a halt, and one of Erini's footmen jumped down and opened the door for her. As the princess descended, she caught sight of a short, graceful man with odd eyes and stylish mustache who reminded her of nothing less than a pet panther her mother had once bought from a merchant of Zuu. Erini felt an almost instant dislike for the newcomer despite the toothy smile he gave her. This could only be Melicard's counselor, Mal Quorin, a man obviously ambitious. What was *he* doing here instead of Melicard?

"Your majesty." Quorin took the tiny hand that the princess forced herself to thrust out and kissed it in a manner that suggested he was tasting her as a predator might taste its prey before devouring it.

She gave him her most courteous smile and withdrew her hand as soon as he released it. *You will not make a puppet out of me, grimalkin.* His nostrils flared momentarily, but he remained outwardly pleasant.

"Is my Melicard ill? I had hoped he would be here to greet me." She fought hard to keep emotion of any sort out of her words.

Quorin straightened his jacket. His pompous, gray military outfit made him look like a parody of some great general and Erini hoped he was not actually commander of the king's armies. "His majesty begs your forgiveness, princess, and asks that you indulge him in this. I trust you were informed as to his appearance."

"Surely my betrothed would not hide from me?"

The counselor gave her the ghost of a smile. "Until word arrived that you had reached the age of consent set down by your father, Melicard had completely forgotten about the pact. Please don't take it as any offense, lady, but you will find he is still trying to cope with it. His physical . . . detriments . . . only add to the difficulty. He tries to see as few people as possible, you understand."

"I understand far better than you think, counselor. You will take me to King Melicard now. I will not shun him because of his past misfortune. We have been paired almost since my birth; his life, his existence, is my tantamount concern."

Quorin bowed. "Then, if you will follow me, I will escort you to him. The two of you will have a private audience . . . fitting, I should think, for the beginning of your courtship."

Erini noted the hint of sarcasm but said nothing. Mal Quorin summoned an aide who was to assist the princess's people with settling down. Her ladies-in-waiting prepared to follow her but she ordered them to go with the others.

"This is not proper," Magda entoned. "One of us should be with you."

"I think I will be safe in the palace of my husband-to-be, Magda." Erini gave the counselor a pointed glance. "Especially with Counselor Quorin as company."

"Your parents ordered—"

"Their authority ended when we entered Talak. Captain!" The cavalry officer rode up to her and saluted. She could not recall his name, but knew he was inherently obedient to her from past experience. "Please help escort my companions to our rooms. I will also want to see you before you return to Gordag-Ai."

The captain, a thin, middle-aged man with narrow eyes and a hungry look, cleared his throat. "Yes . . . your highness."

Erini pondered briefly his hesitation but knew now was not the time to ask about it. She turned back to Quorin, who was waiting with slight impatience. "Lead on."

Offering his hand, the counselor led her up the long set of steps into the towering palace. As they walked, Quorin pointed out this object and that, relating their histories like a hired tour guide to Erini, who pretended to listen for the sake of appearance. Several aides and minor functionaries fell in behind them, as did a silent honor guard. All very out of place, but the princess had been warned that things had taken a strange turn in the years of Melicard's rule. So far, only Mal Quorin and the king's absence disturbed her.

The palace was spacious to say the least, but much of it had an unused look, as if only a few people actually lived or worked within its walls. It was true that Melicard was the last of his line now, but most rulers still surrounded themselves with a gaggle of fawning courtiers and endless numbers of servants. Melicard, it seemed, maintained only what was necessary.

Has he secluded himself that much? the princess worried. His state of mind concerned her far more than whatever scars he bore physically. On that rested the fate of his kingdom.

"Your majesty?"

Counselor Quorin was studying her curiously and Erini realized they had finally come to a stop at a massive set of doors. Two fearsome guards, hooded, kept a grim watch, armed with axes that stood taller than she did. Erini wondered if they were human.

"I shall be leaving you alone now, Princess Erini. I'm certain you and the king will want your privacy."

She almost wanted him to stay. Now that the princess stood within mere seconds of meeting her betrothed, the potential ramifications of her reaction to Melicard's features struck her dumb. Would hate or pity be the only bond tying the two of them together? She prayed it would not be, yet . . .

Quorin snapped his fingers. The two gargantuan sentinels stepped aside and the massive doors slowly swung inward. Within the chamber was only darkness. Not even a single candle glimmered in invitation.

The counselor turned back to her and his catlike face wore a matching feline smile. "He awaits within, your majesty. You have only to enter."

Those words, coming from him, strengthened Erini as nothing else could have. With a regal nod of her head to Counselor Quorin and the two guards, she walked calmly into the pitch-black room.

Her eyes sought vainly to compensate for the utter lack of light, as the doors slowly closed behind her. Erini fought hard not to turn back to the comfort of the light. She was a princess of Gordag-Ai and soon would be queen of Talak. It would be a disgrace to her ancestors and her future subjects if she showed her growing fear.

Not until the doors had closed completely did she hear the breathing of another within the chamber. Heavy footsteps echoed as somebody slowly walked toward her. Erini's heart pounded and her breathing quickened. She heard the other fiddle with something and then a single match burst into brilliant life, blinding her briefly.

"Forgive me," a deep, smooth voice whispered. "I sometimes grow so accustomed to the shadows that I forget how lost others can be. I shall light us some candles."

Erini's eyes adjusted as the burning match lit a candle sitting on a hitherto unseen table. The match died before she could study the hand that held it, but the one that reached for the candlestick, the left hand, gave her a start. It was silver and moved like the hand of a puppet. Neither it nor the arm it was attached to was made of flesh, but rather some other, stiffer substance that played at life.

Elfwood. The tale was *true*!

Then, the hand was forgotten as the candle was lifted into the air and Princess Erini caught her first glimpse of the man she was to marry.

The gasp that escaped her echoed harshly in the dark chamber.

The innkeeper of the Huntsman Tavern was a bear of a man named Cyrus who had once had the misfortune of owning a similar establishment called the Wyvern's Head some years ago. The hordes of the drake Lord Toma had ravaged it with the rest of the countryside, concentrating especially on the grand city of Mito Pica, where the powerful warlock Cabe Bedlam had been brought up in secret. Toma had not expected to find Bedlam there and was making the region an example to any who would dare protect, even unknowingly, a potential enemy of the Dragon Kings. Cyrus, along with many other survivors, had taken what he could salvage and made his way to Talak. The people of Mito Pica were welcome in Talak, for Melicard shared their hatred for the drakes. For a brief time, Cyrus had even been one of the raiders the king had supplied in secret, raiders who harassed and killed drakes with the help of old magic. The innkeeper found, however, that he missed his former calling. A good thing, too. It was the raid on the home of Bedlam and his bride that had led to the king's maiming. The objects of the raid, the late Dragon Emperor's hatchlings, had completely escaped Melicard's grasp.

In all that time and the time that passed after, Cyrus had never told a soul that the warlock Bedlam had once been a serving man in his inn. The beginning of the end of his first inn was etched in his mind. It had started with a vague image. The image of a cloaked and hooded man sitting in the shadows, waiting silently for service . . .

Like the man who sat in the corner booth now.

Had his hair not gone gray long ago, Cyrus felt it would have done so now. He looked around quickly, but no one seemed to notice anything out of the ordinary and there was not a blessed soul to wait on the mysterious personage.

Just when I've set me roots down. Wringing his hands, the innkeeper made his way through the crowds and over to the dark table. He squinted, wondering why it was so dark even though there were candles nearby. It was as if the shadows had come with the stranger.

"What can I get ya?" *Make it something quick and easy!* he begged silently. *Then leave, by Hirack, while I've still got a place!*

The left hand, gloved, emerged from the enveloping cloak. A single coin clattered against the wooden table. "An ale. No food."

"Right away!" Thanking Hirack, a minor god of merchants, Cyrus retrieved the coin and hustled back to the counter, where he swiftly overfilled a mug. He would give the warlock the ale, the fellow would drink it, and the innkeeper would bid him a fond farewell. In his haste, Cyrus bumped several customers and spilled ale on a few more, but he did not notice. Nothing mattered but to serve his unwanted guest and get as far away as possible.

"Here ya go!" He slammed the ale down right in front of the figure and made to leave, but the hand, with astonishing speed and bone-crushing strength, caught his own and trapped him there.

"Sit down a moment." The slight amusement in the hooded one's tone made Cyrus go pale. He sat down with a heavy thud. The warlock released his hand, almost as if daring the innkeeper to run away.

"What city is this?"

It was an odd question, seeing as how a spellcaster of all people should know such a simple thing. Despite that thought, however, Cyrus could not stop himself from responding immediately. "Talak."

"Hmmm. I noticed a commotion earlier. What was the cause?"

Cyrus blinked in a mixture of fear and shock as his mouth formed the answers without his aid. "King Melicard's betrothed, the Princess Erini of Gordag-Ai, arrived only today."

For the first time, the fixture in the dusky hood reacted. Cyrus was certain it was confusion despite being unable to make out the warlock's features. He had been trying to see the man's face for several seconds, but there was something wrong with his eyes, for the other's visage never seemed in focus.

" 'King Melicard'? What's happened to Rennek IV?"

"Rennek died some time back. He spent the last part of his life mad as a sprite." *Where had this man been that he didn't know something common knowledge to everyone else?*

"I've been far, much too far away, innkeeper."

Cyrus shook as it hit him that he had not asked the question out loud.

The warlock reached over and touched Cyrus on the forehead with one gloved finger of his right hand. "There are people of importance that I would know more about. You know their names. Tell me and I will let you return to your business."

It was impossible *not* to tell the hooded figure what he knew. The names that flashed through Cyrus's unwilling mind frightened him, so powerful and deadly the bearer of each one was. His mouth babbled tale after tale about each, mostly from things he had heard from patrons, much of it forgotten until now.

Finally, it ended. Cyrus fearfully felt himself black out.

* * *

The warlock watched with little interest as the innkeeper, his mind fogged, rose from the table and returned to his duties. The mortal would remember nothing. No one would recall that he had been here. He could even stay long enough to finish the ale, something he had not had in ten years. The long lapse made the drink even sweeter.

Ten years, Shade thought as he stared into his mug. *Only ten years have passed. I would've thought it longer.*

Memories of endless struggling in the nothingness that had been his prison, the prison that was a part of his enemy and his friend, flashed through his mind. He had thought he would never touch the earth again.

Ten years. He took another sip of ale and could not help but smile again at circumstances. *A small price to pay, actually, for what I've gained. A very small price to pay.*

Shade put a hand to his head as a sharp pain lanced through his mind. It was as short-lived as the others he had experienced since his return, and he ignored it once it had passed. The warlock took another sip. Nothing would mar his moment of triumph, especially an insignificant little pain.

III

The single torch, left by the mortals, had long ago burned itself out, but Darkhorse had no need of such things, anyway. He did not even notice when the light sputtered and died, so deeply was his mind buried in a mire of concerns, fears, and angers—none of which he had come to terms with yet. What distressed him most was that Shade roamed the Dragonrealm untouched, free to spread his madness across an unsuspecting and, in some ways, uncaring land.

And here I lay, helpless as a newborn, trapped by a mortal fool who shouldn't have the knowledge to do what he's done! Darkhorse laughed low, a mocking laugh aimed at himself.

How he continually underestimated human ingenuity—and stupidity.

His pleas of freedom fell on deaf ears and mad minds. Nothing mattered more to Melicard than his quest to rid the realms of the drake clans, whether those drakes were enemies or not. That Shade had the potential to bring the lands down upon them all—human, drake, elf, and the rest—meant nothing to the disfigured monarch.

"What threat is a warlock compared to the bloody fury of the Dragon Kings?" Melicard had asked.

"Have you forgotten Azran Bedlam so soon?" Darkhorse had bellowed. "With his unholy blade, the Nameless, he slew a legion of drakes, including the Red Dragon himself!"

The king had smiled coldly at that. "For that, he had my admiration and thanks."

"They might've easily been humans, mortal! Azran was no less dangerous to his own kind!"

"The creature you call Shade has existed for as long as recorded memory, yet the world remains. If you wish, you may deal with him *after* you have served me. That seems fair."

It was futile to try and explain that always there had been someone to keep Shade in check and that *someone* had more often than not been Darkhorse. Other spellcasters had fought and beaten the warlock, true, but always the shadow steed had been, at the very least, in the background. Now, he was helpless.

"Well, demon?"

In pent-up anger, Darkhorse had reared and kicked at the unbreakable, invisible wall, screaming, "Madman! Can you not hear me? Does your mind refuse to understand reality? Your damnable little obsession will never be fulfilled, and while you muster your fanatics Shade will bring both drake and human down! I know this!"

At that point, King Melicard had turned to the sorcerer beside him and said, "Teach him."

For his refusal to obey, Darkhorse had suffered. The old sorcerer Drayfitt had surprised him again, intertwining a number of painful subspells into the structure of the magical cage. The pain had not stopped until the jet-black stallion had been no more than a mass of shadow huddled on the floor. Finally, Melicard had simply turned and departed, pausing at the doorway only long enough to give some instructions to the spellcaster. With the king had gone the devious one, the mortal who was known as Counselor Quorin.

Alone with the elderly sorcerer, Darkhorse had pleaded his cause once more. Fruitlessly. Drayfitt was one of those men who embodied the worst and best trait of his race: blind loyalty.

And so here I remain, the spectral horse snorted in frustration. *Here I remain.*

"I once suffered a fate similar to the one facing you now," a familiar voice mocked. "Trapped with seemingly no way out. I think you can imagine how I felt."

Darkhorse rapidly drew himself together, all his power preparing for the worst.

The torch was suddenly ablaze again, but its flame was a deep red that bespoke of blood. Amidst the crimson shadows, a cloaked and hooded figure detached itself.

"Shade . . . or Madrac . . ." Darkhorse rumbled. "Come to mock only when you know for certain your hide is safe from harm."

The warlock bowed like a minstrel after a successful command performance. "Call me Madrac, if you will—or any other name, for that matter. I don't care. I've come to tell you something. I sat quietly drinking in a tavern, absorbing life itself for once. I remember, you see. I remember everything from every life. I recall the fatal day, the agony of being torn apart and restored to existence again and again and again! I recall more than I could ever recount to you!"

As long as he had known the human, Darkhorse had known a man condemned. Forever resurrected after each death, whether his body was whole or not, Shade was cursed to live lives alternately devoted to the dark and light sides of his nature. Each was only a shadow of the original spellcaster, however. Memories were so incomplete as to sometimes be nonexistent. Abilities altered. In desperation to be whole, each new personality even took on a secondary name of its own, such as Madrac, hoping that somehow *he* would be the final, immortal Shade. Now, after millennia, something had changed to make that possible. Understanding this, hope briefly spurred Darkhorse. "Then your curse is lifted; you can live in peace."

Shade chuckled bitterly and stepped forward. Raising his hood, he let the shadow steed stare into his face, or rather, the blurry mask that passed for it. "*Not yet*, my dear friend, not yet, but—Madrac is fading and I cannot be certain what sort of persona will replace him. A different one from those past, that much is evident. I felt the need to speak to you, though, to tell you, but . . .''

"If you can free me, I will do what I can for you, Shade."

"Free you? Don't be *absurd*! I rather enjoy the irony of this!''

The tone of the warlock's voice stirred the eternal's misgivings far more than the actual words did. *Has the curse given way to something darker, something much more sinister?* Darkhorse wondered. Shade's personality seemed to be swinging back and forth unpredictably. If the warlock had not been mad before, he soon would be under the pressure of this new torture.

Putting a hand to his forehead as if trying to relieve pain, Shade continued, "I also came to tell you this: I know where my mistake was made—where my spell went awry. I know why the 'immortality' I *did* receive turned out to be a never-ending agony. That can be rectified—this time.''

He took a step closer to the magical cage. "You—you can do nothing to deter me. Not while you are trapped here. The spellcaster responsible for your pleasant little domain has touched upon Vraad sorcery to create the cage. Do you know what *that* means?''

Darkhorse did not respond at first, stunned as he was by the warlock's words, especially the last. "I know of Vraad sorcery. It no longer exists in this reality! The Vraad only live on in the seeds of their descendents; their magic has given way to the magic of this world!''

Shade inclined his head in a brief nod. "As you wish. Test the spell yourself—oh''—the spellcaster may have smiled; it was difficult for anyone other than him to know for certain—"that's right. You can't. You're inside, of course, and the patterns are outside, surrounding the barrier.''

"Why did you come here, Shade? Merely to talk?''

"I came against my better judgment—but—I felt an overwhelming urge. Call it a whim.''

"Call it conscience.'' Darkhorse retorted quietly.

"Conscience? I no longer have such a wasteful thing!'' The hooded warlock stepped back, growing more indistinct with each step. There was always something not quite right, not quite normal, about Shade's magic, but Darkhorse could not say what.

"Enjoy your vast domain while you can, *friend*. When you

see me next, if you ever do, I will at last be master of my fate—and so much more.''

"Shade—'' It was too late; the warlock dwindled away into nothing. The torch died the moment he was gone, plunging Darkhorse into the blackness again. It was the least of his concerns, though. The brief, puzzling visitation by him who was both enemy and friend interested him much, much more.

To say that Shade's return to him was contradictory to what the spellcaster should have done was putting it so mildly that Darkhorse had to laugh. Shade did nothing without reason, even if Shade might not know the reason himself. To simply come to mock Darkhorse was not enough; it was not the warlock's way in any of his countless lives, at least, the ones that the shadow steed knew about.

How old are you really? It was a question he had asked Shade time and again and it blossomed unbidden now, but there was no answer. The spellcaster could never recall. He only remembered a few vague things; that he, an ambitious sorcerer, had tried to gain mastery over powers that were, at the time, known simply as good and evil, dark and light. Perhaps colored by such primitive perceptions, Shade had made some fatal error in the final steps of his master spell. The powers were not his to command; he was theirs to play with. Perhaps the enchantment had even succeeded, but not the way the spellcaster had supposed. That still did not answer the question that always bothered the jet-black stallion. *How old was Shade before we first encountered one another? Old enough to recall the Vraad? Old enough to—be one?*

The thought was so insane, he cast it from his mind. Generations upon generations of Dragon Kings had come and gone since the brief, fiery appearance of the Vraad in this world. Humans were their descendants, yes, but nothing more.

All plans of immortality eventually fail. Even for the Vraad they did.

Darkhorse knew he was wandering away from the subject. He returned to the reason behind Shade's brief and mysterious visit. If not to mock his helplessness, then what explanation was there for the warlock's return? A warning? Perhaps. Possibly that and more. Darkhorse laughed low as another choice suggested itself. *Could it be . . . ?*

His thoughts were interrupted by the sound of a key unlocking the chamber door. *This is a busy day! I always thought prison was a lonely place!*

The door swung open with a protesting squeal and torchlight flooded into the room. A guard stepped in and, his eyes focused on any spot *other* than the captive, lit the wall torch. As the human departed hastily, a second figure, tall and familiar, entered the chamber in a much more sedate manner. The gaunt, ancient form waited quietly while another guard, as anxious as the first to be gone, placed a stool midway between the door and the edge of the barrier.

When they were finally alone, Drayfitt spoke. His eyes drifted to a spot to the right of Darkhorse. He seemed a bit preoccupied, as if he could sense that someone else had been in the room. "So...demon. Have you reconsidered what my liege has requested of you?"

The shadow steed shifted to his left, trying without success to meet the gaze of the sorcerer. "*That* was a request? Do as he commands—without question—and he *may* free me some day to chase after Shade?"

"He is king and must be obeyed."

"You are well housebroken, spelltosser."

Drayfitt flinched, but he did not shift his gaze. It was apparent he knew what might happen if his eyes locked onto Darkhorse's. "I swore an oath long ago to protect this city. It is my home. Melicard is my lord and master."

"As I said, 'well housebroken'! Every king should have such a loyal pup for a sorcerer!"

"Would that I had never needed to make use of these powers!" Drayfitt's gaze turned upward, toward some memory. Darkhorse cursed silently.

"Why, then, did you?"

"The king needed a sorcerer. Counselor Quorin sought me out, knowing from his spies that I had held one minor political post or another for more than a century, something beyond the lifespan of a normal human, of course. Always before I was able to bury myself in the shuffle of bureaucracy, claim I was my own son or some such lie, and utilize just enough power to make men believe it. I have no desire to follow in my brother Ishmir's footsteps and die fighting the Dragon Kings. I also have no desire to see Talak destroyed, which is a very real threat should the Silver Dragon ever succeed in his claim to the Dragon Emperor's throne."

So many things had happened during the years of Darkhorse's absence that it was difficult for him to say what was the most astounding. That Cabe Bedlam, grandson of the greatest of the Dragon Masters, had bested the Dragon Emperor and fought his own father, mad Azran, to the death cheered the shadow steed, for he had met the young mortal and even travelled with him for a time. The death of the Gold Dragon had broken the drakes; who now could claim the throne of the highest of the Kings was arguable. Cabe Bedlam and his bride, the Lady of the Amber, had been raising the hatchlings of the Dragon Emperor alongside their own children, trying to teach the two races to coexist. Whether the drakes would accept the eldest royal male as their ruler when he finally came of age—whatever age was to a drake—was a question bandied about with no answer as of yet. Meanwhile, at least two of the remaining Dragon Kings had sought the throne of their "brother" on the basis that to wait for the young to mature was too risky, too speculative. Neither of the two could gain sufficient support among their kind, but the Silver Dragon was growing stronger every day. Drayfitt knew that the first step toward reunifying the lands would be to stamp out Talak, the enemy now within Silver's own domain. Having just gained its true independence only a few years ago, the city-state was not going to give in, not while Melicard was king.

"Mal Quorin whispers in his ear at every opportunity, urging him to reckless crusades. Survivors of Mito Pica, the city ravaged by the drake Toma, still call for the blood of the reptiles and their voices are strong. Melicard himself is obsessed with the Dragon Kings. Once discovered, I came to realize that the only way to bring some sense to this chaos was to become an integral part of my liege's court, a voice of reason."

"And so you summoned a *demon*?" Darkhorse responded with false innocence. "Truly you are a master of logic! What genius! Never would *I* have thought of so cunning a plan!"

The sorcerer rose, his brief reverie broken by the stinging words. Almost, he glared at his captive. Almost.

"Mal Quorin would have found another to translate the damnable book! One more flexible to his will! Now, at least, I can control the situation, keep it from growing unchecked!"

"Is this what Ishmir would've done?"

The question was Drayfitt's undoing. Mention of his brother's name gave birth to a rapidly growing rage, a rage coupled with carelessness. He whirled on Darkhorse, intending to punish him for bringing to the surface the thoughts that had been wracking the old man's mind since agreeing to this insane plane. *Would Ishmir have gone through this*; Drayfitt knew the answer and did not like it. He glared at the shadow steed, his gaze making contact with the cold, blue eyes.

Darkhorse froze the sorcerer where he was, seizing control of his unprotected mind. The phantom stallion laughed quietly at the success of his plan, but it was a hollow laugh. Drayfitt was a good, if naive, mortal. Using his brother's name so pained Darkhorse, who had known most of the long-dead Dragon Masters, including Ishmir the Bird Master.

"Forgive me for this, both of you," he muttered, "but I had no choice."

All emotion fell from the spellcaster's face. His arms hung limply. He looked more than ever like a dead man; Darkhorse, who did not want to hurt him, moved cautiously.

"Your mind is mine, mortal! Your soul is mine! I could hurry you along the Path Which Men May Travel Only Once, but I will not! Not if you obey!"

Drayfitt remained motionless, but Darkhorse knew, as only he could know, that, deep within, the sorcerer's subconscious understood.

"You will remove the barrier, and open a gate in this Void-forsaken cage, and let me out! Do so and I will leave you untouched!"

Though his voice boomed, the shadow steed had no fear that the guards outside would give warning. Melicard had ordered Drayfitt to enshroud the chamber in a blanket of silence, meaning that all sounds would pass no further than the walls. A very important guest had arrived and the king, oddly subdued, did not want knowledge of his activities to reach that unknown personage.

The masks of royalty are many, Darkhorse thought snidely. *Who could it be who would make "handsome" King Melicard so nervous?*

Drayfitt worked smoothly, methodically, going through the motions of the spell. Though he no longer had the book, the memory of his first attempt still remained and Darkhorse had drawn that out. Had there been time, he would have had the mortal repeat the steps out loud so that he could study the makings of the spell. Vraad sorcery it was and the black steed was disturbed he had not seen it sooner. Again, had there been time, Darkhorse would have sought out the book—and the one who had discovered it. Vraad sorcery was dangerous, although on the surface it seemed amazingly simple at times.

With a stiff gesture, Darkhorse reversed the outcome of the spell. Instead of creating yet another cage around the first, he tore the present one apart.

The elderly sorcerer lowered his hands and resumed his deathlike stance. Darkhorse took a hesitant step toward the edge of his prison. One limb, stretched to needle-thin, touched the barrier—and passed beyond it. Jubilant, Darkhorse leaped free, not trusting his luck to hold long.

"Freedom! Ahhh, sweet-tasting freedom! Excellent work, my mortal puppet! Most excellent work!" He gazed down almost fondly at the spellcaster. "For that, you deserve a reward of great value, something I think you've lacked these past days! Sleep! Deep, restful sleep! A *long*, restful nap will do you wonders! When you wake, I want you to do one more thing for me; seek out the source of your Vraad sorcery, this book, and *destroy* it! Rest now!"

Drayfitt slumped to the floor.

With one last, contemptuous scan of the chamber that had been his prison, Darkhorse reared, opened a path to the beyond, and vanished through it.

As night prepared to give way to day, the object of Darkhorse's desperate quest materialized in the middle of a chamber that was quite a contrast to the one recently forced upon the shadow steed. Though a bit more austere than the personal quarters of King Melicard, they were elegant and, indeed, also fit for a king.

Shade reached out a hand and ran a finger along the edge of a massive, golden couch. A thick layer of dust flew off. The warlock may have smiled. No one had made use of this room in quite some time, years perhaps.

The rumors were true, then. These chambers had once belonged to the Lord Gryphon, inhuman but just ruler of Penacles, the legendary City of Knowledge. Once, the Gryphon had been a comrade, sometimes a friend, but only at those times when Shade could be trusted. The Gryphon had understood him better than most, save Darkhorse. As Shade wiped the dust from his fingertip, he found he almost missed his sometime adversary. The Gryphon was rumored to be somewhere across the Eastern Seas, fighting some war that seemed unwilling to completely finish itself. Despite numerous pleas by various city functionaries, the man he had left in charge, a minor spellcaster of masterful strategy, General Toos, refused to take on the mantle of king. Instead, the general had chosen to become regent, with powers equal to those of the monarch with the unique option of retiring in favor of the Gryphon if and when he returned.

So much the better, Shade decided. He turned in a slow circle, observing each and every object, whether it stood on the floor, was pinned to the wall, or hung from the ceiling. Most things were as he remembered them, even down to the two lifelike metal statues standing on each side of the door. They were iron golems, animated creatures of cold metal created by the former lord of Penacles to guard his personal chambers. Surprisingly swift, the creatures should have been on top of the warlock the moment he materialized. Unlike most intruders, however, Shade had the key to their control.

There were words, implanted deep in their very beings, that, when acknowledged by the golems, made them no more than fanciful statues. Words that Shade had silently flung at them before completely materializing. There were advantages to having once been privy to the secrets of the Gryphon. The warlock chuckled quietly, then turned to one of the far walls, where the object of his search, a great, intricately woven tapestry of the entire city of Penacles, hung.

That the tapestry hung here, unwanted by the regent, said many things. The artifact was ancient, even older than Shade. He touched it delicately. General Toos had never hidden his dislike for talismans of power, though he tolerated them. The tapestry itself was only a link to another greater wonder, though. Leaning as close as he dared, the warlock slowly studied the pattern. Each and every street, every building, was represented. Despite having been originally weaved during the initial construction of Penacles, the tapestry revealed structures that were no more than a year or two old.

"Even after all this time, you still work flawlessly," Shade whispered. The creator had been a perfectionist and even Shade acknowledged the superiority of this artifact.

For several minutes he scanned the tapestry, seeking a marking that he could not even be certain he would recognize.

Like the city, the mark he sought changed over the years. Sometimes, it was a stylized picture of a book. Other times, it had been a single letter. There had been many symbols over the centuries, a number of them highly obscure.

I need your fantastic eyes, Lord Gryphon! You were always able to spot the mark with little more than a glance!

Then, his eyes fell on a tiny, twisted banner, one familiar to him as it would be to no other creature living today. Shade smiled his hidden smile and the blur of face seemed to swirl with emotion. He memorized the location and briefly looked up at the tapestry in open admiration. "One would think you were living, old thing, and, if so, you have a wicked sense of humor! My—my *father*—might even have been amused!"

Father. The warlock shivered. Not all the memories that returned were particularly pleasant ones. He quickly buried himself in his task.

Locating the mark again, Shade rubbed the banner with one finger, and as he did, the room around him began to fade. Shade may have smiled. He continued to rub the mark as the Gryphon's chambers gave way to *another* room of sorts, a corridor. The tapestry, still whole, remained until the living quarters had completely dissipated. Then, it, too, faded away. The warlock was left standing in a corridor whose walls were lined with endless shelves of massive, bound tomes, all identical, even in color. *The tapestry still worked.*

He stood in the legendary libraries of Penacles.

The libraries had been standing long before the city. His memories returning, Shade recalled some of the truth about the odd structure, a building beneath the earth, beneath Penacles, that was larger on the inside than the outside and never to be found in the same location. Its true origins were unknown even to him, but he suspected that, as with the spell that Melicard's sorcerer had used to make Darkhorse's cage, this was Vraad work.

Other than the countless volumes stored here, there was not much to see. The floor was polished marble. The corridor he stood in and those he could see were all illuminated by the same unseen source. The shelves themselves might have been brand new, though Shade knew otherwise. Time seemed not to matter in the libraries.

"You have returned after all this time."

The matter-of-fact statement proved to be issued by a small, egg-headed figure clad in simple cloth garments. His arms almost reached the ground, due in great part to his uncommonly short legs. There was not so much as a strand of hair on his head.

One of the gnomes—or perhaps the *only* gnome—who acted as librarians here. As far as Shade could recall, the libraries had always had gnomes and all of them had been identical in appearance.

"Ten years is not so long to the two of us," the spellcaster mocked, recalling his final visit here with the Lord Gryphon.

The gnome seemed oblivious to the tone of mockery, replying simply, "Ten years, no. A *thousand thousand* years, yes. Even to the two of us."

Though his face was unreadable, Shade's body was not. He stiffened and tried to speak, but was uneasy about his choice of words. The gnome chose to fill the silence.

"What you seek is not here. It is, perhaps, the one piece of knowledge the libraries refuse to contain."

Speaking of the libraries in terms of a thinking creature irritated the warlock. He had no desire to feel as if he were in the belly of a beast. "Then where is it? It exists!"

The librarian shrugged and slowly turned away, a book in one hand. The book had not been there before. "Seek the caverns, perhaps."

"Caverns?"

"Caverns." The gnome turned back to Shade, eyeing him as one might an inept young apprentice. "The caverns of the Dragon Emperor. What is left of the place where it all began for you."

The place where it all began for you. Shade may have smiled, but, if so, it was a grim smile. He had forgotten that. It was a memory only now restored to him and it was, quite possibly, the one he would have most preferred never to recall—even at the cost of his own existence.

IV

Erini woke to the light of midmorning intruding in her room, her thoughts and feelings a tangled web of half-remembered images and a full gamut of emotions ranging from joy to fear.

The bed was huge and so very soft. She tried to bury herself in it, both physically *and* mentally. Her old bed back home—*no, former home!*—was little more than piece of wood and a blanket compared to this. The entire room was overwhelming, as vast as any chamber she had seen other than the main hall. Multicolored marble tiles made up the floor, partially obscured by the great fur rugs running to and from the various doorways. Columns thrust upward in each corner, festively decorated with golden flowers. Gay tapestries covered the walls. The furniture, including the bedframe, was carved from the finest northern oak, rare after the destruction of so much forest nine years ago during that horrible, unseasonable winter.

To her dismay, Erini found herself remembering how whole herds of giant diggers, great creatures of fur and claw, had torn their way south, leaving little more than churned earth. The princess shuddered, for they had been no more than a day from her city when a disease or something had killed off all of them within hours. Oddly, that was about the same time that Melicard— *Melicard.*

Erini's eyes opened wide as she surrendered to the inevitable and turned her thoughts back to the night before. The princess had expected so many things when she had entered his darkened chamber, the elfwood arm being the *least* of those. Despite its graceful appearance—thanks to some skilled craftsman, no doubt—the arm moved with an awkwardness that would forever remind one it was not real. Even had it been painted so perfectly as to match the king's skin, Erini would have recognized it for what it was.

First seeing that arm in the dim light, however, had
subconsciously made her anticipate the worst. That was why,
when Melicard had held the light close to his face, Erini
had let out a gasp without even actually seeing his features.
When her eyes had at last rested on her betrothed and the
images had sunk deep enough into her shocked mind, that
shock had turned to confusion and, gradually, joy.

Melicard I, king of Talak and once the handsomest of men in
her young eyes, had a visage that, Erini at last admitted to
herself, was everything she had ever hoped for as a girl growing
up. Strong, angular features, athletic, and with a commanding
presence befitting his rank. It was a wondrous thing to behold,
and the princess was so relieved she almost flew into his arms,
barely missing knocking the candlestick from his hand.

Only then, when they were so near to one another, did the
unholy nature of his face become evident. If there was a
graphic indication of her own reaction to this sudden turn, it
was the tightening of his mouth and the narrowing of his
eye—*one* eye—when he saw her stumble and pause.

The "accident" that had claimed his arm had claimed much
of his face as well, even as rumors had foretold. Because of the
ancient magic said to be involved, that face would not heal.
Whole sections of skin had been torn away and Melicard had
even lost his left eye. When all else failed with his arm, the
king had turned to elfwood, rare wood that, legend had it, was
cut from a tree blessed by the spirit of a dying elf, and had his
artisans carve him a new limb.

He had done the same thing with his face.

Erini, remembering what had followed, pulled the sheets
around her. Tears streaked her own features and she whispered,
"I'm *sorry!*"

While his bride-to-be stood where she was in what he could
only believe to be disgust and horror, Melicard coldly lit other
candles from the first. It was evidently his intention to give her
the full effect, so positive was he that she loathed him.

"You certainly must have heard enough gabbers' tales about
my—difficulties—before making your way here! Is it so much
worse than even the stories?"

How could she tell him? Erini could not keep her eyes off his
face. It *was* the face of Melicard, every curve and angle exactly
as it should have been—save that most of the left side was
masterfully carved from the same wood that his arm had been,

even down to the cheekbone and lower jaw. A third of the nose had been replaced; the elfwood spread as high as the middle of his forehead and as far back as his ear. She was certain that unbuttoning the collar of his dark shirt would reveal more of the same.

The damage had not been confined to the left side, either. His right side was streaked by what almost looked like roots spreading from the left. Three major branches split across his cheek and each had one or two minor appendages as well. So contrasting was the enchanted wood to his own pale skin that the entire patchwork face looked like nothing less than that of a man dying of plague.

"You are free to depart any time, Princess Erini," he said after a time.

She shook her head, unwilling to trust her mouth. Melicard, carefully skirting her, came around and offered her a chair. Erini had been so engrossed in his appearance that she had not even noticed there was furniture, or anything, for that matter, in the room. "If you plan to stay, then please be seated. This should be more comfortable than those coach benches, even a royal coach."

With a whispered "thank you," Erini adjusted her ungainly dress and sat down. The king, moving swift and silent, suddenly leaned before her, a goblet of red wine in each hand. She took the proffered goblet and waited until he was seated in another chair directly across from her before sipping. The wine succeeded very little in steadying Erini's nerves, for her eyes could not leave his face even when she drank.

They sat like that for several minutes. Melicard, whose manner had been as politely cold as his words, drank from his own goblet in silence. With each sip, he seemed to draw deeper into his own mind. The princess wanted to say something, *anything*, to ease his pain and her own guilt, but the words would not come out. She grew angry at herself for becoming one of those helpless, useless maidens the storytellers often created for their fables. Until now, Erini had secretly mocked those pitiful women.

At last, the king set his goblet down and rose. The princess straightened, expecting some announcement, some word from her betrothed as to their future—or even lack of it if that was his desire. To her surprise, Melicard turned and walked to the far end of the chamber, where another door stood. Melicard opened it and, without looking back or even saying a word, stepped out of the room.

Erini stared at the door as it closed behind him, not comprehending immediately what had happened. Only when a liveried servant stepped in from the first doorway did realization sink in.

"If you will come with me, your majesty, I have been commanded to show you to your quarters." Through his manner, the servant verified her fears; Melicard was not returning. The king had read her disgust and pity and had been able to stomach it no longer.

She saw no one other than the servants who fed and cared for her and her two ladies-in-waiting. Galea and Madga pressed her for snippets of information about the king, but Erini would have none of that. After dismissing them politely, she had retired early, the combination of the journey and her trial here too much to bear.

Letting the sun now bathe her, heal her mental wounds, she silently swore an oath. *I must make it up to him somehow! I must show I can care without pitying! Small wonder he acts the way he does if everyone reacts as I did!* Melicard could not be faulted for his efforts, the princess decided guiltily. If his own flesh would not grow back, what was he *supposed* to do? Wear a mask of gold and silver? Leave his own, mangled features visible? In many ways, the elfwood face was the best solution, unnerving as it as. Even the king's sorcerer had come up with nothing better after failing to heal his master's wounds.

Her own fingers began to twitch at the thought and she clasped both hands together in order to fight the urge down. She would *not* succumb. There was nothing the princess could do that others more skilled, others who were *trained*, could not do better.

Erini repeated what had become a chant to her—she was a princess of Gordag-Ai and could never be a sorceress or witch. Never. She was destined to be a queen. No king would trust a witch for a wife. Her own people would not have.

Though she fought it down successfully, Erini shook so badly after that, that she rose and dressed herself, not daring to have Galea or Magda or any of Melicard's people wonder what made her shake. By the time the princess was finished, the danger was past. Erini inspected herself in the vast mirror that overwhelmed the wall opposite her bed and, satisfied, dared to summon a servant. If she succeeded in nothing more today, she would at least eat a decent meal.

Neither Melicard nor the unsavory Counselor Quorin met her at breakfast. Galea and Magda joined her, but she made some pretext and left them as soon as she was finished. When none of the palace servants seemed to object, the princess began exploring, trying to understand more about Talak and its monarch through the vast building itself. Erini already knew much of the city-state's "official" history, having been educated about her future kingdom most of her life, but there was more, so much more, beneath the surface of the facts that tutors had poured into her. All she had learned about her betrothed had availed her nothing in his actual presence. It was a mistake she did not intend to make a second time.

As lavishly decorated as the palace was, she soon discovered two things. One was that the vast majority of items had been gathered during the reigns of past kings, to the extent that whole wings had been built to house them. The second and more interesting point concerned those few treasures gathered or created during the years of Melicard's rule. Most of the pieces were dark in nature and not a few of them dealt with the death and destruction of foes, especially dragons. Faces in portraits were always shadowed or, if they *were* fully revealed, were sinister and even hideous. It did not paint a pretty picture of her betrothed. Erini began to have doubts.

At a window overlooking an interior garden filled with hanging plants and blossoming flowers of all colors, she paused to relax. A noise at the far end of the garden made her look there. Her eyes narrowed at an curious sight. Far below, two guards were carrying a third man between them. As opposed to the tall, muscular soldiers, the unconscious figure in the middle was thin to the point of emaciation and as old as any soul the princess had ever seen. He wore a dark robe with a cowl on it, identifying him from Erini's teachings as Melicard's sorcerer Drayfitt. The history that the ancient spellcaster had lived through had always fascinated her, but not nearly so much as why Drayfitt now needed to be carried anywhere. She leaned closer.

Erini glanced back at the direction the trio had come from and noticed the small doorway buried beneath the vines of the far wall. The way to the sorcerer's inner sanctum? Possibly, and, if so, it was also possible that his present condition was due to some spell gone awry.

"What's going on here?" a voice that grated on her nerves snarled.

The two sentries paused and, readjusting their unconscious package, saluted Mal Quorin. He ignored protocol and repeated his question in the same vicious tone as before.

One of the guards, his face no longer visible to Erini, nervously replied, "His majesty gave us orders to seek out the sorcerer Drayfitt and find out why he had not reported to the king this morning. When we arrived, the guards on duty let us in, reporting that no one had entered or left since they had been stationed there." The man hesitated before concluding quickly, "He was lying on the floor! We tried to wake him, but nothing worked, my lord!"

Quorin looked at both of them, evidently not satisfied. "There's *more*, isn't there?"

"The *demon* is loose, my lord!" the other guard finally blurted. "Or, at least, it's no longer in the chamber!"

Erini, listening intently and growing more shocked with each word, fully expected the counselor to vent his rage and power on the two hapless soldiers. Instead, he simply stood where he was, staring. Whether he stared at the sentries or into open space, the princess had no way of knowing. At last, the counselor reached forward and, in a move that stunned not only Erini but the soldiers as well, slapped Drayfitt sharply across the face. The elderly spellcaster's head snapped to one side, but he did not wake. Quorin rubbed his hand.

"Be on your way, then. I want to know when he wakes."

"My lord."

Quorin watched calmly until the trio was out of sight and then whirled back in the direction of the vine-covered door. With tremendous, catlike strides, he covered the distance to his objective in mere seconds. The counselor put one hand on the handle and then, as if sensing he were being watched, turned around and glanced upward. Erini, however, anticipating such a move, was already flattened against a wall.

She counted more than twenty breaths before she dared to look. Mal Quorin was gone, evidently having decided he did not have the time to search for shadows. The princess debated going down to the mysterious door or following the guards and their package. Knowing that the counselor might be waiting for her, Erini chose the latter and tried to guess where the two men might enter. They had mentioned Melicard and his interest in the workings of the sorcerer. If nothing else, they would eventually return to their monarch with some type of report and that report would include Drayfitt's odd condition.

A demon, by my ancestors! Do all the rumors about Melicard have some basis in fact? Am I engaged to a human monster? Have I been so wrong about him?

Drayfitt and the guards. They had to be inside by now. Where might they go? The chamber in which she had confronted Melicard? It was her only real choice. Taking a deep breath, the princess made her way to the central staircase and started down, walking with the air of one who is inspecting her new domain. Erini did not know what might happen if she actually stumbled across the trio, but that was a risk she was willing to take. Her only fear was running into Quorin or the king himself. The counselor was an annoyance; her betrothed . . . Erini was not quite ready to deal with him. There were things she wanted to think about before the two of them spoke again, especially if she had properly understood the conversation between Quorin and the two guards.

At the foot of the stairs, she confronted four sentries, who saluted in simultaneous fashion. Erini nodded imperiously and continued on. No one made a move to stop her wanderings. Once she was far enough away, the princess exhaled deeply, wondering if her heart would ever slow to normal again.

She was turning down the main hall when she spotted the two soldiers from the garden. Drayfitt was nowhere to be seen. The guards themselves were just marching up to the doorway of the chamber she had entered last night. The same sentries stood watch. After a brief consultation, the soldiers who had discovered Drayfitt were ushered inside.

Disappointment washed over Erini. There was no way she could eavesdrop on Melicard and his men. Barging in was also too risky, considering that she might at any minute discover she was no longer to be his bride. Erini began to wonder what room Drayfitt might have been deposited in by the guards. If she could find some way to wake him . . .

"Your *majesty* is awake. Did you sleep well?"

The princess trembled in surprise. Her left hand made an automatic sweep across her midsection and suddenly began to glow, but she reversed the motion, thereby countermanding the

spell. By the time the princess turned around, her hand was
back to normal.

Mal Quorin was standing behind her, his feline features
enhanced by the predatory smile spreading across his face. The
counselor was all politeness as he spoke. "My deepest sympathies
for yesterday, princess. The king is—overwhelming—at times."

"And I was not understanding, Counselor Quorin. I have
every intention of atoning for my lapse. The king has nothing
to regret." She glanced down the hall at the guarded doorway
with a majestically indifferent eye. "I thought I might speak to
him now."

Rubbing his chin, Quorin diplomatically hesitated before
replying, "I regret to say, your majesty, that now would not be
a good time to disturb the king. He has thrown himself into his
work, something he does when his mood grows dark, and I
think it might be best to wait until this evening, when it is time
to sup. I assure you that the evening meal would be a much
better time to mend any rift between the two of you."

The false face of courtesy that the counselor wore for her
irritated Erini and she was tempted to tell him so. The real Mal
Quorin was the man who had been shouting in the garden, an
ambitious, hot-tempered plotter in her opinion. To speak the
truth would avail her nothing, however, and would probably
make matters worse since this man had the ear of Melicard.

"As you say, Counselor Quorin. You will arrange, I trust,
that the meal is a private one. The king and myself. I have
much to make up for."

"I shall do my utmost." He gave one of his sweeping bows.
"If you like, since the king is unavailable, I can have someone
escort you through the city, show you all Talak has to offer its
new queen. Would you like that?"

His tone was that of an adult asking a child if she wanted a
piece of candy. Erini struggled to keep her temper. If there ever
was a reason to let her powers loose, it was the counselor. She
wondered what he would say if he knew how dangerous his
position actually was at present.

"I think not, counselor. Not today, anyway. There is still so
much to see and learn about in the palace itself. I should get to
know Melicard's heritage, for it will be mine as well."

His eyes spoke otherwise in response to her quiet challenge,
although Quorin's words themselves were nothing less than
admiration and the desire to assist. "You are to be recommended,

your majesty. If you will retire to your chambers, I will send a member of the royal archives who will be able to answer all of your questions for you. There are also a vast number of books, some in the handwriting of the king's illustrious ancestors, that I will have pulled from the archives.''

Erini smiled so very sweetly. "You must be a godsend to your lord, counselor. There is no reason to do that as yet. I find I learn so much more just walking these exquisite halls. If you will excuse me now. . . ."

With Quorin watching her back, the princess walked sedately down the opposite hall, visibly admiring the treasures around her. After a few moments, she heard the scuffle of his boots as he turned away. Erini paused, pretending to study a statuette, and looked back out of the corner of her eye just in time to see the man barge into the same chamber that the two soldiers had passed through only a short time before.

More and more, Mal Quorin bothered her. There were times when he moved much like the creature he resembled and others when he made more noise than a full honor guard. He was also her enemy, that much was now completely evident, and she did not doubt that he might even turn to violence. The counselor had no desire for the king to marry, likely because he feared Erini's influence might some day overshadow his own.

Despite her lapses, the princess had no intention of folding up like the heroines of the storytellers. Come an endless army of demons and Mal Quorins, she would still mend the rift between Melicard and herself and, in the process, find out what had truly happened behind that garden door.

If it also meant giving in to her own curse, so be it.

In the eternal darkness of what had once been the throne room of the Dragon Emperor, a searing light burst into life, flooding the entire chamber in its bloodred brilliance. Things that were not entirely of this world, things that had once obeyed the will of the Gold Dragon, scurried back into the safety of cracks and fissures where the light did not reach.

Like a wisp of smoke, Shade uncurled out of nothing and stepped forth into the ruins of the Dragon King's lair.

This had once been the chamber in which the Dragon Kings met in council. There had been thirteen of them until the end of the Turning War, when Nathan Bedlam had succeeded in destroying the regal Purple Dragon who had ruled Penacles

before the Gryphon. The council—and the unity of the drakes—
had broken up for the final time with the madness caused by
the discovery of Cabe Bedlam, Nathan's grandson and successor, who carried a part of the spirit of the great Dragon Master
within him. In this chamber, where some of the huge effigies of
creatures long dead still stood despite all the violence that had
passed through here, two drake lords, the battle-hungry Iron
and his ever-present shadow Bronze, had paid for their rebel-
lion against Gold. In this chamber, Shade had learned, Cabe
Bedlam had defeated the Dragon Emperor, tearing his mind
apart. Here also, it was said, Cabe and the Lord Gryphon had
battled young Bedlam's mad father, the sinister Azran.

Death is so very much a part of this place still, Shade
thought uneasily. If there was a place that could unnerve him, it
was here. As Madrac, he had forgotten that fear briefly, coming
here and using the Dragon Kings themselves to further that
incarnation's goals.

Shade stood and scanned the cathedral-high ruins about him,
marveling at the carnage for several seconds before finally
deciding that enough time had been wasted. The warlock took
two tentative steps toward what had once been the throne itself—

—and paused.

Though no one but the warlock himself would have been
able to tell, Shade blinked. He studied the cavern again—and
then for a third time. When that no longer seemed to satisfy
him, he sought around for a safe place to sit. There, he stared
into the darkness of an adjoining cavern and wondered . . .

. . . wondered why he had come here and why he had
suddenly forgotten that reason.

V

Darkhorse burst from the portal at full gallop, all defenses
ready. He did not stop until he was certain that Shade was
nowhere near. It never paid to be too confident in the Dragonrealm,

especially with the warlock, but still, he could sense nothing hostile within immediate range and decided it was safe to come to a halt.

A wave of sulfur drifted past his muzzle. Had he been less than he was, the treacherous smoke would have left him choking on the ground. Being Darkhorse, he noted it only for its pungent scent.

"The Hell Plains! How aptly titled!" the shadow steed muttered. It was actually more of a shout than a mutter, for even he found it difficult to hear his normally stentorian voice in a land where few minutes went by without some sort of volcanic eruption. All around him, the ground shook. Hills formed, burst open as molten rock was spewed forth, and then collapsed as some new crater redirected the flow. The very earth beneath the eternal's hooves cracked wide and lava began to rise to the surface.

Darkhorse glanced down at the burning, liquefied rock and laughed. The lava licked at his forelegs, but it might as well have been the touch of a blade of grass. Mocking the power of the land with a swish of his thick tail, the phantom horse trotted to stable ground, the better to think.

He had been over a hundred places that Shade might choose to visit and none of those had been sought out by the mad warlock despite more than a day passing. More than a dozen times, Darkhorse had found himself tricked by false or old trails. Darkhorse did not feel defeated yet, but his options were diminishing.

The earth shook, alerting him to yet another crater forming beneath his hooves. Annoyed, the shadow steed began trotting north, toward the more stable regions of the Hell Plains. There was yet one place nearby that Shade might deem to visit. A place hidden from all during its master's reign, but likely to be unprotected now.

Darkhorse kicked up the ash in frustration. He was running blind. He had no idea what Shade planned, where the warlock was, or if the spellcaster had already struck. His only hope was to come across his former comrade in a place of power such as the one he neared even now. *Perhaps this time . . .* he dreamed.

The birdlike skull of a Seeker went bounding into the air, kicked high along with the soot it had been buried under. Startled, Darkhorse came to a halt—but not before kicking up a mangled pile of bones that had come from more than one creature and more than one race.

The bones were jumbled together, the result of continual tremors and eruptions. Treading softly, the shadow steed discovered that they literally covered the earth, hidden from view only by a blanket of ash that had accumulated over the years. Memories of the past stirred. He recalled bits of news picked up concerning the fates of his friends and foes. It was as if time had not passed, for he had been battling the new, deadly incarnation called Madrac when these creatures had died fighting one another. Drake bones mixed freely with Seeker bones. The Seekers, the ancient avian masters of this land, had fought, not for themselves, but for the lord forced upon them, Azran Bedlam. They had died defending his citadel and, when even that was not enough to keep the hordes of the Red Dragon from his walls, Azran had destroyed the fiery legions and the Dragon King with his accursed demon blade. Darkhorse eyed the remains with clinical interest. This, then, was part of the battle site. He was closer than he had thought. The shadow steed puzzled over the remains and then looked up, openly curious.

This had to be the region where Azran's sanctum was located—yet—it was *nowhere* to be found.

He stirred up more ash and bone as he searched the ground. There were a number of jagged hills and craters, but none massive enough to be what Darkhorse sought, unless . . . unless all that remained of the tower was—its *foundation*. The ancient structure, supposedly built by the Seekers to withstand time and the Hell Plains had to be no more than a ruin. It was the only answer and, if true, yet another failure on his part. Shade would never come here.

"Darkhorse, you are a vain, unmitigated fool!" He brought a hoof down on some unidentifiable bone, sending fragments and dust flying. He had been determined to do this alone because he felt the responsibility his. Shade was—had been— his friend. Shade's exile had been the eternal's doing and the warlock's escape had been Darkhorse's failure. Pride ruled the shadow steed as much as, if not more than, it ruled humanity.

A touch of latent power disturbed the edges of his mind.

"What have we here?" he rumbled. That which touched his thoughts was not living, not by any stretch of the imagination. It had the stink of death—no, it *was* death!—and it lay not too far from where he stood. Darkhorse, having few options of his own, followed the chilling trail.

Soon, Darkhorse found himself standing before a long, wide

mound some two or three times the height of a normal man. The jet-black horse stepped up to the front edge of the mound and dug away at it with his hoof, not daring to unleash a spell in the vicinity of such a dark power. Darkhorse had no fear for himself, but he knew that careless action might very well rob him of his only possible chance to find and stop Shade. That, of course, depended on what had sought him out. There were things in the Dragonrealm that even he hoped never to meet.

After a few moments, he uncovered the edge of a wall. It was true, then. Something, perhaps Azran himself, had stripped the ancient castle of its preservative spells. Age and the primitive fury of this cursed region had caught up to the citadel. From what he could see, Darkhorse guessed that an eruption had taken place not too far from the once magically protected grounds. In a few more decades, there would be little or nothing remaining of the lair of Azran.

Somehow, Darkhorse could not bring himself to weep for the loss of such a place. If the Hell Plains buried the evil memory of Nathan Bedlam's treacherous foal, so much the better.

The touch of death returned. Shaking his head to remove the foul feeling, the stallion followed the trail left by the magical contact. Ash, mortar, and yet more bones flew as Darkhorse used the slightest touch of his own power to clear a path. One never knew what might be lurking beneath. The ground rumbled ominously; perhaps decades was too long an estimate. There might be nothing remaining in mere minutes.

He came across what had once been stairs leading down to a room, a room *still* protected by sorcery though the physical structure itself was no more than half a wall and several loose stones. Darkhorse paused only for a moment; then, spelling the ash away, he descended. The protective measures here were bound together with the same unearthly power that had reached out to him, which was why they still remained. Even if the entire region exploded in one massive eruption, this spot would go untouched. Darkhorse laughed, his challenge to what awaited him. He knew with what he dealt now.

His form passed through a spell that would have killed any mortal creature and several entities of lesser ability than he. As the tip of his tail passed beyond the deadly trap, the violent land of the Hell Plains ceased to be.

"I am unimpressed," was his first comment as he surveyed

the chamber he now stood in. "Typical of your masters, who have no imagination!"

How the room had looked before Azran's death was questionable, though, knowing the necromancer's madness, it had probably been much the same. Without Azran's physical influence, however, control of this place had slipped back to the oppressive rulers of the Final Path, the beings known to men as the Lords of the Dead and other, in the eternal's estimation, overly pretentious titles.

I wonder what humans would think if they knew that even these Lords *must die at some time!*

The odor of rotting flesh filled the chamber. Decaying forms, human and otherwise, littered the place. A pool of some brackish liquid—definitely not water—bubbled ominously. Darkhorse laughed again.

"Save your show for those who *believe* in it, Lords of the Overacting! You know that I have no fear of you! If I should ever perish, my ultimate destiny lies elsewhere, not in your slime-crusted fingers! If you have something to say to me, then do so! One who has cheated you over and over for millennia threatens the mortals—mortals who have not yet lived the lives that are their due! Well? Do I need to start dumping this refuse into your little puddle?" He prodded an unidentifiable mass covered with black flies toward the pool.

The bubbling grew violent, creating a green froth that swelled high. The pool became more agitated, waves lapping the floor. Something long, large, and blacker than Darkhorse briefly broke the muck-covered surface before disappearing again. The shadow steed watched all in total disinterest.

In the center of the pool, a new form slowly rose. Accurate description failed, save that it was a hodgepodge of rotting limbs, torsos, and heads combined in impossible ways. Eyes dotted its form, all of them staring at the phantom horse with more than a touch of fury. Several limbs pointed in Darkhorse's direction.

"I feel no more pleasure in seeing your lovely face—*faces, I suppose I should say*!—than you feel in seeing mine! Come! Speak and we can be done with this—or are you going to pass along some unmanageable riddle like those you foist upon mortals who seek your—fools that they are!—*guidance*!"

"Child of the Void." The voice grated, scratched, pierced— it did *everything* as far as Darkhorse was concerned. Despite the irritation it caused him, however, outwardly he revealed nothing. Let them play their little games out as long as they told him something of importance.

"Dweller Without."

The shadow steed kicked the fly-covered corpse into the pool, which caused a flurry of bubbling as the scavengers sought unsuccessfully to escape their sinking home. Darkhorse focused an ice-blue eye on the guardian of the pool.

"Yesss, I have earned my share of pretentious titles as well! Second move to you, my pretty friend! Now, unless you concede this idiotic game and tell me what is so important, I will depart this godforsaken hole forever—but not before *sealing* it so that no one else has to put up with your stench!"

"Kivan Grath." The guardian of the pool spit the name out, along with a number of tiny, vague pieces of matter that Darkhorse did not bother to try to identify.

"Kivan Grath?"

"The Seeker of Gods, demon horse." It was the first understandable reply the thing had given him.

"I know what it is, but why—"

"Kivan Grath. Now." Each of the numerous mouths formed into what Darkhorse could only vaguely accept as a smile. A smile of triumph. "Do not lose him again, unwanted one."

The jet-black stallion met the guardian's multiple gaze. "And *how* many times has Shade departed your domain without more than a nod of his head?"

The guardian did not respond to his retort, instead choosing that moment to sink back into the mire. Up to the very moment its head submerged, all eyes remained fixed on Darkhorse.

He bid the guardian, who may or may not have been little more than a puppet through which his masters had spoken, farewell with a mocking laugh that echoed throughout the chamber. Turning, the shadow steed kicked yet another moldering form into the grisly pool as he burst back through the magical veil and out into the Hell Plains.

Ascending to the surface, Darkhorse scanned the area with renewed interest. "Not so bad a place after all! Almost pleasant!"

His gaze returned to the stairway and the ruins of the chamber. Azran's pool lay in some space between the mortal plane and the lands of the dead, a brilliant piece of sorcery. Almost indestructible, too.

Almost.

"Some doors are too dangerous to leave opened," he finally decided.

The black emptiness that was his form melted, changed. Like the molten rock flowing from the craters, the inky darkness streamed down the broken steps, pressing with purpose toward the magical doorway. As it enveloped the physical portal, a brief touch, a brief moment of protest, tapped at the edges of Darkhorse's consciousness. He ignored it and, as the magic which had created the portal was absorbed within him, the protest faded.

The shadow steed re-formed himself at the top of the stairs. At the base of those stairs was now a clean, flat surface. Other than the steps, there was no sign that there had ever been a portal. Indeed, there was not even a trace of the room remaining.

Kivan Grath. Most majestic of the Tyber Mountains. The name was familiar to Darkhorse and he cursed himself for not having searched there earlier. Lair of the Gold Dragon, long dead. The caverns within Kivan Grath were endless and they predated even the Seekers. Was it possible that one of Shade's rediscovered memories had sent him searching in those caverns?

Darkhorse paused. The rot-riddled masters of human mortality had given him a clue, but did he dare trust it? They cared nothing for him and *that* feeling was returned to them twofold. Why, then, were they aiding him? Was there something greater they feared, should the warlock remain free?

Again, he contemplated seeking out Cabe Bedlam, the one mortal who might be of help, and again the painful belief, that he was responsible for Shade, kept him from doing so.

The guardian had indicated that speed was of the essence and Darkhorse, knowing he had already stalled longer than he dared, opened a path through reality. This time, he would find Shade. This time, there would be no exile.

Only one sentry guarded the room where Erini guessed Drayfitt had been deposited. He stood at the doorway, a bored look on his rough features, his hand on the pommel of his sword. In the palace royal of the king of Talak, no one expected trouble. That, despite what had happened to the old sorcerer.

What exactly she planned to do, the princess could not say. Her ideas had gone no farther than locating Drayfitt and she was chagrined to realize she had no notion as to how to proceed now. Of what use would sneaking past the sentry be, always assuming that Erini could do even *that*, if success only meant confronting the unconscious spellcaster?

She was turning away, defeated for the moment, when she heard the sound of a door opening and the voice of the guard raised high in surprise. Erini, positioned down a side corridor, glanced back in time to see the sentry's face glaze over as a determined Drayfitt stared into his eyes. The sorcerer had an odd look in his own eyes, a fanatical gaze that somehow did not fit the elderly man's appearance. It was almost as if he, like the soldier, were under a spell.

Drayfitt wasted no time. Like a man possessed, he hurried down the hall—toward the corridor where Erini still stood. Quickly, she looked around for some place to hide, not wanting to chance the same fate as the hapless sentry. Sighting a stairway leading downward, the princess scurried over to it. She rushed halfway down and paused, hoping to hear the sorcerer as he passed.

A horrible thought occurred to her. If Drayfitt was returning to the garden, his quickest way to reach it was the very stairway she was standing on. Erini took several steps down and then paused. By now, Drayfitt should have been descending behind her, yet, his footsteps were growing *fainter*. She waited a moment longer and then slowly made her way back up. No sorcerer barred her way. The princess reached the top of the stairs and looked around. The elderly man was gone.

Holding her breath, she listened for some sound. Nothing. Drayfitt had continued down one of the two hallways, but she could not say which. The ancient sorcerer was much sprier than the princess could have believed possible. Now, there was no way she could follow him.

Voices and heavy footsteps down the original corridor made her turn. Quorin was one of them. The two soldiers who had carried Drayfitt to the room were likely with him. The other voice . . .

Melicard!

Erini cursed her luck. If she went down either corridor, they would see her. If she descended the stairs, they might notice her as she hurried across the garden. Either way, things would look suspicious. With her future already in a fragile state, this might be more than it could stand.

Strengthening her resolve, Erini did the only thing she could. It was time to rely on hope and her own ability to act as a princess acted. Smoothing her gown, she strode down the hallway and entered the corridor by Drayfitt's former resting place just as Melicard, Quorin, and at least *six* guards came into sight from her right.

She pretended to notice the stunned guard for the first time. Shock was not a difficult emotion to play; the sentry's slack features and blank eyes were a frightening sight. Without realizing it, she put a hand to her mouth to stifle a gasp.

"Princess Erini! Your majesty!" Quorin's voice. She refused to acknowledge it, instead shaking her head as if ready to break down at the sight of the unfortunate victim of Drayfitt's power.

"Erini."

The new voice was Melicard's and the soft tone of it turned her uneasiness to wonder. She gratefully tore her eyes from the sentry, fixing them instead upon Melicard's face. This time, the princess felt no uneasiness, only uncertainty. Would they suspect why she was here?

"Melicard, I—"

Quorin stepped forward to intercept her as she moved toward the king. "Your majesty, if you will permit me, I will have two of these men escort you to your chambers. There has been some unpleasantness here, as you can see, and we would not want you endangered."

She purposely sidestepped him. "If there is some danger to Melicard, I will certainly not abandon him for my own sake! If there is some danger to me, I will feel safer with my betrothed!" Erini looked up at the king. Melicard met her gaze momentarily, then looked down. "Unless, of course, he does not wish me here."

The king lifted his head and studied her. Erini kept her gaze on his eyes. Her own played tricks; she almost came to believe that both his eyes were real. Would he respond to her bald statement? Did Melicard understand that she would leave Talak now if he so desired it?

Beside her, Mal Quorin grew anxious. He put a hand on her arm, intending to lead her away from both the king and the present, dire situation. It proved to be a mistake. Life seemed to suddenly illuminate Melicard's visage, even that carved of elfwood. He looked from the counselor to Erini and back again.

"It's all right, Quorin. She will be fine with me."

The faces of Erini and Mal Quorin were a study in opposites.

More pleased than she had thought she could possibly be, the princess barely noticed the scowling features of the counselor.

"My liege, I don't think—"

"We'll speak of the other matters later on. I know I can depend on you to deal with the present crisis as I would want it dealt with." The king's tone brooked no argument.

Defeated for the moment, Quorin obediently bowed. "As you wish, your majesty. I shall report to you as soon as we have the crisis under control."

Melicard absently touched one of the streaks of elfwood running across the right side of his face. "Unless you can't control it, I see no need why it can't wait until this evening. I leave it in your very capable hands."

"My liege." The counselor barked orders to the guards. Two of them took the stricken sentry away while the rest followed Quorin down the side corridor Erini had stepped out of before. The king by her side, Erini watched until the party was out of sight.

"Princess Erini," Melicard suddenly began, "I apologize to you for yesterday. You shouldn't have been expected to be at ease with something so ... I sometimes try to provoke a response, I think."

"My conduct was reprehensible, my lord. I should apologize to you for that. As a princess of Gordag-Ai and your betrothed, I should behave better. It could not have been easy for you to accept the fact that you had a bride, not after all these years."

The thinnest shadow of a smile played briefly across the king's mouth. Through some trick of the light, Erini imagined that the elfwood portion of his face flexed and shifted as he talked, as if it believed it was flesh and blood. She wanted to reach up and touch it, just to be certain, but she doubted that Melicard would tolerate such a thing at this point—and she had no desire to do anything that might break anew the bond between them just as it was beginning to mend.

"It was a *bit* of a surprise," he responded. It was as if Erini had met twins, so different was this Melicard from the cold one she had encountered briefly yesterday. "I hadn't even planned on marriage for several years. I have so much to do."

The princess was careful not to press him on what sort of *projects* kept him so busy, instead saying, " 'The years pass as quickly as they once passed so slowly.' An old saying of Gordag-Ai. A king needs heirs if he wishes his legacy to live on. Where would Talak be if something happened to you and you had no heir? The city would fall.''

From the look in his working eye, Erini knew she had struck one of his most sensitive points. Melicard's campaign would be all for nought if he died. There was no one with the drive, the determination, to take over. Mal Quorin had such dreams, but the princes knew that putting Talak in the counselor's hands like that would result in nothing less than civil war. The counselor was a madman and madmen made for short, brutal reigns.

Melicard reached out and took her hand. ''Perhaps we can find a quiet place and talk for a little while.''

Having no desire to destroy what she had so far wrought, Erini made no mention of the fact that, under these circumstances, it was proper for others, specifically her ladies-in-waiting, to also be in attendance. When it came to courtship, the king was a babe. Still, she understood that they could make no progress if he had to endure the stares of other, less flexible souls like Magda or Galea—besides, Erini had no desire for them to be in attendance, either.

Melicard led her down the hall, but not to the chamber they had met in the day before. Instead, the two of them walked toward the cathedral high doors of the main hall, where several startled guards quickly straightened. The king touched his face where elfwood and flesh met, hesitant. Then, with iron resolve, he took her arm and guided her forward. Two guards quickly opened the door for them and several others moved to fall in behind the royal couple.

The king turned and calmly said, ''Return to your posts. We will be within the palace grounds and very safe. That is a *command*.''

With some misgivings evident in their features, the guards stepped away.

''Such loyalty is commendable,'' Erini commented. ''Where are we going?''

Melicard did not look directly at her, but she thought she detected a brief smile. *Twice in only a few minutes,* the princess marvelled. *There's hope.*

''If you'll permit, Princess Erini, I would like to show you my kingdom.''

Her own smile was the only reply he received. Reddening slightly, Melicard escorted her outside and into the sunlight.

* * *

In the caverns of Kivan Grath, a desperate Shade sat silently, his thoughts a raging fury in contrast to his still form. Try as he might, the warlock could make no sense of his memories; he barely even remembered the name by which he had gone for all these centuries. *Shade*. It was the only solid memory he had left. Somehow, he hoped, he would be able to build from it. Somehow.

From the darkened caverns beyond, a single, unseen watcher studied the human. When curiosity was satisfied, the watcher vanished into the darkness to tell the others.

VI

The crimson fire that illuminated the throne room of the Dragon Emperor was momentarily drowned out by the brilliant white glow of Darkhorse's gate as the shadow steed burst through. Chilling eyes quickly drank in the details of the massive cavern, from the few huge effigies still standing, to the flittering, frightened shapes seeking haven in the cracks and crevices. Darkhorse ignored the creatures, knowing them as useless servants of a long-dead Dragon King. There was only one thing, one creature who demanded his attention . . . and though he was nowhere to be seen, the ebony stallion could feel his nearby presence.

"Shaaade!"

The warlock's name echoed hauntingly through the endless labyrinth of caverns. It was said that here, if one dared, a way to the bottom of the world might be found. Darkhorse neither knew or cared. He wanted Shade and each passing second made that hope dwindle.

"Come, Shade! It is time to join the ghosts of our pasts! This poor world can ill afford our constant struggle! Let it end now!"

He waited, listening intently as the echoes of his challenge slowly died away. The things hiding in the cracks and crevices chittered in mad fear. More out of impatience than anything else, Darkhorse looked up in their general direction and laughed, sending them scattering to hiding places farther away from the phantom horse.

Still no one answered his challenge.

There was too much old magic here for him to pinpoint the spellcaster. Old spells abandoned, for the most part. There was also something else, something older *and* newer. Darkhorse sniffed.

Vraad sorcery.

Shade's words to him while the shadow steed had remained helpless in Drayfitt's cage resurfaced. The warlock had said that his elderly counterpart had used Vraad-style sorcery. Now, in this ancient place where Shade himself had come, there were again Vraad traces.

Darkhorse cursed silently. Now there was more than Shade to deal with. If he somehow survived his encounter with the warlock, there were still the legacies of the Vraad. Legacies that threatened more than a world.

Dru Zeree, the stallion thought, recalling the first being to befriend him. *I've need of your guidance. How do I fight what even the Vraad themselves could not?*

There was no answer, of course. It was a friendship of the far past. It was a reason that Darkhorse rarely sought the friendship of others, though he yearned for their trust. Everything passed beyond, save him.

And Shade.

If the spellcaster had come seeking the foul inheritance left by that ancient race of sorcerers, he would be deeper in the caverns, possibly miles below the surface. Though the Vraad were recent by this land's standards, they had been a jealous people and prone to secrets, especially from one another. If one of their number had left artifacts behind, those items would be buried deep—and well-protected.

Mystery upon mystery!

Darkhorse struck the floor furiously, leaving a gouge where his hoof had landed. It also worried him that generation upon generation of Dragon Emperor had made this mountain and its caverns the home of their clans—yet not one of them had ever been known to make use of whatever the Vraad had abandoned.

Scanning the chamber, he chose a likely side cavern. A gate would have been quicker, true, but only if he knew where Shade was. Besides, there was too much sorcery lingering in the air. There was no telling what effect it might have on his own abilities.

Darkhorse trotted cautiously toward the cavern entrance.

A sinewy, metallic appendage wrapped itself around his throat. Another trapped one foreleg and two more snared his hind legs. Momentarily disconcerted, the shadow steed struggled futilely, gouging the earth with the sharp hoof of his sole free limb, as his unseen attackers struggled to maintain their holds from their shadowy hiding places. Then, the true seriousness of his situation jarred him back to reality. No physical bond could hold a creature whose essence was part of the Void itself, not unless master sorcery was at work. Even then, he should have been able to free himself simply by truly becoming a shadow. To his dismay, however, Darkhorse found that the transformation was beyond him. The same sorcery that had been used to create his attackers' weapons also prevented him from utilizing his own abilities. Someone had planned well, though they could have hardly done so with him in mind. It was only unfortunate coincidence that he had fallen prey.

A final, jagged tentacle darted from one of the lesser caverns and snared his remaining leg. Each limb was pulled in a different direction, making movement impossible. The noose around his neck kept him from using more primitive methods to escape, such as biting his bonds in two.

"Hurry, you foolssss! Bind him quickly!"

Slowly, so as not to lose the hold each had, the ebony stallion's attackers abandoned their hiding places and moved toward him. Their identities did not surprise him, not after hearing the hissing voice that commanded them. So engrossed had he become in his search that he had not noticed the spells that must have masked their presence, spells which he, more sensitive to sorcery than most, should have at least felt, regardless.

Despite his predicament, Darkhorse responded to his captors presence with disdain. "*Drakes!* I might have known your kind would be slithering about these holes in the ground!"

The crimson light poured over the newcomers, giving them the appearance of walking dead risen from some terrible battle. Each stood a little taller than a man and, outwardly, resembled savage warriors clad in masterly crafted scale armor that covered all but their heads. The heads themselves were mostly obscured by great dragonhelms that made the humanoid figures

seem even taller. Within those helms, eyes the color of fire
blazed and mouths full of sharp, predatory teeth opened wide in
triumphant smiles. Their noses were little more than slits and,
if one was so foolish as to get close enough to see, their skin
was scaled, like a reptile.

Darkhorse knew far better than most that the armor was
illusion. The scales were real, as real as those on the drakes'
faces. It was not true clothing they wore, but their own skins
transformed by the drakes' own innate sorcery. Even the
mighty helms were false in nature, the intricate dragon crests
being the true faces of the creature and not some craftsman's
design. The shadow steed had seen drakes revert to their
dragon forms, and watched as the fierce dragon head slid down
and stretched, becoming animated with life. It was a sight none
could ever forget—provided they survived the encounter.

Dragons who preferred the forms of men, that was the drake
race. With each generation, there were more and more of those
who could better copy the human form. The females were
already adept—*too* adept, some human women said—but they
sacrificed much of their power for that perfection.

The drake holding the noose wrapped around Darkhorse's
neck gave it a tug. Pain burned the eternal where the metallic
bonds touched his form, and all thought of drakes and their odd
ways vanished as anger resurfaced stronger than ever before.

"Thisss isss our domain, demon," the apparent leader hissed
with gusto. "To enter here meansss to sssacrifice your life!"

Darkhorse chuckled. "You sound like your cousin the ser-
pent, reptile! Is proper speech beyond you?"

The leader hissed, revealing a long, forked tongue. *A throw-
back*, the shadow steed noted in one part of his mind. A drake
whose ties to the dragon form of his birth were stronger than
those of his brethren, those ties manifesting themselves in such
things as the split tongue, jagged teeth designed to tear flesh,
and a savage manner that made them the deadliest of their race.

"Your death will be mossst—most enjoyable, demon! Our
lord will gain great pleasure from watching you perish slowly!
Too many of our race have suffered the unspeakable at your
hands!"

"Hooves, dear lizard, hooves! Those things at the end of
your arms are hands—more or less! Tell me; can you really
hold a sword with those gnarled appendages—or do you scratch
and bite your opponents like a riding drake?"

Riding drakes were huge, swift, wingless dragons of an intelligence just below that of horses. That such mindless beasts were as much a part of the drake race as these warriors before him amused Darkhorse. It did *not* amuse the leader—as the ebony stallion had hoped. "It might prove interesting to see if a sword could cut you now that you are *forced* to remain in the form of a beast of burden, demon horse! I will have to make such a suggestion to our lord when we have dragged you before him!"

Darkhorse looked scandalized. "Drag me before him? Did I say that I would be party to such a thing?"

The drakes grew nervous. A few touched their swords, forgetting the type of creature they were dealing with. The sword was the most useless of their weapons.

"You have no say in the matter."

"Oh, my dear friend, but I *do*!" Darkhorse retorted. He began to laugh, taunting his captors with the very madness of his act. The sorcerous bonds burned into his solidified form, but he turned the agony around, adding its strength to his mocking reply. In the vast maze of caverns, the sound of his voice echoed and echoed, but nowhere with more intensity than in the throne room. The more the pain sought to defeat him, the louder he became.

One by one, his captors lost control as the laughter battered their ears. The drake keeping his right foreleg in check lost his grip on his weapon as he reached up and buried his head in his hands, trying without success to block out the noise. Darkhorse shook the coil loose and used the one leg to pull himself forward. The drakes behind him, barely able to even stand, could not maintain their grips. Freed, the shadow steed whirled and struck at the drake who controlled the coil around his left foreleg. The kick sent the warrior flying into one of the statues that still stood. Though he wrapped around it like a ribbon, the drake never felt his back break; Darkhorse's blow had killed him.

The noose around his throat still burned. Darkhorse, no longer laughing, turned to the source of his pain, the leader of his attackers. The drake was on one knee and slowly recovering as the agonizing sound died away. Throughout all of it, he had maintained a tight grip. One coil, however, was not enough to hold the shadow steed, not now. Darkhorse prodded two of the other coils before him and, as the drake rose, kicked them expertly toward his adversary. The reptilian warrior had just enough time to realize his danger when both deadly toys dropped on him.

He screamed—almost. The power needed to contain an eternal such as Darkhorse was more than enough to consume the drake completely. There was not even a trace of ash.

Desperate, one of the remaining attackers leaped at the shadow steed, beginning the transformation to dragon form midway through the air. Darkhorse made no move to stop him. To what would forever be his dismay, the drake found no solid flesh to rend. He did not land upon Darkhorse but rather *within* him. The now-completely transformed dragon sank into the emptiness that was the jet-black stallion. Smaller and smaller the unfortunate attacker became, dwindling the way a figure falling forever and ever gradually diminished—until there was nothing to see. He would continue falling in that abyss, as still did so many before him, until everything—the multiverse, chaos, and even the Void—ceased to be.

"I am the demon to demons. I am the traveller who defies the Final Path. I am the Void incarnate. *I* am *Darkhorse*." The eternal fixed his chilling stare on the remaining drake warriors as he whispered.

The drakes fled, disappearing in all-out panic into one of the caverns. Darkhorse watched them escape, all the while chuckling in morbid amusement.

Lead me to your master, drakes! Though the cursed light that only Shade could have left behind colors you scarlet, I think that silver *is more to your lord's taste!* Darkhorse began trotting after the vanished drakes, his hooves making no sound despite seeming to strike the stone floor with enough strength to shatter it. This time, the advantage would be his.

Lead me to your master, brave ones, for I think that there might be a warlock I am seeking with him as well—and I will fight all the clans of your kind if that is what it takes to finally face him!

Faces vaguely recalled. Names only beginning to resurface. Images of the ancient dead walking the earth once more.

Shade could not say what urge had suddenly driven him to this subcavern far, far below the throne room. Not exactly a memory, but something more. Something to do with the insignia carved in raw marble and embedded in the wall he now stood before. An insignia he remembered seeing on the Gryph-on's tapestry and which he now traced in an abstract manner with his left hand. A militaristic banner with the stylized image of a fighting dragon.

The banner of his clan. The banner of his *father*.

"What memories do you hold?" Shade whispered, not knowing whether he spoke to the relief on the wall or his own, murky mind. He still could neither recall what he had come to this mountain for nor why the image of a great black beast, a demonic horse, had burned itself a permanent place in his thoughts.

"What memories do you hold?" the warlock repeated. Unable as he was to see his own face—or lack thereof—Shade could not notice the brief clarity which played across it. The change came and went in less than a breath, but it left its mark, though the warlock could not know that.

"Give me your memories." The words were not the product of wishful thinking, but rather a command. The resistance was strong, but not enough, not to one who knew—now. Shade nodded. His own memories were returning again and now he would add new ones as well.

A pale, blue light formed in the center of the chamber and expanded. The warlock, his hand still on the ancient carving, turned to gaze on that light, seemingly fascinated by it as a moth to a flame. The light continued to expand and, as it did so, began to take on shapes. One after the other without stop. Tall. Short. Distant. Near. Simple. Unbelievable.

Memories of a long-forgotten time. Of a race of sorcerers called the Vraad. Of Shade's kind.

The images were indistinct at first. Shade put his other hand on the relief. The memories had been gathered over generations and from countless places. He could not say exactly when he recalled this information, but it was true, just as it was true that this carving had been set in the wall for just the reason he utilized it for now.

"Give them to me!" he swore between clenched teeth.

An image broke from the rest, solidified, and sharpened. Even though it was not yet distinct, Shade inhaled sharply, knowing already who it would be. It was not the one he had wanted—probably one of the *last* he had wanted—but it made sense, given the dragon banner on the wall.

Father . . . Shade raised his left hand to the top of the banner.

With a violent twist of that hand, he banished the image. It flared like a miniature sun—and was gone.

A new image separated from the jumble, grew, and defined itself. A tall figure, female and only recently into womanhood. Shade dismissed it as he had the first, though he briefly wondered why it bothered him almost as much as seeing his father had. There had been no name to put to the woman, but he knew her. He also knew that, whatever her connections to him, she was not part of what he now sought. Still . . .

Caught up in his thoughts, the warlock looked away for several seconds. When he returned his gaze to the blue light, he started in surprise, for another figure, tall and clad in armor, stood waiting patiently. Where the others had been bright, as if the sun of midday had shone overhead, this one stood with the light behind him, blocking the glow and creating a shadow.

A shadow?

Shade glanced down at the rocky surface, eyeing the shadow that stretched long and narrow. This was no memory of the past. What stood before him was very, very real.

"Warlock. Shade." The huge, armored newcomer took a few steps toward him. In the light, the scale armor glittered silver-blue. The voice was a quiet, soothing hiss. "I would have words with you, warlock. Words of things that concern both of us."

The distant sound of mocking laughter echoing through the caverns made both look in the direction of the sole entrance to the chamber. Images of a creature with ice-blue eyes once more demanded Shade's attention.

His new companion stirred visibly. Reptilian features partially masked by the massive dragonhelm were turned once more toward the warlock. Shade caught uncertainty tinged with greed—and fear.

The Silver Dragon spoke again, his words uttered a bit faster than the first time and his eyes continually darting toward the entrance. "I would have words with you, friend—and *quickly*, if you do not mind."

The drakes who fled from Darkhorse led him deeper and deeper into the caverns. Even he, who had known that a fantastic system of chambers lay within and below Kivan Grath, was shocked at the complexity and extent of the labyrinth. Still, it did make sense, for this had been the home of the entire clan of Gold, the most royal of drake clans. In one hot, steamy chamber, a hatchery by the look of it, he had even come across the skeletal remains of a huge female dragon who obviously had been the guardian of the newly born drakes. Her death had been quiet if not peaceful from the look of it. Old age or lack of purpose, he judged. Darkhorse had also not missed the brittle fragments of the second skeleton in that area, a drake warrior who looked suspiciously as if he had been killed by the elderly dam herself.

So many things to wonder about, he thought as he turned down yet another corridor. Would he ever find out what had happened since his exile? There seemed to be so *much*. A sudden uneasy feeling filled him, but it had nothing to do with his unanswered question. Darkhorse paused. No, something else disturbed him. He sniffed the air.

Vraad sorcery—and close!

"Shade..." he whispered to himself. So close the shadow steed could almost see him. Darkhorse opened a path in reality and, without hesitation, stepped through.

The path itself was short, almost nothing, and the ebony stallion emerged from the other end of the portal in mere seconds. He found himself in the center of a chamber, bathed in a pale blue light and surrounded by phantom images that ignored him as they played out their brief lives.

"What manner of monstrosity is this?" the shadow steed bellowed without thinking. Had he fallen into some hell created by Shade?

Two figures whirled at the shout, both momentarily shadowed. Darkhorse stepped quickly from the light, shaking his body as if that would remove the thought of these disconcerting specters from it. They had about them the feel of Vraad sorcery, which made their existence all the more foul.

One of the two figures watching him stepped closer, as if taking a casual walk. "You... you're... Darkhorse... aren't you?"

"As much as you are the warlock Shade, my blurry friend! You know that very well! You remember *everything*—or have you *forgotten* that?"

Perhaps it was his eyes that played tricks on him, Darkhorse wondered, but he would have been willing to swear even to the Lords of the Dead that Shade was smiling just a little. Was it a trick or were those two dark spots his eyes?

Before the shadow steed could take it further, the warlock nodded and replied, "I remembered . . . but I forgot. I am remembering again . . . but not as Madrac. As myself, I think."

Darkhorse's eyes glittered. "Yourself?"

"I can't be certain yet." Shade indicated his companion. "The drake lord asked me the same question. He seemed disappointed. I think he wanted to make some sort of pact. I don't know."

"Thisss isss insssanity!" The Silver Dragon raised a fist. Something crystalline glittered in its grip. "He isss our enemy!"

An oppressing weight crashed down on the black stallion. Darkhorse fell to his knees and grew distorted as the pressure on him increased and he was slowly flattened. The Silver Dragon took a step forward, the light of victory burning in his anxious eyes.

"It worksss! It worksss!"

Shade remained where he was, watching everything with clinical interest. "Of course it does. Vraad sorcery does not fade easily. Still, I doubt if it will be enough."

The drake cocked his head in sudden confusion. Victory had been replaced anxiety. "What'sss that? What do you *mean*, human?"

"He means," Darkhorse forced himself to his feet again, "that you'll need more than that pretty bauble to keep me kneeling before you, lizard!" The shadow steed chuckled. "Surprise was its only useful weapon—and you've used that up!"

The Dragon King cursed and shook the crystal, as if that would make it stronger. Shade shook his cowled head.

"He knows more about it than you do, it seems, drake. I would have to say he probably knows more than I remember, too."

Slowly, the Silver Dragon backed away. "I have my own power! I can deal with him!"

"Ha!" Darkhorse looked down at the reptilian monarch. "Power includes the confidence and will to back it up, my little friend! Do you have enough of either? Somehow, I doubt that!"

Shade crossed his arms and looked at both of them. "He may be right, Dragon King. He may be wrong as well."

"You! He is your enemy, too! If he defeats me, you will be next!"

"Possibly. Possibly not. I *could* just depart—but I suppose he would find me eventually."

Darkhorse moved cautiously. He was confident that the Dragon King would give him little trouble, being the most pathetic of his brethren that the horse could recall. *This is a drake lord? This one would be Emperor?* What worried him, however, was this *new* Shade, this indifferent, even possibly amoral creature who stood talking calmly while two powerful beings prepared to fight to the death—a fight that might very well include the warlock before long.

Desperation was written in every movement of the Silver Dragon. Darkhorse began to understand. This drake lord had lived under the favor of the Gold Dragon and had apparently drawn much of his strength from his emperor—who had been more than a little paranoid about his own position. That paranoia had evidently transferred itself to this Dragon King, who saw himself as the obvious successor to his former master.

The drake hissed and suddenly threw the crystal at Darkhorse.

"That was definitely foolish," Shade commented.

Knowing the artifact for what it was, the stallion stepped nimbly aside. A magical talisman could be deadlier when used in desperation than in planned combat. The Vraad device went flying past him, striking the cavern wall behind. It bounced two or three times on the floor and then rolled to a stop—all without the slightest sign of danger.

Shade leaned over, clearly interested at the lack of reaction on the talisman's part.

The crystal split into two perfect pieces and a gray-green smoky substance began to rise from it, forming into a cloud that swelled with each passing second. The warlock straightened quickly with as much emotion as Darkhorse had seen him convey since his arrival here.

"I *warned* you that it was foolish. I think I may leave after all."

Darkhorse snorted and trotted a step closer to the cloaked figure. "None of us is leaving here, dear friend Shade, until—"

The shadowy warlock curled within himself and vanished with a slight *pop*! before the next word was even out of the eternal's mouth.

"No!" The Dragon King reached toward the spot where the spellcaster had stood, uselessly grasping at air.

"You!" Darkhorse turned on the drake. "Where has he

gone, carrion eater? Where?'' *Notagainnotagainnotagain!* the shadow steed mentally cursed.

Sizing up the chamber and knowing his chances against the creature before him, the Silver Dragon came to a rapid decision. He transformed.

The transformation was quick, almost unbelievably so. Wings burst from the drake's back and the creature hunched forward as his spine arced and his legs bent *backwards*. Taloned hands grew long and arms twisted, becoming more like the legs. The Dragon King's neck stretched high, an ungodly sight at first, what with the humanoid head, but then the dragon-crest slid down over the half-hidden face, slid down and lengthened. The jaws snapped and the eyes opened, the true visage of the Silver Dragon revealed at last. All the while, the form of the leviathan expanded, growing and growing until it threatened to fill the cavern and more.

All this in but a breath. Time enough for Darkhorse to have attacked—save that his limbs were suddenly heavy and the chamber was beginning to *fade*. He blinked, wondering if the ominous smoke cloud had affected his senses. His second thought was that Shade had made a fool of him, had returned somehow without Darkhorse sensing him and struck with some new spell. He struggled forward. The dragon, now whole, did nothing but stare. Shade and slowly smile that toothy smile that only his kind was capable of.

"The nag hasss been sssnared himmsssself!" the Dragon King hissed jubilantly. He inhaled sharply and, as Darkhorse looked on in helpless frustration, bathed the shadow steed in white flame summoned up from his own magical essence. Darkhorse steadied himself, knowing that here was a fire whose burning touch even he might feel.

The flame passed through the trapped stallion without so much as a hint of its unbearable heat. The Silver Dragon roared angrily. Darkhorse laughed, covering his own surprise with bravado. What was happening?

You will come to me, demon! a familiar voice demanded. *Now!*

"Damn the Final Path, *no!*" Darkhorse renewed his struggles, fighting with such ferocity that that Dragon King backed away again. "No!"

The choice is not yours, demon! You will *come!*

He was wrenched from the cavern and the dragon with the

ease that one might reach down and pick up a twig. The
world—everything—twisted and faded. Darkhorse struggled,
but he might as well have been trying to physically run the
boundaries of the Void so futile was his attempt. He had
underestimated an adversary again. His self-exile, he grimly
decided, had warped his senses beyond help.

The world of the Dragonrealm returned then—and with it a
place that he had thought he would never have to see again.

In the dim light of the torch, Drayfitt rose before him,
exhausted but satisfied. The look in his eyes was unreadable,
even to Darkhorse.

"He will not escape this time. We can stare in those dead
eyes until the Dragon of the Depths comes to visit the king for
lunch before the demon will be able to trick one of us again.
His other abilities are stifled as well."

The markings around his magical cage had been altered
slightly. Darkhorse tried to make them out but could not.

Mal Quorin joined his rival and eyed the shadow steed with a
mix of fury and glee. "You've cost us much, demon! That
book cannot be replaced! Rest assured, though, before long,
you will have repaid us for it over and over again!"

"Mortal fools! I am not your fetching slave! Release me! Shade
still wanders free and the danger may be greater than I supposed!"

The Silver Dragon was a bully, strong but with little true
bravery to back it up. Yet, if he was allowed to study the Vraad
for very long, he might become an even deadlier threat. Kivan
Grath might again be home to an emperor, if it did not become
the citadel of Shade first . . .

. . . and Darkhorse, trapped again through his own lack of
forethought, would be unable to do anything about either peril.

VII

Erini woke the next day feeling as if the dreams of her
childhood had become reality. Yesterday had turned the fears of

the future back into hopes. Yesterday, she had met Melicard the man.

In the light of day, the magical aspects of his unique features had taken on a new quality. Erini had thought him handsome *in spite* of the coldness of his elfwood side; now, she saw that the elfwood could enhance as well. There was a beauty to the wood when it became one with the king's pale skin. The rare wood had always been beautiful by itself, but, as Melicard had seemed to draw from it, so, too, had it drawn from him. The two sides of his face had become one despite their differences.

Even the stiff, artificial arm had felt smoother, more supple than earlier.

Galea and Magda came and helped her this morning; a good thing, too, since she found she could not concentrate. Her thoughts continued to be of yesterday's journey out onto the palace grounds and the tower to which he had led her. It was part of the wall and there were three others identical to it spread equal distances apart. This was the best one, Melicard had informed her quietly, to view the city as a whole.

His manners were rusty, as would be reasonable after so many years with so little practice. Still, the more they walked together—*without* the ever-present shadow of Mal Quorin—the more a new man had emerged; a new man, or one who had been locked away for over a decade. More and more, Erini was discovering that the dark, moody ruler of Talak was a creation of Melicard's own fears and, though she dared not suggest it openly, the influence of men like the counselor. This was not to say that the drakes were innocent, not by far, but the princess knew that some, at least, were trying to make peace with humanity. The others . . . she could not entirely fault Melicard's crusade.

He had pointed to the north first. "There you see the old center. After the palace was built here, everything shifted. The buildings in the old center were torn down and new ones put up. Since there's a gate over there, merchants and travellers have taken it over much the way they have the other gates. Also out that way is the main garrison of the city. A remnant of the days when a drake ruled from the Tybers."

Sensing his mood changing at the mention of the Dragon Emperor, Erini had turned west and pointed at a number of fancier buildings. "What about those?"

"The wealthier families. Master merchants and the old blood make their homes there. You probably saw some of that since the gate you entered lies in that direction."

She smiled then, already knowing the effect a smile would have on him. Few women—few people—had smiled at him and meant it, possibly because the king never smiled himself.

In the tower, he had returned her smile. She wondered how she could have ever thought it would be a chilling sight. In reply to his comment, the princess said, "There was so much to see that I cannot recall half of what I passed. Besides, most of the time my thoughts were on meeting you."

Only one other thing disturbed the otherwise pleasant tour. Pointing to a large structure in the eastern side of Talak, the princess asked, "What is that? I saw a building like that in the west. Are they theatres? Arenas?"

"In a sense. You'll find similar buildings in the northern and southern parts of Talak as well. All together, they house a standing force at least five times the size of the armies of Penacles, Zuu, or Irillian by the Sea."

A standing army. The city of Zuu, though far to the southeast of Gordag-ai, was familiar to her by name at least. Though relatively small in comparison to giants like Penacles and the maritime Irillian, their armies were of similar strength—mainly because nearly every adult was willing to take on a foe and being a part of the army was considered an honor. Erini did not understand the ways of Zuu, but if Melicard had a force five times the population of that city-state . . .

The rest of the day went peacefully. She had eaten with the king for the first time and, during the course of the dinner, had carefully broached the subject of their courtship and impending marriage. Melicard's replies were short and vague, but more, she suspected, from shyness than reluctance. Realizing she was starting to push things too quickly, the princess turned to small talk.

Her betrothed had walked her to her room, where both ladies-in-waiting tried not to look disconcerted at the sight of their mistress and the king walking arm in arm. Melicard wished her a pleasant evening and departed. Erini could not recall when exactly she had finally gone to bed, only knowing that she had probably spent several hours either thinking or talking about the king—whether Galea and Magda wanted to hear it or not.

Now, at the beginning of what she hoped to be an even more promising day, the princess found she could not be satisfied with anything she wore. Magda tsked a lot, reminding her that it was Erini the king was to marry, not a particular dress. Erini grew flushed. Here she was acting like the mindless young things that had always surrounded her at the palace back in Gordag-Ai. Always they had spoken of this young duke or that in giddy terms, much to her annoyance. Now, she realized with a wry smile, she was acting every bit as empty-headed.

"Give me that one," she commanded with as much conviction as she could muster, pointing at a dress she had already tried on. Galea shook her head and picked it up again.

Some time later, as Erini studied her finished self in one of the mirrors, she discovered she was still dissatisfied with the dress.

Is this what love is? the princess wondered. *I hope not. I'll never be able to live with myself if I keep acting this way.*

A servant arrived just as she was about to leave her room and informed her that something had come up; Melicard was begging her forgiveness but he would not be joining her.

"What is it? Does Talak face an attack? Is Melicard injured or ill?"

"He did not say, milady. He seemed well, though, and there was no word of an encroaching army in the outlands. I know nothing more."

"Thank you." Erini ended up eating only with her ladies. All through her meal, a meal which proved that, if nothing else, Melicard had someone who could perform miracles with eggs and spices, she found herself returning to the mysterious actions of yesterday. The strange states of the sorcerer, Drayfitt. The anger and fear of Mal Quorin. The door in the garden wall.

The door in the garden wall?

After brunch, she insisted that her two companions learn more about the city so that they would feel more comfortable. With a start, she also realized that she had yet to speak to the captain of the troop that had accompanied her coach to Talak from Gordag-Ai. The hapless soldier had not disturbed her, obviously believing she was too busy adjusting to Melicard to speak to him. Surely, though, the captain and his men wanted to return home as soon as possible, didn't they?

"Magda, before the two of you depart, would you please ask someone to summon—oh, what is his name? The captain of the cavalry troop that my father had accompany us."

"Captain Iston?" Galea piped up quickly. "I'll do it for you, Madga. I know you have some things you want to take care of before we leave."

"Thank you, Galea. I'd appreciate that."

The princess, who felt she had missed something, looked at her other companion as soon as Galea was out of the room. Magda smiled briefly. "Little Galea and Captain Iston have known each other for several months. He is the third son of Duke Crombey and a career soldier himself. That his unit was given to you is a sign of favor on the part of your parents."

"*Gave* to me? Do you mean to tell me—"

"They're staying here, yes. Permanent attachment. Not one of those men has a family to return to. If I may be forward, I hope you'll encourage Galea. The captain is a bit older than her, but they are very serious and definitely a good match. She will bear him strong children."

Erini fought down a grimace. "Is that his main priority with her? Passing on his name to a new generation?"

"It has some importance." The taller woman looked at her curiously. "Your father, King Laris, and Melicard's father kept that in mind, I imagine. Most royal marriages are set up that way and quite a few more common ones as well—but, before you say what your face is already shouting, I think I speak truthfully when I say that Galea and her cavalry officer would marry even if children were out of the question."

The princess looked at her older lady with new respect. "You surprise me, Mag. The two of you aren't *that* much older than me—"

"Fourteen years is *not* that much older? You flatter me."

"As I was *saying*, sometimes I watch you and I see those creatures that my father insisted I associate with, those—those crystalline dolls of the court. Other times, you seem to be in command of the world."

Magda made some adjustments on Erini's dress. "No secret there. I'm a woman. If you want a puzzle to play with, try to figure out men. Now *there's* a mystery."

Erini thought of Melicard and nodded.

* * *

Her talk with Captain Iston was short. Once she had gotten over the fact that her parents had turned an entire unit of Gordag-Ai's cavalry over to her—as a personal guard—the rest was simple. Captain Iston proved to be a competent soldier and one of the few who listened to her without trying to act parental.

"I have only one request, then, your majesty," he said at the conclusion of their talk.

"That is?"

"It makes little sense for your bodyguards to be so far away from you. True, we are cavalry, but any soldier of Gordag-Ai is also a master warrior on foot, too. We were given the honor of becoming yours. At the very least, let me set up a series of watches so that each man can perform his duties."

Erini thought it over and nodded. "I'll have to talk to King Melicard first, captain, but I don't think that *he* will object to my request." Counselor Quorin might, but his likes and dislikes meant little to the princess. "I think I'd also like you to have a permanent place in the palace itself, captain. There will be times when I'll need you and I want you to start developing ties with our new countrymen."

"Your majesty, I'm a *soldier*! I should be sleeping with my men!"

"You won't be far. Besides, an officer is allowed some privacy, I think. You've earned the right to live life a little, too."

Magda and Galea announced themselves almost as if on cue. Iston did his best to maintain a military appearance, though his eyes wandered to the shorter lady-in-waiting more than once.

"We were about to leave, as you suggested, when I thought that there might be something in particular you wanted us to look for. Good day, captain."

"Good day, my ladies."

Erini smiled while the officer's eyes were on other matters. "Nothing, thank you, but a thought occurred to me. Captain Iston, if it would not be inconvenient, I have one more request of you."

He bowed. "Name it."

"I am occupied with many things at the moment, but I want someone to get to know the city. Magda and Galea are performing that favor for me. I'd feel better, however, if they had someone trustworthy to protect them—just in case. Would you be so kind as to take a few of your men and escort them? It would give you a chance to study Talak for yourself, something you were undoubtedly planning, anyway.''

Iston hesitated, then, with a glance at Galea, nodded. "A wise idea, your majesty. If the ladies will permit me a few minutes, I will have horses and half a dozen of my finest join us. Will that be acceptable, my ladies?''

Galea was silent with just the slightest crimson in her cheeks, but Magda took events in hand and gave her approval. "That will be fine, Captain Iston."

"Has the princess any other need for me?''

"None."

The cavalry officer extended his arms. "If the two of you will accompany me?''

Erini watched them depart, Galea's hold on Iston so tight, the princess wondered if it would be possible to separate them again.

Her feeling of joy increased tenfold. She was on her way to strengthening her relationship with Melicard and now her own people were beginning to adjust to their new home. She turned to the mirror for one last look, wanting to be her best when she found her betrothed, which she *would*. Now there was only—

Erini started.

A figure stood visible in the mirror. A hooded figure much like Drayfitt, only younger in stature, but clad in garments a bit archaic for the times. She could not make out his face; something about the angle seemed to make it indistinct, almost a blur. His cowled head had just turned in her direction . . .

She whirled instinctively. Her hands began to move of their own accord.

The room was empty.

Erini glanced back in the mirror, almost expecting to see the figure still standing there. Nothing. She turned and rushed to the spot where he had stood. Kneeling, the princess touched the floor.

There were bits of dirt in the vague shape of a heel.

A feeling of ancient, enduring power caught her by surprise and she fell backward, only barely managing to stifle a scream. It was the first time she had truly sensed another spellcaster and, though she did not understand exactly what she had done, Erini had a fair idea of what she had felt.

She debated for some time what to tell Melicard, if anything. All she had to prove her story was a tiny clump of dirt that even the princess had to admit could have come from her own shoes or, more likely, the shoes of some errant servant. Only because of her increasing sensitivity to the powers did she know for certain that what had been reflected in the mirror was no figment of her imaginative mind. Erini could visualize Mal Quorin's expression should she give in and tell Melicard or anyone else her secret. It would probably be the fatal blow to the betrothal.

Not now. Not yet. I have to wait. Her decision was far from strong and she wavered even as she chose. *Drayfitt! He might understand, but . . . won't he tell Melicard?* Erini knew that the sorcerer was extremely loyal to his liege and that such loyalty might demand he betray the princess. Erini muttered a curse her father did not know she had overheard countless times while growing up. She slowly rose, deciding that she would postpone telling anyone for the time being. Her only fear was that, by doing so, she might let some other danger grow unchecked.

Confused and no longer looking forward to the day, the princess left her chambers. Whatever else happened today, nothing matched the importance of strengthening her relationship with Melicard. Nothing save what might destroy that relationship before it matured.

Princess Erini found Melicard in the least likely of places in the palace. He was holding court—in a sense. What she actually discovered was a huge, nearly empty throne room in which the king sat on a simple chair—not even the throne, which stood empty at the top of a dais—and argued with four or five men whom Erini realized were emissaries from other city-states. Quorin, standing behind the king, looked on in a combination of barely contained anger and contempt.

". . . drake lovers, all of you. I should have guessed as much, especially from you, Zuuite. You've long lived under the *beneficial* rule of the Green Dragon, haven't you?"

The emissary from Zuu replaced his helm, which he had been holding in the fold of one arm. A bear in size, he looked more than ready to trade blows with Melicard. Instead, he retorted, "Tell that to Prince Blane and the others who died defending Penacles from the Lochivarites and the monstrous

forces of the Black Dragon and the drake commander Kyrg!
You recall the sadist Duke Kyrg, do you not, your majesty?''

It was a telling blow. Kyrg's name, Erini recalled, conjured
images in Melicard's mind of his father slowly losing control as
the drake ate freely from the writhing bodies of still-living
animals. Rennek IV had spent the next week babbling on and
on about not wanting to be eaten alive, something he knew that
Kyrg had been capable of doing. Those memories were only
two of the many that haunted Melicard almost every night.

The king's face turned as pale as bone. The elfwood hand
came down on the arm of the chair and broke it into splinters.
Even Mal Quorin stepped back from the rising fury of his
master.

''Get . . . them . . . out of . . . here, Quorin! Get them out before I forget treaties!''

As the counselor rushed around the chair to aid the emissaries in their hasty departure, Erini started forward. She had been
waiting out of sight near one of the side doors to the massive
room with the intention of joining her betrothed once the talks
were finished. Now, the princess wanted nothing more than to
soothe Melicard before his anger drove him to further destruction and possible injury.

A firm hand clamped itself on her shoulder. ''Your majesty, I
wouldn't recommend you speak to him at this time.''

She turned on the sudden intruder, intending to give him a
strong, royal reprimand, and met the sad gaze of the sorcerer
Drayfitt.

''He is in a dangerous mood, milady, and neither of us
should be nearby. Things have not gone well.'' The aged
spellcaster shook his head slowly. ''And I fear that I am the
cause of much of it.''

''So what have your problems to do with me?''

Drayfitt gave her a sour smile. ''Counselor Quorin, in what
may be his finest performance, has been trying to make your
arrival and stay here a detriment to the king's crusade. He's
already pointed out how you kept the king occupied while I
destroyed Quorin's damnable book.''

Erini blinked. ''Book? What are you talking about, mage?''

''I speak too much. Suffice to say, milady, King Melicard is
not quite certain about the courtship. We have to give him a
little time to recall all you did for him yesterday—and it was

significant, I can tell you. He was almost the Melicard of long ago."

"You ramble a bit, Master Drayfitt," the princess paused, "but I will stay clear of him for a short while—providing you give me some answers I seek."

Drayfitt closed his eyes in concentration. When he opened them, he quietly replied, "Don't ask me about yesterday. Even I don't know everything—as Quorin has reminded me again and again."

The spellcaster's muttered words did little to assuage Erini's curiosity, but she knew there were other ways to find out what she wanted to know. The princess was about to ask him a question that she was fairly certain he *would* answer, when the elderly man stumbled against the wall. Erini reached out and grabbed his hand to prevent him from sliding to the floor.

He regained his balance almost immediately, but the look on his face was the most tragic yet. "Forgive me, princess. My powers have been tested beyond their limits lately; I've made heavy use of them much too late in life. Had I continued to train, to practice, while I was still young . . ." Drayfitt's voice trailed off as he stared at Erini's hand, which he still held in his own. After several seconds, he looked up at the princess as if she had sprouted wings. All his grief, all his exhaustion, seemed to vanish as he said, "Step down the corridor with me, please. We need privacy. I think there is something we must talk about quickly."

Not knowing whether she was mad to trust him, Erini reluctantly followed. Drayfitt led her along for quite some time, refusing to release her hand from his own. She began to worry. What if the spellcaster cared as little for her as Mal Quorin did? Despite his polite, sometimes helpful attitude, he might object to the marriage as much as the counselor did. What did he see in her hand?

As if trying to relieve her fears, Drayfitt turned and smiled assurance. He led her around a corner and stopped. There were no guards in sight.

"I could've touched the minds of some of the sentries and had our talk in a more open place, but such flamboyancy always backfires. Knowing something as simple but important as that was one reason I lived peacefully most of my life. I dearly wish it was still true."

"What do you want with me?"

"You have a natural affinity like none that I have ever seen."

The sorcerer continued to hold her hand, studying it closely as if looking for some minuscule marking. Erini had a very uncomfortable idea that she knew what he was searching for. Nevertheless, she played innocent. "What sort of affinity? For excellent fingernails? For having the 'fair skin' of a *maiden* in the tales of the minstrels and players?"

His features grew grim. "Don't play games with me, your majesty! You know what sort of affinity I talk of. Have you felt the involuntary desire to test your skills? What do you see? Most burgeoning spellcasters see the lines and fields of power that crisscross the world. Others see the spectrum, the dark and the light, and choose what they need from that. Which are you, Princess Erini?"

He'll tell Melicard! The thought was an irrational outburst, but Erini did not care. She was not yet ready to face the king with her own curse, not until she was certain her relationship with him was stronger. The princess tried to pull away, pretending to be offended. "You're mad! I am a princess of Gordag-Ai and the betrothed of your own monarch! Release me at one and forget this nonsense!"

Drayfitt's other hand shot forward and Erini had momentary fear that the sorcerer was going to strike her. Instead, his hand went up to the hair above her eyes. Mystified, she stood silent as the elderly man searched for something.

"Aaaah! The growth is slower than I would've thought, but it seems to be different with each magic-user. Interesting. Ishmir was wrong."

"What—what are you talking about now?" She jerked her head away, as if suddenly feeling continued contact would affect her somehow. Simultaneously, Drayfitt released her hand.

"There is a lock of silver amongst your beautiful, golden tresses, Princess Erini. The silver will expand—*magically*, you might say—as your abilities grow. Soon—and sooner than you want, I know—it will be impossible to hide it. Before that point, you must decide what you will do."

This was the last thing she had expected to deal with this morning. Erini stepped back and smoothed her dress, more to try to calm herself than because it needed it. "You don't know what you're saying! If you will excuse me, Master Drayfitt, I believe I will retire to my chambers. I'm not feeling well."

She started to go around him, but the aged sorcerer took hold of her again. His strength was phenomenal, a complete contrast to his weakness a moment before. A fire burned in his eyes. "Don't make the mistake I did, milady. Even if you never need them, it is best to hone your skills. I can help you. I've lived through the pain and the fear—more than most, I regret to say. I can teach you. There is no choice; your abilities will grow with or without your permission."

"Let me go," Erini commanded icily.

Drayfitt obeyed, but he was not yet through speaking. "Think about it. I'll be honest. I may need your assistance later on." As her eyes widened, he immediately added, "What I ask of you will only benefit King Melicard, not hurt him. I want the best for him, as do you. I think that your marriage will may possibly save him from the fate of his father—or worse."

Erini could listen no more. There was too much in what Drayfitt had said that had the ring of truth or, at the very least, conviction. A part of her wanted to turn to him for whatever aid he could give her . . . but the fear of losing everything and the shame of what she was becoming held her back. Perhaps some time alone would let her clear the fog that had grown thick in her mind.

As she walked stiffly away, the sorcerer called after her, "I hope you feel better, your majesty. Let us talk again soon."

She did not respond.

The throne felt proper beneath him. Taloned hands stroked the cracked armrests. He smiled as he thought of the others making obeisance to him, awarding what was due to him after these frustrating past few years.

The hatchlings are tainted, the Silver Dragon decided. *They have lived with humans for too long.* That was the fault of the Green Dragon, master of the Dagora Forest and ally to the humans. When the Gold Dragon had been defeated, the royal hatchlings had been taken by traitorous Green and turned over to Cabe Bedlam, the foulest of the human race. Now, those hatchlings that would have become Dragon Kings were on their way to becoming human sheep instead.

It is the only thing to do. They must be eliminated eventually so that some other traitor does not try to use them as puppets. The line that rules all others will be mine. My claim is strongest. They will see that. I will make them see that.

"I didn't return to you so that you could sit dreaming in a broken-down chair."

The Dragon King jumped. "Curse you, warlock! Announce yourself from now on!"

Shade stepped out of the darkness of a nearby tunnel and looked around. "Where are your brave warriors? Out trying to scrounge up some more toys to replace your crystal bauble?"

"What of it?" The crystal had been a double blow to the drake's ambitions. Not only had it broken, but the chamber of the Vraad and several others nearby were now impassable. The smoky substance released by the artifact showed no sign of dissipating, either. Even Shade, who had come back to look for the Silver Dragon, would not enter.

The shadowy sorcerer had still not explained exactly why he had chosen to finally accept the drake's offer of an alliance. It was not for what the Dragon King had already discovered, though there was *one* item of interest that the warlock wanted— or at least *remembered*—nor was it because they shared common goals. Shade seemed to care little who was emperor, as it long as it did not interfere with his own goals, whatever those might be.

"Nothing," Shade finally replied in answer to the drake lord's question. "Let them search."

"What about you?" Silver's reptilian eyes narrowed sharply. "Did you find it?"

"You said it was in the palace."

"Correct."

The warlock shook his head. "I will try again later. Something went amiss." A slight hint of humor touched his normally indifferent voice. "I ended up in the personal chambers of the king's bride-to-be. She'll probably have nightmares for weeks and drive Melicard mad."

The Silver Dragon chuckled. "Such a tragedy is little in comparison to what I intend to do to that cowardly *scavenger* of a human! Talak will fall as Mito Pica fell—but, this time, there will be not enough left over to rise again. After Talak...Penacles, I think."

"Why not Gordag-Ai in the region of Esedi? Your 'brother' there is dead and few of his clan remain active; you've already taken claim to his kingdom. Teach your subjects that they must obey you. That is the point of having *true* power."

Shade watched the Dragon King visibly mull over the thought.

Gordag-Ai would be easier pickings and boost the morale of the drake's clans. It would also guarantee that his erstwhile draconian ally would remain busy, thereby gaining Shade valuable time—time to remember what it was he had set out to do and whether he had any right to do it.

Staring at one of the majestic effigies lying broken on the cavern floor, the warlock tried to ignore the increased pressure building in his head. He knew his mind had changed again, simply by the added pain. Shade also knew that the fact that he could recall his personality changes meant that he was beginning to stabilize. What worried him was what he would be like at that point.

He felt some shame and remorse for his past actions, especially against Darkhorse, but yet, at the same time, it was his growing feeling that those who stood in his way, regardless of their reasons, were simply in the wrong. If they surrendered to the inevitable, the warlock would leave them be—maybe— but if they continued to oppose him, he felt he was justified in removing them in whatever way necessary.

Shade realized that the drake lord was speaking. "What was that you said?"

"I asked you what you think you are doing, human! Is this how you vent your frustrations?" The Dragon King pointed toward the spot Shade had been staring at moments before.

The warlock returned his gaze to the effigy—or to where it had once lain. Now, there was only a pile of fine dust. Very fine dust. Shade looked down at his hands. They literally glowed with the use of the powers.

"I am *Vraad*," he whispered to himself. "Vraad is power." The words had been spoken millennia before by many, all of whom, save Shade, were dead now. It had almost been a litany to the race, and his remembrance of it was yet another sign of what was happening to him. Still, it bothered the spellcaster that he had reduced the ancient statue to ash without realizing it. A warning beat briefly against the walls of his mind, but the pain drowned it out. He looked up at the impatient and somewhat nervous Dragon King. "Merely a little carelessness on my part."

The drake's burning red eyes narrowed. "Yesss. That is what got you into your predicament originally, is it not?"

"Watch your tongue, drake lord. It might dart too far out of your mouth once too often."

The Silver Dragon hissed anxiously. Because Shade had found a need for him, he had grown overly confident about his power. Only now did the drake realize that there were limits to which he could push the spellcaster. Both knew that the alliance was temporary at best. Quickly, the would-be emperor turned the conversation back to an earlier subject. "What do you sssseek in the book? Most of it makes little sense."

"A key, of sorts. I really don't know what. Not yet, but soon. Soon I'll be my old self again." A vague line that was what now passed for his smile surfaced briefly, faltered, and died. Shade wrapped his cloak about him and, as the Dragon King rose in the sudden realization that something was amiss, vanished.

Through his own words, the warlock had just rediscovered the purpose, the goal, of his search—and why he dared not let anyone, even Darkhorse, stand in his way.

VIII

The pain inflicted upon him was like such he had not suffered in centuries. The human called Mal Quorin claimed it was on order of the king, but Darkhorse, in his more lucid moments, suspected that Melicard knew only vaguely what his underlings were doing. Something in the feline features of the counselor, as if he were toying with his prisoner the way the creature he so resembled toyed with its prey, told Darkhorse that.

It was obvious that the sorcerer was reluctant to question his rival and that alone spoke volumes as to their respective positions of influence with the king. Drayfitt's loss of face was the shadow steed's doing, made doubly worse by the successful destruction of the spellbook by the entranced mage. For that, even Drayfitt had exercised a bit of vengeance.

They had abandoned him for other matters some time back—how long, Darkhorse could not say. Now, the eternal recovered slowly in his accursed cage, his present form little more than a

blot of shadow darker than the rest. Had he been human, he
would have died several times over and that fact had not
escaped him. With one part of his mind, he plotted the torture
of his foes; with the other, he cursed himself for his stupidity
and lack of foresight. Drayfitt had taken care with his original
spell. Had the stallion delved deeply, he would have discovered
the thin magical bond that still tied him to the sorcerer, a tie
that the elderly human had used to recapture him. His escape, it
seemed, had been no more than a farce.

So close! Shade was no doubt laughing at him even now. He
had come so close, actually confronting the warlock. Darkhorse
knew he should have come in striking, beating down Shade
before the warlock had a chance to think. Hesitation had cost
him the battle and his freedom.

Once more, he re-created the equine form he favored. A
hollow victory, creating a form again, but a victory nonetheless. With nothing else to do, Darkhorse began a slow and
thorough scan of his magical prison. Perhaps this time...

Nothing. If anything, Drayfitt had tightened the control of
the pattern, used the power of the cell to cancel out the shadow
steed's own abilities to the point where even eye contact would
not help. The aged sorcerer was a survivor and learned readily
from his mistakes.

Odd, he wondered, that Melicard's spellcaster would have
access to a Vraad artifact at the same time that both Shade and
the Silver Dragon were searching for such things. What was the
connection? What did Shade *want* with a work from so
ancient a time? Surely not to summon a true demon. Its power
would be insignificant compared to his own. Was this latest
madness just the product of his unstable mind? The warlock
had undergone yet another personality change; in centuries
past, he had done stranger things during various incarnations.
These rapid and continuous changes, however, smelled of
something different, something gone awry. When would they
stop? Which "Shade" would be the final result?

Significant questions weaved in a hundred different directions like a swirling mass of tentacles, confusing and unanswer-
able for the most part. He soon realized there was little point in
pursuing them for now, though he knew that forgetting them
entirely would be impossible.

More time passed. All the while, Darkhorse stubbornly
continued to raise, revise, and reject options as they occurred to

him. There was no way that he could physically—so to speak—
pass through the boundaries. His magical abilities all seemed
useless while he languished in his prison. He did not even
know what was going on; the Dragonrealm might be on the
brink of destruction—

Darkhorse did not breathe, though he often pretended to for
appearance. Nevertheless, he came close to holding that
nonexistent breath when it occurred to him that, though his
magical abilities were muted, there were natural ones—unnatural
by human standards—that he might make use of. Regardless of
his careful work, Drayfitt could not hope to completely understand the nature of the ebony stallion.

There were many over the centuries who had called the
legendary Darkhorse the Child of the Void. They were closer
and farther from the truth than they knew. Darkhorse was a
creature of the border regions between reality and the Void who
only *wandered* that empty realm, much akin to the mist
dwellers who guarded the secret paths that crossed into and out
of the world like portals. Through practice, Darkhorse had
made himself stronger than most, though that had tied him to
reality and lost him some mastery over the Void. He did not
regret that; there was so much more to the multiverse. Had it
not proved necessary in his prior struggle with the warlock, the
shadow steed would have chosen never to return to the dismal
domain he had dwelled in for so long.

Yet, it was the Void to which he now turned in hope.

While willing himself back into the form of a horse had
proved difficult after his ordeal, the act of literally *separating*
himself into two parts was sheer agony. The strain alone
threatened to overcome him. Despite the horror, however, he
was willing to suffer that pain and even the permanent loss of
that smaller portion of self. What mattered most was learning
what he could in the hope of using it to engineer his escape.
There might even be a clue as to how he could stop Shade,
though his hopes in that respect were less than nothing after
what had happened.

He willed one of his hooves into a wide circular shape a little
less than a foot in diameter. *That* was the easy part of his task.
The second was far worse, a strain on his already worn
consciousness. There was also the danger of losing too much of
his essence. He planned to separate a tiny portion of himself
from the main body. It was a dangerous thing, risking his very

identity in the process, for a piece of his "self" would be lost along with his essence. Humans who had lost a limb might claim to have lost a part of who they were, but with Darkhorse it was literal. It would take him years to fully recover.

Straining his concentration to the limit, he forced the reshaped hoof to expand away from his leg. Slowly, as the two masses separated, the ankle grew thinner and thinner until it was little more than the thickness of a twig. Darkhorse felt his mind separate into two distinct "selves," one greater, one lesser. With one last effort, *they* broke the remaining physical link between the fragment and the main body.

What must be done . . . He wondered why such a thought would come to him unbidden—then paused in sudden guilt as he realized it was a fading thought from another, that piece of "self" he had sacrificed. Darkhorse stared at the black spot for several seconds before he could bring himself to work the rest of his plan. With great reluctance and a little revulsion, he extended his essence and created a new hoof to replace the old. The shadow steed could not help feeling as if he had abandoned himself.

"It is said," Darkhorse whispered to his other self pulsating on the floor, "that, from the Void, all places may be reached or viewed. The danger lies in forgetting yourself, losing the way home. I am my own home, yet I am also the path to the Void. I will consume you the same way that I have consumed so many of my adversaries, such as the drake in the cavern, over the endless years; but rather than be condemned to floating in the emptiness forever, you, who know the way as I do, will find the path and return through my body, the Void, and the border realms to this world, to the place called the Dragonrealm. Waste no energy in seeking the path closest to this palace, but enter at the first available. Entering reality will cost you your "self" and eventually your essence, but you will provide me with eyes and ears in the world out there—in the hope that there is still something that can be done."

He felt better saying it out loud, though communication between his two selves could have just as easily been accomplished by mere thought.

With a touch of the new hoof, he absorbed the lesser portion of his essence in the same way he had absorbed the drake who had tried to jump him in the cavern. It fell within him, growing smaller and smaller until it was beyond even his senses.

Darkhorse sighed—because it felt right to do so—and then stiffened as the world around him changed.

Mountains passed swiftly before his eyes, smaller than the Tybers, but still majestic in their own right. Green hills dotted the borders of that mountain chain and a few habitations could be seen in the distance.

Darkhorse jerked backwards, falling against the invisible barrier that held him. *By the twin moons! So quickly?*

It was impossible at first to separate the visions from his own sight, but, gradually, they came under control. The journey his other self had taken went beyond things such as time, but even the eternal was surprised at the speed with which it had travelled. That surprise turned to worry, for the images he perceived were weak, as if the strain of the journey had been worse than he had hoped. Little of the fragment's essence survived. There was only one mind, too, for the other him no longer had the strength to preserve its own will. Darkhorse had gained his eyes and ears, but he had lost all else that mattered. Even though it had happened the way the stallion had thought it would, the pain was deep nonetheless.

The northwest. I have emerged into the northwest of the continent. It was now an easy matter to guide the fragment along the simpler paths he knew until it emerged again, this time in the outskirts of the city. Darkhorse could not recall the last time he had seen Talak. He wanted to know what sort of place was ruled by men like Melicard and the foulness calling itself Quorin.

Through the dim vision of the fragment, he observed the people. They seemed healthy, though he was no judge of human conditions, and relatively happy. Darkhorse moved on, intending to work his way to the palace. The more he saw, the more Talak resembled a prosperous and very normal city-state—not what he would have expected under a madman.

No sooner had Darkhorse thought that, when he caught sight of the first soldiers.

They were armored and very definitely hardened veterans. A full column rode through this section, evidently leaving on some military exercise. Darkhorse paused his tiny spy and observed the marching men closely. From the looks on their faces, they were almost fanatical in their devotion to the king. The shadow steed turned his gaze to the banners they carried. The stylized dragon made him chuckle in bitter humor. Melicard was preparing for all-out war and, judging by the size of this column, he was nearly ready.

He will have his glory . . . and the Lords of the Dead will have their bounty. Melicard had numbers, but the drakes had the ferocity. Either side had equal chances, which meant a long and bloody war that would strip the lands further of life.

Is that all there is to these mortal creatures? Are the humans, drakes, Seekers, and the rest all doomed to violent ends? Darkhorse tried not to think too hard about his own role; it was best to believe he had always worked for the quickest and most rational solution.

He wasted no further time. In seconds, his view had changed to that of the palace walls. The fragment, only a tiny part itself of what he had sacrificed, moved through those walls like a specter, entering the rear of the building. He ran it through corridor after corridor, room after room. Most of his observations were of the ordinary type; servants going about their daily duties, guards standing at attention in various hallways, and officials running hither and yonder with no evident purpose. Melicard was not in any of the rooms Darkhorse searched. There was also no trace of either the counselor or the sorcerer. So close, he was forced to slow his search. There were many risks, including excessive activity near Drayfitt, who might be sensitive enough to pick up the magical presence of Darkhorse's spy.

"... and keep them prepared, Commander Fontaine! There's been report of activity in the Hell Plains. The remnants of the Red clans may be moving."

Counselor Quorin marched into sight, another man, a soldier, keeping pace. If Quorin had the face of a cat, his companion was just the opposite. Rough canine features and a bald head gave the human an ogreish cast. Like the animals they resembled, the two men were bickering.

"I've not heard a thing about the Hell Plains! Damnation, man! It's east and north we have to watch! Drakes of the Silver clan have been spotted in the Tybers! *He's* the one we should be moving against!"

"You can always go *back* to the city guard, commander, if you can't obey a directive!"

The officer slammed his helm onto his head and marched stiffly away, muttering something about merchants and functionaries knowing less about wars than conscripted footsoldiers.

Mal Quorin watched the fuming soldier vanish and smiled. It was the same sort of smile he had used on Darkhorse during the "punishment."

The smile quickly soured as some disturbing thought intruded. The counselor turned back the way he had come and moved on, his pace quick and determined. Darkhorse followed closely behind, curious. The path Quorin took led him toward an outdoor garden in the center of the palace. The human was halfway to an old door partially hidden in one of the vine-covered walls when another figure entered the garden from the opposite side. Both Quorin and Darkhorse stopped, the shadow steed quickly backing farther and farther away, hoping he had not reacted too slowly.

"Drayfitt!" The counselor spat out the spellcaster's name as he might have spat out a piece of rotten meat. The look on the sorcerer's face matched his own. There was no love lost between them.

"What do you want now, *Counselor* Quorin?"

As they neared one another, looking all the while like two fighting cocks, Darkhorse moved a bit closer again. Quorin was speaking quietly now, intending his words for his rival's ears alone. The eternal let his fragment drift close to the ground. If Drayfitt's mind remained occupied by the presence of his adversary, then it was not likely he would notice Darkhorse's spy. At least, that was the hope.

"Why aren't you attending to matters below?"

"There isn't much that creature can do at the moment—thanks to both of us! Melicard didn't even know I'd recaptured it, did he? In fact, he seemed quite surprised, *counselor!*"

"What of it?" Quorin bared his teeth in a parody of a smile. "I act in his name."

"Melicard would have never ordered such torture! I should have known better!"

"You seemed to be enjoying it somewhat."

The sorcerer's visage burned crimson. "I allowed my baser emotions to rule me that time, but not again! I care very little about what is ultimately done with that creature, but I will not see it abused!"

Mal Quorin leaned back and laughed loud. "Drayfitt—defender of the weak! That's not a pup down there, you old idiot! That's a demon older than time itself! Remember what it cost us—cost *you*—already! You're fortunate it didn't decide to take your head off while it was at it!''

Darkhorse heard the words faintly, his attention partially focused on the door Quorin had been heading for. The door, he realized, lead down to the chamber where he was being held—and both men had been heading toward it. For a brief moment, Darkhorse adjusted his senses, returning his full vision to the cramped room and his cage. If either man, especially Drayfitt, came while he was engaged with observing the palace, they would recognize that something was wrong. It was proving impossible to keep both positions in perspective and there was the danger that he might become so engrossed in spying on his adversaries that he might not even notice when one or the other visited his prison.

They were still arguing when the shadow steed reestablished contact with the fragment. The images were even more faded, a sign that the fragment was dissipating. Darkhorse knew he should have sacrificed more, but there was the danger of fragmenting himself into two greater yet weaker portions, neither of which could survive on its own. Only by utilizing a *small* piece of his "self" had he been able to do what he had.

"—before long! I expect it to be that way!" Quorin finished up. Darkhorse cursed himself for missing what might have been of great importance.

"We shall see. The book was fairly worthless in any case; most of it was notes, incomprehensible and, more often than not, complete foolishness. What little was useful was also insanely dangerous and destructive. I used what I could—and I still want to talk to the scoundrel you purchased it from. I want to find out *where* he stole or, more likely, scavenged it from."

"Why, if it was so useless to you?"

Drayfitt shook his head, now apparently a bit angry at himself for saying too much. "You wouldn't understand, Quorin. You could not *begin* to understand."

"Pfah! I've no more time for this!" Forgetting that it was he who had started the exchange, the counselor departed—in a direction that took him *away* from the door. Darkhorse hesitated, not knowing whether he should stay with the sorcerer or follow Quorin.

It was Drayfitt who decided for him. The elderly spellcaster started toward the door and then hesitated, as if he were noticing something for the first time. It was evidently not the stallion that had captured his attention, however, for Drayfitt also turned from the door and returned the way he had come.

Darkhorse watched him go, then drifted in the direction that the counselor had gone. *One wonders how anyone gets things done here, what with so many detours along their paths.* The tension in the palace was astounding. It was evident just from the two conversations he had followed that no one in charge trusted anyone else. This was a kingdom in danger of collapsing. Perhaps not now, but some time in the future.

They have no lives, just plots.

Quorin had disappeared somewhere in the cavernous corridors of the building, but Darkhorse did not have the power available to him to find out where. All the fragment could do was observe—and even that ability was faltering. So far, all that he had accomplished was to add to his list of questions. In his cage, the shadow steed laughed in self-mockery. He had outfoxed no one but himself with his trick. The sacrifice of this bit of his essence was proving to be worthless.

Despite the near hopelessness of his search, he endeavored to continue. So long as he could see and hear, there was a chance. Somewhere in this leviathan of a palace, he might still find something of value. Darkhorse regretted that he could not have severed a portion of himself strong enough to free him.

While he pondered his deficiencies, he guided what remained of the fragment through the corridors leading to the main hall, or at least where he assumed it would be. Most palaces, while they reveled in their pomp and majesty, were very much the same inside. Unless the builder and the ruler he had designed it for were both insane, Darkhorse was fairly certain that things would be where he expected them.

He was not mistaken. Both the main hall and the throne room were where they were supposed to be. Regrettably, neither the king nor his underlings were present. The shadow steed cursed as the images grew dark. His lesser self was in the first stages of death—or nonexistence, at least. Something within the eternal twisted painfully at the thought.

"I must insist. He *will* see me."

The voice was female and off to the right. Darkhorse forced his pain down and drifted toward the voice. It had been raised to command, and a female authority in the palace of Melicard I was something worth investigating.

The owner of the voice was a small woman who seemed

twice as tall as the sentries she was browbeating. All three
stood before two massive, wooden doors. By human standards,
she was beautiful, with a long, golden mane that would have
put many a mare to shame. The female was not from Talak; her
mannerisms and a slight accent spoke of the city-state of
Gordag-Ai, which Darkhorse had visited once or twice in
earlier centuries. Why she was here was a puzzle. There was
only one reason that the stallion could think of, but—surely not
with *Melicard*!

Unable to withstand his inbred training, one of the sentries
finally stepped aside. The other followed suit immediately. The
female, a princess if she had the authority to command the
royal guard, waited until the chagrined soldiers opened
the doors for her. Only then did she enter, and only after giving
the two hapless men an imperial nod. It was almost enough to
make Darkhorse laugh.

He followed her in, ignoring the doors as they passed
through the misty form of the fragment.

The room was dark, making the dim images even harder to
discern. Fortunately, the princess's first act was to walk
determinedly over to a set of curtains rising from the floor to
the ceiling and fling them aside. The room was bathed in a
flood of sunlight. Darkhorse shifted to a corner less lit, knowing that the fragment, while insubstantial, would still make an
odd shadow. A sudden movement from the other end of the
room caught his attention. His spirits soared.

Melicard!

The split-faced monarch turned away from the female, but
she would have none of his reluctance. Darkhorse admired her
strength, though he could not say much for her taste. Evidently,
here was a woman bent on saving a man from himself.

A waste of time, my lady, he chided, though he knew she did
not hear him. *Why must mortal women always think they can
bring out what no longer exists?*

"What's happened, Melicard? You act the way you did the
first time we met. Have I given you some reason to think that I
played you for a fool?"

The king did not respond at first, though he did look up at
her from the chair he sat in. Darkhorse could not make out his
face as well as he would have wished, but he thought that
Melicard was nothing if not confused. Here was a man fighting
himself. This was not the same man who had originally visited

the imprisoned shadow steed. Darkhorse studied the female with new respect. She *had* accomplished something.

"I apologize—Erini. My work has become paramount. I cannot say how long it will demand precedence, but I suspect it will be some time. Rather than leave you alone for all that...time, perhaps it might...might be best if you returned to Gordag-Ai. When I can spare the time, I will summon you back."

The princess, "Erini," the king had called her, was not to be put off. With a bluntness that surprised both the eavesdropping specter and the disfigured monarch, she walked up to Melicard, put her hands on his face—on *both* sides of his face!—and replied, "Those are Counselor Quorin's words, are they not? I recognize the ruthlessness in them, a ruthlessness you could never match! Is he blaming me for some error of his? Am I accused of something? Do you remember the things we did and said the other day? Was that all amusement on your part?"

Melicard opened his mouth to respond, but the first try resulted in a silent swallow. After some effort, he said, "It would not be right to make you part of this. Not now. I don't dare allow anything to slow progress. I can't. Not after the setbacks."

Throughout all of this, Erini had refused to let go. Now, she pulled the king closer, so their faces were only inches apart. "Whatever you decide to do, I want to be at your side. Before I came here, it was infatuation with a memory and a dream. After seeing the real you, the one that men like that mouser you made counselor have tried to hide—with your help—it became *love*."

Love? In his cage, Darkhorse snorted in disgust. *Love for this sorry creature?*

Melicard had as much trouble believing it. "After only a few days? Love...like that...happens only in the tales spun by the minstrels and storymen. How can...you be so certain?"

Erini smiled. "Because I know that you love me, as well."

She kissed him before he could even begin thinking of a response. Melicard, unprepared, pulled back. His eyes were wide in almost childlike disbelief at what had happened. He could not have had much experience with the complexities of women, not, at least, in the ten years since he had shut himself away.

This is a predatory woman, Darkhorse thought, amused by it all. *A capable woman.*

The king rose and stepped away from her, but each movement, each hesitation, was an indication that Princess Erini had dashed any argument Melicard might have brought up. He *did* love her; that was obvious even to Darkhorse, who had never quite understood the concept since it did not apply to him. The signs were all there, however.

He whirled on her. "How can you love *this*?" The elfwood arm came up so that the elfwood hand could touch the elfwood face. "This is no epic song. I am no hero. I cannot promise that we will live happily ever after, as they say. You will see this face and this arm every day of your life if you marry me! Do you really want that?"

"Yes."

Melicard, intending to say more, faltered at the quick, simple response. Erini pressed her advantage. "Even if you had neither the arm nor the reconstructed face, I would want that."

A knock interrupted them. The looks on both humans' faces said that an intrusion was the last thing either had wanted. A guard, visibly tense, announced that Drayfitt needed to speak to his majesty. Melicard looked at his betrothed and then at the sentry. "Have him wait just a moment."

"My liege." The sentry closed the door.

Turning, Melicard walked over to Erini and put his hands on her shoulders. She was forced to look up to see his face. "We *will* talk again before the day is over, I promise you that, Erini. I do."

She wanted to kiss him again and Darkhorse, though the images had become so black as to resemble night, could sense that Melicard wanted to kiss her back. Fear held him back, though. The princess smiled nonetheless. "I look forward to it, Melicard. Perhaps, dinner?"

"Dinner." He called out for the guard, who opened the door just in time to let the princess through. Darkhorse slowly followed her. Despite the gravity of his predicament and the definite possibility that the king and the sorcerer would be including him in their conversation, the eternal found himself with an overwhelming desire to know more about this woman who could turn Melicard around so. He wished he could contact her, speak to her, for he suspected she might be his key. Her sympathy might do what his powers could not: make the king forget his idiotic dream of harnessing a demon to his service and cause him to release the shadow steed. It was a futile wish, however, for Darkhorse could only see and hear, not speak, not with so weak a fragment, and what remained of this portion of his essence was no longer enough to even gain her attention.

The princess walked the corridors as one half-dreaming. Darkhorse, who recalled moments of similar reactions from past mortal acquaintances, knew she was picturing the days to come. The stallion wished her best, for here was a true queen who would rule wisely, but he suspected her path still had barriers, chief among them Mal Quorin. The counselor would never accept a role of lesser influence. Already, he had evidently tried to break up the two. Darkhorse wished again that he could speak to her.

She was barely visible now, a darkened figure wandering in the abyss. His sacrificed "self" was in the last stages of dying. With no other option remaining, he drifted as close as he could, hoping to pick up some last words, some last expression. It was foolish and highly useless, but, for reasons he could not understand, he felt drawn to her.

Erini stumbled as if pushed. She came to a sudden halt and looked around, her hands twitching nervously. The shadow steed, his perceptions less than perfect, tried to see what worried her so. He was not long in discovering what, for the princess finally turned in *his* direction.

"Who is that? Drayfitt? Is that you?" She reached up a hand toward the fading place. Darkhorse, stunned, could only watch as her hand went through.

"No, not Drayfitt, it can't be. Did—did I summon you?" She looked down at her hands in growing horror. "Rheena! Not now!"

Summon? In his prison, Darkhorse's ice-blue eyes glittered as the answer struck him. Small wonder he had been drawn to her! *A sorceress! A spellcaster untrained!*

She had the potential to release him! *She* had the power!

The last vestiges of strength burned away. The fragment slowly faded, the last of its essence sacrificed. Darkhorse wanted to *scream*. If she were truly a magic-user . . .

Listen to me! he called out. If she did have a natural ability, it might be enough to establish a link! *Listen to me!*

She looked up—and her image vanished even as the shadow steed sent one last message. *Below! Go below!*

The walls of the underground chamber greeted his eyes once more. The single torch flickered in seeming mockery at his attempt. Exhausted by more than his failed efforts, the shadow steed drew within himself. He had little hope that his final words had gotten through—and without that hope, there was nothing else he could do.

Darkhorse settled down, yearning for the dreamless unconsciousness that was the closest thing to true sleep he could ever know. He hoped his strength, sorely used by this poor attempt, would return long . . .

. . . before the *true* demon, Mal Quorin, paid him yet another *instructional* visit.

IX

In one of the many unused chambers of the vast palace, Shade returned to Talak.

This particular room had been closed down after the death of Rennek IV's young bride, Melicard's mother, though Shade neither knew that nor would have cared if he *had* known. It was a room where he would not be disturbed and that was all that mattered. Cloths, long buried under thick layers of dust, covered the furniture, blocked sunlight from entering through the windows, and hid the painful memories from the old king, who had come here once a year on the anniversary of his marriage. Melicard, while he did not follow his father's example and pay homage here, did leave a standing order that no one was allowed to enter this room unless on his command. As it was, more than four years had passed since a single soul had stepped in here for even a moment. Ironically, Melicard, wrapped up in his campaign, had forgotten about his mother's chamber completely.

"Light," the warlock whispered, as if reminding himself. A tiny pinprick of light, all that he needed for now, glimmered in the center of the room.

Shade studied his surroundings but briefly. In a time long removed from the present rulers of this city-state and during one of his more benevolent incarnations, he had stayed in one of these rooms, the guest of a thankful prince whose life he had saved. The warlock smiled thinly. *There* had been a man who knew how to treat his betters.

Lowering himself down on one knee, the cloaked figure stretched his arms forward, as if reaching for an invisible object. He whispered words of a language long forgotten, the language of Vraad sorcery. Like the spells of the present-day sorcerers, the words were more a memory trick, a way of reminding him how the powers had to be bent by his will so that he could achieve the results he desired. He knew he had succeeded when he felt something squirm within his sleeves.

They say the walls have eyes and ears in most palaces, he thought in growing amusement. *Now they will have noses as well.*

A tiny, wormlike thing poked out of his sleeve. Shade felt a number of miniature legs and hands on his wrist; on both wrists. The wormlike thing proved to be a long and narrow proboscis that twisted and turned as its owner cautiously made its way out from the safety of the warlock's sleeve. From the other sleeve, an identical trunk extended itself.

Shade said nothing, but he shook both arms lightly, stirring the creatures to renewed speed. Drones of his own making, they were prone to be lethargic at first. Given their own way, the simple creatures would remain on his arms for days, trying to draw strength from what they had once been part of. He had no inclination to let them do so. They were nothing to him, who had given them life of a sort. They were tools and nothing more.

A head popped out after the long trunk, a head that was little more than a single, wide orb that was nearly all pupil. Beneath the great eye, a pair each of pencil-thin legs and arms made up the rest of the tiny monstrosity that was the warlock's spy. It scuttled onto the dust-thick floor, crouching, where it was joined by the first from the other arm.

The eye-creatures began tumbling out in astonishing numbers, many, many more than could have been hidden by Shade's garments. As their numbers grew, the creatures began to wander about, inspecting their surroundings with great care, now eager to perform their function.

When he was at last satisfied with the quantity, Shade shook his arms once more, dislodging a final pair of the horrors. He rose and gazed down at his tiny servants.

"Find it," he whispered harshly. "Do not let yourself be seen. Sacrifice yourself, if necessary. When you have located it, I will know. Now *go!*"

Shade watched them scuttle away in every direction, each creature quickly disappearing into the first crack or hole it could find, whether that opening had been initially large enough or not. There were other ways he could have gone about this, but anonymity was his desire for now. Let the destruction of Talak fall to his erstwhile ally, the Silver Dragon. The ensuing chaos and bloodshed would decoy those few who might be able to delay the achieving of his goal and might even rid him of a few annoyances.

The warlock thought briefly about trying to explain to Darkhorse what it was he had to do, but he doubted his onetime companion would understand. There were lives that would be sacrificed in order to correct the error that had twisted him so, and Shade was now fully prepared to sacrifice those lives when necessary. What was the loss of a few transitory souls if it would gain him his proper immortality and the power that should have gone along with it? He was Vraad and the Vraad were absolute. All else was there to do his bidding—even if that meant forcing that obedience by punishing a few. Once he had reclaimed this land...

Something glittered. Shade increased the intensity of the light a bit. The thing that had caught his attention increased by the same intensity. A reflection, which meant a mirrored surface. He walked over to the reflection and tore away the decrepit cloth, unveiling a full-length mirror embossed in silver. With the light floating behind and a little above him, the warlock stared intently at himself in the mirror.

A face stared back at him. The eyes and nostrils were dark spots and the mouth was a thin line, but it was still a face. A face that had been growing more distinct since his return to this world.

Shade put a hand to his reflection and drew a pattern across his face with his index finger.

The mirror cracked... and cracked... and *cracked*. Jagged lines crisscrossed the full length of the mirror. Pieces began to fall to the floor as the warlock stepped away, his face once again buried beneath his cowl.

Though the shattered mirror rained bits and pieces over the chamber floor, they made no sound as they hit. Odder still, the damage to the mirror did not stop there. Instead, those fragments that had fallen continued to crack, creating smaller and smaller parts which cracked further still. Shade watched silently, shaking, as a pile of dust formed beneath the rapidly disappearing mirror.

When nothing remained but a pile of fine ash, the warlock wrapped his cloak about him, twisted his body within himself, and vanished.

Whatever had stalked her was no more. Erini felt its passing, felt that something had disappeared that would never return. Yet, she was also positive that the force behind the misty apparition was still very much alive.

Her first thought was that this was some spy of Drayfitt's, but the feel was not right. He was no more responsible for this than he had been responsible for the visitation in her chambers. Neither was this briefly lived specter the product of that other intruder. This was another presence, one that was somehow not quite *human*.

What sort of place have I come to? Magic flies left and right and, though there are high walls and armed guards, intruders go in and out with ease!

Erini had not spoken to anyone about the stranger in the mirror and she was not all that certain it would be wise to bring this encounter up, either. Again, she had no proof save her growing sensitivities—which would, of course, reveal her powers to Melicard.

Drayfitt? He knew already what she was. If his present conversation with her betrothed did not include exposing her secret, then she might be able to trust him. He *had* offered to help her learn to control herself . . . an idea with greater merit than she had originally supposed. Her initial reaction at discovering the sorcerous onlooker was to reach out with those powers and discover what it was. Only her own fear had held her back. Next time . . .

The princess stirred, abruptly realizing that she had been staring at the same area on the wall for several minutes. So far, no one had come by, but it would not be good to be found acting so strangely. Inhaling deeply, Erini turned and walked in the direction of her chambers. Until she came to a definite decision, it was the safest place for her to be.

As she walked, she could not help feeling that the tiny intruder had wanted something from her, something of importance. The apparition was a sacrifice on its part. Erini had felt the bond, though the fact of that was only just becoming apparent to her. Whatever its cause, the unknown presence was willing to give of itself, if necessary. That was more than most humans would have done.

So engrossed was the princess in her thoughts, she almost walked into two guards patrolling the halls. She succeeded in stepping out of the way at the last moment while they, being only soldiers, were the ones who immediately apologized. Embarrassed with herself, Erini hurried away without responding.

The chance encounter with the guards had steered her to the side of the corridor where windows overlooking the inner garden dotted the wall. Out of pure reflex, she glanced out at this one colorful place as she passed each window. At the fifth one, she froze and moved closer. The door in the far wall beckoned to her with a stronger pull than ever. In her mind, Erini felt the link between the door and the thing following her and found it amazing that she, who had wondered *what* might be down there, below the palace, had never stopped to think that the *what* might instead be a *who*.

Erini would have gone down into the garden then, using the very abilities she had always cursed if that was what it would take to open the door. It was a foolhardy notion, though, for the princess had no idea where the counselor was at this time and, even with sorcery at her command, she did not warm to the thought of confronting as dangerous a monster as Mal Quorin. Even Drayfitt, with much more skill, was cowed by the man.

Her fingers twitched of their own accord as she continued to stare intently at the door. Annoyed, Erini formed fists in an attempt to stifle this latest urge. This was twice now in the space of minutes. At this rate, she would soon be unable to suppress herself.

It's like breathing, Erini thought in defeat, *and I've been holding my breath all this time, building it up into something worse*.

The door still beckoned. Biting her lip, the princess took one last, lingering look—a grave mistake. Her curiosity overwhelmed her caution. She *had* to see what secret the palace held, regardless of the counselor or Melicard's desires. This would be the true test to determine whether she was to be Talak's queen. If Melicard intended on keeping her in the dark as to his plans, then their marriage would be little more than a charade and something she would never be consonant to regardless of repercussions.

Having convinced herself of this, Erini sought out the nearest stairway leading down to the garden. All thoughts of sorcery were temporarily put aside as the anxiety of discovery replaced them. A tiny portion of her mind, buried deep within, warned her again and again about taking part in such foolishness, but Erini paid no attention to it.

The garden itself was beautiful, more so this close up. Any other time, she would have stopped to admire the lush, fragrant flowers and the thick, green bushes. Now, though, she had eyes only for the door. Erini took a quick glance around her, but there was no one else in sight. It disturbed her briefly that there were no guards in sight, but then she realized that the last thing anyone would want to do is draw more attention to the door by placing sentries near it. Unattended, it was just one more seldom-used passage not worth even a second look.

Erini felt a slight tingle pass through, but, unaware of the many abilities just developing within her, she thought it nothing more than nervousness. That delusion was quickly dispelled when a voice quietly but distinctly whispered in her ear.

"Enter there, your majesty, and I cannot promise to save you."

She whirled, saw no one, and whirled around again. Her hands came up in an instinctive offensive gesture.

"Peace, milady, peace! If you continue twirling like a child's top, someone is apt to wonder about your sanity—as I already do!"

The voice was Drayfitt's, but the elderly sorcerer was nowhere to be seen. In what was more a hiss than a whisper, the princess asked, "Where are you? Can you throw your voice a distance or is invisibility a trick you've learned?"

"Alas, invisibility has always been beyond me . . . but the secret of the chameleon is not. Turn slowly, as if admiring the flowers, and look at the wall behind you."

Following his odd instructions, Erini studied the vine-covered wall. At first, there was nothing new to see, but, as she studied it closely—a difficult task since she was also supposed to be admiring the garden flowers—Erini began to make out the shape of a cloaked figure standing at ease among the ivy and brick. His clothing and even his skin were colored and streaked in the same way as the wall, including the vines. The princess knew that if she ever hoped to see him clearly, she would have to walk straight up to him and touch his face.

"How do you do that?" Erini asked quietly. Unspoken was the second question: *Why did Drayfitt feel it necessary to disguise himself if only to reveal his presence to her? Because of Quorin?*

"Your majesty, if you would do an old man a great favor, I would ask of you that the two of us retire to a quieter place—such as my workroom."

"Why?" She was not entirely certain she was safe in trusting him after this peculiar display of his magical talents.

"Because I felt your struggle to control yourself even while I conversed with the king and I know you will not be able to hide your secret much longer. That was why I came, feigning weakness from some research."

Erini glanced wistfully at the door. "Very well."

"Excellent. We've been fortunate so far in that none of the guards have happened by here, but I assure you that our luck will not hold—and some of them are more loyal to Counselor Quorin than they are to King Melicard."

With that warning hanging over her head, Erini carefully made her way to the nearest exit. Her visible attitude was that of someone who has enjoyed the peace of a short walk but who now has become bored with matters. It was a look she had cultivated well over her short life.

Departing the garden, Erini continued to feign her disinterest in all things until she was well away. Certain that she was at last safe from prying eyes, she turned, expecting to see Drayfitt with her. The princess instead found herself to be utterly alone. Erini was about to call out his name when the sound of footfalls echoed from down the hall.

The ancient spellcaster stood before her, all smiles. "My dear princess, how nice to run into you!"

Confusion reigned supreme. "Why—?"

Her question went unasked as marching feet warned her that

the two of them were no longer alone. Erini caught a glance from the sorcerer. *Play along!*

"I've just finished an interesting walk in the garden, Master Drayfitt. A pity you weren't able to join me; we could have walked while you told me more about Talak. There is so much I still have to learn and you must know more than anyone about the city."

Four well-armed guards turned the corner, marching with the same exacting precision that all Melicard's soldiers seemed to march with. The apparent squad leader, a stout man with a thin, graying beard, called his men to a halt. He stepped toward the anxious princess and bowed.

"Guard leader Sen Ostlich at your command, your majesty! May I say it's an honor then to meet with you! May we be of service to you?" He pointedly ignored Drayfitt.

This was something that Erini could handle with ease. Her face became a mask as she imperiously replied, "Nothing at this time, guard leader, but your attention is noted. Is there something you wanted of me? Has the king requested my presence?"

"Not to my knowledge, your majesty. We're merely making our rounds. It wouldn't have been proper to pass without acknowledging our queen-to-be. The captain would've had us all on double duty." Ostlich allowed himself a rueful smile.

Erini granted him a royal smile. "Then, I shall not keep you from your duties. Carry on."

"Your majesty."

Bowing, the guard leader returned to his squad and gave the order to resume the patrol. The princess and Drayfitt watched them go, a sardonic smile creeping across the lined visage of the elderly sorcerer.

"How *gracious* of them. How curious that they purposely changed their route to march by here while you were nearby."

"Isn't this their regular route?"

"By no means. Oh, they'll claim that it was changed only today—if you ask them, that is—but I've the distinct advantage of having seen them turn from their normal patrol because one of the other guards reported seeing you in the garden. The chameleon trick has its advantages. I saw the sentry just as you were leaving. He didn't see me." Drayfitt smiled, pleased with his own success.

"I wondered why you vanished."

"Enough of that. Now that we've *officially* met in this hall and you've expressed your interest in Talak—an *excellent* request and good, quick thinking on your part—I think no one will suspect, anymore than usual, that is, that we have anything else in mind. If you will accompany me to my workroom . . ."

"You are my guide," Erini answered gracefully. As Drayfitt led her down the hall, already into the beginnings of a lesson on the history of Talak, the princess looked back in the direction of the garden and the door. While she was grateful to Drayfitt for his concern for her well-being, the sorcerer's actions had not deterred Erini but rather fueled her determination. One way or another, she would return to the garden before long and discover the truth.

Drayfitt's workroom was not what Erini had expected of a sorcerer. She had pictured a dark, moody place of vials and parchments, bones and the various parts of rare and magical creatures. There should have been ancient tomes on subjects such as necromancy and magical artifacts from civilizations long dead.

"Looks rather like the office of a minor bureaucrat, doesn't it?"

It was true. A high desk stood in the center of the tidy room, a set of candles and several sheets of parchment on top. There *were* books, countless books on shelves that ringed the room, but they were neatly stacked and fairly new. Some of them sounded fairly mysterious, but others were on classical plays or theories on government. Erini had not known that so many books on so many subjects even existed.

"Do you like them?" the sorcerer asked a bit wistfully. "I wrote most of them over the years. It's a shame that most city-states are not like Penacles, where writing and education are paramount. I understand that a few of the copies I made are now a part of the collection gathered first by the Lord Gryphon and now by Toos the Regent. I've made certain that at my death, accidental, natural, or otherwise, the Regent will get this collection."

Erini could not help smiling. "You do not remind me of what I was always told a spellcaster was like."

"Head bowed over a cauldron, arms waving in insane motions, and sinister, inhuman things waiting at my feet for some command? Some of those things are true, and, if you know the tales of foul Azran Bedlam, those images pale in comparison to what he was like. I was never happy with sorcery. I was quite happy to find myself a little niche in the controlling of Talak and stay there.'' The spellcaster's face darkened. ''*Counselor* Quorin insured that I would never be able to return to that and so I've made a special point of making him regret that action ever since.''

A twinge in Erini's right hand reminded her of why they were here. If Drayfitt could help her or, better yet, find her a way to rid herself of this curse, then she would take advantage of it. As if reading her thoughts, the sorcerer took her hands in his and looked them over.

''Tell me, when you observe the powers around us, do you see the lines and fields?''

She shook her head. ''No, I see a rainbow, bright on one end and changing to black at the other.''

''A spectrum. Pity. I see the former, myself. Well, at least you see the powers as something understandable. There are those who see them in radically different ways than we do, though such folk seem to be rare. The lines and the spectrum seem to dominate the minds of most—and before you ask, I have no idea why we see them at all. Some people discover them naturally; some, like myself, need training.'' Drayfitt released her hands. ''You are a natural adept. With some assistance on my part, you could become very skilled.''

Erini shook her head violently. ''No! I want you to help me get *rid* of this curse, not *enhance* it!''

''Your majesty, the abilities you have are a part of you, a gift from—from whoever watches over us. It's the spellcaster who makes those abilities work for good or ill. How else could one family produce both a fiend like Azran Bedlam and good, strong men like his father, Nathan, or his son, Cabe. I understand your feelings. For years, I lived with the memory of my brother, Ishmir the Bird Master—Aaah! I see by your face that you know of him. Ishmir perished in the Turning War with most of the other Dragon Masters and it took me years to forgive him for that.''

''Forgive him? For dying?''

The sorcerer looked chagrined. ''He left me, a young man, then, half-trained, uncertain of what I was. I had your qualms, too, but Ishmir saw I had the potential, though it was buried deep. I forgave him eventually, but I kept my powers hidden, utilizing only those that would help me secure a place in Talak's government and keep me alive—I'm a coward when it comes to death. Since my forced re-education in the world of sorcery—only a short time ago—I've learned much about its benefits. If not for my efforts, Counselor Quorin's influence with the king would be much stronger. That alone I count as a reason to hone my skills.''

Erini turned away, walking over to a shelf and running her fingers along the spines of some of Drayfitt's books. ''It might be different if I were not a member of royalty, Master Drayfitt. Such things are not for us. In the eyes of my people, I would be considered tainted, a demon in human form.''

''I think the only demon is in your own mind, if you'll pardon me for saying so, your majesty. There have been rulers aplenty who command in part through sorcery. The Lord Gryphon of Penacles is the best example. During his reign, it was his skill more than anything else that kept the Black Dragon at bay. He was even instrumental in the Turning War.''

''The Gryphon was a magical creature, Master Drayfitt. The powers were a part of him.''

The elderly spellcaster chuckled. ''He may not like all this talk in past tense; he still lives, they say, but fights some war across the Eastern Seas—hence the title of Penacles's present ruler, Toos the Regent. That is neither here nor there, however; what I am trying to tell you is that the skill to manipulate the powers is as much a natural part of humanity as it is of the elves, the drakes, and the Seekers. We merely have a greater tendency to stifle those skills. *I* ought to know.''

Erini slowly turned back to him, an idea forming. ''Then, if you cannot help me rid myself of it, teach me how to control it so that I will never find myself 'accidentally' unleashing some spell at a courtier who has happened to annoy me. That is what I fear; the *powers* taking control instead of the other way.''

A relieved sigh. ''Thank you, your majesty, for making my task easier. Had you demanded I help you rid yourself of your growing abilities, I would have endeavored to do so, despite the impossibility. After all, you are to be my queen.''

''That still remains questionable, Master Drayfitt.''

''I doubt it. One reason it was so easy for me to leave the king abruptly was because he seemed distant himself, and the look on his face I have only seen when he thinks of you—favorably, that is.''

The information earned the spellcaster one of Erini's few true smiles. "You have no idea how happy I am to hear that."

"I do and it makes me happy to say it. The two of you are well matched. Though it's only been a few days since you met as adults, I'm not above believing that a bond of love has already developed. There are those who are meant to be together. I—" Drayfitt suddenly paused, his eyes darting about the room.

"What is it?" Erini asked in hushed tones. To her horror, the sorcerer raised a hand toward her. She felt both the pull as he unleashed some powerful spell and her own instinctive response as she prepared to defend herself.

"Not *you*!" Drayfitt muttered at her. "Remain where you are!"

She froze in place. Behind her, the princess heard the thump of books falling from the shelves and—*the patter of tiny feet?* Something quick was running along the shelves, seeking a place it could hide from the spellcaster's attack. It might as well have been running from time itself.

Erini heard a tiny squeak, then Drayfitt's curse as something the old man had evidently not expected happened. A moment later, he lowered his arm, a look of disgust and worry on his face. He rose from the table toward the spot where the intruder had evidently met its fate.

Standing, the princess joined him. There was a strange odor emanating from the shelves and she sensed the remnants of some odd, disturbing sort of magic, something she had sensed briefly before. There was no sign of any creature.

"What was it? Did you destroy it?"

Abandoning his brief search, Drayfitt began picking up and reshelving his books. "As to what it was, I can only describe it as a little monstrosity obviously created to spy on others." He looked at Erini. "It's head and body were no more than an eye and a snout. A creature of magic. As to destroying it, that was not my intention. The creature destroyed itself. I wanted it alive—if it truly was—so that I could track it to its source, which is probably Quorin."

"He has no magic."

"Yes, you can tell that, can't you? Probably better than I. The only reason I noticed our spy was because this workroom is laced with spells sensitive to unwanted visitors. Here, of all places, I am most secure."

Erini hesitated before finally admitting, "I've felt something similar to that creature. The same sort of magic, different from you or me."

"What? When?"

"In my—my chambers. I was looking in the mirror when I saw him. When I turned around, there was nobody there. I thought I'd imagined him, but there was dirt on the floor where he had stood and—and when I touched it, the strangeness of it startled me so much I fell back."

Drayfitt's eyes narrowed and he scratched his head in thought. "Can you describe him, milady?"

"Not well. He wore a cloak and hood like you do, only they seemed older, out of style." The princess closed her eyes and tried to picture the dark figure. "All his clothing seemed a bit archaic."

"We are not always known for our sense of style. Forget his clothing, then. What did he look like? I may know his face if you describe it well."

She looked flustered. "I cannot help you there, Master Drayfitt. I was not able to get a good look at his face. My eyes must have been watery, because, no matter how I looked, it remained shadowy or blurry."

"His face was unclear but you could see that his clothing was old, archaic?"

"Yes, strange, isn't it? I remember them clearly enough, but not his visage. I think he had dark hair, perhaps brown, with a streak of silver."

"But his face you can't remember." The sorcerer pursed his lips in mounting frustration. "I wish—I truly wish, milady— that you could have given me a face to go by."

Erini could sense his worry. "Why? Who was it? Is it whoever you hide down below? Did he escape?"

Drayfitt gave her a dumbfounded look. "Soooo . . . you know about *that*, too. This gets worse and worse." He looked up at the ceiling, staring at something beyond it with eyes filled with dismay. "Aaaah, Ishmir! Would that you were here instead of me!"

"What is wrong, sorcerer?"

He went to the desk, opened a drawer, and pulled out a bottle caked in the dust of ages. Without asking whether the princess desired any, Drayfitt poured himself a goblet of what must have been wine and practically swallowed it in one gulp.

Eyeing the shelves of books, he finally replied, "The one you described can only be the warlock Shade, who can only be here for two reasons; the first of which is caged deep below in a chamber forgotten until recently. Another creature of legend, a shadowy steed called Darkhorse."

"Darkhorse?" While everyone knew one tale or another concerning the tragic existence of Shade, forever cursed to live alternating incarnations of good or evil, it was the demon known as Darkhorse that had fascinated the princess more. Here was a magical creature from elsewhere, immortal, and the terror of drakes. Some stories made him as tragic as the warlock and there were many who feared him as much, but the image of a great stallion, blacker than a starless night, had captivated her. She had even dreamed, now and then, of riding through the darkness on its back.

A legend and a reality were two different things. The thought of riding whatever Drayfitt had imprisoned down below made her shiver—and not in anticipation.

"Darkhorse." The sorcerer nodded. "They have been friends and enemies for millennia. Yet, if he wanted the stallion, he could find him easily. There'd be no reason to materialize haphazardly in the palace unless he was searching for something better hidden, something like the book."

"What book?" Erini was becoming more and more confused.

Drayfitt sighed. "The book I used, half in ignorance, to summon a demon, or rather Darkhorse, to our world. A book he tricked me into destroying when he thought I wouldn't be able to recapture him again." The elderly spellcaster smiled a bit proudly at that; it had been a coup in ways, defeating the eternal twice. Then, he frowned. "I hope it's not the book he's after, though I can't think what else it might be."

All thought of her own problems had long ago vanished as Erini tried to make sense of everything. She had wanted answers for so long, but now that she had them, the princess was more at a loss than before. "Why do you say that? Is it something he should not have?"

"Probably not. That's academic, I'm afraid, your majesty. As I said, I destroyed it. He'll find nothing but ashes now."

In a darkened corner of the ceiling, a small form scurried deep into a crack that should have been too tight for it. The sacrifice of its brother had proven worth the cost, for it had discovered what its master had wanted to know. Soon, it would be able to return to the warm nothingness he had summoned it from. Perhaps even as soon as it relayed the news to him.

Shade's eye-creature did not understand how its master would react to this particular bit of news. It would not be able to comprehend the fury nor would it comprehend that the warlock would destroy it, not because it had served him well, but because of a need to strike out at someone or something.

Least of all, it would not understand the danger the success of its mission had placed the sorcerer and the princess in. Nor would it have cared.

X

The Silver Dragon watched from the throne he had usurped from his dead counterpart as his loyal subjects began the long process of clearing the central chamber of rubble. Under the light of many torches, warriors watched over the servitors, who seemed uneasy at invading the caverns of their cousins. The Dragon King shifted to a more imperious posture, the better to build the confidence of his people. It mattered not that the clans of Gold—those that still lived—were outraged at his actions. They had three choices: become part of the clans of Silver as the survivors of the clans of Bronze and Iron had, flee to their other cousins, or face execution. So far, none of the three choices had become a clear-cut victor, which was the best choice in the Silver Dragon's mind, for it meant that the remnants of Gold's people would never band together in sufficient strength to fight his rightful rule.

I should have taken this place after Gold's defeat. So many years wasted—but now the throne is mine. The days of the Thirteen Kingdoms are at an end. Eventually, the Dragonrealm will bow to one monarch alone with no council to voice their dissent. . . .

So far, none of his counterparts had raised more than an

angry voice against him; proof, he believed, of their gradual willingness to accept him as emperor of all. Only Green openly denounced him, but that was to be expected from a traitor whose domain housed his race's greatest enemies, the Bedlams.

Ssssoon, he thought with a smile. *Soon we shall begin the cleansing process, sweeping down and bringing the upstart warm-bloods to their knees, where they will learn once again to give obeisance in the proper manner.*

One of his younger hatchlings, an unmarked male who served well in the hopes of securing a dukedom in the new regime of his sire, knelt before him. His false crest was less elaborate than some of his elders, a choice that the Dragon King approved of. He gestured for the warrior to speak.

"My sire, I give thanks to the Dragon of the Depths for your ascent to the throne of emperor."

Silver hissed as the flattery made him swell with pride. "What word of our chaotic ally?"

"None. Our spies search for him—cautiously, as you commanded. There *is* word on the book, however,"

"And that is?"

"That the book is *ash*," a voice from behind the throne announced.

The Dragon King leaped from the throne and whirled around. The other drakes looked up from their tasks, but a chill glance from their monarch, who realized he had lost face by this cowardly action, sent them scurrying back to their duties with greater effort than before.

"How?"

"The sorcerer Drayfitt. Why would you give such an artifact to a human sorcerer?" Shade cocked his head, his voice soft and smooth, companionable even.

The Dragon King was not fooled for a moment. He knew that he was facing yet another variation of the warlock, one that he suspected was closer to the original than any of the rest. "He was to translate it. All others failed. It was said he had the skill and knowledge."

Shade walked slowly around the throne. The two drakes stepped back. "So the creature Mal Quorin is yours."

His draconian ally did not argue the point. "Only after the book wasss brought to him did we discover the truth. The human king was quickly made to believe that a ssspell had been found that would give him a demon servant and all he had to do was find a sorcerer—which proved *sssurprisingly* easssy. The one called Drayfitt would continue the translation—at the command of his king, of course—and also test the validity of his resultsss.'' Silver forced himself to stare into the two dark spots that passed for the warlock's eyes. ''He would either fail and disssgrace himself or succeed, at which point, sssome accident would overtake him and the book would be returned to me. Any demon he had sssummoned would then be mine to control!''

''You are quite a gambler, evidently. I doubt if *I* would have done the same as you.'' With great deliberation, the warlock sat casually down on the throne. The drake who had reported to the would-be emperor hissed and bared his claws. Shade looked him over.

''One of *your* get?''

''What of it, *human*?'' the defiant warrior hissed.

''He bears no markings,'' the hooded figure commented to his ally, ignoring the growing anger of the younger drake.

''What if I do not?''

The warlock finally seemed to notice him again. ''Just so I know that I've eliminated nothing of importance.''

The furious drake reached for him, then hissed in consternation as a great, black hole materialized in his stomach. While the rest of the drakes—unable to keep from looking despite their master's earlier glare—watched in horror, the hole expanded. The hapless victim, in a state of insane calm, put one hand into the gaping maw, unable to believe his eyes.

The hand and the arm were sucked in.

In less than a breath, the shoulders, head, and remaining arm followed after and, when they, too, were gone, the torso and legs vanished into the hole. A single black spot remained floating in the air for a second or two, then vanished, seeming to swallow itself.

Shade glanced in the direction of the Dragon King. ''You've desired the power of the Vraad; that was a taste of what we could do.''

''Am I next?''

''I was under the impression we had an alliance of sorts.'' The warlock leaned forward. ''Don't we?''

''You recalled the book. That wasss why you returned to me. The book—*your book*—was destroyed. I assumed you had no further need to pursue our alliance and so I have moved on with my plansss.''

"Subjugation and/or destruction of Talak. I remember. I would think it simple with the king's counselor at your beck and call.''

"Nothing is simple except the belief in simplicity.''

Rising, Shade straightened his cloak. "Continue with your plans. They coincide with my needs. There is only one thing you must remember.''

"That is?''

"The sorcerer Drayfitt must not be harmed. I've need of him.''

A wary look passed across the drake lord's half-hidden face. "Quorin's followers are to assassinate him—soon—while he travels with the army. What need do you have for a human spellcaster with little more than adequate ability?''

"It's not his abilities as a sorcerer that I want. It's his mind. You did say he set out to translate the entire book, didn't you?''

"So?''

Shade sighed, wondering how this creature could miss the obvious. "Never mind. Return to your plans.''

"But *your* part of the bargain—''

"That?'' The warlock smiled, a shadowy line slightly bent upward on each end. There was something dreadfully cold about his smiles, Silver thought.

"Neither Darkhorse nor the Bedlams will interfere. You may rest assured on that. They will be too busy with other, weightier matters.'' That said, the warlock curled within himself and vanished.

Almost the Dragon King felt sympathy for the warlock's adversaries—almost.

Another day had passed and Darkhorse once more studied the cracks of the chamber walls. Studied them while his mind sank deeper into a bottomless abyss.

Failure. Utter failure.

Darkhorse looked *again* at the chamber that was his world and would *be* his world for some time to come, apparently. His one hope had been crushed—and at the moment of greatest potential.

The human female called Erini, Melicard's betrothed—now *there* was irony—was a natural spellcaster of high potential, possibly as high as Cabe Bedlam or the Lady Gwen. She had noticed the fragment of self although even Drayfitt had not. In the last moment of vision, he had seen how her hands itched to reach out to the powers, manipulate them. The female was stifling those powers, though; that much he had seen as well. If that were the case, he would receive little aid from her. Likely, she had not even told Melicard her secret.

His thoughts were interrupted by the unlocking of the door. That made him chuckle in sour humor; who would want to come in and what would they do once they were here? If it was not to keep someone out, what other reason was there for locking the door? Darkhorse would have been as secure if the entire palace had been leveled. Even then, the barrier enclosing him would have stood.

The door swung open and Melicard himself, accompanied by his foul shadow, Quorin, and the pitiful mage, Drayfitt, entered. There was something different about the king, a humanity that had blossomed almost overnight. It was not complete humanity, not by far, but a great touch more than the split-faced monarch had had during his first visit.

Given time, this princess would make him a whole man again. The shadow steed studied Melicard's visage closer, especially the living eye and the set of his mouth.

Apparently, there will not be time after all.

The king was here with an ultimatum. Darkhorse could read that even before Melicard spoke.

"My army marches against the clans of Red in the Hell Plains at tomorrow's dawn. Men will die so that their children will live free. The Plains will drink their blood as it drinks the blood of drakes."

"A pretty speech . . . and very old."

"You have been told not to be disrespectful to his majesty, demon! Perhaps you need another lesson—"

Melicard curtly signalled for silence. "Quiet! I want this creature, this legendary Darkhorse who fought alongside the Dragon Masters, Cabe Bedlam, and other humans throughout the centuries, to tell me why he will not save the lives of men by ending those of drakes!"

The ebony stallion sighed. "You who would make history, have you not studied it? Are not the lessons of the Quel, the Seekers, and those who preceded even them evident? This land we now call the Dragonrealm is a harsh mother. It has watched the glory of many races and it has watched the downfall of each—all through bloodshed. Even the Quel, who succeeded where others failed and held onto a bit of their power when the Seekers took control, even they did not learn from their mistake and eventually lost what little they had in trying to destroy the new avian masters! As for the Seekers, in putting down the last gasp of the Quel, they planted the seeds of their own destruction!''

Melicard was silent, but Darkhorse could see his words had had no effect. *And I scoffed at his tired speech!*

The king's eventual response was what he had expected. "Though you are our prisoner, for some reason we cannot make you obey. Drayfitt has tried to explain, but that means nothing. Tomorrow, I will send the army out—without your magical aid. It will take them a week to ten days to reach the northern part of the Hell Plains, where the Red Dragon's revitalized clans prepare for their own assault. We shall catch them unprepared, however; and, where Azran Bedlam failed, we shall wipe them out to the last egg. One less clan. The other twelve will follow.''

"All hail the conquering heroes!" scoffed the shadow steed.

"Your *majesty*—" the counselor began to protest.

"You were overzealous before, Quorin. We will not punish this one, not this time. Perhaps he will reconsider before the deaths have grown too many.''

Darkhorse refused to look at the king any longer, instead choosing to alternate his piercing gaze between Drayfitt, the weakest link, and Mal Quorin, the treacherous one. The elderly spellcaster looked pale, worn, as if he had just suffered a great disaster. If so, the malevolent cat who counseled the king had something to do with it because there was now a slight hint of satisfaction on Quorin's face that, under the circumstances, should not have been there. The counselor almost seemed pleased by events.

Something is not right where this tabby is concerned, Darkhorse decided. *What can I do about it now, though?*

"Come," Melicard commanded his two advisors. "There are more *fruitful* endeavors to pursue at the moment.''

"The only fruitful endeavors will be those of the Lords of the Dead—after the battle.''

The door shut behind them with a sinister note of finality. Darkhorse kicked at his invisible cage, frustrated more than before.

"Fools!" he cried, though he doubted they could hear him, sound-absorbing as this room was. "This will be far worse than the Turning War!"

He brooded after that, unheedful of the hours that soon passed by and wondering again and again if they now intended on abandoning him down here indefinitely. *Perhaps, as the years fall, some scavenger searching through the ruins of this once-proud city-state will find his way down here and pass on a word or two before leaving me alone again.*

The door jostled. Someone was trying to open it—but with little success. Darkhorse gathered himself together, his interest in things revived by this sudden and possibly trivial incident. *It may only be a guard testing the lock. . . .*

Nothing else happened for more than two minutes. The shadow steed's hopes sagged again.

A sudden groan of twisting metal informed him that the first time had not been an illusion. The area of the door where the handle and lock were situated had been torn asunder, rendering the whole thing useless. Someone standing on the other side of the door pushed it forward.

The eyes of the Princess Erini stared at him in awe and growing recognition.

"You. You were the shadow in the hall. The one that—that followed me and then vanished." While she talked, her hands continued to twitch, as if they were eager to perform yet more sorcery.

Darkhorse dipped his head in acknowledgment. "Princess Erini, I would assume." He indicated the door. "A trifle overdone, I'd think."

She looked embarrassed. "I was only trying to open it. Drayfitt said that if you concentrate, you can manipulate the spectrum and unlock it with little more than a look."

"Can you try that with my accursed cage here? Have you come to set me free?"

"Are you—are you Darkhorse?"

That made him laugh loudly. "Of course. Who else could I be? Who else would dare to be Darkhorse—or *want* to be, for that matter?"

"Not so loud, please!"

His manner became subdued. The shadow steed knew that this human held his freedom in her anxious hands. "Why did you come down here? Won't Melicard become wroth when he discovers his future bride has uncovered one of his secrets?''

"Melicard is busy. *Quorin*—'' the look of disgust on her young face was evidence enough of her hatred for the man. The shadow steed's opinion of the princess rose further. ''—has convinced him that the time to move is now. Melicard is completing final preparations.''

"He was here earlier. This is madness, you know.'' The ebony stallion shifted impatiently in the confined space of his prison. *Free me!* he wanted to shout at the human.

Erini looked up sharply. "I don't know if I should. I don't know if I can.''

"Your powers are very formidable, gentle lady. I think you could undo the spell the elderly human wrought. The key is in the symbols on the floor. Look closely at them.''

She started to, but then shook her head. "I can't! If I do, Melicard will never forgive me! If I betray him, he'll find out about these!''

"Your hands? They seem lovely, though I'm no judge of human standards. . . .''

"You know what I mean. These powers. I do not want them. They are a curse. If I thought that cutting off my hands would rid me of them, I'd be tempted to do it.''

"It will not, so do not think about it again.'' *Madness! Am I to be tormented by the key to my freedom?*

If Erini caught that thought, she did not respond to it. Instead, the princess said, "Drayfitt told me the same thing. I know that.''

"Is that why you came to me? To tell me you don't like your gifts and you won't use them to release me? Are you a greater sadist than the 'lovely' Counselor Quorin, then? He has only assaulted my physical form; you've torn at my hopes!''

"No! I—''

"Princess!'' Drayfitt stood at the doorway. He had become even more worn and pale since the shadow steed had seen him hours before. Caught up in their own thoughts, neither Erini nor the eternal had noticed his nearby presence. He, on the other hand, had felt them all the way in the main hall, where he had just left the king after an unsuccessful attempt to, if not call off the march, postpone it until events became clearer. The intensity of the two had been enough to pierce the cloud of worry smothering his mind—and probably would have been enough had he been outside the walls of Talak itself.

The elderly mage inspected the damaged door and grew even more dismayed. "This will never do!" He touched the torn handle and lock. Before the eyes of Darkhorse and the princess, the metal reshaped itself, returned to what it had been like before Erini's impetuous entrance. Drayfitt glanced up again. "Your majesty! What do you hope to gain by coming here? I warned you to stay away!"

"I could not help it, Master Drayfitt!" She stepped back from both of them. "I saw the three of you come down here hours ago, then leave a few minutes later. When I saw the guards depart as well, I knew something had happened. I—I was not thinking properly. It took me this long to build up my determination, but eventually I had to come down here—I do not know why. Perhaps to see . . . to understand . . ." Erini trailed off, at a loss.

"She came to see a curiosity, sorcerer!" Darkhorse bellowed arrogantly. "She came to see the demon her love had chained to this world! Rest assured, she would not want to hurt his feelings by granting me my rightful freedom, oh no! I pleaded with her long enough to know that!"

Erini looked as if the shadow steed had kicked her violently— which was just what Darkhorse wanted. It was a terrible thing, he knew, that he was forced to resort to shaming her, but if the stallion had read her correctly, the princess would turn that shame around and come back to him—this time to free him.

I will make amends to her after Shade has been dealt with Darkhorse swore, shielding the thought from her already impressive abilities. He tried not think that by forcing her to look at her own conscience and free him, that she might lose the man she loved.

There were times when he did not envy humans the ability to love. It seemed to have more to do with pain than any other emotion.

Ignoring his outburst, Drayfitt confronted his queen-to-be. "Your majesty, tomorrow, thanks to the slippery words of the *loyal* Master Quorin, I will be enroute with the army. I must ask that you watch yourself while I'm gone, stay with the king at all times. The more Quorin has him alone, the more he can poison his mind—and diminish your hopes of a true relationship. I shall return when I can."

"*If* you can, spellcaster. Your kind has a limited lifespan in war. What happens to the city, then?"

"I will see to it that *nothing* happens. I've a stake in my life, Darkhorse." The elderly man took hold of one of Erini's arms in a gentle but determined manner. "Come, milady. Judging by your mishap with the door, there are things I need to show you before I leave come the morn."

"Wait, Drayfitt!" The shadow steed shifted as close to the door as the barrier would let him. "What about Shade? I've felt him here! You cannot deny his existence, I think."

The two humans looked at one another in a manner that answered one part of Darkhorse's question. The warlock had returned to Talak at least once and both of them knew about it. It was Erini who finally responded, much to the evident consternation of the sorcerer.

"He's been here at least *twice*, Lord Darkhorse. Once, for a brief moment, in my chambers; the second time, to release some foul creatures to spy on the palace."

"He wanted the book, apparently," her companion interrupted. "It was his, you know, but thanks to *you*, demon, *I* destroyed it."

"Then, you are in danger, human!"

"He's your foe. *You* were the one truly responsible. He has no further argument with me." The tone of Drayfitt's voice suggested he had worked hard to convince himself of that.

"Don't be a fool, mortal!"

Drayfitt turned from him. "Come, your majesty."

She accompanied him, but slowed long enough to study him in detail. Darkhorse returned her frank stare. This was a female who did not give in easily. There was hope after all.

As the door closed, the shadow steed laughed quietly. Now, if only it was not *too* late.

The climb up was long and especially slow, despite Drayfitt's continual urging. Erini only partially heard him, her mind on the confrontation below.

Living darkness. An abyss that threatened to swallow all that stood too near it. More than a shadow, yet also less.

All these were apt descriptions of the astonishing being she had met. All were apt but greatly insufficient descriptions of the jet-black stallion calling itself Darkhorse. Majestic and terrible at the same time, he was far more than the legends had even hinted at. Small wonder he was held in both awe and fear by those who knew of him. There was a sense of time beyond eternity in his very presence. His chilling blue eyes, crystalline and lacking pupils, seemed capable of capturing her very soul.

His words came back to Erini and the shame burned brightly within her once more. For the sake of her relationship with Melicard, she had been willing to leave him a prisoner. It went against everything she believed in, and the fact that she had not done anything about it cut her deeply. She had once dreamed of a marriage based on love and trust; could she be satisfied with one that was also built on the sufferings of others?

Erini realized that Drayfitt had asked her something. "I'm sorry; what was it you asked, Master Drayfitt?"

The elderly man sighed. Somehow, he seemed even *more* drawn than when he had first discovered Erini. "I asked your majesty if she trusts her personal guard and her ladies-in-waiting."

"Completely. Why?"

Drayfitt's face revealed nothing. "No reason, milady. Only pleased to hear that there *are* those who can be trusted."

Neither spoke again, more to save breath than because of any other reason. The journey downward had seemed so much easier. At last, though, the door finally came into view.

I cannot leave him! the princess suddenly thought in a swelling panic, the sight of the door resurrecting her shame concerning her ill treatment of Darkhorse. *I have to do something for him even if—even if—*

"I've been wondering," Drayfitt began, "wondering why Quorin removed the guards from in here. They weren't necessary, but he seemed to think them so important before. If they'd been here, you wouldn't have gotten this far."

Erini neither knew nor cared what reason the counselor might have had to send the sentries away. Only one thing concerned her. The princess was not even certain it would work, but, based on what little she had learned from the sorcerer, it should at least be *possible*.

On the next step, she fell forward.

"Princess!" Drayfitt reached for her, almost losing his own balance in the process. He was unable to stop Erini, who turned so that her back was facing her would-be rescuer.

While her face and hands were not visible to Drayfitt and his mind was concerned solely with her safety, Erini unleashed a crude spell formulated only from half-formed thoughts and wishful thinking. The elderly spellcaster had explained that hand gestures were not necessary and mostly acted as a guide, but the princess did not trust her skills well enough to do without them. Her fingers wiggled in a maneuver that was pure instinct. Unfamiliar with the world of sorcery, she could not say whether she had accomplished her task or not. Whatever the case, Drayfitt was now standing over her and Erini knew that trying any longer would only give her away. As it was, she remained uncertain as to whether he knew or not. He had shown her how to shield her thoughts during their one session, but theory and practice were never the same, that held true in sorcery *and* governing.

"Are you all right, Princess Erini?"

She nodded slowly, trying to act dazed. "Yes—I missed my footing. Thank you."

The sorcerer helped her to her feet. "A fall here could prove fatal, milady. You would not stop for thirty or forty feet at least. Come, the sooner we leave here the better, as far as all is concerned."

Drayfitt opened the door, guiding Erini up to the surface with his other hand. The sun was going down and the garden was full of deep shadows, though none as deep as that which was Darkhorse, the princess thought.

Closing the door quietly, Drayfitt quietly said, "We will forget this happened, your majesty. Best for both of us, I'd say. Now go before someone asks why we were here."

"This is ridiculous! I am a princess! Am I not to be queen of Talak? Should I go skulking about? I won't be like you, Drayfitt! Not even for the love of Melicard!"

He frantically waved her quiet. In the distance, Erini heard the sounds of men in armor. "I only recommend it from past experience, your majesty. What you do is up to you, of course."

"Princess Erini."

Erini started and Drayfitt cursed under his breath. The princess calmed down, however, when she realized who it was. "Captain Iston!"

The Gordag-Ai officer bowed to her and, after a moment's hesitation, nodded briefly to the sorcerer. "Princess, you are making it extremely difficult for my men and I to perform our duties. So far, you've succeeded in evading every one of them."

"The princess is skilled at such things," Drayfitt interjected. To Erini, he said, "Think on what I said, milady, and, by all means, make use of such loyal men as your captain here."

"What's that supposed to mean, then?" Iston asked, his suspicion roused.

"Only that I hope her majesty will allow you to perform your function. It's sometimes hard to find a person you can trust so much. Good evening."

His eyes on the departing sorcerer, Iston frowned. "That sounds like a warning of sorts."

"It's nothing."

"As you command." Nevertheless, the captain continued to look thoughtful. "Might I be permitted to escort you back to your chambers, your majesty? I have a handful of anxious bodyguards waiting for the two of us."

"Why did you not bring them with you?"

Iston smiled enigmatically. "Some things are better handled by one man."

They walked quietly through the garden, the officer falling in place just behind his mistress. Erini allowed her thoughts to turn back to the events below and the question as to whether her spontaneous actions had freed Darkhorse or not. She also wondered what Melicard would say if it turned out the shadow steed *was* free. Drayfitt would be unable to say anything; come the morning, he would be gone with the army. Both the king and Quorin might assume that Darkhorse had either escaped on his own or that Shade had taken him away somewhere.

Her secret would remain safe . . . unless *she* chose to tell Melicard. He had to learn some time . . . but when?

As before, her questions went unanswered. She exited the garden, followed by Iston, of course, with the knowledge that sooner or later the truth would come out and that it might benefit her if it was *her* admission, not Quorin's, that Melicard heard first.

Guard leader Ostlich abandoned his hiding place overlooking the garden the moment the would-be queen and her lackey vanished back into the palace. His mind was aglow with the thought of the gold Counselor Quorin would pay him. What the princess from Gordag-Ai had been doing mattered as little to him as why Quorin had ordered the guards away from the area in the first place. He only knew that the counselor would pay for the knowledge that she had been down there and reward him further once the reins of rulership changed hands.

What happened to the princess was none of his concern.

XI

With the grand crusade now ready to commence, no one had time to inspect the chamber where the King's reluctant demon had been locked away. Caught in the midst of final details that would keep them secluded all night, the king and his advisors saw no one except those who came to deliver information specifically on the march. Thus it was the Counselor Quorin remained ignorant of a fact that would have been of great import to both him and the king . . . for the barrier, the magical cage, and its sole occupant were no longer there. Had he received a message from one of the guard leaders to the Counselor Quorin, the advisor might have excused himself and investigated for himself, venturing down to the shadow steed's prison, and discovering something of such importance that even the king would have taken interest . . . because the barrier, the magical cage, and its sole occupant were no longer there.

The bulk of Talak's great army moved in swift and orderly fashion despite its impressive size. By dawn, more than half the column was outside the city gates. Around them, the citizens cheered their husbands, fathers, sons, and brothers. Cohorts four hundred strong marched by, most of them veterans eager to teach the monstrous drakes that humans of this particular city-state would never bow to the Dragon Kings again.

Lost in the cheers and commotion was one pessimistic sorcerer and several irritated commanders, all of whom felt they were moving in the wrong direction; but it was their duty to obey, and obey they would. The city was not undefended. There were garrisons posted all around the countryside, especially the northern and western borders. The city guard would keep order in Talak itself and the palace would be well-protected by the royal guard.

Unbeknownst to these forces, the northern garrisons, in response to orders received that very dawn, were preparing to move westward to meet with their counterparts there. For the next week, they were to face off in a series of war games designed to test their effectiveness in guerrilla fighting, much like the sort of war waged by Melicard in the early days of his crusade. While the commanders silently questioned the need for this, it was not the first time that some functionary in the government had decided to play up his own reputation by *cracking down* on the common soldier; and besides, the war was to be in the east for now, so no one would miss them for a few days, anyway.

No one argued the validity of the orders themselves; after all, they bore the king's seal, didn't they? Nobody but Melicard and his closest advisors used the seal.

The king saluted those riding out to do battle in his name, his visage somehow more regal than frightening this day. He had planned to lead them, as he had done in the past, but some of his advisors had recommended that he remain in the city. It would not do to have the crusade's driving force accidently struck down in the heat of combat. At the palace, Melicard could coordinate *all* of his activities. There was also continued talk of the eventual marriage of Melicard and the princess from neighboring Gordag-Ai, an event most everyone was looking forward to with eagerness. Those near enough to see the king were able to get a glimpse of the Princess Erini standing at his side. Counselor Mal Quorin, Melicard's chief advisor, stood on his other side.

In the shadow of a building near the city gate, a lone figure watched the ongoing procession with growing impatience. The shadows draped his visage, but even if they had not, it would have taken a long, close look to make out his patrician features and his arresting eyes—eyes with great, wide pupils not of any color, but instead glittering like fine crystal and seeming to see much more than the view before them. It was the face of one born to his place in the world, one who knew that all within his grasp was his. Azran Bedlam had worn such a look, but it paled in comparison with this one. This was the face of a Vraad sorcerer.

The true face of Shade.

* * *

Food. Eat. Eat. The others in the herd kept urging him. They had been doing so all day.

Provider. Walks-on-hind-hooves-and-smells-of-herd. Brings more food. Eat. The herd tried to watch out for one another, but the dark one kept refusing to be part of the herd, though he had said he was.

Not hungry. The dark one allowed the strange creature with the odd, loose skin to guide him. *Drink? Walks-on-hind-hooves-and-smells-of-herd leads to water. Smells puzzled. Not thirsty, provider. Provider smells of fear. Why fear of self? Self not harm provider.*

Self . . . not right.

Before him, the provider called to another of his own herd, a smaller walks-on-hind-hooves who often came to this herd and smoothed and washed their coats. The dark one could not recall ever having this done to him, but the others, who seemed very stupid to the dark one, had told him this. It was one of the happy times they had. The dark one did not care for their happy times. Their happy times were for stupid ones.

"Andru! When did they bring in this one?"

The boy—boy?—shook his head, his mane flying back and forth as he did. The dark one realized the boy could not speak.

The man—yes, *man!*—looked at the dark one. "He's magnificent, but he spooks me for sure! More like a demon than a horse!"

Horse? Demon? The dark one's mind stirred. He did not question for a moment that he understood the *man* so well, even though the rest of the herd seemed to only hear the tone of his voice. He was different. Far different. Memories began to stir, memories of confinement, of evil men and shadowed figures. Memories of a need to escape.

"Here! What's wrong with you?" The man—for the first time, the dark one saw that the man was tall, well-muscled, and graying—sought to bring his skittish charge under control. The dark one—there was *another* name!—easily fought him off.

"Andru! Boy! Get the others! We've gotta rogue on our hands!"

The young one ran off. The older man tried to get a grip on the bit that someone had dared put on the dark one, but failed.

Not dark one. Dark . . . horse. Darkhorse!

The shadow steed's memories returned in a torrent of mixed images and scraps of thought. Darkhorse froze as he tried to assimilate everything, and the handler chose that moment to grab the bit.

"I don't know which mule-headed lord or lady left you in the royal stables, but you're goin' to have to learn who's *master* 'round here!" He tugged hard on the bit, trying to force Darkhorse's head down. The horses around the ebony stallion shied away, already familiar with the strength and tactics of a man who had not yet met an animal he could not break.

Of course, the jet-black steed before him was far more than an animal.

Darkhorse, at last himself again, finally took notice of his would-be master. Soul-snaring blue orbs met the narrow eyes of the human—causing the latter to scream and release his hold. Stumbling backward, the man made a sign against evil.

Darkhorse laughed. Laughed, not only because of the futile gesture, but because he was *free!*

"Hela and Styx!" The horseman fell to his knees. "Spare me, demon! I couldn't have known!"

"Not known *me*? Not known Darkhorse? I am no demon, horseman, though neither am I one of your charges! Tell me quickly now and I will leave you be! What place is this and what day?"

The answers both amused and angered the phantom steed. This was *Gordag-Ai*, the Princess Erini's homeland! He could see what she had done. In haste, perhaps because she was still with the sorcerer, she had wanted him to be safe and secure. Her mind, however sharp, had thought of him in terms of a true animal—and why *not?* Very few people truly understood what he was. Therefore, when she had attempted to free him, her crude spell had sent him to a place her memories recalled as safe—the kingdom where she had been born and raised. Since he was a horse, her rescue attempt had sent him to the royal stables, surely the most secure place for one of his kind! Unfortunately, the side effect of so haphazard a spell had nearly made him just such a creature; and as much as he admired their forms and their loyalty, he had no desire to become one.

What frustrated him were the results of that side effect. Almost a full day had passed while he slowly reverted to himself. The massive army of Talak must already be far beyond the city, heading toward the Hell Plains; and though he had no proof to back up his fears, Darkhorse suspected that something terrible, something that Shade would have a hand in, was going to happen. Not just in Talak, either.

He realized that the human was still kneeling before him and that several others were standing at the entrance to the royal stables looking quite dumbfounded. Darkhorse laughed bitterly and said, "You have *nothing* to fear from *me*, little ones! Darkhorse has always been the friend of humanity, though there are those for whom my love has been tried! Fear not, for my time here with you is over!"

Rearing, the shadow steed summoned a portal. It flickered uncertainly for a moment, but the stallion, impatient to move against his adversaries after so long, paid it no mind. After his confinement and the stifling power of Drayfitt's magical cell, he expected his own abilities to be less than they should be. That was why it was time to include others in his battle with his friend/foe. It was time to seek the help of Cabe Bedlam.

The gate he opened flickered again—then *vanished*.

Cursing loudly—much to the panic of the few humans who had *not* run off already—Darkhorse tried to resummon the portal. It blinked into and out of existence almost too fast to be seen, enraging the frustrated eternal even more.

"I am Darkhorse!" he shouted at the disobedient hole. "A gate is less than nothing to me! Materialize!"

He was greeted by a complete lack of reaction. There was not even a flicker this time. His confinement had sapped his abilities far worse than he could have believed possible.

This was a spell with Vraad origins, the shadow steed finally concluded. *A treacherous, destructive thing like its creator!*

"Very well," he rumbled. "If, for the nonce, the paths beyond are forbidden to me, than I shall travel through the world of humanity!" Darkhorse looked down at the humans. "Be vigilant, mortals! The clans of Silver are awake and, though I suspect they look toward Talak, it would be safe in assuming that Gordag-Ai is also among their desires!"

When it appeared that his message had sunk in, the huge stallion reared and charged east. At first, the men in the stables grew panicked again, for there *was* no eastern entrance, only a solid wall. Then, before the unbelieving eyes of people who had thought they had already seen all there was to see, Darkhorse melted into the obstruction, like a ghost.

* * *

Darkhorse had no time for patience with the failings of humanity. If the fiery presence of a huge, jet-black stallion charging over their heads was enough to set them running in a hundred different directions, then that was their misfortune. What the shadow steed fought to stop was far worse than a little fear left in his wake. Shade, a Vraad sorcerer, would not settle for a little fear. As a Vraad, he would expect to control everything. It was not because he was necessarily evil; if anything, the Vraad had been, in Darkhorse's limited knowledge, amoral. They could not comprehend that something might be out of their reach unless another, stronger representative of their race had already claimed it. Even then, it was a matter of who had the upper hand.

The warlock would be working to divide and eliminate rivals, even potential rivals.

Darkhorse quickened his pace as Gordag-Ai fell quickly behind him. Princess Erini's homeland had been given a warning about the drake menace near them. What concerned the phantom steed now was the very person he had looked to for aid. Cabe Bedlam and his family were in danger. A Vraad sorcerer would not let a spellcaster of young Bedlam's potential go unchecked; if he could not enlist their servitude, then he would destroy them the way one would destroy a pest.

Darkhorse pushed himself harder, only now realizing how accustomed he was to his magical abilities. Though he raced more swiftly than any common horse, the pace was infinitely slower than travelling the path beyond. Seconds, even minutes, had now become hours.

Hours he might not have.

What was occurring in Talak worried him also, but there was nothing he could do, and speaking to Cabe Bedlam and the Lady of the Amber was paramount. The city-state of mad Melicard would have to wait, despite the debt he owed its future queen—future queen *only* if Talak had a future. Darkhorse needed the mortal's aid.

Time continued to be his enemy, passing with a swiftness he could never match at his best. Night came, grew old, and began to dissolve. The lands of Esedi, where the Bronze Dragon had once ruled and where Gordag-Ai was situated, had given way to the southwest edge of cursed Silver's domain. As the sun began to climb, relief touched him. He was now in a region on fair terms with humanity and the Bedlams, the forest lands of the Green Dragon. Through the hateful words of Melicard and the confusing ones of Drayfitt, the stallion had learned how this one drake lord had done the unthinkable, worked it so that there might be a place for both races, so that his own would survive and not give way, which was inevitable to all save the other Dragon Kings.

His hooves grazed the tops of the tallest trees. Something large stirred and fluttered away into the depths of the woods below. Darkhorse thought it at first a small drake, but the glimpse he had of it showed it to be birdlike, yet with the shape and form of a man as well.

Seeker.

There were very few of them now. The brief, horrible winter that had taken place a year after the shadow steed's exile had apparently claimed many of these once-mighty rulers, predecessors to the Dragon Kings themselves. Confidentially, Drayfitt had indicated that the hordes of hungry, gigantic, digging creatures from the Northern Wastes, monstrosities who had followed the soul-numbing chill southward, had been responsible for the depletion of their numbers more than anything else.

Darkhorse suddenly hesitated, almost landing on top of a tree. Of all creatures, the Seekers would surely know the Vraad. The avians had controlled this land before the coming of that race of men—and had fallen afterward to the might of the upstart drakes. Perhaps the Vraad had had something to do with that, though it was also possible they had no longer existed as a race by then. Something had changed their descendants into the humans of today. It was a time period that the eternal knew little about, having only known it through encounters with one Vraad, a good man. The shadow steed had not returned to this reality until long after the Dragon Kings had established their rule, long enough for all to have died who might have answered him.

Turning, Darkhorse dove into the forest. If he could only catch the Seeker...

The foliage whipped about the stallion as he entered the forest. The change in his form from phantasm to solid flesh startled him, as it had not been his desire. Darkhorse slowed and landed hooves-first on the ground, leaving deep imprints.

Thanks to the thick vegetation, it was impossible to locate the avian by normal sight. Those other senses that *should* have been able to aid him in his search failed just as miserably. The Seeker was nowhere to be found. Darkhorse trotted cautiously through the forest in the direction of his original goal, the Manor, while probing the visible world and those beyond for some sign of the Seeker or of any other creature out of the ordinary. It had occurred to him, belatedly, that the Green Dragon might not see him as the ally and friend of the warlock Bedlam. As peace-minded as this particular Dragon King had seemed, he might still consider Darkhorse as the enemy of *all* drakes.

He came upon a path that showed signs of regular use and chose to follow it, trying to indicate to any hidden sentinels of the Green Dragon that he was friendly. In times past he had travelled this region unharmed, but one could never completely trust what had once been. Perhaps the monarch of the Dagora Forest had not sought his death simply because of his strength. A struggle between titans would have destroyed this wooded land that the drake loved so much. Now, though, he was dealing with a much weakened stallion, a much more tempting target to those who believed they had a legitimate reason for vengeance.

Still the Seeker evaded his senses. It had either been able to shield itself or had fled long before. He knew the power of the avians could be formidable and that they might find him a useful tool in their efforts to regain the Dragonrealm, but if this was a trap, it was an odd one. Darkhorse cursed his present state; he was no longer certain if he could trust what his senses told him.

Darkhorse moved through the woods. The hours continued to become new memories, most of those concerning traipsing through endless forest and all thought of the Seeker was gradually abandoned as the shadow steed passed by tree after identical tree. As much as Darkhorse enjoyed nature, he soon lost all admiration for the color green. There was just too much of it. He was tempted to take to the sky again, but, with his abilities questionable, he preferred to be where he had the best chance of spotting hidden watchers, as futile as that seemed at the moment. The lush treetops made it virtually impossible to see anyone, either in the branches or on the ground. Here, at least, he could study both areas more thoroughly. His eyes and ears were now his foremost senses; they were far sharper than those of his animal counterparts' and thus afforded him a fairly accurate picture of what lurked nearby.

Though he appeared to be alone, he soon discovered that there *were* others. Those nearby, insofar as his limited skills could tell him, included small animals, a variety of birds and insects, and three creatures of vague shape and identity who could only be servants of the forest's master. It was possible, then, that there was presently a welcoming party of some sort on their way. Whether they would merely follow and shadow him was debatable. They *would* be there, however.

The land before him began to take on a familiar appearance. Darkhorse slowed to a more cautious pace, knowing that, like his cage, what he sought would be invisible to the eye. A decade was long enough in the mortal plane for an entire world to rearrange itself and, though he was not completely certain he had arrived at the outer grounds of young Bedlam's sanctum, it was best to approach things with the thought of traps in mind.

Darkhorse neared a copse of trees that had grown so close to one another as to be one. The shadow steed knew with little more than a glance that magic had been at work, for the trees wrapped around one another as loved ones might. The sight was a marker of sorts, for it told him that he was indeed close to his destination. The Manor grounds could be no more than—

He felt a great desire to go no farther. It was as if something pungent had been left under his nose. Darkhorse throttled back several steps, trying to recover. He snorted and glared at the location of the aromatic assault.

"Come now, Amber Lady," he jeered, certain that the horrid scent was a product of the Lady Gwen, Cabe's mate. "A little smell will not repel your enemies—nor those you insist of *thinking* as your enemies!"

The jet-black stallion reared and charged swiftly forward.

He found himself running the way he had come from.

"*What?!*" Darkhorse came to a dust-filled halt. He turned and stared at the direction he had originally charged. There was nothing to indicate when and how he had been turned. The spell was one of the smoothest he could recall seeing in centuries. Unlike many, there had been no sense of reversal, no noticeable tingling.

"Perhaps I've underestimated you, Lady Gwen!" He backed up and charged again, building his own defenses as he ran. No mere reversal spell would stop him *this* time.

It did not—but the sudden panic that he must have been *mad* to have even come this close to such a deadly, horrifying place sent him reeling back out of control.

Some distance from the stunning attack of nerves, he gathered himself. Darkhorse eyed his destination, then reared back his head and laughed. "My compliments, Lady of the Amber! This is far more an annoyance and far more creative than the original spell!"

She had placed at least three spells over the magical barrier that protected the Bedlams and their people from outsiders, and Darkhorse was not yet ready to see if there was a fourth. Each had been progressively better, and he suspected that any deeper level would stop being a deterrent and start becoming very, very painful. That left the eternal very few options. Once, when he had first met the confused young mortal name Cabe Bedlam, a Cabe who did not understand who he was and why the concerted efforts of more than one Dragon King had been focused on him, the shadow steed had called out in his mind to the untrained warlock. Had not Cabe responded, the sorcerer would have fallen victim to the wiles of three temptresses, drakes in human disguise. Now, with his powers failing, Darkhorse would have to try again. Out of sheer pride, the shadow steed hesitated, but, in the end, there was not better way.

Slowly, his concentration on the mind of his human ally, Darkhorse made his way around the edges of the barrier. It was ironic, he realized, that he who had spent so much time fighting to free himself from one cage was now desperately seeking entry to another, possibly deadlier one.

Minutes passed. There was no response. He could not even feel the presence of another mind, though that did not necessarily mean anything. It was possible that this new series of spells, so intricate compared to the old one placed on it by one of the Manor's former tenants, also shielded those within from his silent plea. If so, he might find himself circling the grounds hour upon hour until either of the spellcasters or one of their servants happened to step without. Darkhorse's eyes narrowed to slits as he thought of the time wasted.

When he had circled the warlock's domain once, he paused, trying to assess the situation in the hopes that he had missed something earlier. The sun was almost gone and, standing in the midst of the deepest, darkest forest, Darkhorse was already in deep shadow. In a fit of unleashed fury, he gave up all thought of appearance and caution and, backing just a bit away from the edge of the barrier, called out in his loudest voice.

"Cabe Bedlam! Come! Give me entrance! I am Darkhorse, your friend and ally! Hurry, before the hand of Shade tears at the foundation of the Dragonrealm and lays waste to all!" *A bit flowery,* he decided once he had finished, *but it will bring him to me! It must!*

Several seconds later, something began to rustle through the brush. It kept itself well hidden behind the trees and bushes, but Darkhorse soon saw that it was too small for a human of Cabe's size.

"Darkhorse." It was a statement, a child's statement, but with something odd about its tone.

"I will not harm you, youngling! I am indeed Darkhorse, friend and ally to the master of this place!" He tried to talk soothingly.

The boy moved closer, though he still kept himself fairly obscured. There was something a bit odd about his gait and his breathing was fast, as if he had been running. Perhaps he had. He might have been far from this place when he heard Darkhorse.

"Come closer to me, youngling! I mean no harm! If you will take a message to the warlock Cabe Bedlam, I'll be forever in your debt!"

"I don't like you. Go away."

Darkhorse kicked at the ground. He had little experience in dealing with young. Better a trial of combat with a Dragon King than to have to try to placate a child. It was a wonder humans survived to adulthood. "Your sire would do well to teach you manners, youngling!"

The boy straightened and hissed. Darkhorse, about to add further in the hopes that what humans termed a scolding would make the child obey him, hesitated. The boy's reaction was too violent, too—

"My sssire is dead."

The words were far too chilling for a human. The ebony stallion voiced his next words quietly and calmly. "You have my sorrow. Who was your sire, young one?"

He knew it would not be Cabe Bedlam, not after hearing the sibilant tones. It seemed impossible that the child before him could be what he believed it was.

As if emboldened by the question of his heritage, the boy

stepped out of hiding. From his height, he was likely a decade old, maybe a year or two more. His height was the *least* of his characteristics. Darkhorse, who had once again come to believe that he had seen everything, found that the child left him speechless.

He had dark hair that flashed a hint of gold. His eyes were narrow, red ovals that burned bright in the darkness. His nose was tiny, almost imperceptible, and his mouth had a cruel yet majestic cut to it, thin-lipped and knowing. He was a child with a mind beyond his years.

The boy was handsome, but in an inhuman way.

The layer of scale that covered his face told the shadow steed what he was even before the boy opened his mouth and revealed sharp teeth and a tongue slightly forked. This close, Darkhorse could see the hatred in his eyes, an overwhelming hatred that no young one should have been allowed to grow up with. It had already twisted him.

"My sire'sss color wasss *gold*. My sire wasss an emperor." The drake child stared resolutely into the eyes of Darkhorse— and it was the eternal who looked away first.

The hatchling of the Dragon King Gold triumphantly added, "*I* will be emperor, too."

XII

"*Kyl! Where are you?*"

The unnerving drake child turned at the sound of a voice obviously familiar to him. Darkhorse looked up in the direction of the newcomer's voice as well. He *knew* who it was who called out, though it was hard to believe that something had turned out right for once.

"There, guardian! He's there!"

"I see him, Grath. I see—*Darkhorse!*"

The shadow steed dipped his head in acknowledgment. "Greetings to you, good friend Cabe!"

Kyl, his visage now a mask hiding his earlier savagery, stepped aside as he watched the lean human clad in dark blue robes approach, accompanied by another child. Ten years had and had not changed Cabe Bedlam. With his masterful abilities, he could extend his lifespan and keep himself young for three hundred years or so, possibly longer if violent death, a common problem among spellcasters, did not claim him. He seemed taller, though that might be because of the confidence with which he walked. Cabe looked exactly as he had years before, like a youth in his twenties, but only until one studied his roughly handsome features. The basic face had not changed—attentive eyes that kept track of the disobedient hatchling while still maintaining a focus on Darkhorse, a nose slightly turned, and a strong chin reminiscent of his grandfather, Nathan. Yet, put together, they had an age and experience to them that had not been there before.

He will be greater than his father and his grandfather, the stallion decided. *May he live a more peaceful, fruitful life than they.*

"Darkhorse!" With a bit of wonder recalled from their time together, Cabe reached out to touch the shadow steed. However, just before he reached the limits of the protective barrier, he paused. His eyes narrowed and literally blazed with built-up power. The great silver streak in his otherwise dark hair seemed to glitter. "You *are* Darkhorse, aren't you? I'd hate to think what I might do if I found you were some drake from the Storm Lands or from Lochivar who thought he could sneak in here in the guise of an old and trusted friend. I might do something very, very damaging to you—say, turn you inside out."

Darkhorse laughed. "Friend Cabe, you have picked up a wicked streak in the years since we met! Of course, I am Darkhorse! Who would dare or *want* to be me, I ask you?"

To the side, Kyl, whose face had become animated at the talk of damage, lost interest again. The other boy—now the shadow steed saw that this, *too,* was a drake, but one more human, more *gentle*—looked relieved.

Cabe's grin returned. "Enter freely, then, old friend."

It was as if a portal had opened up in the protective barrier that had for so long frustrated him. Darkhorse stepped through as the others backed up to give him space. Grath, the other hatchling, wanted to touch him, but Kyl suddenly shook his head and hissed, "He'll suck you in and sssend you to the dark places!"

"That'll be enough of *that*!" Cabe reprimanded. He looked up at his former companion and apologized. "He hears the tales from other drakes—and humans, too. Stories, but what can I do? They've been around longer than me."

"Perhaps it might be best if I altered my appearance a little." Darkhorse became a true stallion, even altering the appearance of his eyes. "Is that better?"

"Much."

"I should speak to you as soon as we have some privacy, young Cabe! It concerns my—return—to your land."

As the four of them started out for the Manor, the warlock nodded. "I thought so. I didn't think you were ever coming back. The Gryphon said you'd sacrificed yourself to keep Sh—"

"Of *that* we shall talk—when we have more privacy, if you don't mind." He indicated the hatchlings, both of whom were openly curious about what the two were saying.

"Sorry."

Darkhorse shook his head. "There is no reason to be sorry! Come! While we have a few moments, tell me of yourself and what has become of the Gryphon. I only know tales that have been told to me by untrustworthy sources."

Cabe informed him first of the Gryphon's journey across the Eastern Seas to the land of his birth. The Gryphon had discovered his people, the denizens of some place called the Dream Lands, under siege by the black-armored wolf raiders, the Aramites. D'Shay, a particular wolf raider who had dealt with various Dragon Kings over a period of time, had evidently survived an encounter in Penacles that once supposedly had climaxed with his death. The missives, delivered to the Dragonrealm by drake ships of the neutral city of Irillian, did not go into detail on the subject of D'Shay. For the past few years, though, the lionbird had been aiding the revolt of many of the Aramites' conquered enemies. The wolf raiders' empire was crumbling, but it was a slow, bloody conflict. The ebony-armored soldiers had not conquered most of their continent by luck.

"Toos runs Penacles in his absence," Cabe concluded. "The general refuses to be named ruler, despite the pressure on him.

He and I both wanted to go and aid the Gryphon, but that would have left no one to keep an eye on certain troublemakers.''

"A wise decision, Cabe! Now, what of you? The Lady of the Amber is your mate, yes?''

It was informative to the shadow steed the way the mention of his wife made the otherwise confident warlock turn red. Darkhorse recognized the deep love the mortal had for his enchantress.

"She's my... mate. Yes. We have—we have two children.''

"But this is *wonderful* news!'' Darkhorse roared, unmindful at the moment of how his voice carried. After so many dismal events, the progression of life, something that both fascinated and puzzled him, cheered the stallion, especially as it dealt with one of the few mortals who fully trusted him. "You must introduce them to me—if that is acceptable to the Lady of the Amber!''

Cabe smiled in wry humor. "She doesn't like to be called that. It's either 'Lady Gwen' or 'the Lady Bedlam.' She's very much into the control of this place and our children... but then, so am I.''

Darkhorse quieted as the four exited from the forest and entered the clearing where the unique structure called simply the "Manor'' stood. Seeing the place reminded him again of that time when he had come to Cabe's rescue. The Manor was a perfect complement of nature and planned design. It was difficult to tell where the building ended and the natural contours of the great tree that made up at least half of the structure began. Some walls had been completely shaped by the tree; others had been built. It was at least three stories high, with windows everywhere. The grounds had been carefully shaped to match the land. There were other buildings as well; and, though they had not been designed with the efficiency and beauty of the ancient citadel, someone had taken great care to ensure that they did not detract from the splendor of the forest.

People looked up from their tasks—people and *drakes*, Darkhorse amended, trying to cope with the idea of such cooperation—and stared at the horse beside their lord. It was the stare of the mildly curious, not the panicked, which evidently meant that his disguise had succeeded. Both hatchlings suddenly ran off in the direction of the Manor itself, perhaps to give warning. The shadow steed wondered what sort of reception he could expect from the Manor's mistress. A cool one at best. Better that than open warfare.

There had to be several families of both races living here side-by-side, but everyone seemed to be taking it with stride. A man and a drake dealing with the horses broke off from their discussion to first acknowledge the warlock, then to admire the magnificent black animal trotting beside him. Darkhorse watched them in turn, amazed at such cooperation, such friendship. Even the humans of Irillian or Zuu, cities in which humans and drakes had lived together for centuries, were more polite and respectful to one another than they were friendly.

"She was in the garden when I went out to search for Kyl," Cabe whispered, nodding in turn to those who paid him homage as he passed. The embarrassed look on his face was a humorous sight to Darkhorse. "Hopefully, we should find her there."

With a brief nod of his head, Darkhorse signalled his understanding. Certain questions were beginning to eat at his patience, however, and he hoped that he and the two human spellcasters would be able to converse before long. As enjoyable as this reunion had been, Shade was a problem that could not be cut off.

They did find Gwen in the garden. Kyl and Grath stood patiently off to the side. With the witch were two strikingly beautiful women. Though no judge of human tastes, Darkhorse knew that they were capable of tempting many a man. He also knew that these women were not human. They were female drakes, far more adept at shapeshifting into such forms but less talented at sorcery.

Despite their beauty, however, the two drakes paled in comparison to the woman kneeling before them, who was bent on adjusting the clothing of a small human male perhaps two years younger than the hatchlings. Long, thick tresses crimson in color fell well below her shoulders and a silver streak, smaller and narrower than the one in Cabe's hair, added to the intensity of the fiery image. A form-fitting gown the color of emeralds revealed curves that were, by the standards of most human males Darkhorse had known through the ages, quite arresting. The Lady Bedlam rose and glanced their way, her perfect face with its glittering eyes—eyes that matched the gown absolutely—tiny nose, and full red lips marred only by the anxiety in her expression. Anxiety and distrust.

As they neared her, Darkhorse could not help feeling both relieved and disappointed that he was unique, that there was no female counterpart to him. Had there been, she surely would have resembled Cabe's mate in thought and action.

Even the multiverse is not ready for that! he thought with much humor and some passing regret.

"S'sseresa," Gwen called. The nearer of the two drake dams stepped closer. Her eyes still on the black steed, the witch said, "Take Aurim and the others to their rooms and please check on Valea. She should be waking from her nap soon."

"As you wish, Lady Bedlam." The two female drakes seemed to have no difficulty dealing with taking orders from a human, and Darkhorse slowly realized that they had probably had several years to get used to it. One dam took the two hatchlings; the other reached down and, whispering a few words to the golden-haired boy, took him by the hand. They followed after the others at a slower pace.

"Now, then." Gwen's expression was cold. "Kyl told me that *you* have somehow come back, but I was hoping he'd been imagining things. I see he wasn't."

"You were a bit warmer when last we parted company, Lady Bedlam—may I extend my congratulations?—and I see no reason for your continued distrust of me. I hardly came back by *choice*, much as I enjoy this world. I was *forced* back here by one of *your* kind."

The ice melted. Barely.

"Things have been fairly peaceful here the last few years. I have children now, Darkhorse. Children who should grow up in peace."

Darkhorse laughed, ignoring the fury on his hostess's visage. "I am so sorry that I have to awaken you from your dream, witch! If you have eyes at all, you should know that, despite their unwillingness to band together, the Dragon Kings are far from harmless! Even now, the clans of Silver prepare to strike—and with Shade loose—"

"Wait! What's that you said?" Cabe stepped between the two, his original intention being to keep one or both from striking out. Now, however, he was interested only in Darkhorse's words. "Is that what you came to tell us?"

Backing away for the sake of his friend, the shadow steed nodded. Even the Lady Gwen was now listening in rapt attention. The anger had vanished, replaced by concern—concern for her husband and children.

"*Now* I have your attention! Good! It should have been obvious to you, Lady of the Amber, that if I've returned, then so has Shade! Our faceless comrade is worse than I can ever recall seeing him! Something in the spell that tore us from our exile has caused a reversion! Shade has been as a man gone truly mad, with personalities vying each time I've met him! I fear he is returning to his original mind-set—and I fear it may be the worst of all!"

Gwen sat down, her hands rubbing together tightly. "I owe you an apology, then. If what you say is true—"

"There is worse! I have sorely underestimated the age of my onetime comrade! If I am correct, a Vraad sorcerer walks among us again!"

The name meant nothing to Cabe, though he carried within him some of the memories of his grandfather, who had studied the ancient races thoroughly. Gwen, on the other hand, turned pale and spat out an epithet concerning the shadowy warlock that made her husband look at her in mild shock.

"What's a Vraad sorcerer? Is he different from us?"

Lady Bedlam nodded slowly. Her jaw set tight as she looked at Darkhorse. "We've heard nothing out of the ordinary from the northern lands. The only reports that reach us concern the fact that Melicard is supposed to marry some princess from the west. I pity the woman."

"They are a fair match, witch. She may be his salvation. She is also a latent sorceress."

Cabe put a hand on his wife's shoulder. She reached up and placed her own on his. The warlock smiled sadly, as if acknowledging the end of a beautiful time. "You seem to know quite a bit, Darkhorse. Maybe you could tell us how you know so much."

He did. Drayfitt's abilities came as no surprise to Cabe, though the elder's actions in the name of his king did. Cabe had only met the man briefly, but he had come to respect him. Both spellcasters knew of Melicard's crusade and his overzealous advisor, Mal Quorin, but spies had reported nothing except the usual raids, though those had become fewer in the last couple years.

Of Shade and the plots of the Silver Dragon, they knew nothing, and what Darkhorse conveyed to them stunned both

Bedlams. To Lady Gwen, it was the culmination of fears she had always harbored about the hooded warlock; to Cabe, it was a tragic conclusion to someone he had both befriended and pitied. That the true Shade might be a less than savory being saddened him further.

"I'd always assumed he was a basically decent man behind that curse."

"A fairy tale! This is true life! Shade is a Vraad and, with few exceptions, they were arrogant and amoral! The world did not weep at their passing, so I'm given to understand! It amazes me that you and yours could be descendents of their kind."

"Cabe." Gwen squeezed his hand tight. "If all he says is true—"

"I would not—"

She cut him off. "*As* all he says must be true, then we have been purposely led astray. Someone has been lulling us into a false sense of security."

The warlock nodded. "The Silver Dragon or Melicard; more likely it's his counselor, Quorin. I wonder if the lord of Dagora knows anything. He's been extremely quiet himself."

Growing unsettled, Darkhorse stamped the ground with his hoof. The words that fled his mouth had almost become a an automatic ritual. "I was a fool! I should have come to you the moment freedom was mine! It may already be too late!"

Cabe grimaced. "It doesn't do any good to continually condemn yourself; I did that enough to know. What we have to do now is contact the Green Dragon and, with his aid, discover why there seems to be a curtain of silence between us and the north. You said that there may be a pact between the Dragon King Silver and Shade. Do you have any idea what that pact might entail?"

"I suspect part of it might have to do with a book—Shade's notes on his vile spells—but that book is dust, thanks to me. Without it, Shade will have to plan from scratch. At one point, he seemed to recall everything, but I think that must have proved a temporary state, else why his search?"

"Then you think he plans to recreate the original spell—but *why* if the curse is lifted?"

"It may not be lifted. Even if it has been, where would that *leave* him? Friend Bedlam, if Shade sought immortality long ago, why would he not seek it again?"

The warlock's mate, who had remained silent during this part of the exchange, turned to Darkhorse. "I worry about Talak. It sounds like a volatile situation. Do we dare let it continue that way?"

Darkhorse saw what she feared. Now would be a perfect time for the drakes to strike at Talak. "I would go back there now, since I owe the Princess Erini for my freedom, but I lack the strength and will to form a proper portal."

"Let me see." Gwen reached out with her hands, standing as if she were trying to ward off the stallion. Darkhorse could feel her probe as it danced over his essence, stopping here and there as she sought the cause of his weakness. When she was through with her examination, the Lady Bedlam lowered her arms and nodded to herself.

"There is a thin link between you and . . . someone else."

Incredulous, he searched for himself. His own probe was less efficient than hers, suffering as it did the way *all* of his abilities suffered, but he eventually found what she had located. Darkhorse laughed at the thin, magical strand, invisible and insubstantial, but virtually impossible to sever.

"Drayfitt's link! That's twice! Curse the mage! Am I never to be free of him?"

"Is it the same?" Lady Gwen asked. "Most links are forged in the same manner, but not this one."

Darkhorse inspected it again. "*No* . . . and it explains my weakness. I have become—a source—of strength for Drayfitt. The link is draining me slowly, but . . . this is too haphazard. I think the Princess Erini did this to me unintentionally."

"Sever it now," Cabe suggested.

"He cannot. If he does, he loses what Drayfitt has already." Gwen made a face. "You might say that the old sorcerer is stealing Darkhorse's essence, his being."

"I am being *devoured* alive, is what you're saying!"

"Essentially."

Cabe looked disgusted. "How can we stop it?"

"Killing Drayfitt is one way. With the link, all that he stole will return to its original place. Darkhorse might even gain something."

"I want nothing of Drayfitt's! I am not a ghoul—or a murderer!"

Lady Bedlam paced. "Nathan never taught me anything like

this; I think he was as disgusted with the concept as you are, Cabe. Yet . . .''

"Yet what?" Darkhorse grew anxious. He enjoyed existence and planned to continue to enjoy it, despite the increasing odds against doing so.

"If you can persuade him to break the link from *his* end—"

"Why should *he* be able to do that when I cannot?"

"He forged the original." She looked at Darkhorse as he thought she must look at her children when they asked an obvious question.

"Forgive me, Lady of the Amber! I have not suffered so many calamities in centuries! I fear I am not taking them well! The frustration of being kept in check while Shade—"

Gwen cut him off. "Forget your apologies, eternal. Perhaps you're not quite the demon I cannot help thinking you are, but you always seem to be the harbinger of disaster. For the sake of my family and the peace of the lands, I want Shade stopped— even if that means dealing with you. I don't say that I'm right, but I'd feel the children especially safer with you far from here."

Darkhorse tilted his head to one side and looked at the two spellcasters, finishing up with Gwen. "Humans are a strange, convoluted people, and you, Lady Bedlam, are a prime example. There is a part of you that would accept friendship with me, but there is a part of you . . . I need not go on. When this is over—if it ever is—we must talk again."

More to turn the conversation to a safer course than because it was necessary to say, Cabe interjected, "If you need Drayfitt to break the link, then that means *you'll* have to go to him."

"I am aware of that. The thought does not stir joy within me. Drayfitt is not in Talak, I believe. That leaves the city virtually under Mal Quorin's control."

"We'll take care of that. It might be time for the master warlock Cabe Bedlam and his lovely bride, the powerful enchantress—enchantress of my *heart*!—Lady Gwen, to visit the city-state in typical sorcerous style."

His wife gave him a coy look. "Materialize on the steps of the palace?"

"Probably not a good idea. If it was that easy, the Dragon Kings would have done it long ago. I was thinking more at the city gates with a great fanfare and fireworks—all illusion, of course."

"What reason do we give, husband?"

"An offer of peace. Melicard was always good enough to hear such things out. There is still a good man beneath that horrible face."

"Princess Erini has brought much of that man out to the surface," Darkhorse added. "She would make a good ally, providing they *do* marry. Very well. I will leave now, then, since you seem to have things in hand! My relief is beyond measure—but what of the children while you two are gone?"

"Even Shade needed permission to enter this place. The children will be safe here."

Darkhorse did not ask the other question. *But can you trust the children?* he had wondered, thinking of the taller of the two hatchlings. What would this Kyl be like when he was mature? Already, he seemed too much a reflection of his sire.

There will be time to worry about that only if we succeed in solving the present crisis! Through habit, Darkhorse reared, intending to summon a portal for his journey to the north. Only when nothing materialized did he remember the extent of his plight.

Cabe was the first to understand what was wrong. "You don't have the strength or the will to summon a gate, do you?"

"I fear not."

The warlock thought about it, then, with some hesitation, said, "Neither of us have been in that region for years; most of our portals would depend upon blind luck, except . . ."

"Except?"

Cabe looked at Gwen. "I think there's one place I could never forget. Azran's citadel."

"There is little more than wreckage there. The spell protecting it from the violence of the Hell Plains and the ravages of time has long fled from it."

"You've been there?"

"Yes." Darkhorse decided it was better not to go into his encounter with the emissary from the Lords of the Dead.

"Still, I think I remember well enough to get you there safely. What do you say?"

"Since I have little to fear even if you should land me in molten earth or during some great tremor, I suppose so."

Cabe gave him a sour grin. "Thanks for your confidence."

The gate was there even as Cabe finished speaking, a sign of how accustomed he had become to his abilities since they had last met. Darkhorse inspected it briefly, more because of his own recent lack of success than because he did not trust the warlock's skill. When he was satisfied, he turned to bid the two farewell.

"Thank you for your aid, Cabe Bedlam—and yours, too, Lady of the Amber."

"Please don't call me that."

"My apologies! I was warned and I forgot."

She slowly shook her head. "*I* apologize. This is not the time for trivialities."

"Good luck, Darkhorse." Cabe waved a hand. "We'll leavel on *our* journey as soon as possible."

"Do that. Things may be calm, but best not to take chances, eh?" The ebony stallion reared. "Beware, dear friends! Shade may strike at any time and in any way! Be vigilant!"

He heard Cabe call, "We will!" and then the world shifted as he crossed through the portal. Ahead of him, the fury of the Hell Plains exploded in a mocking salute to his return. The gate vanished as the shadow steed emerged. Darkhorse, wasting no time, immediately reached out through the link itself and noted that his quarry was somewhere south of him.

Darkhorse prayed that he would have some idea of how to convince the sorcerer to break the link before the two of them came face-to-face again. He was uncomfortably aware that he stood a good chance of becoming, for the *third* time, Drayfitt's prisoner.

The last thought might have been humorous . . . if not for the fact that he knew there would be no escape this time. Drayfitt would surely see to that.

In the garden of the Manor, Cabe stood with one arm around his wife. The two of them stood staring at the spot where, moments before, the portal that Darkhorse had used had stood.

Cabe blinked and smiled. "We should do this more often."

"I keep telling you that. Why do you think that I bring the children out here? There's something about a walk around this place that puts one at ease."

The two walked slowly to one of the benches. The Lady Bedlam sat down, looking briefly confused.

"What's wrong?" Cabe asked, sitting down beside her.

"I keep thinking that Aurim was out here—but that's silly. He's not."

"You sent Aurim, Kyl, and Grath to their rooms, remember? We wanted privacy."

"Privacy." She kissed him. "We don't get enough of that, do we?"

"No. Still, we can't complain. Things have been pretty peaceful over the last few years. Even Talak's been quiet for months."

Gwen settled into his arms. "Let's hope it stays that way. I'd hate for something to ruin as lovely a day as this."

They kissed and then sat quietly on the bench, listening to the birds and enjoying the day. Neither of them spoke of the return of Darkhorse, Talak's army marching, or Shade's plot. What point *was* there in talking about such things?

None of them had *happened*.

XIII

A day had passed since the departure of the column, and it had been a day of change. It was not something that Erini found she could put her finger on at first. A glance from one of the palace guards, the curt words of one servant to another, and the politeness of Counselor Quorin. The last worried her most, for if the advisor had reason to be polite to her, it probably meant trouble.

Melicard's manner seemed to be the only positive result of yesterday's events. He was actually jubilant.

One final change confused more than worried her. After insisting that she allow him to protect her better, Iston had found reason after reason to summon his men away. From Galea, she had been told that the captain was out somewhere, honing his troops to battle-fitness as every good commander should; while from Magda, she received only an amused smile, a response to Galea's simplistic explanation. Erini suspected that neither of them really knew what Iston was actually doing.

Breakfast with Melicard went swimmingly, as her father

would have put it. The princess was astounded at how pleasant he could be. More and more, his talk turned to peaceful times, times without the Dragon Kings and what he would then hope to accomplish. He even began talking about bridging the chasm that he had set up between himself and his neighbors, especially Penacles and Irillian. It would have been an idyllic world, the one he built up over the course of the meal, if it had not had one major flaw.

There was no mention of the drake race in his new world. From the way the king spoke, Erini knew that there would be no room for the drakes. It marred an otherwise wonderful morning. Finally, she put the thought aside, assuring herself that she would press him on it once they were married.

For the first time, Melicard broached the subject of marriage.

The two of them had walked outside onto one of the marble terraces that seemed to have been a preoccupation with one of the palace's designers. Two sentries stood stiffly at attention as the royal couple glided by. At home, Erini would have expected to see at least a dozen guards nearby—just for *her* protection. Melicard, however, seemed confident of his own safety. Erini was not so certain.

"You've made a change here, my princess. You know that, do you not?"

"What could I have done? I've only been here a short time."

The king closed his one eye (though the light made it seem as if *both* eyes closed) and appeared to make a rapid calculation. He opened his eye and smiled with the good half of his mouth.

"It *has* been only a short time, hasn't it? I've begun to feel as if you have been here always. Quorin says the same thing."

With a very different meaning behind it, the princess thought in grim satisfaction. "This is my home. I feel that way, too."

Melicard turned his gaze away from her, embarrassed. This was not the sort of thing he understood well. Battles and vengeance were his forte. "I told you something to the effect that love at first sight exists only in tales. I think I was wrong."

"You were. I know from personal experience."

Without thinking, he brought up the elfwood arm and took her hand. The arm was pleasantly cool to the touch, smooth without feeling lifeless. Erini noticed how its feel seemed to be dependent upon her betrothed's mood.

"I cannot say how long this crusade will last, or if it will even end during our lifetimes, for that matter. Regardless, if you are willing, I think it's time that we put an end to the 'royal courtship' and began planning for—the future.''

She laughed lightly, positively delighted with the way he had put it. "Marriage? Is that the word you sought, your majesty?"

Melicard nodded with mock severity. "Yes, I think so."

Her kiss proved to be the proper response. As with the false arm, she hardly noticed that a part of the lips that touched her own was not real. The elfwood was wood only if the two of them saw it so. Now, their belief made it flesh.

"Your—*majesties*." Quorin's voice threw a deep chill on the day, dousing even the fires of happiness that had enveloped Erini during Melicard's proposal. Still, there was some pleasure in seeing the look on the counselor's face. He was confused and livid, and both those emotions were barely being kept in check. Erini gave him a polite but false smile.

"What *is* it, Quorin?" Melicard, unlike his future bride, bared his teeth in something that could never be termed a smile. Its ferocity surprised the advisor, who had probably never had it turned on *him* before. "I left orders that *no one* was to disturb us. That *included* you, I believe."

"Forgive me, my lord... I was under the impression..."

He stared at the princess, who had the feeling that the man had not expected to find the two of them in so intimate a moment.

"Since you are here, Quorin, I have something for you to do."

"My lord?" Feral eyes drifted to Erini.

"Announce that, with the campaign underway and a new era beginning in which Talak will be at the forefront, the Princess Erini of Gordag-Ai has consented to be my queen. We will be married in a citywide ceremony in—how long would you say, my princess?"

She gave Melicard a smile. *At last!* "Since this marriage was arranged before I could walk, there is little preparation needed on my part. I would prefer it as soon as possible."

By now, the counselor had recovered somewhat. With a slight gleam in his eyes, he quickly said, "It would be remiss to have a less-than-regal wedding ceremony, your majesty. The princess's family will wish to attend and all of the nobles from both city-states will demand their rights, too. Such an event calls for extravagance."

Erini grew cold. "I've never been one for extravagance. If there is someone who can marry us now, so much the better."

Melicard patted her hand. "My sentiments exactly, but Quorin is, unfortunately, correct. We owe your family and the people a ceremony—a festival even."

"One month, your majesty! If I can help organize several thousand soldiers, a wedding will seem simple in comparison! One month!"

"That long?" The king seemed more reluctant now. "I was hoping two or three weeks at most. Make it a smaller ceremony. The nobles and the royal family of Gordag-Ai. Announce that a festival for the people will commence two weeks after that. They'll understand."

Quorin sighed in evident defeat. "Two weeks, then. May I be the first to extend my congratulations to both of you."

Melicard thanked him, but Erini could only nod her head. As the advisor turned to leave—supposedly to begin those preparations, especially the announcements that would have to be carried by courier to Gordag-Ai—the princess could not help thinking that he had given in too easily. In fact, it seemed that his main purpose had only been to assure that the wedding did not take place immediately. A month or two weeks; a delay was a delay.

"Is something wrong?"

"No. I just wish we could be married now."

"That would be pleasant, but we're already ignoring protocol. By rights, the courtship was to last a full month and the wedding date should have been set from four to six months later."

"Months in which anything could happen. Our fathers actually decided that?"

"It was how they were married to our mothers. Royalty sometimes requires setting odd examples. Enough of that. Now that Quorin has succeeded in interjecting his presence into my day, I am reminded of work that must be taken care of. The campaign has begun, but I have people to govern, too."

"If I am to be queen, should I not learn how you govern your people?"

Melicard smiled. "You have a point, though I fear that you will only distract me from my duties. Very well. Come with me and see how I protect my children. Perhaps you will even have a few suggestions on ways I can improve."

She refrained from commenting, wondering how he would react to her opinions.

As they left the terrace, Erini noted how the guards appeared to have been rotated. These were two new soldiers, men the princess vaguely recalled seeing in the patrol that had stopped her when she had been leaving the garden with Drayfitt. Ostlich's patrol.

"You're leaving me again," Melicard whispered from her side. "You have a mind that certainly loves to travel."

Erini suddenly tightened her grip on the king's arm. Had it not been the one made of elfwood, it was likely she would have cut off blood to the limb. Melicard's final words had struck her hard, for, as if having a premonition, she *had* seen herself leaving her betrothed—but only because both of them were dead.

Shade watched the column come to a halt from what little remained of the tower he had usurped.

The tower had been built long ago as a sister city to Talak, but, as Talak was flexing its muscle, so apparently had this one. At some point in recent times—recent time to the hooded spellcaster being anything in the past few centuries—it had been destroyed. The expedition steered clear of it, possibly because they felt that the ghosts of the dead would put a curse on their crusade.

It is not the ethereal phantoms of your minds that you must fear, the warlock thought with something almost approaching indifference. What became of Talak's great army did not interest him; what became of Drayfitt *did*. The elderly sorcerer was the only link he had to the spell. There were things he needed to know, things that had again escaped his mind after his brief fling with omniscience. He cursed the personality that had been dominant then. Instead of working with that knowledge, it had chosen to relax, to taunt, and to play the fool. There was little to redeem in any of his past incarnations. Madmen and fools all of them. To Shade, they were different people, not worthy of the Vraad race.

It had taken an accident to change things. To his regret, however, Drayfitt's misuse of the one spell offered Shade both immortality and final death. All that mattered was time.

I am Vraad. Tezerenee. The dragon banner rests in my *hands now.* Which tent would be the gaunt mortal's tent? Shade blinked and his view changed to a closeup of the massive camp, despite the fact that they were more than an hour to the south. He had no qualms about altering his body to suit his needs. Shapeshifting, however, was a costly and difficult spell for most sorcerers, and actual physical change was only a last resort because it required the most delicate of manipulations. They feared disrupting the natural forces of this world, something that had never stopped the Vraad. It was so very hard to believe that these people were descendents of his kind—except that there had been those, like the Bedlams, who had proved that magic was still the ultimate tool.

"Cabe," he muttered, recalling the first time they had met. The young boy had been frightened out of his senses, not understanding what he was.

A movement in the camp disturbed his reverie. Shade frowned, wondering why he should spend time reminiscing about something so inconsequential. This was not the first time, either. Everything he had done in the last few days had stirred some memory—and with the memories came emotions. The Vraad had never been immune to emotion; they had, in fact, been slaves to their passions at times. Yet, the memories he found he could not purge concerned these lesser creatures or those who could now only be called his enemies. It made no sense. They were transitory lives for the most part; thralls for his will as had been the way before the journey to this place.

He was saved further introspection by the appearance of his quarry.

Drayfitt looked worn out, unaccustomed, it seemed, to riding long distances. Shade clucked his disapproval; a competent spellcaster would have created his own, more comfortable transport and, since his companions were apparently mundane in nature, travelled at the head of the column as its supreme commander. Any idiotic officer who tried to argue otherwise would find himself without a mouth to curse with.

Shade watched as Drayfitt spoke briefly with two officers. Their words were of unimportant matters—the coming battle, what they possibly faced, and the continuing agreement that this was folly and the expedition should have actually been sent north or northwest to deal with the suddenly active clans of Silver. The warlock smiled; Talak would get to fight the Silver Dragon sooner than they expected.

The night would soon be upon them. Then he would go to

the elderly sorcerer and relieve him of the burdensome knowledge locked in his subconscious. After that, the wrong that had
been done to Shade could finally be corrected. He would be
immortal, have control of the powers of this world, and have
no rivals to argue his claim. There were good points to being
the last of his kind. The Dragonrealm would be his to mold into
a proper domain, and its inhabitants would adore him—because
he would will it so.

A harsh voice, an old memory, thrust through his mind like a
well-sharpened sword. *Do not dream! Act!*

The corners of his mouth curled downward as he observed
Drayfitt departing for one of the larger tents.

"Yes, father," he muttered coldly to the ghosts in his head.

As the last vestiges of an ignoble day departed beneath the
horizon, Drayfitt discovered an odd thing about himself. The
first few minutes on his feet—after a whole day's journey on
the back of the monster some fool of a soldier had chosen for
him—he had been totally exhausted and sore to the point of
numbness. Now, only minutes after sitting down on the cot in
his tent, he felt refreshed and actually stronger than ever. His
abilities, too, seemed sharper. Drayfitt stared thoughtfully into
space for several minutes, then looked up at a lantern someone
had lit for his use. Pursing his lips, he whistled to the flame. To
his delight, a tiny red figure immediately leaped out of the fire
and down to the ground. Miniature plumes of smoke trailed
after him. The figure was little more than a doll, lacking even a
face. It walked up to the spellcaster and bowed gracefully.

Drayfitt whirled his finger once. The flame-creature did a
flip, landing on its feet again. It repeated its bow.

Laughing quietly, the sorcerer whistled for another figure.
The one that leaped out this time was female in shape. She
joined her counterpart and executed a curtsy. At a silent
command from their creator, the two fiery dolls stepped together and began to dance. Around and around they spun. Drayfitt
watched them with a child's glee; Ishmir had performed a trick
like this when Drayfitt had been little more than a baby. It was
one of the reasons he had later tried to follow in his famous
brother's footsteps. It was one of the first tricks he discovered
he did not have the aptitude for. The potential was there, but
the powers, for some reason, refused to respond properly.
Ishmir had claimed on several occasions that the only differ-

ence between a Dragon Master and a simple street showman was strength of will.

Finally tiring of his little dancers, he dismissed them back to the flame. It was silly, he decided, to waste his newfound strength on so childish a spell. With his present level of competency, the aged spellcaster realized that an entire world had opened up to him. Up until now, his skills had served him adequately at best—lengthening his lifespan and blurring the memories of those around him when necessary. Now, he could take his place as a true sorcerer, one who did not have to worry about the Seeker talismans that Counselor Quorin wore upon his person to keep him safe from magical assault by *outside* foes. He, Drayfitt, would guide the king to a more reasonable course of action, make Talak truly a city guiding the Dragonrealm to peace.

"I hope you will excuse the intrusion," a mockingly polite voice asked quietly.

Drayfitt spun around, all his newfound strength at the forefront for this sudden attack. He knew whom he faced—even though he had not expected to actually *see* the other's visage.

"Yes, I am Shade." The hooded warlock bowed in what seemed a perfect imitation of the fire elemental's bow. He had something unidentifiable in each hand. For some reason, Drayfitt's stomach churned uneasily.

"I bring you—offerings." Shade threw the two objects to the ground. As they landed, legs and tails formed. Two very large and very nasty scorpions trundled toward one another, preparing to lock with one another in battle.

"They were partners in crime once. Sent by someone who would see you dead. Poison was to be their weapon, poison in your food this very night. Enough to kill a dragon."

Drayfitt turned pale. The scorpions sparred with their claws, their wicked tails waiting for some opening.

"I thought it only appropriate that they suffer justice akin to their crime. Don't you agree?" The expression on Shade's face—Drayfitt still marvelled over the fact that there *was* a face—was one of indifference. He might have been watching a leaf blown along by a gust of wind.

As if released from some spell, the two scorpions attacked in earnest now. Claws tore at legs. The tails darted forward and snapped back as if some mad puppeteer were controlling them. One creature succeeded in tearing a leg from his adversary.

Overconfident, he was almost struck in the head by the wounded one's stinger. As it was, the near disaster put him off guard and his opponent, dripping ichor where the leg had been lost, forced him back.

Drayfitt looked from the scorpions to the warlock. Shade noted his emotions and snapped his fingers at the two duelists. Both backed away just far enough to separate themselves from one another, their stingers tensed.

Shade lowered his hand. The scorpions struck one another on the head again and again, piercing each other's brain. They continued to strike one another long after each should have been dead from the physical damage alone.

"Enough," the hooded figure commanded.

Two lifeless husks dropped to the ground. They decayed rapidly and within seconds there was no trace of either.

Summoning his courage, Drayfitt glared at the intruder. "Why have you come here? What was that damnable display supposed to prove?"

"Prove? They were going to kill you on Counselor Quorin's command."

"What?" Even having expected the answer to his second question, it was unsettling to actually hear it. "You could have left them alive rather than torture them so! This would've been what I needed to rid the king of that feline's poisonous words!"

"I wouldn't worry about your king. I think he's due to be toppled tomorrow." Shade scratched his chin. "Yes, tomorrow is correct."

"What sort of mad game are you playing?" Drayfitt readied himself. How his newfound strength would hold against the power of the eldest, most skilled spellcaster alive was difficult to say. *Not very well*, he supposed after a moment's consideration. "If you planned on killing me, why not simply have those two poor souls do the work for you?"

"*Kill* you?" The warlock looked openly startled. "I have no desire to kill you. Just give me what I want and I'll erase your memories of this night. Simple as that."

"Erase my memories? After you tell me my king is in danger?"

"He'll be toppled whether you know or not. Besides, I made a pact and I will abide by it. Be reasonable. I just want a piece of your mind." The ends of Shade's mouth tilted upward and

he stretched out a hand toward the elderly sorcerer. Drayfitt
found that Shade's sense of humor escaped him.

Where are the sentries? he suddenly wondered. Shade was
talking loud enough for anyone within the general area to hear
him, yet no one had come to investigate. *And I didn't even
notice the spell—whatever it was,* Drayfitt concluded. *What
chance do I have? What* choice *do I have?*

"You will not take memories that are not yours!"

"Ohhh, but they *are*! My memories, I mean! You studied
that book from end to end; I know. Even if you cannot recall its
contents consciously, it remains trapped within you. I merely
plan to sift through until I find them. You should be reasonable
about this."

As Shade spoke, Drayfitt felt his arms and legs grow heavy.
He took a step toward the warlock, thinking ruefully how much
this resembled his failure during Darkhorse's temporary escape.
That reminder seemed to give him the impetus he needed.
Summoning his strength, he broke the spell the warlock had
wound around him with such ease that it left him startled.

Shade did not look too pleased, either. "Do not resist me.
You only play the role of mage; I *am* magic! Give me what is
mine and I will leave you be."

Drayfitt made a circular motion with his left arm. "Anything
of such value to you should be kept from you at all costs. I
know what you are. I know the destructive effects of Vraad
sorcery."

The sand began to creep up Shade's legs at a rate that caught
the warlock unaware until it was up to his waist. He stopped it
there with little more than a frown and sent the granules flying,
creating a man-sized dust devil that swarmed over Drayfitt.

The elderly spellcaster dispersed it, but the motion cost him.
Shade reached out with one hand and touched Drayfitt on the
temple. Drayfitt let out a gurgle and fell to his knees. The
warlock cradled his quarry's head in both hands.

Though physical resistance had failed the old man, Shade
found his path no easier now. Drayfitt's will was stronger than
Shade would have imagined it could be. It was almost as if the
sorcerer were drawing from some secret reserve. He was
actually succeeding in repelling the invasion of his mind.

Stepping up the intensity of his mental assault, the warlock
began picking up random, insignificant memories. At first, he
was pleased, thinking he had broken through. Then, he realized

that Drayfitt had turned him toward a blind alley of sorts and that the other's resistance was still keeping him out.

Annoyed, Shade ceased holding back his full power.

Drayfitt's eyes widened and his mouth opened in silent agony. His hands clutched at his attacker's, but the will behind them was failing.

The memories began flowing like a river newly released from the winter ice. It did not take Shade long to find the ones he had wanted, for, being recent memories, they were clearer, more obvious. There were memories of Darkhorse mixed among them, but the warlock let them dwindle away, seeing no use in them. What could they tell him about the shadow steed that he did not know already?

When at last he had absorbed all he had desired, Shade released Drayfitt's head. The king's sorcerer crumpled to the ground, eyes staring sightlessly ahead. Drayfitt breathed, but that was nearly all he could do.

Shade knelt down beside him, putting one hand on the stricken figure's forehead. There was a mind there, but it was slowly ebbing away. He would be dead within the hour. The warlock generously closed Drayfitt's eyes. There was no remorse; had Drayfitt not resisted, Shade would not have been forced to take stricter measures. It was as simple as that.

Lying in the dirt, though, seemed an ignoble end for a mage who had, however briefly, had the strength to check him. Shade stared at the cot and slowly smiled.

It took him one breath to complete the scene . . . and then the warlock was gone.

Just beyond sight of the sprawling encampment, Darkhorse stumbled backward as what he had lost to the King's spellcaster returned to him in a heady rush. His initial thrill at becoming whole again was quickly smothered by the echoes of pain and suffering that accompanied the return. He knew instantly what had been wrought and by whom. Despite regaining everything, Darkhorse chose to continue on toward the camp and the tent of the sorcerer. There were things that Drayfitt might still be able to tell him—if the shadow steed could only reach him before the elderly mage expired.

He hoped desperately that one of those things might be *where* Shade would strike next.

XIV

From the midst of the somber Tyber Mountains, another army set out on a crusade. A larger force coming from the west would join with them before dawn. Together, the combined legions of the new, self-proclaimed Emperor of Dragons would sweep down on the kingdom of the upstart human monarch and claim it for their lord. So as to seal his authority, the Dragon King Silver rode at the front of the horde, the huge riding drake beneath him the largest and deadliest of its kind, as befit an emperor.

The Silver Dragon's eyes burned hungrily as he stared south, where, if one used imagination, the gates of Talak already stood open to greet him.

Someone else sensed the shock of Drayfitt's passing.

Erini had retired early and had just fallen asleep. The princess did not wake at that moment, but rather began to dream. She dreamed of the elderly sorcerer collapsing, his life ebbing away. She dreamed of a fearsome, hooded face made all the more terrible because the emotions that it displayed were not even evil; there was annoyance, irritation, and a cold indifference to the fate of the king's spellcaster. It was as if the life was next to nothing to this face.

The princess knew somehow that it was the face of the warlock Shade.

She dreamed of another, as well: the ebony stallion Darkhorse. He stood poised above a fairly stable hill, staring down at the camp. Though he had not yet entered, he *also* knew of the death and the bitter knowledge that he was too late.

Drayfitt had had his faults, but Erini mourned his passing. There had been a bond between them, the sharing of her secret, her *curse*. In a sense, she felt that Darkhorse had a similar bond with her, and her dream-self drew some relief from that. At that point, her subconscious turned to the one time she had truly met the shadow steed. The chamber beneath the palace. The meeting was fixed in her mind, as was the fact that she *had* succeeded in freeing him.

"Princess?" Darkhorse turned, as if realizing for the first time that she was there.

Erini woke—and found herself on a cold, stone floor in total darkness.

Fear struck, but it passed quickly. She seemed in no immediate danger, and hysteria might only lead her into something worse. Pulling her nightclothes tight, Erini wished for something warmer to wear, then almost panicked again when the fabric covering her form tingled and altered. For a moment, she thought something was trying to swallow her feet; only after touching them did she realize that she now wore boots.

With her growing skills, Erini had succeeded in reclothing herself. She so marvelled at the feat that it was some time before the princess returned to the problem of her present accommodations, and when she did, Erini decided that the first thing needed was light. Only then could she get an idea of where she was.

How? was something the novice sorceress already knew. Her abilities had brought her to this place, wherever it was, and those selfsame abilities would, the princess hoped, return her to her room. First, though, came the light.

Not knowing exactly how she was to do it, Erini tried picturing a candlestick in a holder standing no more than three feet away from her. According to Drayfitt, a spell as simple as this would be almost automatic. She would not have to visibly reach out to the spectrum and touch the powers. Her natural skill would do that—hopefully.

When her first attempt yielded nothing but a slight throbbing in her temple, Erini shut her eyes tight and pictured the candle over and over, hoping that through constant repetition, she would achieve her goal.

The smell of melting wax informed her that she had succeeded. Then, the smell became a stench and brightness suddenly sought entrance through the lids of her eyes. Erini opened them wide and stared in disbelief as over a hundred candles, all burning like miniature suns, flickered and melted before her, an army come in response to her summons. The scene brought a brief smile to her lips—a smile that died when she recognized the room she had teleported herself to with her magic.

It was the chamber where Darkhorse had been held prisoner by Melicard.

There was no sign of the diagram that had made up the boundaries of the magical cage. Even the marks Drayfitt had etched into the stone floor were gone.

With the discovery that she was still within the palace and not that far from her chambers, Erini decided it might be best to *walk* back. Her success with sorcery had, thus far, been fair at best. Erini had altered her clothing—evidently to the type of brown leather and cloth riding suit, including pants, that was famous in Gordag-Ai—but the other spells had had wild results. Instead of one candle she had called up a hundred. In her sleep, she had teleported herself to another location. If she tried to send herself back to her bed, the princess knew that she *might* materialize there; however, it was just as likely she might appear back in her bedroom in her *father's* palace. Explaining *that* to the king and queen of Gordag-Ai, even despite the fact that Erini was their daughter, might prove scandalous. At the very least, her secret would be out before she had control of her abilities.

She picked up one of the candlesticks and, after a minor internal debate, snuffed out the rest as quickly as she could. Erini wondered what Quorin or Melicard would say when they came down here and found Darkhorse free and dozens of half-melted, unlit candles standing in the middle of the floor. While it had its amusing aspects, Erini knew that she wanted to be far away when it happened. If there was one thing that might still shatter her hopes with Melicard, it was her implication in the shadow steed's escape.

Erini stepped to the door, found it unlocked, and opened it.

Two bored guards turned in sudden shock and stared at her, openmouthed.

She tried to close the door, but one of the guards, quicker to react than his fellow, kept it open by thrusting one meaty arm against it. He was already pulling out his sword when the princess acted without thinking and thrust the candle toward his face, wishing desperately for something more effective to combat the two soldiers with than the tiny flame.

A ball of fire swelled *out* from the candlewick, engulfed the two hapless sentries, and dwindled back to a tiny, flickering flame . . . all before Erini had a chance to understand what she had wrought this time.

There was no trace of the two men. The flames had swallowed them completely, not even giving them time to recognize their fate—a minor blessing, the princess thought, her hand shaking. The candlestick and what remained of the candle itself, most of it having melted from the great burst of heat, fell from her untrustworthy grip and clattered to the floor. The stunning truth, that she had just *killed* two men with her unpredictable abilities, horrified her. Two men. Erini understood that they had been trying to kill or capture her, but that made it no better. She had not even been trying to hurt them; her desire for something deadlier had merely been in the hopes of stalling them long enough for her to think of something—anything.

Sleep! I could have put them to sleep! I know it! Instead, I murdered them! There's not even anything left for their families to mourn!

She knew then that she must not marry Melicard. She should not even be around people. Any passing thought might be the death of someone close to her—as if the death of some stranger was any better. Tears gave of themselves in great numbers as the princess stared at her hands. Even knowing that the magic was a part of her, hands or not, Erini could not help thinking of them as *the hands that have killed*.

Tonight, she decided abruptly. *I have to leave!* She refused to even consider utilizing her growing abilities to send herself far, far away by that method. There would be no sorcery. Everything would be done by physical means.

Torchlight illuminated the long, winding stairway. Erini, recalling the last trek up the maddening steps, took a deep breath and started up as fast as possible. She was able to keep her pace for the first fifty or so steps and then slowed continuously from there. Perhaps it was only because of her anxiety concerning her situation, but Erini felt as if the stairway had grown to twice its normal height, so long did it seem to take to reach the door to the garden. The princess was so happy to have finally arrived that she swung the door open carelessly. Only after it was out of her reach did she curse herself for forgetting that there might be sentries here, too.

There were none. The garden was dark and empty. Abandoning everyone was a bitter thought and, deep inside, she would have welcomed Melicard's sudden presence, even if his love turned to hate when he discovered what she was and how her lack of control had killed two men. The unfortunate guards had probably merely been performing their duties. They certainly could not have expected to see a royal princess step out of a chamber that supposedly housed only a magically ensnared creature from beyond. Their actions had made sense; an intruder had been emerging from a secured place. For their obedient performance, she had rewarded them with instant incineration.

Pushed forward by a new wave of guilt-ridden thoughts of the guards who had just been doing their duty, Erini started out in the direction of the royal stables. There, she would be able to find a proper steed, perhaps the bright devil Iston had ridden. She despised the thought of stealing another's horse, but her requirements included speed and stamina. Iston's horse more than measured up in both categories.

"A strange time of the night for walking the garden, don't you think, Princess Erini?"

Erini did not jump, though the voice floating from the darkness had actually shaken her already taut nerves badly. She stood her ground, putting on a frosty look and acting as if anything she did was not the business of a mere noble, even the king's special counselor.

"You weren't in your chambers, princess, and I became worried about you." Quorin stepped out from an entranceway to her right, looking unruffled. Behind him, Erini could barely make out the hulking shapes of at least two guards, one of whom was holding a torch.

"Of what concern is it to you whether I am in my chambers or out taking a walk in the garden? I find the night air and the life in the garden to be soothing."

"If you find walking so suits you, then I insist you join me. There's something fascinating you should see."

Mal Quorin took her arm. There was no pretense now, for his hand squeezed painfully tight. His men, four of them, formed an escort around the duo. Even though the counselor had not yet said what it was he wanted her to see, the princess knew already. She struggled briefly in what proved to be a futile attempt. Quorin was even stronger than his appearance indicated.

"*Counselor Quorin*," she grated angrily, trying a new tactic, "I have no desire to walk anymore, especially with you! If you do not cease this disrespectful manner, I shall be forced to mention it to my betrothed, *your king*!"

"Do so," the advisor responded indifferently. Without warning, he began walking, practically dragging Erini for the first

few steps before she matched his pace. Two guards moved in
front and the other two fell back to the rear, creating a square
of sorts with the princess and her captor in the center. A glance
from Quorin convinced Erini that it was not in her best interest
to shout or make noise of any sort. She doubted he intended her
any physical harm, but that might change at any moment,
especially once they reached their destination.

There was only one way she could extricate herself, but it
meant trusting in the very curse that had placed her in jeopardy
initially. Erini could not bring herself to trust her abilities, not
after the wasted death of two men. Even the slightest error in
judgment might add five *more* lives to her burden of guilt, and
as much as she despised and distrusted the counselor, Erini did
not want his death on her conscience.

One of the men opened the door in the wall. Quorin pulled
his reluctant guest bodily to the stairway and led her down.
Whereas the journey upward had lasted an eternity, this one
seemed to pass in little or even no time at all. Erini was down
at the base of the steps, staring at the door through which she
had released death, before her thoughts could even organize
themselves.

"No," she gasped so quietly that her smiling escort did not
hear her.

"These aren't your new quarters, your majesty," the advisor
said wryly, mistaking the reason for her hesitation. "I thought
you might like to see again what your *beloved* has wrought
here. You do want to know what the true Melicard is like, don't
you? I find it hard to believe that you could still stomach him
after seeing his 'guest.'"

"Have you lost your mind, counselor? Do you think Melicard
will let this pass? Even if I do not tell him, he will discover it
for himself!"

"Undoubtedly. Given the opportunity, he might even be
tempted to hand me my head—as he has done to so many!"

Erini had no time to ask for a clarification to the enigmatic
statement, for Mal Quorin shoved her roughly against a wall
and reached for the handle to the chamber door, evidently
desiring to give the moment his personal touch.

In desperation, the princess gave in to temptation. Her
muddled thoughts came up with a solution she believed would
not result in death and, focusing her will, she struck out at her
captors.

Nothing happened.

The princess tried again, gritting her teeth in frustrated concentration. Her original idea became murky; a solution of some sort was all she desired now.

Again nothing... nothing save that Mal Quorin, who had looked inside the chamber, was now stumbling back, his face red with rage and his anger focusing on the most likely target—her.

"What happened here? Where is he? Answer me!" Quorin slapped her hard, forgetting who it was he was assaulting and why he had dragged her down here in the first place. "This was Drayfitt's doing, wasn't it? He's the only one who could've done it!" Quorin the animal had resurfaced. His feral visage was filed with the need for blood.

It was that which strengthened Erini in the face of terrible danger. If she had so frustrated the counselor by freeing Darkhorse, then she had struck a heavy blow against his plans, whatever they were.

The soldiers had backed away from their master, obviously more familiar with his violent temper. He eyed them ferociously, knowing that someone had discovered the escape earlier but had been afraid to alert him, then sneered at his captive. One hand darted toward Erini's face, causing her to flinch. It stopped short of striking, instead seeming to caress her bruised chin. When his hand came away, there were drops of red on two of the fingers. For the first time, the princess tasted the blood on her lower lip.

Quorin took a deep breath. "You were an unexpected impediment! Melicard to have a queen? What sane creature would want that pathetic fool? You should've been well on your way back to Gordag-Ai within a day of meeting him, but *no*, you chose to play the heroine in one of your fainthearted ladies' tales, the woman who would rescue the enchanted king! This is what it gets you!" He held up the hand with the blood on it so that the stained fingers were directly before her eyes. "Even knowing that he would dare to summon up a demon, a fiend that might have killed hundreds of innocents if it got out of control, you convinced yourself that you loved him!"

Erini simply stared back. She knew Quorin's words for the twisted lies they were, however, and finally could no longer hold back. "And who was it who first suggested he seek out

demons? Drayfitt would have never suggested such a dangerous, mad spell!''

"Drayfitt." Mal Quorin took hold of Erini's arm again and
wiped the blood onto her sleeve. She did not give him the
satisfaction of struggling, no matter how disgusted she had
become with his true manner. Her abilities had failed her for
reasons she could not fathom, but the princess had survived
without them all of her life and would continue to do so,
despite the odds. "What did he tell you? It doesn't matter now,
princess, because that old charlatan is dead. Poisoned, I'd
think."

Erini did not respond, and simply clamped her mouth shut,
continuing to glare.

"Perhaps later," Quorin continued. He was slowly growing
calm again, as if the discovery of Darkhorse's escape and
Erini's questionable involvement did not really matter. "Perhaps
later, when the last few items have been taken care of, we'll
speak again. Your presence initially threw everything into
chaos, but you may prove to be the key to adding Gordag-Ai to
our winnings without so much as a struggle."

Responding to some silent signal, two of the guards took
hold of Erini by her arms. She finally gave up all sense of
caution. "You've overstepped yourself! Melicard will not stand
for this! Your influence over him is nothing now! He'll—''

He gave her a genuinely puzzled look. "Princess Erini! Do
you mean to tell me that you, an intelligent if somewhat
troublesome female, can't understand what's happening? Do I
sound as if I care what your crippled lover does to me?''
Quorin smiled as he watched Erini's belated reaction. "This is
a *coup*, your majesty. Tonight, Talak will be without a *king* for
the first time in centuries. Fortunately, the *rightful* one is on his
way even now . . . and the gates will be open in greeting.
Remove her from my sight but try not to damage her."

As she was dragged past him, Erini struck out at the
counselor with the full force of her will, not caring what the
results might do to her or even the palace, if it came down to it.
The sole response to her efforts was a sudden movement of one
of Quorin's hands to his chest, where he seemed to be reassuring himself that something still hung around his neck. He
stared at the princess intently, his expression a mixed one of
doubt and curiosity, until the twisting stairway took her out of

sight. Erini wondered if he knew now what she was—and what that would mean to her eventual fate.

Melicard! Even though the evidence was all there, she could not bring herself to fully believe that the counselor's minions had taken over the palace so swiftly and silently. She had retired for the night only a few hours ago! Yet, Mal Quorin had had years to plan for this, slowly insinuating himself into the hierarchy of Talak, becoming the fellow crusader obsessed with the same goals as his master. The longer she dwelled upon it, the more the truth of those final words became evident. Probably more than three-quarters of the palace guard obeyed the advisor's commands. Melicard—Melicard had likely been cut down while he slept, a victim of the very men he had thought were protecting him.

Drained, Erini made no effort to free herself as she and her two companions reached the top of the stairway again and exited into the garden. The nearly starless night seemed a fitting symbol of the twilight of Melicard's rule. He had not needed her worthless curse to tear him down; his own obsession had done that.

Why her skills had suddenly abandoned her, she could not say, but, even if it had cost her his love, Erini would have utilized those abilities however possible to save his kingdom and his throne.

Her mind was numb and so she did not struggle as they passed through the garden and into one of the adjoining halls. Erini had never been through this area, but that made little difference to her now. All she wanted was to find some quiet place where she could bury herself in the darkness and not come out again.

Evidence of the coup mounted as they marched through the palace. Armed figures prodding men wearing the same uniforms, that of the palace guard, walked past them in the opposite direction. Erini rose from her stupor long enough to watch the unfortunates as they were herded away, wondering in the back of her mind where *she* was being taken, since it was safe to assume that the other prisoners were going to cells. Perhaps, Quorin had a separate area for prisoners of royal blood. Perhaps, Melicard's body would even be there.

They had gone through a number of unlit corridors, left darkened apparently because there were far more important things to attend to than lighting torches, and so neither Erini

nor her captors paid any attention to the latest one. The two
soldiers muttered to one another, but not loud enough for her to
understand. By this time, they were leading her more or less as
a puppet master might lead a marionette. Thus it was that she
was totally caught unaware—as were her guides—when *hands*
reached out from the walls and caught the soldiers by the
necks.

Erini fell to the ground, bruising her shoulder but succeeding
in preventing her head from striking the hard surface. She
looked up and tried to make out more clearly what was
happening. What little she *could* see left her completely baffled
and even more frightened.

The hands had been joined by partial bodies. A darkly clad
figure, consisting of the upper half of a man's form and one
lone foot that seemed to hop by itself, had one victim down on
his knees. The other attacker, no more than a head and two
arms, was slowly dragging the other hapless soldier backwards.
Both newcomers were using something akin to wire or string to
choke their victims. With their windpipes expertly cut off,
neither guard could even gasp loudly, much less summon help.

It was over in less than a minute. When both victims lay
limply on the floor, one of the dark figures moved toward the
princess. The other began removing evidence of the attack—
that is, the bodies.

"Your majesty! I give thanks that we found you!" The
man's voice was only a faint whisper, but Erini still recognized
the tones of one of her own people. Were there *sorcerers*
among her own subjects?

As if reading her thoughts, her rescuer pulled off the hood
obscuring his features. In the darkness, she could only make
out a soldier perhaps ten years older than she was with a face
that only now, as her savior, could possibly have been termed
handsome. "Don't be frightened, Princess Erini, of either what
we did—or what I look like without a mask." The attempt at
levity failed. "If you could please see to rising, my lady, we'd
like very much to lead you to somewhere safer."

"Safer?"

He nodded. "Captain Iston holds a portion of the palace;
he's been planning for this for days, ever since the rumors were
first reported by our network here."

"Network? Days?" Reality was returning with less than
savory surprises. "What do you m—?"

"Please!" he hissed. "When you're safe, your majesty, the captain will answer all your questions!"

The other man joined them. He was younger, almost as young as Erini and only a little taller. It amazed her to think that he had taken on a veteran more than a third again his size.

"We've gotta move! There's another batch comin' this way!"

"*Please, your majesty?*"

Too many men had died because of her already and the princess would not allow these men to become the next ones. Rising in one swift motion, she gave her hand to the first man, who immediately led them down the corridor in the same direction the guards had been taking her. At the first intersection between halls, however, they turned left. The sound of marching feet echoed for a time, then drifted away as the patrol the second man had noticed apparently turned in a different direction than the trio had gone.

As they moved, Erini caught a glimpse of the cloaks the two men were wearing. At first, they seemed incongruous, serving no apparent purpose, but then she noticed that, depending on how the cloaks twisted, her rescuers seemed to fade—no, not *fade*, but *blend* into their surroundings. The cloaks somehow cast some sort of illusion. Erini had heard tales of such things, though she had never seen anything like them before.

Twice, she tried to ask them something and twice they signalled for silence.

The second warning was punctuated by a short cry. The younger of her two companions suddenly clutched at his side where an arrow protruded. Stealth had required that neither of her rescuers wear much in the way of protection and that requirement was proving costly now.

Something thin and sharp appeared in the hand of her remaining guardian. He threw it at the archer who had seemed to materialize down the corridor. Though Erini could not see where it struck its target, the weapon did its work. The archer fell, his hands clutching at his chest.

More soldiers appeared, too many for any one of them to get off a safe shot at the escaping duo, but more than enough so that the odds against the two fugitives were overwhelming. Seeing that, Iston's man tore off the cloak of his dead companion and shoved it into his mistress's hands. Pushing her down the corridor, he whispered, "The stables! Head toward the

stables! Down this corridor and then turn right at the third one
you see! Keep running! It's the only way, my lady!''

"But *you*—"

"I do my duty! Run!"

Erini did, but there were more soldiers coming down the
other way, cutting her off. As she slowed, trying to find another
route, her lone defender went down. Another death on *her*
hands.

Thinking of her hands, Erini suddenly noticed the subtle,
familiar tingle in her fingers. How long since that feeling had
returned, she could not say. Perhaps if she had kept her wits
about her she would have noticed in time to save the others.
Perhaps not. In a fatalistic move, Erini turned so that one
outstretched hand pointed down each end of the corridor. If the
results killed her as well, so be it. *These* men she felt no pity
for. These men must *pay*.

She might have been influenced by the cloaks that had
allowed her two rescuers to fade into their surroundings. The
concept struck her as perversely appropriate for those who
would play at loyalty and betray their good lords at first
chance. They were not men; they were only the shadows of
men, less than nothing—and Erini would make them so.

When the first screams rose, she tried to force her eyes shut
and keep them shut, but failed, drawn somehow to the hideous
tableau playing itself out on each side of her. From her fingers,
glittering tendrils slithered forth, like serpents of the purest
light, hungry avengers of her pain. As each broke free of her
fingertips, they shot unerringly toward the nearest of her
enemies. Nothing stopped them. One man put a shield up, but
the tendril went through it like a ghost, continuing on unimpeded
until it pierced the unfortunate in the chest and buried itself
completely within his torso, leaving not the slightest trace of its
passing.

As the man scratched desperately at his chest, a light seemed
to come from within him, filling his eyes and his mouth with
the same glittering illumination of Erini's creation. While Erini
stared, unable to believe in what she herself had released, the
light within intensified, becoming so brilliant that its glow
shone *through* the soldier.

The man tried to take a step forward, but his body only
rippled, as if lacking substance. For the space of a breath, a
walking skeleton was outlined within the thinning frame of his

body, then the struggling guard's legs collapsed underneath him, perhaps because those bones had finally melted away. He fell forward, arms outstretched in an instinctive effort to save himself, but, in a final sequence that would return in Erini's nightmares, first the hands and then the arms crumbled like ash against the hard surface and blew away. Unhindered, what remained of his torso struck the floor—and scattered into tiny particles that dwindled to nothing.

Not one man escaped that fate. The tendrils moved with the speed and tenacity of a plague, catching them even as they turned to run. By the time the first man had perished, the rest were infected. Even had she wanted to, Erini would not have been able to save them. The young princess, her face a sickly white by the glow of her instruments of vengeance, could only stand where she was, both fascinated and revolted by the results of her spell.

She had wanted something else, something *cleaner*. Only now did the princess know that there was nothing clean about death, especially death bought about by hatred and anger. They had killed two of her own and possibly the man she loved, but *this*—this was not what she had wanted. As the last man faded, still trying to remove his executioner from within his body, the last of her anger faded as well.

Erini slumped against the wall and slid down to a sitting position, her gaze focused on, but not seeing, the now-empty corridor where only a few loose weapons and an odd item or two were all that remained of probably a dozen men. Had anyone come now, she would not have fought them. It was as likely the princess would not even have noticed them. Now, she only saw darkness—a darkness she quickly welcomed as the one friend she could trust.

Her head tipped to one side as exhaustion and remorse finally carried her off to the only place she could now find peace.

XV

Fully restored, Darkhorse nonetheless moved cautiously investigating the tent of the sorcerer Drayfitt. He could not feel the presence of Shade, but if there were anyone with the talent to muddle his senses to the point of uselessness, it was that one being who knew him best.

A careful probing of the areas surrounding the tent revealed nothing. There was a trace of strong, violent magic in the air, but such was to be expected when two spellcasters met. It said something for Shade's abilities that the two men had battled freely, yet no one knew even now that the king's sorcerer lay dead among them.

An interesting and devastating surprise awaits you all on the morrow, Darkhorse thought, wondering what the loss would mean to the crusade. If Shade was indeed working with the Silver Dragon, a killing as potentially demoralizing as this might send the entire military expedition back to Talak, the last place the drakes would want them, if the eternal had read the situation correctly.

Fairly certain he was not about to enter into a trap but unwilling to put his complete faith in such a belief, the shadow steed trotted quietly down toward the encampment. A portal would have been quicker and probably made discovery less likely, but materializing in an area that his adversary had just departed from was something he did not want to take a chance with this time. Besides, with Drayfitt dead, he faced only human soldiers, men whose weapons were nothing to him.

The tent was not quite on the edge of the camp and Darkhorse slowed as he entered the region. Whole at last, it proved little trouble for him to make a guard's eyes avert or cause a passing soldier to turn in another direction. A young recruit peeling an apple suddenly dropped his knife and, while

he searched the dark ground for it, failed to notice the ebony
form that flitted silently past. The shadow steed reminded
himself what he had been through already so that the ease with
which he now succeeded in his tasks did not create deadly
overconfidence. It was at times like that when disaster struck—
and Shade was a master of disaster.

Around the tent, the grounds were noticeably deserted.
Though a sorcerer was generally invaluable in terms of combat,
most of the soldiers, up to and including their officers, preferred, whenever possible, to keep a safe distance from those
such as Drayfitt. One never knew what might crawl out of a
spellcaster's confines.

Hmmph! Ice-blue eyes blinked as Darkhorse stared disbe-
lievingly at the display only Shade could have wrought. The
hypocrisy of his longtime friend/foe astounded him. *I grow less
and less enchanted with the true* you *the more time that passes,
dear Shade!*

There was no doubt that the warlock had honestly meant this
as an honor of sorts, else he would not have taken the care with
both the body and the bier that he had wrought. Darkhorse
doubted that there had been much remorse; it hardly seemed the
way of the new—that is, the *old and original*—Shade. Still, the
stallion wondered how even his adversary could have not seen
what he had created. Not a monument, but a mockery.

Drayfitt lay peacefully—the first time the shadow steed could
recall seeing him so—with his arms crossed and his worn robes
replaced by a fascinating, multicolored garment that the sorcerer would have never worn in life. A false smile graced his lips,
obviously the warlock's doing, as Drayfitt had, in the shadow
steed's limited experience, never been a man to smile freely.
This was not the elderly sorcerer but some cruel parody.

The funeral bier was worse. As had been his people's way,
Shade had created what might have been called a typical Vraad
monument to opulence. Gilded and decorated freely with what
were likely actual gemstones, it seemed more like an attraction
in a city bazaar than the resting place of the unfortunate
spellcaster. The base, in fact, was composed of four, intricately
carved figurines designed to seem to be holding the bier level
and representing the drake, human, Quel, and Seeker races.
Darkhorse pondered briefly the potential significance of the four,
but could think of nothing that related to his present situation.
Desiring a closer look, he probed the immediate area again.

A thin tendril of life flickered *within* Drayfitt's body.

Untrusting, Darkhorse probed again. It *was* there! Only a trace and barely even that. He knew he could not save the aged mortal, but there was a chance, then, that Drayfitt might be able to tell him something about Shade's plans. Anything.

The essence of his probe altered. Where in the past few days he had twice been forced to part with a portion of his very being, Darkhorse now willingly gave of himself, a handful of water to a man dying of thirst. It was a slow, careful process. Too much and he might finish what Shade had started; too little, and he might not revive the sorcerer in time.

The cracked, gaunt face twisted suddenly as life fought back. Drayfitt coughed and choked, his fingers reaching out to claw at the air, perhaps in an unconscious attempt to further gather life to his thin shell.

Darkhorse silently cursed those who had given the original Shade his own life.

Eyelids fluttered open, but the eyes within did not see. The shadow steed moved closer, hoping that, even if the dying mortal could not see, then he could at least hear.

"Friend Drayfitt, it is I, Darkhorse," he whispered in one ear. "Do you hear me?"

Nothing.

"Drayfitt, I have done my best for you, but your time is short. Talak and your people still depend upon you, as they have for more than a century."

The sorcerer's mouth opened and closed. Darkhorse waited. The human's mouth opened again and a hiss escaped as Drayfitt sought to speak. Uncertain as to whether he might push too far, Darkhorse gave of himself again.

"*Draaa . . . aaa . . .*" the failing spellcaster managed to say.

"You are Drayfitt. That is true." Inwardly, the stallion wanted to roar. Would this be all his efforts came to? Was there nothing left of the human's mind?

"*Draaag . . . King!*"

Dragon King? Which one? The lord of clan Red?

"*Tallll . . . aaak!*" Drayfitt's left hand sought out his own chest. "*Quorin!*" It was the clearest, most precisely spoken word so far, an indication of the sorcerer's hatred for the counselor. Drayfitt clutched at his chest again, as if seeking something that had hung around his neck—or *Quorin's*.

While what he had heard had begun to form an ugly picture

in Darkhorse's mind, none of it concerned the one the phantom steed was hunting. "What of Shade? Tell me of Shade!"

"Memmm . . . mrriess. Focus . . . child?" The eyes turned, seeing perhaps, at least shadows of what was around him. Drayfitt, with forethought that had kept him alive and secure for so long, was trying to economize his words to those that would mean the most. He knew that his life was ebbing away and that even Darkhorse's gift was failing him.

"Focus? Child?" *What did it mean?*

"Mistake again . . . again—"

"*Master Drayfitt!*" someone shouted from without. Darkhorse turned, then realized that the sorcerer was still saying something. By the time he turned again, Drayfitt had grown silent. His eyes were still open, but the only thing they might be seeing now was the final path that all mortals took at the end of life. His last words had been lost.

"Drayfitt!" An officer in his middle years barged through the tent flaps. Unlike most humans, who were properly in awe of the eternal, the newcomer took one stunned glance at the immense steed before him, drew a sword, and *charged*.

The image was so incredulous that Darkhorse laughed despite all that had happened. Ignoring the laughter, the soldier cut expertly at the stallion's legs. A true horse would have been too slow and would have fallen to its knees, its front legs useless. Darkhorse, though, nimbly stepped aside. Pulled off balance by the force of his own swing, the officer left his side open. Darkhorse seized the opportunity, sending the man flying with the gentlest of taps with his front hooves.

"*Now,*" he roared, ignoring the other humans who rushed through the entrance, "if you will be so kind as to *listen* instead of trying to kill everything in sight, I will—"

"You'll do nothing, *demon*!" A man clad in armor decorated intricately enough to designate him as the commander of the expedition pushed aside the rest and strode toward the shadow steed. He carried no sword, but something in his right hand emanated so much stored energy that Darkhorse grew uneasy. There had been, throughout the millennia, objects created by one race or another with more than enough killing power to destroy a hundred Darkhorses.

"Listen to me, you fools! Talak—"

"—will not suffer your masters' reign of tyranny ever again!" The commander held up a small black cube.

"My masters? I am no thrall of the Drag—"

Darkhorse got no further. The tent interior melted into a surreal, fog-shrouded picture. Darkhorse shook his head, trying to focus on reality. Through the haze, he could still hear the voice of the human.

"Think our king did not imagine your drake masters would try to summon such as you? This talisman is proof against *your* kind!"

The shadow steed tried to argue, but his words were muted by whatever trap he had been caught in.

"Would that I could command you to tear your masters apart, but such is not within the power of this object! I can only command *it* to perform its original function—and send you back to whatever hellhole spawned such as you! Begone now!"

"*Foooolssss!*" was all Darkhorse had time to cry.

"Utter, abysmal fools!"

"Once there was a tiny dot," a voice floating in the nothingness commented blandly. "A tiny hole in reality, he was."

The shadow steed kicked uselessly at the empty space around him. He knew where he was—how could anyone fail to recognize a place as barren as the Void?

Whatever hellhole spawned me! This is the hellhole that spawned me, curse all meddling mortals! I should stay here and let them suffer their fates!

"The tiny dot grew over—*time* doesn't work, does it? I shall have to find something else later, when I have the—" the owner of the soft-spoken voice giggled insanely—"*time!*"

Darkhorse focused on the direction the voice seemed to be coming from. "Still composing your tales?"

"I compose *epics*; you *wear* tails." Another giggle.

"I've no time for your witticisms, gremlin."

"My name is *Yereel*, if you do not mind, and even if you do!" A tiny figure, like a child's doll, coalesced before him. It had no distinct features and was as black as Darkhorse. "And here, as you so well know, there *is* no time all the time! Have I said 'welcome home,' by the way?"

The shadow steed looked around him, noting, as he always did, the densely packed regions of empty space. Nothing crowded against nothing, which jostled even more nothing. Some of the nothing was forced to climb on top of the rest of

the nothing just so there was room for all. It was astonishing
that so much nothing could fit into so little space.

I begin to sound as bad as this one, Darkhorse thought
wryly. To his puppetlike companion, he replied, "A welcome is
hardly on my list of desires; I plan to leave here in a moment!
You *know*, too, the mortal who saw you cried out 'You're real!'
Hardly a masterful way of choosing a name!"

The puppet did a headstand in the emptiness. "And *you*
chose *your* name so cleverly! You haven't commented on the
start of my latest epic, dear one! I was thinking of calling it
something nonsensical, like, *Darkhorse, the Hole That Would
Be Whole*!" The tiny figure giggled again, then struck an
upside-down orator's pose. "The hole, as it grew, matured into
pretensions and delusions of grandeur. . . ."

Darkhorse had had enough. He physically turned himself
from the other. "Goodbye, *Yereel*."

"Let me *come*!" The black figure shifted form, becoming a
miniature version of the shadow steed. It trotted through space to a
point within eye-level. "Take me back! You know what it's like
when we've touched the reality! I can't stand this emptiness!"

Darkhorse sighed. "I understand—more than you could ever
imagine—but I cannot and *would* not even if I could! You were
ousted and exiled here by those with greater power than
me—and I cannot blame them!"

"It was all so glorious, I couldn't help myself!"

"Mortals *die*, Yereel," the stallion reminded his tiny twin.
"*You* didn't care how many, either."

"I was *living*! I had *purpose*!"

Moving around his counterpart, Darkhorse began to drift
away. He knew that Yereel could not follow him. Even the vast
reaches of the Void were forbidden to him. The puppetlike
creature could only travel in a small circle again and again. "*I*
journeyed to reality. *I* learned about life and death. Your failure
was your own, Yereel."

"I should *never* have *formed* you!" the other cried testily.

Darkhorse did not look back. "Perhaps, that would have
been better."

As he moved faster and faster through the Void, the stallion
heard the dwindling voice of Yereel.

"Then the hole, now a vast and mighty sea of false dreams
and misconceptions. . . ."

* * *

In the Void, a trek could take no time or all time, including any interval in between. Had Darkhorse been the demon that others proclaimed him—or even one who had *played* at being a demon, like Yereel—it might have been different. He would have been condemned to stay here until some other spellcaster summoned him back. His self-exile had been such a one-way spell, though, in that instance, it was his cooperation that had given it the strength. Darkhorse, however, had a tie to the world of the Dragonrealm that was now at least as strong as his tie to the place that had spawned him. It should have been simple to pierce the barrier between here and there. Should have been, but was not.

He could sense the path, but it seemed endless. For a moment, he wondered if this were some trick of his counterpart, but Yereel's powers were limited to his tiny piece of emptiness. Nothing could change that. No, whatever interfered now, was the work of some *other* influence.

His intended destination had been the Manor, where the shadow steed had planned a quick discussion with Cabe and the Lady Gwen about all that had transpired in the short time since he had left them. Slowly, it occurred to him that the difficulty might not be with *him*. If there was a threat to Shade besides Darkhorse, then it was Cabe Bedlam. More and more, it seemed to make sense, although Darkhorse had little other than a feeling to go on.

"Well, if I cannot enter near the grounds of the Manor, then I shall open a path farther away!" He felt foolish that it had taken him that long to think of so simple an answer to his quandary. He recalled the area where he had entered the forest last time, the place where the Seeker had escaped him. This time, he felt the portal form. Pleased with his sudden change of luck, he laughed quietly and, when the shimmering gap fully materialized, he abandoned the Void without further delay. Had it been at all possible, Darkhorse would have wished that he would never have to return to this dismal, empty region again.

It was still dark when he emerged into the Dagora Forest. Another stroke of luck. With time only an imaginary concept in the ageless Void, it sometimes happened that whole days, even weeks, could go by back in the worlds of reality. Darkhorse's journey had been, relatively speaking, a brief one and so he was fairly positive that this was still the same night that he had left only a short span earlier. Hopefully, he would not be proved incorrect.

Cautious of a trap, Darkhorse moved silently through the forest. Last time, his senses had been at their weakest. Now, though, they were at their peak, and he chose to make full use of them because of that. Whether those senses would prove equal to the task of locating and outwitting Shade was something that he would only discover at the worst possible moment.

The boundaries of the protective barrier were almost upon him before familiar landmarks informed him of where he was. The shadow steed backed away, not wanting to risk suffering through Lady Bedlam's attractive little curses again. He trotted back and forth for some time in an attempt to locate someone who could relay his messages. After a few minutes, however, he gave that idea up. Unlike Darkhorse, the humans—and even the drakes, for the most part—were creatures of the daylight only. With the spell protecting them, most, if not all, were asleep.

There was something amiss, but whatever it was, was not readily evident. He probed the area surrounding the grounds and found no trace of the presence he had felt earlier while still adrift in the Void. Something confusing attracted his attention and he extended his search. A low, disquieting laugh escaped him. He had found the paradox. A spell had been cast to prevent detection of another spell—but it had, at the same time, made magical detection of the Manor's protective measure impossible. Understanding that, Darkhorse adjusted his senses to a different level of comprehension, reaching into an area well beyond human limits, even Cabe's.

Well, well, my feathery little fiends!

The trees around him were aflutter with entranced Seekers. There were more than a score of the avian humanoids, all of whom seemed part of a pattern focused on the region of Cabe's home.

The threat was not Shade, then, but the former lords of this realm once again attempting to assert their power on a land that had passed them by so long ago. Darkhorse snorted in derision. He had no idea what the ultimate purpose of this pattern was, but, since it had been created by the Seekers, it could only be trouble.

Eyes glittering in anticipation, Darkhorse reared high and struck the nearest inhabited tree a harsh blow with his hooves.

Panic broke out above him as Seekers from the tree he had

assaulted and many from those next to it took to the skies. He received confused images of indistinct attackers and realized he was picking up the avians' mental projections, the Seekers' method of communication. Some of them thought that the hordes of the Green Dragon had found them and were even now tearing down the trees. Others tried to calm their brethren while still maintaining the pattern. The latter, at least, proved an impossible task. With almost half their number fully awake, the avians lost control, breaking first the spell that had hidden them and, with much more of a struggle, the mysterious pattern that they had formed over the area.

Darkhorse laughed loudly, in part to keep his adversaries as confused as possible, but also to wake and alert those within the Manor confines.

"Come, oh lords of glories past! Darkhorse invites you to join him!" He kicked at another tree. The Seekers flew hither and yonder, trying to organize themselves. More images passed through the ebony stallion's mind, distorted views of himself as some horrendous creature from the netherworlds. There were few creatures that the avians feared; Darkhorse was among them.

"Come, come! I promise only to bite a few wings, pluck a few feathers, and stomp a few bony, beaked heads!"

One foolhardy male accepted the challenge, diving at Darkhorse with all four sets of claws ready. The shadow steed reared up and caught him in the chest with both hooves, smashing the creature's rib cage with that single blow. The Seeker squawked and collapsed to the ground. Darkhorse looked up at the others and laughed mockingly at them.

Slowly, the Seekers began to organize. Several older ones flew up above the rest and, as Darkhorse watched suspiciously, they formed a small circle. The shadow steed smiled grimly. *Think you that the air is safer?*

Other Seekers tried to form a protective wall in front of the circle. Darkhorse allowed them to organize no further, leaping into the air and soaring toward the avians at a velocity that sent the defenders scattering in sudden panic. One slashed wildly with its claws, sinking its hand into the eternal's body. Darkhorse absorbed him without noticing. Nothing would keep him from the circle.

He was halfway to them when, as one, they cocked their heads to one side and stared. Darkhorse knew then that he had *underestimated* the speed and ingenuity of the avians. That knowledge did him little good, however, as force buffetted him aside. He tried to counter it, but was then buffetted from another direction. One blow after another threw him back and forth across the sky. The constant battering made it impossible to think at all. Darkhorse cursed his own overconfidence and bravado. While he was struggling just to maintain some sort of defense, he knew that other Seekers would be preparing an attack of far more lethal measures than this.

A brilliant flash illuminated the heavens, sending *all* the Seekers into renewed confusion. Darkhorse heard shouts from below. Human and drake voices. The assault against him dropped abruptly as the members of the circle joined their retreating brethren. Darkhorse righted himself and gave chase, furious beyond the point of reason and more than ready to strike a few blows out of pure frustration.

He picked out one of the avians who had formed the circle and was probably one of the rookery elders. Even as he closed in on the creature, an image leaped to life in his head. Shade was in it, a tall and ominous monster whom the Seekers feared even more than they did the stallion. Darkhorse caught hints of a promise made and the results that failure would bring. There were random images of renewed glories and a land that the avians would have ruled again if they had succeeded.

I wonder what his draconian ally would say about such promises, Darkhorse thought as his prey continued its desperate, but seemingly hopeless escape.

The shadow steed slowed abruptly, soon letting the Seekers fly off into the night without further battle. For their failure to the rookery, many of them would pay dearly. For their failure to Shade, who *had* instigated this entire ploy, those who had *sent* this flock would also pay dearly—to the warlock himself. Darkhorse could think of no better justice than that. He turned, descending to the ground at the same time.

"Darkhorse!" a familiar and welcome figure cried out. Reforming himself into something more earthbound, the shadow steed touched earth just in front of the lord of the Manor.

"I'm glad you're safe!" Cabe wrapped his arms briefly around Darkhorse's neck, something that unnerved the eternal more than a hundred avenging Seekers would have. So open a display of affection for *him* was a rarity that he could count on one hoof. Several humans and drakes, who talked among one another like old friends, looked at their lord with renewed awe.

After a decade they might be used to seeing many startling things, but how often did their great and powerful master greet a demonic horse with a simple hug?

Lady Gwen's greeting was cordial, but far less affectionate. "You have our gratitude, Darkhorse. When you broke their spell and woke us with your voice, we realized what had happened to us. My only regret is that we could not capture or kill a few more of those arrogant birds! They sometimes make the Dragon Kings seem *pleasant* in comparison!"

"And make *my* company acceptable, is that it, Lady Bedlam?"

She grimaced, then nodded her head slowly. "Sometimes, dark one. *Sometimes*."

"What happened to you, Cabe Bedlam?"

The young warlock scratched his head. His open honesty was a great contrast to the secrecy and moodiness of Shade. After a moment's thought, Cabe smiled sourly and replied, "We've been living an idyllic life, thanks to the Seekers. They've had us taking walk after walk in the garden, playing with the children, relaxing, and," Cabe glanced at his bride and reddened, "doing whatever else gave us pleasure and took our minds off of the world."

Darkhorse laughed, but not at that. "What a fool I was! Never did it occur to me that the Seeker I pursued briefly might have some purpose for being so near! Now I see why I failed to find him, too! With my 'self' diminished and my impatience guiding me, I never noticed what they were about! They must have freed you briefly and in a subtle manner so that you would not be aware of what games they were playing! Tell me. Do you remember everything?"

Both humans nodded. Gwen added, "I can't help feeling that Shade had *something* to do with all of this."

"He did." Darkhorse explained what he had picked up from the Seeker's mind. There were benefits to the avians' method of communication, but there were disadvantages, too. Seekers, when in dire straits, often emitted their thoughts so powerfully that spellcasters of some ability could pick up the images in their own minds. For Darkhorse, it had been even easier.

"What now?" Cabe wanted to know. "Somehow, I don't think our original plan holds."

Darkhorse nodded. "I would say not. If only I knew where Shade was and what he now intends to do! Drayfitt is dead, Cabe, and his final words, if they were not another ploy engineered by the hooded warlock, are a mystery that I must solve before very long! Shade was never one to be inactive!''

"One thing," Lady Bedlam interrupted, "that we should still do is contact the Green Dragon. He may have some information for us or, at the very least, some suggestion."

"You do that, then," her husband suggested. "I want to check the area out. I want to make *certain* that there are no other surprises."

"That leaves only myself."

"What do you plan on doing?" Cabe asked the shadow steed.

"Return to Talak. If I am incorrect, things will be as they were when I—departed. If, however, things have gone the way I think they have," Darkhorse stared at them and his eyes glittered coldly, "it may already be too late to save the city."

XVI

Shade stood staring in open contempt at the putrefying column of mixed body parts and dripping ichor that was the guardian of this opening to the realms of the Lords of the Dead. He was not impressed. Not at all.

"Shoddy. I would've expected better of your masters. It appears that they, too, have fallen from the ranks of *pure* Vraad." He waved his hand and the guardian, with a wailing sound, crumbled into its component parts. "Is that the best you could do?" he called out to the mire-filled pit. The cavern around him echoed his growing annoyance.

Tendrils of thought reached out to him, some contemptuous, some defensive, all of them a bit fearful. What had *he* accomplished in all his existence? What had *he* accomplished other than creating an endless game between the opposing poles of his existence?

The warlock smiled coldly. "Too true. That changes now. *Your* existence changes now. You have a bauble of mine that I require." Protesting thoughts bombarded him, but he shook them off like droplets of water. "Don't bandy words with me! Return to me the *tripod*. Now."

Open fears now. Fears of control lost and rifts opened.

A sigh. "This world *has* changed you. Like all the rest. You are not worthy of the name Vraad. You are especially not, my cousins, worthy of the name Tezerenee."

A breath, perhaps two, passed before a dark and unprepossessing object formed at the warlock's feet. He picked it up and examined it thoroughly. It was, as he had termed it, a tripod perhaps a hand's length high. A black sphere, no bigger than one of his pupils, rested securely on the top. Finally satisfied, Shade thrust the artifact into the voluminous confines of his cloak.

"Thank you so *very* much," he acknowledged with a mocking bow. "Having taken such great care of it, I can almost forgive you for stealing it from my workshop after my—*death* just doesn't sound right, does it? My *temporary* displacement." He started to fold within himself, then changed his mind. "I did say 'almost forgive you,' didn't I?"

Panicked protests went unheeded as the warlock struck out.

When Shade at last left what remained of the cavern—and the now-ruined island that had once housed it—his thoughts turned immediately to the culmination of his millennia-long dream. Time was running out for him, he knew that. In two, maybe three centuries, his forcibly extended lifespan would reach its limit, but not with the normal aging results. The shadowy warlock knew what awaited him would be far worse, a last fifty or so years as a withered, decaying creature, a consciousness trapped alive in a dry husk. Only when the last vestiges of his earlier, more desperate spells dissipated would he be freed— freed to a death he had no desire to embrace. The others had given in to this world, let it *master* them, but not him.

He reentered the world in the emperor's cavern, only to find it abandoned. The Silver Dragon *had* moved on with his campaign, likely fearing that whatever Shade had in mind for Drayfitt would upset his carefully laid plan. He had taken everyone with him. The Dragon King's ideas had merit; planting a loyal human among his kind's worst enemies and then manipulating that man into a position of great authority had been a plan worthy of a Vraad—and why not?

He dropped that line of thinking, deciding it was hardly worth his time now that his dreams were nearing fruition. He had mapped things out carefully in his mind, seeing where he had made his mistakes, reassuring himself of those results with the memories taken from the sorcerer Drayfitt. It *had* to work this time!

With the tripod returned to him, there was only one other item he needed, but it was the most intregal component of all, outweighing even the artifact that he had taken back from the Lords of the Dead. The tripod was the means of summoning, something Drayfitt could never have known since it had not been in the notes, but it could not function as the focus, the means by which the powers would be drawn together, bound, and turned to his will. His prior mistake had been making *himself* that focus. Forced to both contain and bind them simultaneously, even *he* had failed. No, the only way for the enchantment to succeed would be to find something else to serve as a focus.

Something? *Someone.* It had to be a living entity, one with the open gift that made one a spellcaster. As untrained as possible and young, for the spell would tear at the lifeforce, eating it away. Untrained and young also because those minds were more susceptible to the sort of commands he needed to ingrain upon them. A child would be perfect. A child was malleable.

A child with the potential he sought would also be nearly impossible to find. Since the days of the Turning War, when the human mages had almost defeated the Dragon Kings, the latter had tried very thoroughly to assure that there would never be a second such war. They had missed Cabe Bedlam because of his grandfather's interference. Likely they had missed others as well, since their control had slipped harshly after that near disaster. A long search might prove fruitful, but Shade knew that searching for an infant with latent abilities might very well consume more time than even he had.

There *was* one possibility, likely more, but he had found himself strangely reluctant to consider it. Memories of his addled past, the centuries of swinging back and forth between one mind or another, invaded again. A curse escaped his lips and a fissure suddenly burst into being in one of the cavern walls to his right. He paid it no mind. Breathing deeply, the warlock buried the alien thoughts and memories. It was not the first time he had done so, but he swore silently that it would be the last.

He had sworn so more than a dozen times this one day alone. Each time, they had returned stronger than before. Care. Guilt.

Friendship. Unbecoming memories for one of his stature. Feelings for those who were not Vraad.

That settled it. He would hesitate no more. Not with so perfect a focus awaiting him. One whom the family would not even notice was missing, if he could help it. The last thought gave him a feeling of benevolence, like a master taking good care of his pets. For their sacrifice, they deserved that much. It would be as if the boy no longer existed.

Still, a tiny shadow of guilt lingered on.

Melicard.

Erini stirred, her eyes slowly focusing on the darkened corridor. Her mind, a sluggish mire of self-disgust and defeat, refused to clear. She closed her eyes again. Melicard's visage was the only thing she could think about with any success. Her image of him had a strange quality to it, almost as if he were actually before her, propped up against the opposing wall. She saw him as unconscious. Dirt and blood streaked his face and—Erini choked—someone had torn the elfwood mask from his face, revealing the torn and burnt flesh that would never heal. She did not have to see his arm to know that the false one had been removed as well. It was a wonder he was still alive.

Still alive? The odd thought brought clarity to her clouded mind. Why would she think such a thing about her own imaginings? Why would she subscribe reality to delusion? Yet, there *was* something about the images, a continuity that seemed too real to be her own doing.

Could it be?

Erini tried to concentrate on his face, but that only made it less substantial, more that of a phantom than a living person. The princess thought quickly, recalling her state of mind. Leave her mind open? Let it happen naturally? Melicard's features were already almost invisible, little more than a true memory. Erini settled back and dreamed of Melicard the man. Where was he and what was he doing? She thought about him, but not at him. That, she hoped, was the key. If Drayfitt had only had the chance to teach her . . .

Melicard's face, which had been solidifying, dwindled away again. The princess quickly dropped all thought of the dead sorcerer. It was all to easy to let one's imagination turn to other things, even in times of a crisis.

Slowly, the picture of her betrothed returned to full clarity. It was almost as if, with her eyes closed, she could actually reach out and *touch* him. She saw the blood from his wounds, the bruises on his face and body. Mal Quorin's ogres had not been kind to him. Another thing the counselor would be called to account for—if Erini survived this terror.

She had, without thinking, reached out in an effort to ease his pain. The Melicard in her mind suddenly stirred, as if waking. The princess, startled, lost her concentration. Melicard's image faded away, this time permanently. Try as she might, Erini could not make it return.

He was *alive*! Battered and wounded, but Melicard was alive! New life surged through the princess despite all that had happened. As long as he was alive, there was reason to hope. Erini straightened into a standing position and gazed around her, finally realizing that more of Quorin's men might come pouring down one end of the hall or the other before very long. It was a wonder they had not already—unless there were other things on their minds. Like Captain Iston. Possibly loyal guard units, too. The suddenness of this coup could not have been completely planned. Despite the counselor's attitude earlier, there was too much evidence that all was not well in hand. Another sign of hope, as far as she was concerned.

What mattered now, Erini decided grimly, was to find Melicard. She could not draw Iston and his men into this. Two of them had already died on her behalf when she could have saved them. Her powers, the princess was slowly coming to realize, were as potentially beneficial as they were detrimental; it was her own attitude that determined which way she went. If she could turn her abilities to finding the king and overwhelming the rebels ... The thought of a stunned and grovelling Quorin made her smile with dark pleasure.

How do I find him? came the unbidden thought. What little she recalled of the image had revealed a place far from the elegant rooms of a mighty king. More likely, he was in the lower depths of the palace, a dungeon or something. Unfortunately, Erini had a fair idea of how immense that network of underground passages and chambers was. She did not have the time to search *everywhere* and her attempts to recall Melicard's presence had, thus far, failed miserably.

There remained one option, then, that promised hope. It was the only possibility her mind could dream up. Given rest and some peace, the princess might have been able to devise something less daring, less risky. Time, however, was something she had already used up too much of. No, her only choice was to follow through with her decision.

She would simply *ask* someone where the king was held.

Drawing herself together, Erini stepped quietly down the corridor in the direction *opposite* that of where her loyal defenders had wanted her to run. Iston's stronghold—she wanted to know more about how *that* had come about—was probably watched by too many of Quorin's men. What she wanted was a lone sentry or two left to guard some secured hall. She would probably find such a place deeper in the sections of the palace that the treacherous advisor had under his control. Erini also suspected that, given Quorin's way of doing things, it was where she would be nearest to Melicard.

The nagging fear that her plots were all askew never left her during the entire nerve-wracking journey.

In the dark, Talak's royal palace proved to be quite a maze. Matters were not helped by her own lack of familiarity. Erini only hoped that by trying to keep a parallel course as much as possible, she would not lose herself in the vastness of the ancient structure. The palace of the king and queen of Gordag-Ai seemed almost like a cottage in comparison to the monstrous creation the princess was now forced to wander.

When she finally found what she sought, Erini hesitated. There were two of them, tall, ugly, and armed with blades longer than her legs, it seemed. The princess cursed herself for being so stupid as to not have taken one of the weapons scattered on the floor by her unfortunate attackers. Better still, a sharp, thin blade like the one the elder of her two defenders had utilized. *That* was a weapon she could use properly.

That would also not solve her present dilemma. Sorcery was her *only* chance of success. What sort of spell, though?

One of the men nodded off briefly and was knocked awake by his companion, who seemed none too lively himself. Their exhaustion reminded Erini of her own, but she dared not dwell on it too long for fear she would collapse. Still, the scene had given her the answer. It should not be too difficult to make men who were already tired slip far enough into slumber. From there, she could take one of them and try to coax the information from his unprotected mind.

Relaxing despite the natural tendency for just the opposite in such a situation, Erini found she knew which areas of the spectrum would aid her spell. In her mind, she saw the colors blend and shape themselves, forming a pattern. A part of her understood that what was happening was actually taking place in less than the time it takes a person to blink. This was what Drayfitt had been steering her toward. Soon, it might be so automatic to her that the actual process would seem instantaneous. Drayfitt had said that.

The results of her spell became noticeable instantly. The guard who had dozed off only moments before collapsed completely, falling back against the wall and sliding to the floor. His grip on his sword relaxed, but not until he was almost all the way down. The resulting clatter was hardly audible.

The second man's fall proved more nerve-wracking. He fought the spell, almost as if he had enough sense left to understand what was happening. He raised his sword arm up to his forehead, as if trying to support his sleep-laden mind, and *dropped* the blade. The weapon struck the hard floor with an echoing rattle that Erini was certain would bring new men rushing down the hall at any moment.

Unable to resist any longer, the second guard fell to his knees, then face-first onto the marble. His helmet added to the distant reverberations of the sword.

When neither man had moved after a minute and battle-ready newcomers had not charged madly into the hall from every direction, Erini stepped out from the corner she had been hiding behind and investigated the two men. The first guard was sleeping soundly; there was even a satisfied smile on his lips. The second man was not so well off. He slept, but his nose had been broken from the fall and blood spilled on the floor. Only the spell kept him sleeping. The pain was evident in his twitches. Erini wondered if the pain would eventually give him the strength to overcome her enchantment. If so, it meant that she had to work even faster than she had planned.

Turning back to the first man, she leaned near one of his ears and whispered commands...

The ensorcelled guard's arms hung limply by his sides. His eyes were closed. He looked as if someone had strung him up. That would never do. She gave him a few extra commands, hoping there was no immediate limit to such things. It would not do to have confusion stir him from the spell.

A minute later, he was ready. To all eyes, it now appeared as if *she* were *his* prisoner. The scowl on his face was very real. The gleam in his eyes made him a man carrying out orders from the *highest* authority: Quorin, of course. If anyone stopped him, he would say that the counselor had decided to give the two one last moment together so that the princess could see how handsome her betrothed was *without* his false face. Erini had trouble with the last, but it might prove necessary. Such comments would hopefully put the other men at ease.

While she stood there, assuring herself that all was in readiness, a sudden, horrible notion burst forth. She looked up at the mesmerized figure, who stared straight ahead, waiting to begin his new role. "Do you know where King Melicard is being held?"

"Eas'rn t'nnels. Rat land."

Rat land? She let that slide, happy that she had not gone to all this trouble for nothing. In her haste to test her abilities, Erini had totally forgotten to ask him the all-important question first.

From the other guard she took a small dagger. Not much of a threat, but one never knew. The princess secreted the blade in one boot, hoping she would not be forced to run very quickly while it was still hidden in there. Then, Erini turned to the guard and whispered, "Lead."

The next few minutes made the previous few seem almost heavenly. Erini's heart sounded like a stampede of heavily laden warhorses. It was astonishing that the sound did not echo through every corridor. She kept one hand close to the blade— on the off-chance that the soldier had completely fooled her and was even now bringing her to her own cell. The trek was taking her into regions of the palace that she had not known even existed. It amazed the princess to think that there was still so much she had not investigated. If she survived, Erini intended to survey every plan of this behemoth and then double-check every corridor and room personally.

Dreams of entering into such minor crusades kept her from going completely insane with anxiety. Too many things seemed to count on her. She had welcomed them in the past, but none had ever involved death—and so *much* of it—or the use of questionable abilities. Erini was no coward; that was not her fear. What ate at her was the fact that she might not be enough. Melicard, Iston, Galea, and Magda . . . they and so many others would likely die if she did not succeed.

A rough hand grabbed her arm. She almost lashed out with whatever her abilities would give her, then realized that she had fallen behind the ensorcelled sentry. He looked at her as if seeing someone else.

"Come on. This way." His voice was slurred, something that could be explained away as from exhaustion. She quickly reminded him of that fact. He coughed his acknowledgment of the command—a trick Erini had mixed in with the original commands—and resumed the journey. Erini kept pace with him this time, noting that they were heading toward a darkened stairway.

Down below the earth again. I should have known! It would make things that much *more* difficult—and that much *more* dependent on her abilities.

They descended together and, at the bottom of the stairway, her plan received its ultimate test. Four sentries stood guarding the underground passageway. Unlike the one beside her, these men did not look in the least bit tired. They studied the newcomers, first with veiled curiosity, then with eye-widening interest when they discovered who it was they were seeing.

One of them, possibly the leader, possibly not, pointed the tip of his mace at Erini's companion. The others were armed with blades of varying wear. All looked far more skilled at using the weapons than the mesmerized figure at her side. "The cripple's woman! You've caught her!"

"Yeah." The answer issued forth easy enough, but Erini's guard had been ordered not to continue unless pressed.

"Why bring her down here? The master said no one's to see the prisoner."

Erini forced herself not to look at her companion and try to guide his answer. It would have to be his response alone. "New orders. The counselor wants her to spend a last few minutes with him. See how pretty he is. See what she would've married."

There was a moment's hesitation, but then malicious grins began to appear. This was something they would have expected from a leader such as Mal Quorin. Destroy the last good memories of Melicard. Turn his betrothed's love to disgust. None of them could fathom a woman continuing to care for a "cripple," though Erini was of the silent opinion that, even without the elfwood to mask his face and replace his arm, Melicard was worth a thousand of these men.

"Go on," the leader signalled.

The princess's guard stumbled a little, nearly causing her heart to fail. Had they looked closely, they might have noticed the glazed look that was returning to his eyes. Fortunately, they assumed it was something else.

"You'd better report to Ostlich when you're through with her. He don't want anyone dropping on duty. Not tonight." The leader indicated a scar running across one of his men's face. "Edger here stays real alert now, don't you Edger? Sometimes up to *four* days!"

The one called Edger nodded, but said nothing. Erini's companion returned the nod automatically and added a slow "Yeah." His words were becoming more slurred. Fortunately, he was already leading her past them.

When they were out of sight, she started to breathe a sigh of relief—only to cut it short when two *more* guards came into view. They leaned against a wall in which several cell doors stood as grim reminders of some of Talak's less-than-pleasant history. One of them looked up.

"What's goin'? Why's *she* here?"

Her puppet did not respond. Erini pretended to stumble, prodding him into activity as she bumped into his side. He repeated his short explanation concerning Quorin's sadistic little game. His words were slow, but understandable.

The look that passed between the two sentries at the cell indicated that they thought something besides exhaustion had taken its toll on the newcomer, something with more than a little kick to it. One man licked his lips, evidently dreaming of what it would be like to have a drink after so long on duty.

Seemingly convinced, they unlocked the door. The princess wanted to rush in, take Melicard in her arms, but could not so long as she needed the charade to continue. That meant agonizing heartbeats as she forced herself to keep pace with the shuffling soul beside her.

A figure huddled against the far wall, chained by his hands and feet. There was no light in the cell; the prisoner's upper body was in complete darkness and the lower was only a vague shadow. Behind her, the cell door slammed shut. That was the ensorcelled soldier's cue. He released his hold on the princess and stared blankly in the direction of the prisoner. To outside eyes, he would be watching the two.

No longer able to contain herself, Erini rushed over to the worn figure. "Melicard?"

The head slowly turned toward her. It *was* Melicard! Until this moment, she had still feared that something was amiss.

His face, when she saw it, threatened to tear her heart asunder. They had *tortured* him! She forced herself to look closer and saw that she was not entirely correct. There were bruises and cuts, true. He *had* been beaten and badly. Quorin would pay dearly for that. What she thought were burns, however, were what had been hidden beneath the elfwood mask he had always worn. *This* was what was left of his true visage.

Deep pits of scorched and torn flesh streaked across the one side of his face. That was horrifying enough. The other side, the one that had received the brunt of the wild magic . . . Erini recalled only one thing in her life that had ever looked like this. A fire in the royal stables of Gordag-Ai. A fire that had burned to death four horses and injured one of the young boys that helped take care of the animals. One of those horses had broken free of the fire toward the end, a maddened, flame-drenched beast whose face, neck, and body had been burned to the bone at various points. It had run in confused circles for more than a minute, nearly spreading the fire further, before the life within that twisted shell had finally abandoned it. Like the horse, Melicard's face had been torn open to the very bone and, thanks to the power of the artifact that had caused it, those wounds would not heal. Even now, even in the dark, she could see them glisten moistly, as if inflicted only this day.

"The fruit . . . of . . . my labors." Melicard smiled grimly. The open side of his face looked like nothing less than a grinning corpse. Despite herself, Erini had to turn her eyes away for at least a moment.

He noted the reaction. "The storytellers never speak of this type . . . of scene. Either that . . . or they gloss . . . gloss over it."

"I'm sorry. It's not you—"

"It's never me." The sarcasm was biting.

Erini looked him squarely in the face. "It's *not* you. When I saw your face, I felt your pain, wondered how you could have gone on—I don't know if I could have—and cursed dear Counselor Quorin for every day of his existence!"

"Quorin." Melicard grew cold. "I was a fool of the highest rank, wasn't I? How many loyal humans and drakes did the Silver Dragon sacrifice to assure brave, clever Quorin's place at my side? How many? I never saw it once. I was so . . . so proud of myself and so ready to take them all on. Look what it has cost me. Part of my body. My kingdom. My life.'' He closed his good eye. "Worst of all, it's cost me you.''

"No." She touched his hand. "It hasn't.''

"I doubt if our future together is longer than another minute or two. Surely my esteemed advisor's man there has orders to drag you out of here. This is just a torturous game, letting us see one another and then separating us again.''

It was time to explain. Erini leaned forward. "This is no game of that foul grimalkin! That is what the sentries outside are supposed to think. My guard is under my influence.''

The king eyed her in open curiosity. "Influence?''

"Like—like mesmerism.''

"Mesmerism.'' He did not seem completely convinced. Melicard indicated the chains that held him. "What about these? Mesmerism will not work on these, my princess.''

"I—I can deal with them.'' She tried to reach for the cuff around his wrist, but he refused to let go of her hand for the moment. Trying to hide the worst of his face, he tilted his head to one side and gave her as honest a smile as he could manage.

"My princess . . . my queen.''

When their hands finally separated, Erini took hold of the cuff and examined it. It had a simple lock on it—not that she knew anything about picking locks—and was worn with age. The rust interested her the most. She had succeeded in lulling to sleep two men who had already been tired. Could it be possible to use the same concept to encourage the spread of rust across the cuff? Make it so brittle that a simple tap or two would shatter it?

As she thought about it, her fingers unconsciously rubbed the cuff. Tiny streaks appeared. Erini gasped. Melicard, who could not see as well from his angle, grunted his curiosity. The princess did not respond, watching in fascination as the entire cuff and even part of the chain turned dark in the space of a few seconds.

She took his arm by the wrist and, sobbing like a grief-stricken, frail princess, muttered audibly, "Oh, Melicard! What will happen to us?''

The king offered no resistance, leaving things in her care. As Erini moved in what appeared to simply be a desperate hug of

her beloved, she brought the cuff down against the wall. The
sound was buried by her words and the rattle of the chains.

The cuff shattered.

"Impo—" was all that escaped from Melicard before he
succeeded in smothering his surprise. Erini immediately went
to work on the leg cuffs and found, to her joy, the spell working
perfectly both times. She did not, however, try to share her joy
with Melicard. Erini feared to even look at his face now. Not
because of his appearance, but because of what he must by now
have come to realize; his bride-to-be was a sorceress.

"Erini—" Melicard whispered.

"I think *that* verifies it, then," came the one voice she
feared to hear.

Leaping to her feet, Erini shielded Melicard. Whatever aid
her abilities would give her she would gladly accept. Anything,
especially if it meant the end of Mal Quorin.

One of the guards unlocked the cell door and opened it.
Quorin stepped through alone, confident in his power. Erini's
mouth twitched upward. Not *this* time. She understood her
abilities better. The traitor would soon find out what *power*
actually was.

Behind her, Melicard had risen to his feet. He would not
have someone like Quorin stand above him. Erini drew strength
from his act.

The counselor still advanced, slowly and silently. He appeared
very much the cat he resembled. His habit of always seeming
to show up where and when others least expected him added to
that effect. Even the smile.

*Perhaps I will turn you into the mangy rat-eater you really
are, Master Quorin!* The thought appealed to the princess
greatly. She would even let him stay and keep the stables free
of other pests.

"Did you realize only now that your bride was a sorceress,
your most royal majesty? I suspected as much, though I wasn't
certain until she escaped from my men earlier." Quorin looked
at Erini. "Of course, my lady, I knew where you would be
rushing to and took a quicker, more direct route. Now I have
you again. All that remains are your stubborn countrymen and
a few random guards who escaped my net. Talak will not even
know of its change of rulers until the northern gates open and
my master comes riding triumphantly through."

"Bearing a silver banner?" Melicard asked grimly.

"Of course. This will be the true mark of his destiny, his right to be emperor of *all* races. The capture and destruction of the monster king. Your crusades will be at an end. A sign of strength will bring his brethren around—save the outcast lord of the Dagora Forest. With the united strength of the others, however, *no* opposition will stand in the Dragon Kings' way. They will bring this land back to the glory it had before the Turning War."

The king laughed, though it was evident that to do so hurt him further. "Did your master train you to say all of that? Look—look at him, Erini. Would you ever believe that he and these others were actually men and not drakes in disguise?"

The barb struck Quorin harder than he pretended it did. Erini, who had seen and felt his rage, watched him closely. She had just about formulated the sort of spell she felt appropriate for one such as him. Something *decorative*. A few seconds more and she would be ready.

Turning his attention to her, Mal Quorin said, "There was a chance you might have been useful in regard to Gordag-Ai—or even to my tastes in entertainment—but I don't care for the thought of a sorceress alive and neither does my lord. Your betrothed will get the opportunity to see you die more or less painlessly before we prepare him for the coming of Talak's new ruler."

Erini unleashed her spell at Quorin. If it worked, he would envy the men who had died trying to recapture the princess.

Nothing.

No! Erini stood drained, horrified. *Please! Not now!* Her abilities had abandoned her again!

"Have you never wondered why I feared no tricks by that doddering old fool, Drayfitt?"

To one side, the ensorcelled guard suddenly moaned and shook his head. Her other spell had failed now. Erini stared at Quorin, who was reaching into his uniform for something that hung around his neck. It proved to be a medallion the diameter of a walnut.

Melicard groaned, though whether from pain or what he saw was debatable. "A Seeker medallion, Erini. One he received from *me*. It mutes a spellcaster's abilities. Makes them . . . helpless."

"Helpless. Yes." The counselor snapped his fingers. Two of the sentries from the hallway joined him. One he ordered to assist the man who had just woken up. He looked at the second, then nodded toward Erini.

Beaten and worn, Melicard still tried to save Erini. He rushed past her and tried to tackle the oncoming soldier with his one good arm. Quorin's servant, however, was a massive ox and he threw the one-armed king against the far wall. Melicard slipped to the floor, still conscious but stunned.

As the man turned toward Erini, she saw Quorin watching her from behind him, his cat's smile wide across his face and a thin, jagged blade now waiting in one hand. Waiting for her.

XVII

While the night had brought chaos to Talak, it had brought something even more ominous to the Dagora Forest. Just beyond the protected grounds of the Bedlams' domain, a tree curled and twisted, becoming a gnarled thing that soon cracked and died. From its withering roots, a black blot seemed to spread to the plant life around it, creating a dead, barren patch of earth several yards wide.

Within the boundaries of the Manor, a separate but hauntingly similar incident passed. This one would have been less noticeable, save its victim was one of the birds that nested in the trees. The fate the lone tree had suffered had been kinder. What was left of the bird was barely recognizable.

In the darkened room of a young lad, a golden-haired boy who dreamt of amazing feats of magic he would some day perform, the night seemed to have eyes. Eyes and shape. A shape that slowly detached itself from the rest of the darkness and loomed over the sleeping child, noting even without light the tiny streak of silver in the youngster's hair.

Shade smiled almost fatherly. *Blood will tell, my young one! Great power courses through your parents' veins! Great power that has pooled together and formed you!*

There was a young girl, too, but she was too young,

unpredictable. If this vessel proved insufficient, he would wait a few years and take the second. By then, she would be ready.

He touched the boy's forehead. A name came to his lips and he mouthed it in silence. *Aurim. The Golden Treasure.* The warlock frowned. He could feel the love the parents had for this child—both children—and it was beginning to disturb him in ways that were alien to him. He had taken subjects for his spells before. It was not as if they were Vraad. They were just . . . others.

His face resembles Cabe's, though his nose is his mother's. The uneasiness began spreading through him. Why was he not already gone? The task was a simple one! Take the child and depart. The defensive spells surrounding the Manor were laughingly simple to one with millennia and the powers of Vraad sorcery on his side.

Take the boy! he demanded of himself.

"Shade."

The hooded warlock looked up. Another figure stood on the other side of the bed, hands clenched and eyes narrowed. He wore a dark blue robe and much of his hair was silver.

"Cabe."

"My son, Shade. He's not for you to do with as you please. Get out of here now while I can still remain civil with you."

Moving almost like the shadow he resembled, Shade looked closely at the youngster. "He has striking golden hair . . . how is that possible?"

Cabe tried to contain himself. This *was* Shade. This man had been his friend. He had also tried to kill the younger warlock. Which stood before Cabe now? "We named him Aurim because, being our first, he seemed so precious. When he was old enough to understand what his name meant, he decided he should have golden hair. The next day . . . it simply was."

"A lad of great potential."

"If he lives to adulthood." The edge had returned to Cabe Bedlam's voice. "Which he won't if you take him."

"He might. He might not. I have need of him, though."

"You've no right to him." It was becoming harder for Cabe to maintain his composure. "You've no right to anything!"

The other warlock wrapped himself in his cloak. "I am Shade. I am Vraad. My existence is my right. My *continued* existence is my demand."

A hand rose. It blazed with green flames that danced about

the fingertips. "You've lived long enough, Shade. He deserves his chance—and I won't let you take him."

Shade chuckled. "No longer the uncertain novice, are you? Is ten years enough? The skill is easy enough, but the reaction time is always the questionable part. Do you know your limits? I have *none*."

"You have more than you think. You still thought the Seekers controlled us until I materialized here. I made it seem so. I thought you might come back, Shade. I prayed you wouldn't, so that I wouldn't have to fight you. I'll see you dead a thousand times before I let you take my son."

"And I shall return a thousand and one times." The cowled visage lifted enough so that the glow from Cabe's hand allowed him to see Shade's true features for the first time. Cabe's mouth dropped open. "Or I will just take him *now*."

Tendrils burst from the cloaked figure of the one warlock and enshrouded sleeping Aurim. They started to withdraw into Shade's form until the hooded spellcaster checked himself.

"This is *not* your son."

"No, he and the other children are safely hidden—even from you. I've learned. I thought you might come back, so I laid a few snares. You chose the false Aurim, though I don't care to think why. It almost fooled you long enough. In fact, it *may* have."

A clear liquid showered down on Shade from nowhere. As it touched him, it solidified, becoming harder than marble. The torrent continued, forming a shell about its victim. Shade struggled, but seemed unable to move more than his fingers. Oddly, nothing but the warlock was covered by it.

"I never thought I would thank Azran Bedlam for an idea," Gwen said as she materialized out of the darkness behind Shade. "I never thought I would want to condemn anyone to this sort of hell—until *you* came back here for our child."

The shower ceased. As Gwen had once been imprisoned in a shell of amber by Cabe's mad father, so had she sought to snare Shade. Only Azran's fabled demon sword, the Nameless, had succeeded in breaking that prison, and only with an unconscious boost from Cabe.

"It's over," she continued, speaking to her husband. "It wor—"

The amber prison exploded, sending deadly fragments spilling across the room in every direction. A fair number flew with unerring accuracy toward the Bedlams. Only their automatic defensive spells saved them at all. Razor-sharp pieces tore into the walls, ceiling, and floor. Minor objects in the room were punctured or shattered. Cabe and his wife were battered into unconsciousness, though bruises were all they suffered. Not one jagged fragment had flown their directions.

When the last particles of the devastating assault had drifted floorward, Shade shook himself free of any remaining fragments and eyed the two spellcasters. Oddly, he was not angry, but rather, impressed.

"I am myself once again and there is *no* equal to me, Bedlams," he whispered. Shade turned to the false Aurim, undamaged by the assault. With a glance, he disposed of it in another realm where the surprise within would not threaten him. Two very deadly traps. Together, they might have succeeded.

"I am Vraad, Cabe. That was your undoing." He took a deep breath. "But you have earned the right to your children. I think there may be another who will serve instead—that is, if *his* memories serve me right."

He looked down at each of them and concentrated briefly. The walls groaned as if weakening, but he paid that only the least bit of attention, assuming the damage was due to his last assault. A new spell placed on each of them would assure that they would sleep a full day, maybe even two. More than enough time to deal with the other situations.

Taking one last—almost *fond*—glance at Cabe, Shade departed the Manor.

How could there be so many? Darkhorse wondered grimly. *How did so many still survive?*

The legions of the Silver Dragon were the stuff of epic. Not since the combined forces of Bronze and Iron had attempted to overthrow the emperor had there been a dragon host as great as this. Not all of them were of clan Silver, either. The two clans that had rebelled now had a new master. Remnants of both now rode, ran, or flew along with those of the Dragon King. There were even a few drakes of clan Gold, though they were the fewest of all. Darkhorse suspected that there *had* been other survivors, but not for very long. The would-be emperor had taken over their caverns, stolen their birthplace. Many drakes were too proud to stand for such things. Most of those that rode with him now were likely the dregs, perhaps even treacherous fools like Toma the renegade.

Though he could see them, Darkhorse knew that the night still gave him protection from the oncoming army. He had come here, rather than return immediately to Talak, because he had feared this very thing. His fears had proved far more than even he had supposed. The host here would have given a fully armed and ready Talak trouble—unless King Melicard had a trick or two up his sleeve. Perhaps that was one reason why he had agreed to summoning a demon; it was possible that he had suspected this invasion was coming.

Darkhorse laughed quietly. *Even a demon would think twice about taking on a legion of fiends such as this!*

A drake army was not an army in the traditional sense. The host included several castes and species from the lowest minor drake—huge reptiles almost as intelligent as horses and often used for the same purpose—to the elite of the ruling drake class, the humanoid warlords who drove their beastlike cousins and their lower-caste brethren before them. There were dragons in the air and on the ground. Some carried riders, others did not. Each one was as deadly as a score of more trained men; yet, they had been defeated in the past. There were weaknesses that men had learned to exploit, Talak most of all. That was why the Dragon King had worked to separate the forces of his human foe. He wanted an easy victory to prove his worth as emperor. Darkhorse knew he also wanted it because, of all his brethren, this drake lord was the most craven.

Yet, even this bully has the muscle to flex, the shadow steed thought with bitter humor. Alone, Darkhorse could harass the drakes and cause great damage, but he would eventually fall. Despite his cowardly ways, the Silver Dragon was quite possibly his equal or better in power; it was difficult to say. Surrounded by his own followers, each with their own measure of power, he would be nigh on invincible compared to Darkhorse.

Talak had to be alerted to the menace. If they had weapons to combat this host, so much the better. The Bedlams would lend their hand, also. This was not a battle to be won by a lone warrior, but only with the effort of many, himself included.

I shall see you before long, Dragon King. This I swear.

Summoning a portal, Darkhorse departed for Talak. He hoped and prayed that what he found there would be an improvement over this dismaying sight. He had his doubts, though.

May the gods who grant me my luck be cursed with the same ill sort!

As he stepped out into Talak, into the great hall near the front entrance of the royal palace, he sensed the wrongness of the place. *Blood had been spilled here! Much of it and only recently!*

Things were beginning to move too swiftly for him. A dragon host that would, by his estimate, be here just after dawn. A royal palace under attack—yet the city seemed its normal self! Was he mistaken about the bloodshed? Drayfitt could give him no answers, especially to the question that still plagued him from the back of his mind.

Where is Shade while the world turns mad? Is he orchestrating all of this?

He dared not linger on thoughts of Shade now. Like it or not, his first duty was to Talak and warning it of the threat moving toward its gate. Darkhorse concentrated his will on seeking the Princess Erini. As a sorceress—and an untrained one—she would unconsciously radiate a powerful presence. Training or pure luck would teach her to mask that presence. Death would completely eliminate the problem. For the moment, however, her ignorance was to Darkhorse's advantage.

Find her he did, in a place buried beneath the palace much the same way his prison had been, though not as deep. She was the only distinctive presence. There were others, perhaps as many as a dozen, but something interfered with his senses, making them appear as less than individuals. He did not have to think long to realize that she was probably a prisoner. There were fear and hatred; they were so strong they nearly radiated auras all their own.

If the Princess Erini was in danger, he could not hesitate. Summoning up a portal, Darkhorse reared and, laughing mockingly, leaped through it.

"Well! If there is to be a party, then surely Darkhorse is welcome, yes?"

His sudden, overwhelming appearance, coupled with his brash, confusing speech, stunned the humans in the chamber—a prison cell, he saw. There were several people in the room, as he had thought, and among them were two others he had wanted to find. The first was Melicard, mighty Melicard, looking more like something left behind by a playful and only slightly peckish dragon. He stood—with the aid of one captor— against the wall nearest the door.

The second and somewhat more irate of the two—and only *he* would be irate in the face of a creature as devastating as Darkhorse—was Counselor Mal Quorin. He had a long, ugly blade in his hand and had apparently been toying with the princess. There were no marks on her, but the look on her face indicated that, had she been able to, the advisor would have been dead a hundred times over. That verified what Darkhorse had already suspected. Quorin was the source of whatever was dampening his senses and the princess's abilities.

All this the ebony stallion took in during the first glance around him. He took a step forward now, his attention focused specifically on Quorin, who, with more courage than many, immediately moved closer to his prey. The knife touched the princess's throat.

"She dies if you even flinch, demon! She dies if you so much as blink my direction!"

Unimpressed by their master's defiant rhetoric, several of the guards deserted for safer climates. Only the ones in the cell, who probably knew they could not run away in time or were insane fanatics like the counselor, remained.

Darkhorse laughed in the face of Quorin's threat. "You are a true servant of your master! As much a fool as he!" An ice-blue eye narrowed at the traitor. "Think on what sort of mercy you will receive from me if you *do* kill her!"

"I can draw her agony out, demon! I will!" The counselor's eyes widened. Averting his gaze suddenly, he shouted to his men. "Don't stare into his eyes! He'll try to snare you like he did that bag-o'-bones charlatan!"

There was some nervous shifting. The man holding Melicard finally broke down and tore through the doorway, but not before shoving his charge to the floor. Melicard did not rise.

Cursing, Quorin stepped back a little, directing the others to do the same. Not once did his blade leave Erini's throat. She, in turn, continued to watch him with an obsessive loathing that disturbed even Darkhorse.

"Your men abandon you, Master Quorin! Their deep faith is *so* touching to observe!" The advisor was a very dangerous adversary. Even with his plots crumbling, he refused to give in to his fears. As long as he held the knife and prevented both himself and his men from falling to Darkhorse's gaze, there was little the eternal could do without causing harm to the princess. Anything he tried might still give Quorin enough time to cut her throat.

The key to this situation was whatever Quorin utilized to keep Erini's abilities in check and the shadow steed's senses a bit muted. It was likely a Seeker artifact—there were always too many of the blasted things around!—but Darkhorse knew of no way he could remove it from the chamber without Quorin reacting first.

It was Melicard who finally decided it. Melicard, ignored by all but Erini, considered helpless by even her. Beaten and minus one arm, he had lain as still as a corpse after being tossed to the floor. Quorin, of course, had had other, weightier matters on his mind. He did not, therefore, hear or see the king rise quietly from the floor, his one good eye fixed on the counselor's back. The advisor's remaining men, also more concerned about the foreboding steed pawing at the floor before them, paid him no mind, either. As for Erini, her view was obstructed by Quorin until the last moment. Even then, to her credit, she gave no sign, not even stiffening.

Darkhorse saw all and acted accordingly. Whether Melicard succeeded or failed, if there was an opening, the shadow steed would seize it.

The king stretched out his one good arm, tottered. Darkhorse quickly filled the silence that had been extending far too long already.

"What do you hope for now, human? To stand ready until the Dragon King himself stalks into this room?"

"If *need* be," Mal Quorin grated. "I doubt I'll have to wait that long. My only problem is to get rid of you somehow, and I think—"

Reaching forward, Melicard grabbed his treacherous aide by the collar and pulled him back. Quorin's hand went up, the blade briefly nicking Erini's chin, but no more. One of the remaining soldiers grabbed the two, who were falling down in one tangled pile of arms and legs.

Darkhorse struck. The man holding Erini, panicking, tried to shield himself with her. Against a physical attack, he would have succeeded. Darkhorse had other tools at his command, though. He hit the floor with his right front hoof, creating a wicked split in the stonework and the earth below. The crack that formed shot unerringly beneath the legs of both the princess and her captor. The soldier looked down in horror as an eye stared back at him from within the crevasse. In his shock, he loosened his grip on his prisoner. Erini suddenly went flying from his hands, pulled free by the power of Darkhorse. She landed softly by the eternal's side. As her feet touched the floor, the guard's left it, or rather, *it* left him. The floor where he stood collapsed into the crevasse, the guard with it. His screams had barely died before the floor had sealed itself back up, looking remarkably untouched.

"I was always a slave to the dramatic," Darkhorse rumbled to anyone who could hear him.

Erini was ignoring him, her only concern Melicard, whom she probably imagined dead by now. Her rescue had taken only a few seconds, though to her and her unfortunate captor, it must have seemed far longer. Darkhorse laughed. Concentrating now on Quorin, he used his powers to pull the hapless counselor into the air and, while the traitor struggled to regain control of his limbs, transported the medallion to a place that burned hot enough to melt even Seeker magic away. Darkhorse contemplated sending Mal Quorin there as well, but he knew that there might yet be need even for something as foul as this creature was.

The princess, however, was not so understanding. While her abilities had been hampered by the protective artifact the counselor had worn, her fury had grown unchecked. Now, feeling the release of those abilities, she struck without thinking. Mal Quorin screamed and tried to scratch off his own skin. The last of his men had run off the moment he had been thrust into the air. There was no one here left to save him. Erini planned to have her revenge now for everything he had done or planned to do.

"*Erini!*" Melicard's faint call went unheeded, so caught up was the princess in the full force of her own power.

"*PRINCESS!*" Darkhorse roared. His voice cut through where the king's had failed. "Princess Erini! Stop and think!"

Stop and think? The look on her bitter face indicated that she planned to do anything but that. The time for thinking was long past. Now, it was time for vengeance.

Darkhorse persisted. "Think what you do to *yourself*, princess, not this piece of rotting offal! You might become like Shade, so in love with your power that you lose your humanity.''

She seemed to stir then, for her eyes travelled from her prey to the ebony stallion and finally to her betrothed. Melicard and Erini matched gazes briefly. Whatever the princess saw in the one eye of the king drained the need for vengeance from her heart. Darkhorse felt her withdraw her power back into herself. Above them, Mal Quorin, drenched in sweat and pale as bone, sighed and collapsed. The shadow steed brought him slowly back to the floor.

''Melicard.'' The princess looked ashamed, as if somehow her madness had made her less a creature than even Quorin was.

The king would have none of that. He had used the last of his strength in his battle and could only force himself up enough to lean on his elbow. He shook his head as his bride-to-be continued to berate herself and whispered something. Darkhorse, though he could have eavesdropped without either knowing, chose not to. There were some things that were meant to be private.

Whatever Melicard said soothed, if not completely convinced, Erini. She smiled and seemed to regain some of her confidence. Tenderly, the novice sorceress touched Melicard where he had been crippled by the one artifact so many years before.

His visage and arm became whole instantly. Darkhorse had to look closely before it became apparent that Erini had only given Melicard back his elfwood mask and limb and had not actually restored the missing pieces. Even for Darkhorse, that would have been an astounding achievement.

Aided by the princess, Melicard rose to his feet and walked up to the shadow steed. For a time, neither human said anything to the eternal. He waited patiently, knowing some of the limits of their kind. Both of them had suffered greatly at the hands of the crumpled heap on the floor.

''Thank you, dem—Darkhorse,'' Melicard finally began. He looked angry with himself. ''And I dared to try and make you my slave. It's a wonder, great one, that you would even help one such as me.''

''The past kindnesses of Counselor Quorin made it nearly impossible at first, I must admit,'' Darkhorse responded wryly. ''I did it as much for my *own* benefactor here,'' he indicated the princess, "as anyone else, your majesty. I did it for your people as well. The Dragon King Silver is on his way even now with a host that may make all this subterfuge rather unnecessary."

"And Quorin's men still hold the palace and the northern gate."

"That is so, your majesty. Tell me, would your army turn back from its crusade into the Hell Plains if the sorcerer Drayfitt was found murdered?"

Melicard's mouth dropped open. "Drayfitt? Murdered?" He turned toward Quorin. "I should kill him now and forgo the niceties of a public trial and execution!"

Darkhorse shook his head. "While the effort was there, the true criminal is the warlock Shade—who has his own hand in this enterprise. He and the Dragon King have made a pact, though I would not trust either to adhere to it for very long. *Shade* is my true quest, but I will do what I have to in order to save your people from the more immediate threat."

"They will likely go on," Melicard said, responding to the stallion's original question. "We have many other tricks. Drayfitt is a great loss—both to my plans and personally—but his death does not mean that all is lost."

"Can you hold against the Silver Dragon's host?"

Melicard looked at Erini. "If my bride-to-be will add her strength, perhaps."

"My—what I am doesn't turn you?"

"No more than what I am turned you."

Perhaps it was a trick of the light, but Darkhorse swore that the elfwood mask moved exactly as the king's face would have. *There are all sorts of magic . . .*

Erini smiled gratefully. "I don't know what I can do, but I will help as I can."

Seeming to draw strength from that, Melicard looked up and said, "Then, the first thing we must do is take this palace back."

XVIII

The warlock Shade haunted the halls and chambers of the vast imperial palace of Talak undetected amidst the chaos commencing around him. Sentries rushing to and fro—whether loyalists or traitors Shade could not say and did not care—did not so much as glance at the hooded figure they passed, even those within an arm's reach of him.

Unfolding himself at his destination, the warlock knelt down in the midst of the garden. Here, in such an excellent, centrally located area of the palace, he would release the last and largest clutch.

When emerged from his sleeves were little more than amorphous shapes that flittered and darted about, as if in silent impatience. Unlike the bizarre searchers that he had summoned that other time, these were not living creatures in any sense of the word, merely bits of magical energy shaped to do a particular task. Shade counted out an even dozen before he broke off the spell. His head throbbed briefly, but he assured himself that it was only a headache this time. There had been no further losses of memory—as far as he knew—and his personality had been stable for days. He was himself at last and nothing would change that again.

Without a word, he sent the tiny shapes out and about. They would spread through the palace. No corner of the massive edifice would remain uninvaded.

He drew back into the shadows then, wondering how long it would take Darkhorse to detect him once the masking spell that had protected him thus far was removed. Not too long, he supposed, but long enough.

The warlock smiled to himself as pictured the scene to come.

Retaking the palace was child's play, as far as Darkhorse was concerned. Melicard found and freed a number of the prisoners the counselor's men had captured in the cells surrounding his own. Though still outnumbered and without weapons, they were a force to be reckoned with, even forgetting that the king also had a sorceress and a "demon" to aid him.

After a thorough search through more than half the building, it became apparent to all that the palace was, for the most part, deserted now. Only a few stragglers, looters generally, were uncovered. Melicard's men rearmed themselves quickly on weapons left abandoned in the corridors. The reason for the abandonment soon revealed itself to them, thanks to a looter caught trying to ransack the king's chambers. Staring up at Darkhorse all the while he spoke, the prisoner informed them of how Quorin's men knew now that Melicard had unleashed his personal horde of demons that he had saved just for this moment. Allowing the traitors to seize the palace had only been a ploy to discover who was guilty and who was not. Even now, men were fleeing for their lives from the monsters they knew were following them relentlessly.

Darkhorse understood. Seeing him and knowing that he had come for their master, Quorin's underlings had panicked. In their haste to get as far from the shadow steed as possible, they had likely rushed past their fellows without pausing, spouting out garbled warnings as they ran. As was always the case with fear, the stories had grown, each man shouting some tale of a demon come to get them. Panic escalated.

The eternal chuckled as he told Melicard, "Apparently, I *was* too pessimistic about your chances of quick success! You have my apologies, King Melicard!"

"We have you to thank for our easy victory. Let us hope that those at the gate surrender so easily."

"Shall I go there and see to it?"

The king shook his head. "I am grateful, but your appearance may panic people near the gate. I need as much order as possible."

Erini, who had vanished momentarily from the throne room, returned at that moment with another man, an officer in the dress of Gordag-Ai. Melicard knew him, but the princess introduced him to Darkhorse, who learned the man was a Captain Iston or something. Iston seemed in awe of the ebony stallion, but his military training succeeded in keeping him from making much of a spectacle of himself.

Captain Iston apologized profusely to the king for his failure to keep the princess safe. From the look on her face, Darkhorse hazarded a guess that Erini had heard the same thing only moments earlier.

"I've already explained to you," she said, interrupting his fourth apology, "I am a sorceress, captain. I transported myself out of the room by accident. There was no way for any of your men to keep watch over me." Beneath her calm tone, the eternal noted some bitterness. Erini had still not forgiven herself for the men who had died trying to rescue her.

While they talked, rather too idly in Darkhorse's opinion, something nagged at the corner of his mind. Something obvious that they had all been missing, something about the crooked counselor . . .

Of course! Darkhorse cursed himself for not thinking of it sooner. He turned immediately to King Melicard, who was engrossed in a discussion concerning the chameleon cloaks Iston's two men had worn. "*Your majesty!*"

When a tall, pitch-black stallion demands attention, he receives it instantly. Melicard fell back under the glittering gaze. "What is it? Is Shade within the palace walls?"

Darkhorse snorted. "I doubt I would be able to tell even if he was, but that is not what I wanted to say! I have a request of you!"

"Name it. I owe you too much to deny you anything."

"Mal Quorin's chambers. I want to see them."

Erini's face darkened. Melicard nodded grimly and looked rather irritated with himself. "I should've thought of that long before. He's the link, after all, to the Dragon King—and likely Shade, too."

"Yes! It was he who provided Drayfitt with the book that the drakes had uncovered! I wonder what else remains hidden in his rooms?"

"I'll have someone drag him back up here!" Melicard rubbed his chin. "He'll show you everything even if I have to remove a few fingers and toes to get him to do it."

The eternal disagreed. "Mal Quorin is the last creature I would want in that room. From the tricks he has already played, I would not put it past him to have a few more ready and waiting for him. No, I think I would prefer to probe his room on my own. Your good counselor is best left admiring the cobwebs of his new abode."

"There's much in what you say. Do you need someone to lead you to it?"

"It is not a place I think I would care to enter without some prior inspection. I am *not* impervious to everything."

Melicard smiled. "I was beginning to think you were unstoppable. However, if otherwise is the case, I can have one of my men show you the way."

Darkhorse dipped his head in the closest he could come to a bow. "That would be appreciated."

Little more than a few minutes passed before he was being led to the ex-advisor's personal sanctum by one nearly panic-stricken soldier. Even knowing that the great leviathan trotting next to him was an ally of the king did not stop the man from shaking and stuttering. It was an amusing sight, a soldier who was obviously a longtime veteran shaking in his boots, but Darkhorse forbore from saying or doing anything that would shame the human.

At last, they came to a set of doors that somehow arrogantly proclaimed power even though they were as plain as any Darkhorse had seen here. He was interested also to note how far they were from the king's chambers. Quorin had set up his own tiny little kingdom in the palace. It was a wonder that he had, according to Erini and Melicard, always seemed to be around when you expected him least.

Darkhorse dismissed his guide, who happily departed at the quickest walk he could manage while still seeming to keep his dignity. The ebony stallion waited until he was alone and then began to inspect the entrance for traps or tricks.

The first was simple yet devious. There was an intricate triple lock in the door. A normal key would merely cause one lock to be exchanged for another, all without the one turning the key realizing it. He would then find that the door was still locked. Trying again would set the third lock into play. It was an endless cycle. The secret, evidently, was a special key that Quorin had no doubt carried on his person, one that caught all three lock mechanisms simultaneously. A very impressive piece of work, the stallion decided, but not one that would give *him* any trouble. Darkhorse did not need a key and, in fact, could have ignored the lock altogether. The door was so reinforced that nothing short of a raging, full-grown bull would have been able to break it down, and that only after several painful attempts. That meant nothing to the creature who could create fissures in a mountain with the mere tap of his hooves. In respect to King Melicard and Princess Erini, however, Darkhorse decided to forgo splintering it into so much scrap. Instead, probing the locks again, he caused all three locks to open at the same time, as if the key were actually in there.

After that, it was an even simpler task to make the door open up by itself. Darkhorse laughed silently at the picture he knew he must have made. Not once, however, had he considered giving himself hands and arms, useful though they might have been. The form he wore was more his own than the shapeless mass he had originated with. With his abilities intact, it would serve him as well as any other.

The shadow steed peered inside.

"Curious," he finally muttered before stepping into the room.

Mal Quorin's personal chambers had an odd feel to them, as if the rooms, at least the front ones, were more for display than actual use. Things were just too perfect, too much what one would have expected, almost as if even the placement of the chair by the fireplace had been choreographed. This was *not* the sort of room a man like Quorin would have been happy with. This was a place where he spoke in private to the king or pretended to do work.

Moving swiftly to the next doorway, he noted that the bedroom was the same. Again, everything seemed appropriate for a man of Mal Quorin's rank and position. Too appropriate. The fixtures were just too gaudy to be believed. The bed was large, well-built and expensive, but hardly right. A row of well-preserved tomes on a shelf revealed the typical books concerning politics and history, including, ironically, several by the late Drayfitt.

Darkhorse laughed, his tone somewhat bitter, wondering if any of them had been read.

These were *not* Quorin's personal quarters, he concluded. These were the ones that the traitor had made up for the sake of appearances. Where then . . . ?

He backed out of the room and looked down both ends of the corridor. One would take him back toward the Princess Erini and the others. The opposite direction ended in a cul-de-sac and included two other doors on one wall. Darkhorse stared at the blank wall across from those two doors. Elegant paintings and intricate sculptures adorned it. Nothing seemed amiss . . . from the hallway.

Darkhorse reentered Quorin's chambers, heading straight into the bedroom. Probing with his mind, he soon discovered what he sought. There was a spell masking it, a strong one that even he had not noticed at first, caught up as he was by the general wrongness he had felt upon first arriving.

Not so clever, dear one! Someone, perhaps Mal Quorin, perhaps not, had sealed the other rooms on this side of the corridor, making it seem as if they had never existed. The only true way to enter them now was through the counselor's chambers. He found a switch of sorts hidden in the back wall of the bedroom. Darkhorse wasted no time, tripping the switch and immediately stepping back. After so many mishaps, the shadow steed was trying to be cautious. His senses had proven too little too often in the past few days.

The wall slid open without the slightest hint of any danger. Searching, Darkhorse detected nothing potentially threatening in the walls, ceiling, or floor. There was, though, a subtle spell emanating from the secret doorway that tried in vain to turn his thoughts to anything but the desire to enter. A human would have been affected and would have likely walked away, suddenly caught up in some other notion. Darkhorse overwhelmed the spell easily, eliminating it so that the king's men would have no difficulty entering at some later time. That done, the stallion nosed the secret door open further and slowly entered. Before he was even halfway in, he already sensed that here, indeed, was the true domicile of the traitorous advisor.

It was dark in here, as dark as the former inhabitant's life. Adjusting his physical senses, Darkhorse brought the world of Mal Quorin into focus. It was not a place he would have invited the Princess Erini.

"And they call *me* demon when abominations such as this roam freely, advising heads of state!"

The room he stood in was filled with grisly trophies. Skulls adorned one entire shelf, all of them polished smooth. Darkhorse wondered if each had died at the hands of the counselor himself. Possibly, they had all been rivals for power at one time or another. Hanging from the opposing wall, as if to allow the skulls something to gaze at, was an array of sinister and unusual weaponry. Most had not been designed to bring about a quick and painless death. Mal Quorin seemed to have a fondness for serrated edges.

Perhaps I should have let Princess Erini erase his existence from this world! Better yet, perhaps I should have done it myself instead of preserving his foul life!

Death had come freely to this room many times, he noted. The stench assaulted him on many planes. The room beyond emanated even worse. Darkhorse did not even bother stepping toward it. He knew what he would find. Quorin's *playroom*.

Does this truly fall under the definition of humanity? Darkhorse wondered. He knew there and then that he *should* have let the princess have her way with the fiend while they were in the cell. When this was over, Mal Quorin would pay . . . and pay . . . and pay. Darkhorse was not like humans; he had no qualms about the rights and wrongs of punishment. Mal Quorin had now forfeited any right he had to a continued existence. Whatever use he might have been, it was not worth it. Not now.

None of what he had discovered so far, however, had any bearing on the reasons he had come here. Quorin's personal atrocities aside—though not *too* far aside—the man had left little other trace of his double side. Darkhorse had expected charts or something that would give an indication of what had been planned. There seemed to be nothing. His search would need to be more thorough. Frowning, the shadow steed concentrated.

Drawers slowly opened. Cabinets doors freely swung forward, revealing their contents. A panel hidden in the wall snapped into existence. Even the secret door through which he had entered opened wider.

"Show me what you have," he whispered to the room.

Parchments, maps, talismans . . . everything that had been stored over the years in one place or another came flying out into the air. One by one, they flew past the gaze of the eternal, who studied each with eyes that saw more than the physical. As each piece was dismissed, it would return to its point of origin, even placing itself in its original position. The last was not due to any courtesy toward the treacherous counselor, but rather because Melicard might find reason to inspect these belongings himself. What might have been of no significance to Darkhorse might prove vital to the king.

The speed with which he inspected each and every item would have horrified Erini or the others. Things flew by as little more than blurs, depending on what they were. Time was of the essence, true, but that in no way meant that Darkhorse was being careless. If there *was* something of importance to him among Quorin's effects, he would find it.

He *did*, though it took him more than half the search to find even that one item.

A tiny box, quite ordinary in appearance. To most, it would have seemed the sort of thing the man might have kept a keepsake or two in, save that the imprisoned counselor was hardly the sort of person to keep remembrances. Moreover, the box was not quite what it was supposed to be. Power had been infused into it; so much, in fact, that the lid refused his first attempts to open it, something that impressed upon him the abilities of the creator. There were few entities alive now with such power. A Dragon King would have the ability.

Darkhorse cursed and set the box aside. It would require his full concentration and that was not something he had command of, not, at least, until he was through with his search. Impatience was eating at his thoughts and Darkhorse knew he was going to grow more and more careless if he was not careful. So much to do and, despite what seemed an endless night, dawn was fast approaching. If the Silver Dragon and his host were not within sight of Talak already, they soon would be.

His search progressed with very little else to show for his efforts. Even the items of these rooms revealed little of Quorin's misdeeds or what the plots of his master still entailed. It was as if the man had only started his life a short time before joining the lower ranks of the city-state's government. Possibly it was so. Possibly it was also the case that Quorin kept most of what he needed to know in his head. Such an agent would be useful to the Dragon King.

Just as the shadow steed was about to concede defeat, a yellowed parchment giving off a very distinctive aura caught his eye. Its age was uncalculable, save that he knew with only a glance that it was Vraad in origin. Darkhorse did not take time out to study it. Instead, he completed his search of the rest of the effects, moving more slowly and cautiously now.

Three other pieces caught his attention before he was finished. The first was a dagger with an inscription dating it to the time just prior to the Turning War. It had a taint to it that Darkhorse suspected belonged to Cabe's father, Azran. The second of the trio was another parchment, one of recent origin. While he could not sense anything overly malevolent about it, something disturbed him. The final addition was a talisman, obviously of Seeker origin, that he found in the same drawer as the box. Its purpose, too, escaped him for the moment, but any such item that Quorin would deem worthy of keeping interested him for that reason alone. The shadow steed's spirits both rose and fell as he surveyed his tiny collection. It was possible he had found what he had originally sought, but now came the difficulty of understanding just what it was he *had* found.

The box interested him most, but it would also probably be the most exasperating piece of the lot. He inspected the dagger first. It was, as he had suspected, a creation of Azran's and definitely one of his first attempts. The madman's mark was on it. The dagger would kill with only a touch. Even a nick was fatal. Close examination revealed the blade as nothing more than that. Unlike the other items he had looked over, Darkhorse did not replace the dagger in its original location. With some satisfaction, he raised it into the air before him and sent it on a journey that would only end when it reached the sun. Even a toy left behind by Azran had limits to its capacity to survive.

The Seeker talisman seemed to have little in the way of power and, though its use remained a mystery, Darkhorse doubted it could be of any importance. He returned it to where it had come from. That left the parchments and, of course, the box. After some deliberation, he had the Vraad parchment rise up before him. Defenses ready, the shadow steed slowly made the yellowed and crumbling sheet unfold. It had not survived the millennia as well as Shade's book apparently had, but that it still existed at all said something for the power invested in it. He only hoped that it was not protected by some secondary spell. His probing had revealed nothing of the sort, but one could never be too certain where the Vraad were concerned.

He recognized the mark, though he had seen it only once or twice, and that in the far, far distant past: the dragon banner. There was a Vraad clan name attached to that banner, but it escaped his memory at the moment. He could only recall that the warlock had been part of this selfsame clan.

It was a map. A map detailing the division of a land. There was a list of almost two dozen items, names perhaps, some of which had been crossed out and all of which were more or less illegible. Darkhorse discarded the parchment in disgust. Only the Vraad would think of preserving something so minor as a list of their division of spoils from some plot. The great conquerors. Despite himself, he laughed.

That left him only two items: the newer, or, at least more *recent* parchment and the box. Once more he tried to pry it open with his powers and once more he failed. Furious, he allowed it to drop heavily onto the floor. Darkhorse used his skills to snatch up the parchment in its place and, with thinning patience, unfurled the new item completely before common sense reminded him of the traps that might lurk within.

Something briefly struck at him. A human would have died from the blow, his heart literally bursting open. Darkhorse, on the other hand, suffered nothing more than annoyance at his own lack of thought. Had this been a stronger spell, he might have been injured—or worse.

The blow lessened until it was no longer noticeable. The ebony stallion inspected the parchment. It was blank. Its sole purpose had been to kill whoever had opened it. Darkhorse wondered if it had been meant as a last resort for Quorin should he have failed his master, or if the foul counselor had intended to give it to Erini or the king at some late point. Whatever the case, it was now no more than an unused sheet. He returned it to its original resting place and once again began inspecting the box.

"You, my friend," he muttered to the object, "have a story to tell! I wonder what lies within your maw—and what I must do to pry that maw open . . ."

The spell keeping it closed had an odd feel to it, almost as if it were incomplete and that, somehow, it was that incompleteness that gave it strength. The spell was a lock and completing it would be like using the key—but *what* key would fit?

I have no time for your little games! Darkhorse ranted silently at the box. The key would not be obvious to someone who had not searched the entire area already. If would have to be magical in some sense, but subtle as well. Only a tiny link was missing from the spell binding the box shut. What he needed was something almost insignificant in power but—

He recalled the Seeker talisman from where he had sent it. *Could it be?* It would explain why Quorin had kept such a weak artifact and why it seemed to have no detectable purpose. Add to that the fact that it had been located in the same drawer as the box. Why not put the key in the same place as the lock it was meant for, especially since most people would never connect the two. Like hiding something in plain sight. More and more, Darkhorse convinced himself that he had chosen correctly. In the end, however, there was only one way to find out, and that was to see if his "key" fit.

Recalling some of his past mistakes, he surrounded the container and the talisman before beginning. With so much effort put into keeping the box sealed, it was possible that what he unleashed might be devastating. Possible, but doubtful. Unlike the parchment, Darkhorse sensed that this item had a more useful purpose.

With his mind, he brought the talisman to the box and laid it on top. The pattern he sensed did not seem right. Darkhorse shifted the talisman to a standing position in front of the container. The binding field altered, but again it was not the complete pattern that he sought.

After a moment's thought, he caused the medallion to lay flat. This time, he brought the box to the talisman, carefully placing it directly on top of the Seeker device.

A perfectly formed pattern momentarily flickered into existence, then cancelled itself out completely. He had succeeded in unlocking the box.

That success did not ease his mind. Darkhorse still had to *open* the container.

Something nagged at the corner of his mind. He was beginning to dislike those feelings and, under present circumstances, chose to ignore it as simple growing paranoia. It might even be, the stallion decided, that the box itself was trying to turn him away before he opened it and discovered its secret.

Still, there was no sense in taking too many chances. . . .

He turned the container so that the lid would open toward *him*. In this way, the brunt of any blow would be away from where he stood. The precaution might be all for nought, but there was no harm in taking it.

With a careful touch of his will, Darkhorse raised the lid high.

Briefly, there was a flash of brilliant light, so brilliant that it illuminated the far half of the chamber as well as the sun might have, had it been brought inside. The flash lasted no longer than two, maybe three seconds and then died completely. Darkhorse's eyes, adjusted to the dark of the room, needed a moment to readjust. When they had, the shadow steed scanned his surroundings, searching for any minute difference. There was none. Despite the fact that he had shielded the box, he had expected some altering. Curious, he dissolved the shield.

The box looked and felt harmless. Darkhorse probed it closely. It was as if Quorin's toy had used up whatever power it had contained and now needed to be recharged. Where had the power gone, though? Darkhorse almost wondered what would have happened if he had taken the flash full on. It had been more than raw power, though time had not allowed him much of a chance to discover what *else* it had been. Some spell, but for what purpose?

In frustration, he dropped the box to the floor and crushed it beneath one of his hooves. "Curse your creator! If I should ever find that our paths have crossed . . ."

It was a foolish act and one he instantly regretted. Darkhorse kicked at the remnants of the container, knowing that it was likely he had destroyed his only clue.

Darkhorse was about to return to Melicard when he became aware of something—no! *Someone*—in the outer rooms. There was no mistaking *that* presence. Not so *close*.

"Your madness has finally led you to—" he burst into the room, defenses and offenses at the ready . . . only to find no sign of his adversary.

No sign of Shade.

Or was that the case? Darkhorse moved toward the wall to his left, sensing a slight trace emanating from that direction. Shade's magic. It was too distinctive, too *Vraad* to be any other's. There were cracks in the wall, too, as if the warlock had struck out against it before his abrupt departure.

Darkhorse laughed. Even now, he could sense the warlock's presence elsewhere in the palace. This time, there would be no escape. This time, Darkhorse *would* confront him.

And one of us will play the final hand . . . perhaps both of us, if need be!

The shadow steed laughed again, but it was a hollow laugh, devoid of even the least bit of humor.

In the place where he had chosen to wait, Shade nodded to himself and whispered, "So. Now comes the time. At *last*."

XIX

Two men had been left to guard Mal Quorin's cell. Even though at the time the king had been shorthanded and no one had known that Quorin's men would rout, Melicard had decided that sparing two men was still worth the price. It said something about the importance of the prisoner—and how much King Melicard desperately wanted his former advisor to remain where he was until Talak could mete out proper justice to a man who had betrayed everyone.

For the last few hours, their prisoner had remained quiet. It had been a welcome change from the first hour, when Quorin had recovered somewhat from the princess's assault and started ranting how they would all pay when his lord and master crushed the city beneath his paw. The guards, still weak themselves from their own ordeal, had been taking turns napping, trying to build up their strength. Once in a while, the one awake would look through the barred window in the door of Quorin's cell and make certain that the prisoner had not slipped through the cracks in the cell walls or some such impossibility. Each time, Quorin had still been there. The ten-minute ritual quickly became something of a joke—until one of the sentries stood up, stretching his worn legs, and glanced inside.

The chains hung loosely. Of the traitor, there was not the slightest sign. The cell had no other openings . . . unless the prisoner *had* slithered through the cracks.

Though the panicked guard and his soon-to-be-panicked companion could not have known it, Mal Quorin had vanished from his place of confinement just about the time Darkhorse had opened the lid of the box. Even had they known and been able to make the connection, there still remained one more question, one that greatly outweighed the question of *how* he had escaped.

That question was, of course, *where was he?*

Melicard paced the room, trying to explain again to his headstrong bride-to-be what he wanted of her and *why*.

"Erini, I want you to stay back here—"

"Where it's *safe*?" The princess shook her head vehemently. "This will one day be my kingdom, too—unless you've changed your mind about me—"

"Never!"

"Then let me defend it with you, Melicard." Erini took a deep breath and stepped away from the king. She was more nervous than she wanted to admit. *Does it ever become easier?*

Darkhorse seemed to take the entire thing in stride, as if combatting immortal warlocks and sinister Dragon Kings was an everyday matter—and perhaps it was with *him*. The princess, on the other hand, while ready to give her life for the protection of her people, still contained within her a very human desire to be safe and secure from the troubles around her.

"Without Mal Quorin to lead them, the traitors have no one to turn to. It will be over in an hour, maybe less. We have a fair idea now who belonged to him, thanks to some of our prisoners. At worst, we shall round up everyone, replace the gate complement with men loyal to me, and sort out the innocent and guilty here in the palace. Crude but effective. Hardly something requiring your talents—which I *will* need when the drakes arrive."

"The drakes . . ." Erini shook her head, not because she disagreed with Melicard's summation but because the lack of sleep was finally taking its toll upon her. She stumbled momentarily.

Melicard succeeded in grabbing her arms, preventing her from causing herself any harm by slipping. "*This* is the reason I especially do not wish your aid in this matter. I *want* to protect you; I will not argue that point. I know, however, that your abilities make you invaluable to the safety of my—our—people. That is why I want you to take the time you have to *sleep*. Rest. You have not fought the battles I have. You have not had to go without sleep for days. What happens when the Dragon King arrives and you don't have the concentration to make use of your abilities? What happens then?"

What, indeed? Erini knew he was correct. Knew it, but did not like it. She wanted to be there at his side for every moment that became available to them, even in the middle of a battle if circumstances warranted it. Yet, if she truly wanted a future here, the princess knew that she would be best able to guarantee that by being fit and ready when the drake host arrived. Melicard admitted he had many tricks of his own, long-term preparations for just such a day, but the aid of a spellcaster of any sort would only strengthen their chances. They were hardly assured of victory. The Silver Dragon had been preparing for this day as well—with better success so far.

"You will face danger enough," her betrothed continued. His grip had changed from a spontaneous one designed to keep her from falling to one that threatened to never release her from his side. Erini would have been happy enough to suffer such a fate. "The Dragon King will note fairly quickly that there is a sorceress aiding in the defenses. You may be personally assaulted."

The princess shivered. She felt herself brave, but . . .

"I have something for you." One hand released its hold reluctantly, vanished, then returned, this time bearing a familiar-looking object.

"This is Quorin's talisman." Erini tried to push it away, wanting nothing to remind her of the insidious man.

"Not his, but one similar. Stronger. It was once mine. I've not worn it for some time, not since after the . . . you'll need it more."

She accepted it reluctantly, knowing this was one point it would be useless to argue over with him. As he placed it around her neck, a sudden, insane fear crept over her. "Melicard. Do you think we have any chance?"

"Talak has stood before. We also have Darkhorse. He's promised us the aid of the Bedlams, and I know from past experience that they are up to the task."

"Where are they? Why haven't they arrived yet?"

"Who can predict what these spellcasters will do?" He leaned closer and whispered, "I have enough trouble with just one. The one who so readily saved my soul after I twisted it into something of a mockery."

"It wasn't that difficult. You'd had nearly twenty years of free life. I only reminded you of what that life had offered once."

Melicard broke away from her. "Which reminds me also of the tasks at hand." He snapped his fingers, summoning four men he had borrowed from Iston's complement. "Escort her majesty to her quarters and remain there. See to it she gets some rest."

Both of them knew that the princess could easily bypass her watchers with the aid of her abilities, but Melicard also knew that Erini felt guilty about the trouble that her accidental departure had caused them during the coup. The princess knew he was counting on that.

Before allowing herself to be escorted away, Erini stepped over to Melicard for one final time, reached up, and kissed him in full view of the others. She was going to get a reputation for being brazen at this rate, she knew, but there was always the chance that something terrible might happen while they were separated. Reluctantly separating herself from the stunned king, Erini rejoined her escort and gave them permission to depart. For her own sake, she dared not look back until she knew for a fact that Melicard was no longer in sight.

In the halls, it seemed impossible that there was still a great threat to the safety of this city—*her* city. The palace was nearly silent. Only if she listened closely could she hear men running or marching in the distance. One last patrol was searching through this massive edifice in the remote possibility that some of Mal Quorin's men were still in hiding.

Captain Iston, on his way back to the king, stopped her in the hall. His face was worn, but he looked willing to take on the entire horde if that would keep his mistress safe. His mistress and one other, based on the first words that escaped his lips. "Galea! Your majesty! I—I beg your pardon! I wanted to ask—"

"—if I could see how Galea was doing?" Though they had failed to spirit her away, Iston and his men had succeeded in rescuing her two ladies. Unfortunately, Iston had never had any time to actually speak with Galea. Knowing how difficult it had been for her to leave Melicard, Erini smiled and added, "Of course, I will. You have my promise."

"My deepest gratitude, your majesty." The officer bowed and hurried on his way.

The walk to her personal chambers was uneventful, with the exception of the notion, which rose twice in her thoughts, that Shade was so very nearby. Once, she stared at one of the walls, thinking he was there. The second time, Erini had the oddest feeling that she had just walked *over* an area where the warlock should have been standing. It puzzled her once she realized that he was in neither of those two places. Why would she imagine such a thing? Had recent events finally taken its toll on her? Was Erini losing all sense of reality?

Sleep began to look very wonderful, very precious. Melicard was correct; if the princess did not sleep, she would be useless to him when the siege began.

Before dismissing her escort, she peeked into the rooms belonging to Magda and Galea. Magda, ever in control even after surviving a coup attempt, looked up from where she was sitting. Beside her and lying asleep in bed, was Galea. The tall woman rose and walked quietly over to her mistress.

"Yes, your majesty?"

"How is she? How are both of you?"

"She feared more for your life and that of her dashing captain that she did for her own. Galea is worn out, nothing more. I promised to sit with her for a while in order to calm her nerves. As for myself . . . I get along."

Erini could not help smiling slightly at Magda's attitude. "You are a rock that both of us sorely need."

"I live to serve my mistress."

"I'd be lost without you. When Galea awakes, tell her that her officer asked about her. He's fine. I also want you to get some rest, Magda. Even you have to sleep."

"The same could be said about you, your majesty. I'll tell her and do as you say. I must admit to some difficulty with keeping my eyes open."

"I know the feeling. Sleep well, Magda, for we may all need our wits about us come the morrow."

"The morrow is almost here already," the plain woman commented. "May you sleep well, also, my lady, and please summon me if you have need of my services."

"Thank you."

Her escort stayed with her to the very end, even insisting on following her into her chambers. Not until every corner and every closet had been inspected, evidently at Melicard's command, did they deign to depart. Even then, two of them went no farther than the corridor outside. Erini was tempted to tell them the futility of such an action, but knew it was likely her betrothed's way of easing his own fears—though he knew as well as she that sorcery made it too easy for her to leave without anyone noticing.

Alone, the princess was tempted to fall face-down into her pillow and lay there until sleep overcame her, which would not have proven much of a struggle, judging by the way she felt merely *gazing* at the bed. She found her thoughts intruding again; this time concerning the terrible situation they would probably find themselves in come daylight. *If only Darkhorse had been able to warn them!* she thought wearily. *They would be here by now!*

He *had* tried. She knew that. Unfortunately, the commander had assumed it was the eternal who had killed Drayfitt and that he was a servant to one of the Dragon Kings. It was a wonder that all the stallion had suffered was a momentary exile to—to—whatever plane had apparently spawned him, if she understood correctly.

If only Melicard could have spoken with his men. He had mentioned once having methods for that, but, as with so many things, those methods had fallen under his ''loyal'' counselor's control. Now, they were no longer available. Quorin had been very thorough in his work.

Drayfitt, Erini thought sadly. *Drayfitt could have created something. He could have—*

It occurred to her at that point that she had the potential to do *anything* the elderly sorcerer had been capable of doing.

The notion excited her, brought new energy to her worn body and mind. If *she* could somehow contact Melicard's forces in the Hell Plains, she might be able to convince them to turn around. Then, it would be up to Talak to hold out until the army returned. Surely with foes coming at him from two sides, even the Dragon King would be forced to capitulate or flee. Melicard had also mentioned his smaller armies of the north and west. While the princess did not quite understand under what circumstances Quorin had tricked them, she could only assume that if she was successful with the first, then she stood a good chance of contacting them as well. From there, time would be what mattered. Erini hoped the Bedlams would arrive before it was too late.

How would she do it? Drayfitt had shown her little. Yet, the one thing he had always emphasized was, magic, in any form, worked more easily if one allowed it to come to oneself naturally. Allow her inner self to make each spell almost automatic. Few people had the ability or the patience to do that, which was why there had never been *that* many spellcasters of significant ability even prior to the Dragon Kings' secret purgings following the unsuccessful Turning War.

The first thing she needed, Erini decided, was a comfortable but firm place to sit. Had she been, say, the Lady Gwendolyn Bedlam, she knew that it would have taken perhaps just the blink of an eye or the wave of a hand to perform the deed. Not having experience or the feel of sorcery, the princess was forced to do everything step-by-step. Hopefully, there would be time later on for someone to assist her in her practice.

While the bed looked most comfortable, the floor seemed

more practical. Erini did not want her spell ruined because the
softness of her bed made her too sleepy. The floor was
comfortable, but in no way conducive to rest—at least, not yet.
Erini knew that, once her initial enthusiasm faded away, it
would be near impossible for her to stay awake regardless of
where she was or what she was doing.

Seating herself on one of the carpeted areas, she closed her
eyes and tried to picture men encamped in a violent, smoke-
filled land. They would be rising about now, Erini supposed.
She pictured the tents, saw the sentries, and imagined the
details of their armor, the last based on those she had seen the
palace guards wearing. The images faded briefly as exhaustion
tried to seize the moment while her eyes were closed tight.
Blinking, the princess cursed under her breath and tried again.

The images grew sharper in her mind, but that was all they
were—images. She could feel no connection between herself
and anyone in the encampment. With growing disgust, Erini
realized that she knew none of the officers by face, much less
by name. How, then, could she hope to make contact with
them? Was her only hope the possibility that she might be able
to transport *herself* to the encampment? Would that even work?
To date, her abilities had worked haphazardly at best, even
taking into account Mal Quorin's damnable medallion.

Her concentration was interrupted for what she considered
permanently by the return of the feeling that there was *another*
in the room with her, another by the name of Shade. Erini leapt
to her feet, teetering ever so slightly. Nothing. For the space of
a breath, she had felt his presence so near that it would not
have surprised her to find him staring over her shoulder. Her
weary mind succeeded in coming up with an answer that
satisfied her for the moment; her erratic senses had no doubt
picked up on the traces left behind by his previous visitation.
That she had not noted them in the days between now and the
time of that incident did not occur to her.

Defeated, Erini slumped onto her bed. The appeal of falling
asleep in her clothes renewed itself. Her arms were lead; the
weight of the palace seemed to have been placed on her head.
She wanted nothing but sleep now. Perhaps after some rest, the
princess hoped, she would have some success.

A hesitant knock on her chamber doors stirred her. "You
may enter."

It was Galea. There were rings under her eyes and it looked

as if she had just woken up. She had dressed hastily, for her
clothes were wrinkled and her hair was in complete disarray.
"My lady?"

"What is it, Galea?"

The other woman looked perplexed. "You *summoned* me,
your majesty."

Had she? Try as she might, Erini could not recall doing so.
Perhaps Galea had only dreamt that she had. "I've no need of
you now, but if you have a moment, I have a message for you
from someone important to you."

From the way her companion's eyes lit up, the princess knew
that Galea had already guessed who that certain someone was.
Trying to smooth her hair into something more organized, the
robust woman stepped respectfully inside, closing the door
behind her. She hurried over to her mistress, unable to hide her
anxiousness.

Erini started to speak, then clamped her mouth shut as the
feeling of the two of them not being alone threatened to
overwhelm her. She glanced quickly around the bedroom.

Galea looked at her in slight confusion. "Is something
amiss, my lady?"

"I'm not—" the princess turned to her, intending to calm
both Galea's worries and her own—and found herself staring
into eyes that no longer saw, but gazed blindly into the
emptiness next to her. "Galea?"

The gentle woman did not move. Erini could not even tell if
she was breathing.

It had *not* been her imagination and in her weariness she had
failed to understand that.

"Greetings to your majesty," a voice uttered indifferently.

Even before her gaze turned on him, she knew it was Shade.
He stood near the mirrors, which had turned black and opaque
in his presence. Erini idly wondered whether there was something the warlock did not want to see.

Shade slowly strode toward her. His face, though shadowed
by the immense hood, was quite distinct this time, a complete
change from their accidental meeting. A lock of silver hair
hung down across his forehead. Erini shook her head, not
believing any of this. *Not now! Not after everything else!*

"I find I have need of you, Princess Erini. Other matters . . .
well, you wouldn't understand, I imagine."

She tried to open her mouth to scream for help, not knowing

who or what could save her from this, but her lips seemed sewn shut.

"My apologies, but I have more to say and much to do." He reached forward, not for her, Erini noticed, but for Galea. The princess reached out to block him, but her movements were uncoordinated for some reason and she only succeeded in falling over herself. As she tried to rise, Erini caught a glimpse of Shade whispering to the other woman. Galea nodded, still deep in the trance.

Darkhorse! Where was Darkhorse? Managing to come to a kneeling position, the novice sorceress tried a spell, any spell, that would alert someone, preferably the ebony stallion, to her predicament.

"Mustn't do that," Shade's hand was suddenly on her shoulder, though the warlock had been elsewhere a moment before. Galea was nowhere to be seen. Tears of frustration tumbled down her cheeks. She looked up into the cursed warlock's visage and tried to convey her anger with her eyes.

He almost looked sympathetic. His next words even carried a tone of slight remorse with them. "I do not know why I am explaining myself to you. You are my only choice. I have to act now—who can say how long a better choice than you might take to come along? My time is limited and I find I grow more impatient."

Her eyes narrowed as she pictured Darkhorse confronting and defeating him. Shade smiled knowingly, almost as if he could read those harsh thoughts. "Your savior will not notice your absence for some time to come. At present, he is chasing . . . me, you might say. Something to keep him busy." Shade held up the fingers of both hands and counted names off. "The Bedlams sleep. I owe them that much for now. They will sleep for quite some time. Your Melicard has a mighty horde approaching his very doorstep and, counterwise, the Dragon King Silver has an entire city prepared to face him. Poor Drayfitt, my sad benefactor, is dead—an unfortunate accident of his own doing. Finally, Darkhorse is chasing phantoms."

There were still several fingers up as the warlock completed his insane recital. Erini studied them closely, still keeping a faint hope alive. Shade looked from her to the raised fingers and then slowly lowered them. "The rest were merely spares, I'm afraid. There's no one else."

He pointed a single finger in her direction and indicated that

she should rise. There was no choice in the matter; Erini's body
responded without her cooperation. The hooded warlock nodded in satisfaction.

"I could have taken you in a much more violent manner,
princess, but I'm trying to be reasonable. You have no idea
how calm I've been. I could have leveled this city with your
precious Melicard in it. The Dragon King would've been
annoyed; he so wants to take Talak in one piece. There's so
much I could have done, but things turned out for the best after
all, so I suppose there's no use pursuing the subject."

Erini could say nothing, do nothing. Only her eyes allowed
her any opinion at all. They spoke volumes, mostly concerning
the madness of the creature before her.

Shade frowned and purposely looked away, only to find the
blackened mirrors confronting his gaze. Turning back to his
captive, he smiled again. It was a different sort of smile,
though, one tinged with guilt; an emotion Erini found it hard to
accept that the warlock would feel under the present circumstances.

"You may survive," he added, almost hopefully. "If you
do, I'll return you safe and sound to here—or Gordag-Ai if the
drakes succeed here. You have my *oath* on that."

She gave him one last glare, telling him what she thought of
his promises.

The warlock grew oddly unsettled. "We have to go now."

As Erini struggled futilely to make her body respond, Shade
wrapped his seemingly endless cloak about both of them and
pulled her toward him. The world seemed to warp around
them—and then they were elsewhere.

XX

"Shade!"

Darkhorse struck the wall of the cellar he had materialized in
only a few seconds before. As with his previous stops, the only
trace of his adversary was a minute trail left behind by the

warlock's method of travel. The previous thread had led him
here—but then, the last trail before that and the ones before
that had *all* led him along.

That was the truth of the matter, Darkhorse finally admitted
to himself. He had been *led along*. He had fallen for yet
another ploy by the warlock, who had spent each and every
lifetime during his curse plotting and planning tricks for the
incarnation yet to come, not to mention the hundreds of
enemies he had gathered over the centuries.

"Damn you!" The shadow steed kicked through the wall.
He stepped back, annoyed and embarrassed. If he was not more
careful, he would do the Dragon King's work for him. How
ironic it would be for the inhabitants to discover that the palace
had collapsed due to the efforts of one of its defenders.

After his fourth miss, Darkhorse suspected he was being led
astray; suspected it, but could not be certain. There was always
the chance that Shade *wanted* him to believe he was on a false
trail. As he had thought so often in the past, the only thing
predictable about the warlock was his unpredictability. That
convoluted sort of reasoning had forced him to pursue the trail
again and again. This visitation, however, had finally settled
it for him. Shade had made a fool out of the eternal once
more.

*What is your purpose for all of this, Shade? What plot have
you unleashed now?*

Was there danger to Melicard or the Princess Erini? The
possibility was too great to ignore. Darkhorse departed the
damaged cellar posthaste. In his imagination, he saw the king
and all his soldiers scattered about like so many toys. Worse
yet, he pictured the novice spellcaster, Erini, desperately battling for herself and her betrothed against a foe she could not
hope to withstand. It was not that she was weak or that she was
a female; it was because the warlock had the experience of the
ages to draw upon, whereas she had only a handful of suggestions given to her by Drayfitt and him.

He burst through the portal's other end, landing amidst a
conference between Melicard and several officers. A few could
not help gasping at the imposing sight. Melicard flinched, but
otherwise held his shock back respectably.

"Darkhorse! Where have you been? Dawn is almost upon
us! The first rays are already doing battle with the weakening
night!"

"Already?" The eternal sought out a window facing the proper direction. Sure enough, there was an aura of light growing steadily upward from the horizon. Had he been occupied *that* long? Either his obsession had finally grown completely out of control, or Shade had added a slight twist to the trail, secretly slowing Darkhorse's time perspective. True, he had also taken quite some time with his search of Quorin's belongings, but that still was not sufficient. It would have been an astounding feat, slowing time, that is, but hardly something beyond the abilities of a Vraad. Darkhorse prayed he was incorrect; if Shade was playing with time, then the entire world was threatened. The Vraads had a tendency to eventually destroy everything they utilized.

Melicard sensed Darkhorse's sinking mood. "What is it? What did you find in Quorin's chambers? Something of great importance?"

Shaking dark thoughts from his mind, the shadow steed finally replied. "There is nothing of value to us that I could discover. Perhaps you will find it different. My sincere recommendation, however, is to either seal or strip those chambers as soon as you can. I, myself, would prefer everything burned— with the fiend bound, gagged, and laid out on top of the pyre!"

"Gods! What *did* you find?"

"That is unimportant to us at the moment! The Princess Erini! Where is she?"

"I sent her to get some rest some time ago. We'll need her if we're to stand off the Dragon King's oncoming host. By the way," Melicard gave him a triumphant smile that somehow stretched across the mask, too, "the gate is ours. It was almost too simple—even more so than retaking the palace. They virtually threw themselves at us and begged for imprisonment rather than face the demons! You have quite a reputation now, Darkhorse."

"One that I would gladly trade for another, I think. Is the princess guarded?"

"I believe so. She will be safe."

Darkhorse shook his head. "I think I would prefer to look in—"

"Your majesty!" An officer clad in the same sort of uniform as Erini's Captain Iston barged through the heavy doors. He had apparently been running all the way from wherever he had come. "I brought the news myself, in case you had questions!"

"Questions about what, man?" Melicard demanded.

Between gulps of air, the soldier replied, "The lookouts have identified the first signs of the drakes' approach!"

"Already!" Melicard took a deep breath and looked at everyone, even Darkhorse. "Come. I want to see it for myself and I want each and every one of you to give me *any* observations about them as they draw nearer."

Darkhorse hesitated, caught between his fear for his benefactress, the princess, and his concern for Talak. Talak won out, though the steed swore to himself that he would look in on Erini once he had seen whatever there was to see of Silver's horrible army.

Out on one of the highest balconies of the palace, they gathered to watch. One of his aides handed the king a long tube, which Melicard put to his eye. Darkhorse did not have to ask the purpose of the device, which obviously gave the king a better view of the distant reaches. Sorcerers had created similar tools before, though this one had evidently been crafted by hand.

"I see them," Melicard commented at last. "By my father, it looks to be a vast legion! I don't think there's been a drake host this great since perhaps the siege of Penacles!"

While others gazed on or waited for the opportunity, Darkhorse adjusted his own senses, allowing him a view that even the mechanical toys of the king could not match. Melicard was correct; this was a vast host—and at its head rode the Dragon King himself. Oddly, Silver seemed almost apprehensive. Bully and coward though the drake lord was, Darkhorse would have expected him to be in a far more triumphant mood. With such an army behind him and the city gate supposedly ready to welcome him in without a struggle, he should have been confident. Was it just the drake's way, or did he know something?

Surveying the drake warriors who rode beside their master, Darkhorse finally discovered the horrible truth. Seated behind one warrior and looking distinctly distressed was none other than *Mal Quorin*.

"King Melicard!" The eternal returned his senses to normal.

"What now, friend Darkhorse? Do you see something?"

The shadow steed laughed. "Do I *see* something? Your

majesty, was it your intention to perhaps draw the drakes unsuspectingly to your gates? Did you hope to fool them into thinking that the traitors still controlled the city?''

From the flushed look on Melicard's face, he had intended something very close to that. Darkhorse was not surprised; it would have been a fairly logical maneuver.

The stallion dipped his head so that he was almost on a level with the mortal. ''Your majesty, the plan will fail now! Mal Quorin *rides* with the drakes!''

''Impossible!'' Melicard raised the tube to his eye again and tried to see what his ally had. Unfortunately, the device was not up to the task. He threw it to the floor in disgust, where the glass lens on one end cracked from the force. The king did not even notice. ''I believe you, Darkhorse, even if I can't see it for myself! How, though? What sort of trick?'' He turned to one of his aides. ''Alert the gate! Tell them that our plan is known!'' To another, he added, ''Go to our treacherous counselor's cell! Find out from the guards posted there what happened and why I was not informed!''

''Go easy on the sentries, your highness,'' Darkhorse commented, somewhat subdued. His mind had been racing and he suspected he knew the secret of Quorin's escape. ''They are probably confused and fearful. I think that I may have accidently been the catalyst for the devil's escape.'' He did not elaborate, intending that for a time when things were more peaceful—if such a rarity were ever to occur.

Melicard nodded, reading the eternal's attitude and knowing Darkhorse was angry toward himself. Fear suddenly raged across the monarch's odd features. Not fear for himself, but for his bride-to-be. ''Erini! He might have done some something to her!''

That was doubtful, in Darkhorse's opinion. He suspected now that the box was a last resort saved by Mal Quorin on the off-chance that he had to flee to his master. In opening up the container, the shadow steed had unwittingly unleashed the spell, which apparently had been specifically tied to the imprisoned advisor.

The king would not listen to those around him. If he had not been informed of Quorin's escape, then it followed that he might also have not been informed of any new attempt to kill or kidnap Princess Erini. Darkhorse was on the verge of stating that *he* would investigate, having already desired to do so since first arriving, when a new voice broke through the chaos.

"What's wrong? Darkhorse! Melicard! Are the drakes already at the gate?"

"Erini!" At the sight of his beloved, the king rushed to her and took her in his arms, ignoring the embarrassed looks on the face of his subordinates. The princess held him briefly, but seemed more interested in what was going on that would require everyone's presence here. "I couldn't sleep any more," she commented as she broke away and walked toward the rail of the balcony. "I was worried that something might happen while I was resting."

Melicard, a little at a loss due to the chaos his mind had been struggling with, joined her. "The drakes are out on the horizon. There. Darkhorse says that Quorin is with them."

"Quorin? That's terrible." Erini stared northward, as if trying to see the drake army without the aid of any device or her own sorcery.

Darkhorse snorted. *Terrible?* He would have expected a far more virulent response from the princess, who probably hated Quorin more than anyone else here. Studying her closely, he noted her pale, almost unresponsive features. It was likely that her lackluster response was due in great part to a surge of fatalism concerning the coming day or even simply because she had only slept a short while. Unlike Melicard and his men, who were long used to staying awake for a day or more, she had never had the need to do so. *Would that I could sleep! I would sleep for a year if such was possible!*

But not until Shade has been dealt with, he reminded himself.

Shade. Darkhorse still wondered what purpose the warlock had had in setting him off on the endless and pointless chase. Shade had wanted him occupied. Why?

He realized belatedly that Melicard was speaking to him. "What was that, your majesty?"

"I asked what might be taking your friends so long? We have need of the Bedlams, Darkhorse. I would like to discuss our options with them beforehand—unless they feel they can arrive at the last moment and remove the threat with a wave of their hands." The king's voice was tinged with aggravation. His kingdom's existence was hanging in the balance and two of his greatest allies were among the missing.

Darkhorse, too, began to wonder. Cabe had fallen prey to Shade's machinations earlier. Had the warlock struck twice? "I will go seek them now! There is still time before the Silver Dragon can strike! Will you be safe?"

"I would never leave my kingdom defenseless against a threat like the drakes. I swore that Duke Toma would be the last of his kind to ever enter Talak with his head still attached to his body."

The shadow steed chuckled. "Indeed. You also have your personal sorceress, too." He indicated a somber Erini with a nod of his head. She looked at Darkhorse, smiled briefly, then returned to her dreamlike gazing. "Yesss. I will return before long, King Melicard! You have my oath on that!"

"I would prefer your presence instead. We will await your return."

Summoning a portal, Darkhorse leapt from the balcony and vanished into it. The transition was swift this time and he barely noticed his brief passage through the emptiness. In mere breaths, he was exiting the other side, his destination as near to the protective barrier as he could get. This time, he hoped for a simpler visit.

He sent a probe first, hoping that it would engage the attention of one of those he sought. With the Bedlams sorely needed elsewhere, Darkhorse wanted to keep his return as quiet as possible so as to not panic the others who lived here. Unfortunately, he received no response, which, when he thought about it, left him few other choices than to call out.

Trotting closer to where the Manor itself stood, Darkhorse shouted, "Bedlams! Cabe! It is I, Darkhorse! I have need of you!"

He heard confused shouts and the mutters of angry folk. Several anxious minutes went by before someone responded to his summons. It was *not* Cabe. It was an uncrested drake, one of the servitor caste, who finally dared to challenge him.

"What isss it? What do you ssseek?"

"What do I *seek*? Your master and mistress, drake! The warlock Cabe Bedlam and his mate, the Lady of the Amber!"

The drake seemed more interested in the ebony stallion than locating those he served. "I have never ssseen a beassst such as you!"

"I was here earlier! I am Darkhorse!"

"Darkhorsssse!" The drake hissed in pleasure. "The massster has ssspoken of you! I wasss sorry that I misssed you! I am Ssarekai, one who trains and cares for riding drakes and sssteeds such as your magnificent ssself!"

As much as Darkhorse normally delighted in being appreciated, he had no time for such flattery now. "Your *master*, scaly one! I have need to speak with *him*!"

"Yesss, forgive me! Your appearance here has excited me! Others have been searching for them!"

"Searching? No one knows where they are?"

"They were not in their room."

Ssarekai would have said more, but a human female materialized through the trees and rushed to his side. Glancing at Darkhorse with more than a little fear, she whispered to the drake. It was an odd sight. Though humans and drakes intermingled in some places, such as Irillian, there was generally a sense of separation even when they spoke to one another. Here, on the other hand, the woman stood somewhat behind Ssarekai, as if she depended on him for protection from *Darkhorse*.

Curious things are being done here, the shadow steed thought wryly.

The drake looked upset. His hissing became more evident and his blunted, nearly human tongue darted in and out every now and then as he spoke. "Great Darkhorse, sssomething is amissss! No one can find the massster and mistress! Someone sssays—"

He did not hear what the drake had to say next, for another voice intruded, this one threatening to tear his mind apart, so intensely did it strike him. Ssarekai stepped back, his next words forgotten. Behind him, the female human tried to make herself as small as possible.

Darkhorse!

That was all. His name. His name echoing again and again. Shaking his head, he succeeded in clearing the echoes from his mind, but not from his thoughts.

"Great Darkhorse?" Ssarekai tentatively called.

The eternal paid him no mind. *Erini!* She was calling for his help! The Dragon King must have struck somehow!

His task here forgotten, the eternal summoned forth a new portal. Had the drakes waited until *he* was gone before beginning some insidious assault? What?

"Great One?" the drake Ssarekai called again, this time more urgently. His voice went unheeded.

"Stand fast! Those who would touch the friends of Darkhorse must be willing to pay in full for their misdeeds!"

The fearsome statements were out of his mouth before his eyes acknowledged the obvious fact that *no one* standing within sight appeared to be under attack by so much as a flea. Nothing seemed to be happening at all, save that Darkhorse once again found himself facing a sea of startled looks from every pair of eyes in the room. It was something he was becoming very annoyed about. The stallion was beginning to feel as if *he* were the intruder, not Shade or the Silver Dragon.

Scanning those around him, Darkhorse spotted Erini. She was staring at him in mild surprise. Confused, the shadow steed turned away from her gaze and focused on Melicard. The king flashed an uncertain smile in his direction.

"While we—appreciate—the sentiment, Darkhorse, I think the time for theatrics is long past."

Something is dreadfully wrong here! Had it been possible, his face would have turned crimson. "I received a desperate summons for help—from the Princess Erini!"

Melicard looked at his future queen. "Erini?"

The princess shook her head silently. She seemed almost disinterested.

The king turned back to the imposing figure before him and said, "Nothing has happened since you departed a moment ago save that the drakes have moved a little closer and we still await your friends, the Lord and Lady Bedlam. When do they arrive? I would rather not put my faith entirely in my own tricks, not if there are two master spellcasters available."

"I—I cannot say when they will arrive or if they even *ever* will. There was no sign of them. Their own people cannot find them!"

"Cannot find them?"

"I fear Shade has struck again!" Darkhorse could not help looking skyward. "I rue that this time should have ever come! He was my friend during many an adventure, but he has also been my sworn foe in times past! This day, however, washes away all the good that he has ever performed! If Cabe and his mate have suffered because of the warlock..." Darkhorse could not finish, unable to find a punishment strong enough to mete out.

The cry had seemed so *real*. He studied the princess, who idly stood by, waiting for something to happen. Why was she so indifferent now? Even with the lack of true sleep, she was not acting as he would have imagined her to act. The Erini he had met would have continued pushing until unconsciousness took her. This one seemed to hardly care.

There was one other thing that disturbed him—or perhaps it was the *absence* of something.

Several men came marching into the chamber, Captain Iston in their lead. A gasp escaped Erini and she took a tentative step forward before catching herself and settling back into her look of indifference. Darkhorse's ice-blue eyes narrowed.

Iston saluted. ''My men are ready when you give the signal, your majesty.''

Darkhorse listened to the officer's words, but his eyes remained fixed on the princess. There was a look of longing growing in her eyes that had nothing to do with Melicard. Her attention appeared to be focused on the captain.

He knew that the princess was a woman of passions, but the shadow steed knew that her love could have never turned so easily. Erini had been prepared to give her life several times over for the sake of her betrothed. This Erini acted as if she had never cared at all.

This Erini?

Forgetting Melicard and the others, he trotted toward the princess. She could not help turning to him, so impressive a sight he was, especially moving toward her with such evident purpose. Strangely, there was a level of fear noticeable in her eyes that also did not match the Erini he had come to know well, even despite what little time they had spent together.

''Your majesty is not looking well,'' he rumbled.

''A lack of sleep,'' she murmured. It was evident that the woman before him did not want him so near.

''How is your concentration? Will you be able to aid in the cause?''

''I hope so.'' Her tone suggested otherwise.

Darkhorse fixed his glittering eyes on hers. Erini tried to struggle, but her will was surprisingly weak and she quickly succumbed.

"I know *now* what so disturbed me about you! I know now that you could not have summoned my aid!"

Behind him, Melicard moved quickly to stand beside his bride-to-be. He faced Darkhorse with blood in his good eye.

"What *are* you doing to her? What in the name of the Tybers are you doing?"

"Resolving my own uncertainties about a few things—and cursing myself anew for missing the obvious!" Darkhorse drew Erini toward him, repelling Melicard at the same time. While the king struggled in vain and his men watched in stunned confusion, the shadow steed probed the human before him. He was not surprised at the results.

"This is *not* your future bride, King Melicard! This woman has no sorcerous ability whatsoever! She who stands before you, though she looks like the Princess Erini, is but a poor creature caught in a spell whose origins can only derive from that master of mayhem, Shade!"

Melicard's jaw dropped. "Not Erini?"

"No, *not* the princess! I should have noticed instantly that she projected no sorcerous presence! Princess Erini did not have the skill yet to mask that presence, at least not so completely!"

The false Erini was struggling with the spell that held her. A spellcaster she might not have been, but whoever—and that was likely to be Shade—had ensorcelled her had shrouded her in a few defensive spells. Darkhorse, though, strengthened by his own fury, tore away each of them, until only the illusion remained. While everyone waited—Melicard shaking—the shadow steed removed that last spell, revealing a shorter, slightly stout woman.

"Galea!" Captain Iston surged forth, trying to reach the woman. Darkhorse nodded imperceptibly. The female's deepest emotions had forced themselves to the surface the moment the officer had entered the room. Only strong love or hate was capable of that and Darkhorse knew enough to tell which was which. He released the confused Galea, who turned to her soldier and buried herself in his arms. A quick glance into her thoughts had already revealed that she knew nothing.

"Erini! Where's Erini?" Melicard demanded of him.

"I do not know, your majesty! When the summons reached me, I paid its point of origin no attention, assuming that since

little time had passed, she must be in the palace with you!''
The ebony stallion laughed madly, mocking his own stupidity
and carelessness. "Every turn! Every direction! He trips me
each time and I continue to take the falls!''

The king's split visage became a grim mask. Staring at some
point in space, he calmly and quietly commanded, "Find her,
Child of the Void. Find my queen and save her. I don't care
what the cost might be. Start now.''

"Now?" Darkhorse studied the human incredulously. "I
cannot search for her now, though a part of me screams to do
just that! Talak is endangered and the life of one being cannot
outweigh the fate of an entire kingdom!''

"I have no need of you. We *will* hold. We will hold until the
end of everything, if necessary. Go! I refuse your help! Will
that free you of your obligation?''

The shadow steed stamped a hoof against the marble floor.
He knew what the king was doing and liked it not at all. All of
Talak! "King Melicard . . . I cannot do this—''

"Get out of my sight, then, *demon*! I want nothing of you if
you will not do this for me!''

Melicard's subordinates were finding everything else to do
other than stare at their ranting monarch. Darkhorse knew that
the king's ravings were only an act. An act of love.

Sighing, Melicard visibly pulled himself together. "We will
still be here when you return. As I have said, Talak has long
been prepared for such an invasion—even if most of my forces
are scattered elsewhere.''

They would be arguing until the Silver Dragon himself burst
through the chamber doors, Darkhorse finally realized. There
was no changing the king's mind. The eternal knew that
accepting the human's decision was not the correct thing to do,
but it was too close to his own desires for him to fight it. He
felt he owed much to Erini for releasing him—and much more
because there was a quality about her that he had found in so
few others, making it all the more admirable. There was no one
name for it and he did not care to think of one. What mattered
was the princess.

"Very well," he finally replied, his words as close to a
whisper as he could manage.

The look he received from Melicard was a mixture of
gratitude and relief.

"I do not even know where to look.'' That was somewhat of

a lie. Darkhorse did know where to look; the only trouble was that there were *too* many places and certainly not enough time.

"You do what you can." With that final statement, the king turned away, momentarily unable to continue.

Deciding silence was more appropriate than any response he could give, the shadow steed departed immediately—for where, he could not say.

With the imposing presence of Darkhorse gone, Melicard was slowly able to get his thoughts under control. He had sworn that he would make Talak hold, and hold it would. The defenses had never been tested in actual combat, but he tried not to think about that. Ironically, Melicard no longer thought about the potential for destruction. That hundreds of the cursed drakes would die meant little to him. His own people would die as well and the kingdom might fall.

"Captain Iston!" He had come to rely heavily on the foreigner, impressed as he was with the man's loyalty and experience. If they somehow survived, he would offer the soldier a permanent position on his staff—if Iston still wanted to remain in Talak. Should Darkhorse *fail*—and the horrid thought refused to die—the complement from Gordag-Ai would likely return to their homeland, having no further ties with his own kingdom.

"Your majesty?" The officer reluctantly abandoned his woman's side. Melicard felt a twinge within.

"You have your orders. I must ask that you now follow them."

"Yes, your majesty."

As an afterthought, the king added, "You may say your farewells before you depart."

"Thank you." Iston saluted, took Galea's hand, and led her away.

Melicard turned to the others. Several already had their orders and these he dismissed immediately. The rest waited, somewhat reassured now that their liege had taken control again.

The king surveyed the horizon. Was it his imagination or was the Dragon King's host moving more slowly? He grimaced. Wishful thinking, no doubt.

"We have," he finally began, "only a few hours before

havoc reigns. The others know their duties. What I want from each of you are suggestions—or comments on anything I've forgotten about. I want anything that will buy us time." He also wished he had at least one spellcaster. Thanks to the talismans he had kept, despite his own dislike for them since his disfigurement and what little Drayfitt—*poor Drayfitt*—had succeeded in accomplishing, the king had assumed his palace was fairly safe from the invasions of spell-throwing drakes and such. Now, however, he was not so certain. Darkhorse's ability to come and go as he pleased did not bother him. Shade's did, but here was a warlock with the knowledge of millennia. What bothered him was that an agent of the Silver Dragon had worked actively underneath his very nose and there was no doubt that Quorin had been in contact with his true master several times. It would take only one breach in those sorcerous defenses . . .

"My lord!" A guard stood by the doorway, awaiting permission to enter.

"Yes, what is it?" Were there not enough troubles?

"There is a drake demanding entrance to the city!"

"A drake?" How had they missed that? No doubt an emissary from the Silver Dragon, here to issue the demands of his lord. Best to kill him . . . no. Best to send him back with a message! "Tell the reptile that his master will never have this city and that I have said his head will hang alongside the banners when we have crushed gaggle of monstrosities!"

"My lord—"

The king knew it was emotion speaking, not thought, but he hardly cared. The *audacity* of his foe angered him. "You heard me! Go!"

The sentry bowed low, but did not move. He had something he felt *had* to be said, regardless of the king's anger. Melicard nodded permission.

"The drake is not at the northern gate, my lord, and he does not appear to be of the clan Silver."

"No?"

"He claims to have ridden from south."

South? "The Dagora Forest?"

"That was what he said."

Melicard did not know whether to laugh or curse. The Green Dragon had sent an emissary, but, considering that Talak and the monarch of the Dagora Forest had clashed in the past, the question was—was he here as an *ally* or a new *foe*?

There was only one way to find out.

XXI

Erini was frightened, though she tried as best she could not to show it. She was frightened of many things, but what frightened the princess most was the curious behavior of her captor.

Despite his claims to the contrary, she doubted that Shade's mind was as complete as he thought it to be. His personality seemed fluid to her, changing from one extreme to another. So close to what he believed would be his triumph, Shade was beginning to recall more and more about his tragic failure—and he insisted on sharing each detail with her, as if trying to purge himself of the memories.

"When men came back to this land," he was telling her companionably, "and settled, bowing for a time to the will of the first Dragon Kings, I moved back among them. Weaklings! Their ancestors had given in to this world, taking up its magic instead of strengthening their own! There were a few who could do outstanding things with that magic, though, and from them I learned much of what I had dared not attempt for fear of losing myself as my counterparts had."

Erini, held by his spells in a standing position with her arms outstretched—as if challenging the world, she thought bitterly—did not understand half of what he said. He was talking for himself. As long as it kept her from the fate he had planned, Erini did not object.

"I took many names and many guises in those days, learning what I could. Several times, I renewed my lifespan. Someday, though, I knew that *those* spells would fail me. I would die and the Vraad would pass from this world forever, a world ours by *right*." He smiled coldly. "There were a few others who survived, in a sense, but they had also given themselves over to this world's nature, becoming less Vraad and more—more—''

Shade rose, seeming to forget his tale completely. It was not the first time he had changed so abruptly. Shade stretched out one arm and caused the blue ball of light floating high above them to increase in intensity. The warlock's stronghold, little more than shadow prior to this, was revealed to his captive for the first time. Erini was properly awed.

Erini had never seen the throne room of the drake emperor, so it was understandable that she would miss the incredible similarity between that place and this. Grand effigies of people and creatures long dead or vanished lined the walls on each side. Some were so real as to force the princess to look elsewhere, for fear one of them would start staring back at her. Erini was brave, but, even with her limited experience in magic, she could sense the cold presence within each one. These things *were* alive, although hardly in the sense that most people thought of as living. In some ways, they almost reminded her of Darkhorse, though she hated even considering such a thought.

''My cache. Plundered by those scaly wretches above. This was where I formulated my spell and stored all my notes and special—toys. A Vraad habit. Though I performed my spells among humans and lived in human communities, it was here, in this place, that I first conceived of my notion. It was here that I found and began to travel the path of immortality and *true* power such as even the Vraad had never dreamed.''

As he spoke, Shade reached into his cloak and removed a rather ordinary-looking tripod. The care with which he handled it told Erini it was anything but ordinary. She watched in helpless frustration as the warlock placed it at her feet.

''The concept came to me early on, but the doing of it escaped me for centuries. I feared I was lost. To understand what I needed, I would have to give myself. Become changed by this world—have I said that already?'' Shade looked up from what he was doing, uncertain. There was a slight trace of fear in his tone, as if he were finally realizing that his mind was not as it should be.

While he puzzled over his own question, Erini continued her own struggle. Though she could not move, her mind was still free. Shade needed her mind free yet malleable. The princess desperately tried to capitalize on that, continually summoning

up whatever strength she could find within herself and sending
out a sorcerous cry for aid that she hoped Darkhorse would
detect. It was a slim, almost mad hope, but it was all she
had. She lacked the skill and experience she needed to break
free of her physical predicament. The warlock knew too many
tricks.

"It won't even hurt—not much, that is," Shade suddenly
told her, coming within a hand's width of her face. She tried to
close her eyes, but his spell prevented that. Instead, she was
forced to stare into his glimmering, seemingly multifaceted
orbs. There were those who said that the eyes were the mirror
of the soul, and what there was of Shade was more reflection
than substance. More than life, but also less.

He was no longer human and likely had not been since
the very day that he had fallen victim to his own obsessive
desires.

His hand came up before her eyes, his voice was soothing,
yet with that undercurrent of anxiety and fear. "Listen to me
now. I'm going to begin. I don't need your cooperation, but I
ask it. Give me what I want and I'll see what I can do for you
afterward. You will give it to me regardless of your desires, but
the transition will be easier on both of us if you do your part
willingly."

Frozen as she was, Erini could only respond with her eyes,
which she did promptly. Shade backed away, his face initially
the picture of remorse, then, in an abrupt change, arrogant and
lordly. "Very well, then. I offered for your sake, really. Suffer
if you like. Here is what you will do for me."

The warlock reached up and touched her forehead. Erini's
mind was suddenly filled with images and instructions. She
found herself unable to continue her desperate summons under
such circumstances and finally gave in. Her only consolation
was the thin hope that something in the shadowy warlock's
instructions might give her an idea.

Erini's task, as he had defined it, was to be the vessel in
which two radically different forms of sorcery would be meshed
together. Unlike the tales the princess had heard as a child, it
was not the powers of darkness and light that Shade had sought
to master. It was the vestiges of a power that lingered from
whatever world the Vraad had originated from and this world's
own strength. The images both horrified and fascinated her.

"We will begin *now*." Wrapping himself deep within his

cloak, Shade leaned forward and focused his gaze on the tripod.

Though she could see little, Erini felt everything. She felt the power that she summoned forth fill the chamber—*she* summoned forth? No, it only appeared that way. From the instructions that the warlock had implanted in her mind, she understood that he was utilizing the tripod in order to draw energy through *her*. To draw upon so much power himself would be to risk the success of his plan. He had to be free to control the situation, and without her that would have been impossible.

Erini knew that there must be defenses she could summon, things that would disrupt his spell permanently, but her mind was not skilled enough to cope with the influx of power and still concentrate on shielding herself. The princess now saw why Shade desired an untrained and inexperienced spellcaster with high potential. Even Drayfitt's mind would have been too closed for Shade to have trusted the outcome of his experiment. Erini was like a child, uncertain of what her limitations were; an open book on which Shade could write what he pleased.

"You feel the power flowing into your soul." A statement, not a question. "Hold it there. Let it gather."

She did as he bid her, unable to do anything else. It was frustrating to feel so strong and yet be so helpless. The strength of the world seemed to flow into her. For the first time, Erini saw the world in terms of the lines and fields of energy that many spellcasters did. Yet, the spectrum remained there as well. The two were one. It was impossible to tell if one had resulted because of the other or if they had both sprung into existence simultaneously. There was so much potential here that even the greatest sorcerers of legend had probably never known the like. There was power enough here to make one almost a god—

—and this was only a *part* of what Shade desired. Shade, not her. She was a vessel, the princess reminded herself, for all the power that she contained was for her captor, not herself.

"The flow will continue slowly. You must guide its intensity, make certain it does not overwhelm you—and be prepared to accept the next offering."

It was too much! Erini panicked. How could she hope to contain so much energy, so much pure power? Erini struggled to assert her mind. *Darkhorse! If only I could summon him!*

Erini?

It was brief and lost to her completely after that single word, after the calling of her name, but she knew that she *had* touched the eternal's thoughts. Her mind filled with hope.

A cold, loathsome essence entered Erini just as she sought Darkhorse again, caressing her soul as if tasting a treat. Caught unaware, the princess wanted to scream and scream and *scream*, but Shade's earlier spell prevented such a release of her horror at the unthinkable invasion. The world around her shrank away, as if she were looking at it from above. The warlock looked into her eyes, curiosity and anticipation at the forefront. She wanted to ram him through the earth, peel away every layer of skin while he writhed in agony—*anything*—as long as it would free her mind from the unspeakable presence seeking to become a part of her.

"Accept it, princess. You have no choice."

She didn't. Erini wanted to destroy, to tear her *own* body apart and remove the cancerous thing from her soul. Shade's commands prevented all but the weakest resistance. This was the essence of the power that the warlock's kind had utilized in that nameless hell they had been—forced?—to leave. It was alien to the Dragonrealm, following different, twisted laws of nature that should not—could not—exist here.

There is a way around that.

The thought was not her own, but rather one of Shade's imprinted instructions, rising forth, now that its task was at hand. It felt like something almost alive, as if it had been imbued with a tiny piece of the Vraad's being.

There are points of binding, places where the two realities may be joined. You have only to look.

Joined. They had to be joined. Erini saw that now. It was the only possible way to keep herself from suffering a similar fate to that which Shade had suffered, if not something worse. Either force within her was capable of scattering her body and mind beyond the reaches of forever. If she was to have any chance to survive, she would have to do as her captor's instructions indicated.

Of course you do, the piece of Shade reminded her. Erini wondered if it was her own mind that made it seem so *much* alive and, if so, was she going mad?

You have a task. Do it.

That was the only truth she did have at the moment. With growing disgust, she accepted the foreign sorcery completely into her being. In her imagination, it seemed to squirm like a worm trying to burrow deeper. Erini almost rejected it then, but knew that, by doing so, she would condemn herself. What sort of world had the Vraad come from, and how could they possibly be the ancestors of the humans alive today? There were hints of those answers now and then, vague, ghostlike images that danced around her, almost distracting her from the horrid task. None of them were distinct and Erini felt some relief at that. Despite her wonder, these were things she actually had little desire to learn about. They all bore the same stench as the sorcery.

See the points. Take them and marry them to their counterparts. Here. Here. Here.

This part of her task seemed almost laughingly simple now, though she knew that here was where Shade had originally begun his downward spiral to damnation. Erini could not see why. The points her mind saw met willingly with one another. Perhaps it was, as the warlock had indicated, only because she was the vessel—or rather the catalyst—and not the final recipient of the spell's outcome. She had only one purpose, not several as he had had.

While a portion of her consciousness worked automatically, having no choice to do otherwise, Erini found a change occurring throughout her mind, throughout her very *soul*. The princess could no more deny the transformation than she could her earlier acceptance of the alien sorcery. After a few seconds—perhaps minutes or even *hours*, she could not say—Erini even began to *welcome* the change. Her perspective grew and grew and her comprehension of what her world was truly like expanded until Erini felt she *was* the Dragonrealm, the vast eastern continent, the smaller southern continents, the islands, the seas . . . everything.

Shade's spell became a secondary thing to her, something that had to be done but that did not require more than a trace of her concentration. All events, all people, became known to her. Unconsciously, Erini focused on Talak and her betrothed.

It was there before her gaze, a thought came to life. The drakes were within striking range of the city. The princess gained some perspective on how much time had passed, for the sun was already high and it appeared as if the first blows had already fallen. There were dead drakes on the landscape between the Dragon King's host and the city walls, and settle-

ments unfortunate enough to have sprung up near the northern
wall were little more than splintered wood and scattered arti-
cles. The inhabitants, she remembered, had been ordered in at
some point before her kidnapping. There was also damage to
the city itself. *An aerial assault,* 'some corner of her mind told
her. It sounded astonishingly like her grandfather, general-
consort to her grandmother, the queen at that time. He had been
dead for almost seven years. She studied the dragons. Something pierced their hearts. *Something magic.*

Melicard. Her view did not alter, for she saw all things at
once, but the image of the king somehow was foremost among
them. He was in the throne room, giving orders, caught up in
the battle. A few of his men were injured and there was a
sticky, dark fluid covering one of the walls. Erini belatedly
noticed the sky where the ceiling had once been. A drake had
nearly broken through *all* of their defenses. Somehow, though,
the magical defenses of Talak—she could not recall if she had
ever known about them prior to this—had been restored and, in
fact, improved. The Dragon King would find Talak a costly
victory.

Victory. It was still within the drake lord's grasp. At the very
least, Talak would be in shambles and most of its population
would be dead. Another Mito Pica.

The two magics were nearly one now. Erini's perspective
altered again, this time in a puzzling manner. A bit worrisome,
too, though that emotion was becoming less and less a part of
her. The princess, despite the understanding of her world that
she had gained earlier, could not fathom what was happening
now. In some ways, it reminded her of how the world looked
when the spectrum was visible to her. Like one image superim-
posed upon another. It was an apt comparison, she decided, but
hardly one that explained *what* was overlaying the Dragonrealm
and the rest like a shroud.

There were mountains where mountains should not have
been. There were seas and rivers where only dry sand or lush
forests existed now. Where Talak stood, another city, smaller in
width yet stretching far higher into the heavens, also rose,
ziggurats of Melicard's kingdom fighting for supremacy with
odd, twisted towers that ended in spearlike points. It was and
was not the same world.

Though she felt life on this world, something warned her not
to seek it out. Instead, she turned her inner gaze to the most

fascinating and most chilling sight visible. The heavens themselves. The beautiful blue of her world had been replaced by a green of dark intensity. Not a green such as a leaf might be colored, however, but a green that reminded Erini of nothing more than rot. Decay. A world that was festering and had *been* festering for over thousands and thousands of years.

The world which Shade and the Vraad had abandoned for this one. A world they had *made* into this putrifying abomination.

This was the potential that Shade represented.

Without willing it, her view turned to the warlock himself. He knelt before her, enraptured by the progress of his spell, almost ready to accept the fruits of her forced labor. To her shock, she saw things about him she doubted even *he* had ever known. Not just his myriad incarnations, but what the distorted spell had done to his essence over the millennia. Shade was far from whole, far from untouched by the world his people had fled to. He was possibly in a worse condition than he had been during the time of his previous incarnations—and he refused to see that.

She was astounded at his latent abilities. He had held back throughout all of this, the princess realized. In the hooded warlock was the potential to devastate a region larger than the Tyber Mountains themselves. Shade had hinted at the godlike powers of his kind, but the truth was far more overwhelming. It had only been his desire to complete his lifelong goal that had checked a madness that might have seen the Dragonrealm in complete ruins in less than a week. That and a tiny, nagging doubt—*guilt*, she correct herself—about what he was doing. There was more good in Shade than he realized. There had been more in the original, too. His own memories were playing him false.

This is a new form of incarnation, Erini concluded. *Shade has not escaped his previous failure; he has become even more mired in it than before.*

What would happen when his power increased a hundredfold?

Erini found she was growing beyond the point of caring. Her perceptions continued to expand. Soon, she would no longer be a part of her world, not in the true sense. This was the fate that Shade had suffered, but Erini would not be returning in any form. Shade's variation on his original work would guarantee that. He would gain command of the powers he sought, but lose his vessel in the prospect.

What remained of Erini sought to fight that fate, but she lacked any weapon with which to do it. She did not have the concentration to strike back with her own insignificant talent—and what good would it have done, anyway? Shade would have dismissed any assault on a magical level with as much effort as what he needed to breathe.

Erini felt herself beginning to fragment. Her task was almost complete, but she would never see the outcome. The strain was too much.

She thought of Melicard, who would have no one to keep him from falling into the same darkness that he had lived within before her coming. His image, commanding his aides in the defense of Talak, flickered before Erini. She thought of her parents, who would never know what fate had befallen their daughter. Melicard seemed to fade as the king and queen of Gordag-Ai took precedence. Lastly, Erini thought of Darkhorse, a being she had known only for a short time, but with whom she felt a rapport, a bond.

Erini?

The image of Darkhorse strengthened. He stood, confused, in an area she recognized from its ungodly bleakness as the Northern Wastes. The cold and snow did not bother him in the least. Darkhorse remained where he was, his head cocked to one side, almost as if he were listening to something.

Erini!

Had he sensed her? The novice sorceress was no longer certain she cared. Still, because of their bond, she acknowledged her presence to him.

Now he stood ready, seeking a direction in which to run. *Erini! Where are you?*

Where was she? "Everywhere" seemed the most appropriate response, but she knew that was not what the shadow steed meant. He was searching for her physical form.

A wave of urgency washed across her consciousness. Erini could not be certain whether it was a stray emotion of her own or one of Darkhorse's, relayed somehow by their contact. Whichever was the case, she acted upon that urgency and allowed him to see, to experience, where she was.

The eternal grew very grim and shot back, *I know where your are! Do not lose yourself! Keep a hold on your existence, Erini!*

She lost track of him, then, for, to obey his instructions, on top of all else, the princess was forced to concentrate her remaining will on maintaining her essence. She was uncertain as to how long she could do this, for the intensity of the warlock's spell was becoming more and more difficult to withstand. It would not be long, regardless of her efforts.

Erini wondered whether Darkhorse would find her in time—and whether even *he* now stood a chance against the powers of Shade.

In that part of her that was puppet to the warlock, the final binding was at last completed.

In the chamber, below the watchful eyes of the effigies, a triumphant Shade, hood pulled low over his face, reached forth with those abilities at his command and prepared to at last accept what he felt was his due. The faces of Vraad he had known, most of them clan, others friends or, more often, foes, drifted in and out of his memories. He would have life eternal now, and power to make even those who watched over the Dragonrealm and the other lands, those would-be gods, acknowledge his mastery.

He would have a world to play with. No Vraad had ever had an *entire* world to play with.

Most of all, he would not *die*. The Vraad would not become a shadow of the past.

A presence oh so familiar to him forced the sorcerer from his dreams. He felt a barrier form about the princess.

"The last false trail has been removed, Shade! Come! Turn around and greet your old friend! Have you no words for Darkhorse—words that I may have them etch upon your crypt?"

The hooded warlock turned slowly toward his ancient adversary, his friend of old. "You took long enough getting here."

Darkhorse stepped back anxiously, but not because he was frightened by the Vraad's confident words. Of course, Shade had known the shadow steed would be coming. He would have expected nothing else. No, what disturbed Darkhorse was something that Shade from his angle, could not see—and, as a matter of fact, neither could the stallion.

Nothing met his gaze from beneath the deep hood save a blur that *might* have been a face.

XXII

The Dragon King Silver hissed bitterly as he watched Talak fend off another assault. Somehow, the crippled vermin that fancied himself a ruler had overcome all obstacles placed before him, save the loss of much of his army. The drake lord glanced briefly to his right, where his human agent stood surveying the same scene with emotions that mirrored the Dragon King's own. He had no idea why he was letting the creature Quorin live, save that he had a desire to prove to him, to prove to *all* of them, that he would take Talak if it cost every possible weapon and life at his command.

Shade was next. The alliance had been a fallacy, one the drake lord had thought he needed during a desperate moment and one that neither had followed from the first. The Silver Dragon wondered if the warlock knew yet that his curse had not been lifted. That had been obvious to him, but the arrogant warm-blood had been certain he was whole once more. The drake laughed, making those around him eye him discreetly while they tried to discern what it was their master found amusing at a time such as this.

Shade had taken his information from the mind of the sorcerer Drayfitt, knowing that the elderly spellcaster had studied the warlock's book thoroughly. Unfortunately for Shade, Drayfitt had never seen some of the final notes. Though the drake lord had had to wait until the sorcerer's translations of the other pages were passed on to him, that wait had been worthwhile. They had provided the dragon king with the basis of translating the remaining sheets, which were where he had successfully guessed the most valuable information had been written down. The pages contained clues to the foundation of Vraad sorcery and, by sheer coincidence, integral comments that the warlock had written about his original theories. Somewhere along the way, those notes had been forgotten by Shade. The Dragon King had ensured that they would remain forgotten until *he* could find some use for them.

Yes, Shade would be next . . . if there was anything left of him for the drakes to kill.

The Dragon King straightened and gave a signal to one of his dukes, a warrior whose clutch he himself had fathered. Most of those around him were his offspring, though none bore the markings of succession. They could never be heirs. All they could be were warriors who gave their lives for him—as they might do now.

The signal was what the main host had waited for. The Silver Dragon King knew what defenses were weakest now. He would throw everything he had at them. He had wanted Talak in one piece. A prize. Now, the drake lord did not care if one stone remained standing, even if it took the last of his force.

One of his offspring had argued that such an assault was madness, that it would only cost lives. His carcass was even now being digested by the Dragon King's riding beast. No one else had dared speak out and no one else would ever dare hint that he was an incompetent ruler, that he had only thrived in the shadow of his more powerful brother, the Dragon Gold.

No one else would dare call him a coward.

There was no reasoning behind the last, but none was needed. A Dragon King was answerable to no one save himself.

They moved on Talak.

A blur.

The passage through the barriers between the Void and reality of the Dragonrealm had *not* reversed the spell Shade had unleashed. It had, evidently, altered it in such a way that there was no telling what would happen next. The period of sanity had been little more than a time of dormancy while the next phase of the warlock's "disease" built up. From his manner, Darkhorse knew that his companion of old did not even realize what had happened. Shade still believed he was back to where he had started, that he was mortal, but whole.

What would this new spell do to him, then?

Erini, locked frozen in the final stage of Shade's gambit, seemed to fade just a bit. Darkhorse turned his gaze back and forth, his fear for Erini, but his fury for the warlock. The female had little time remaining to her. Darkhorse's quick action had bought her a delay, but how long that delay would be was questionable. He was forced to expend energy at a growing rate merely to keep the forces gathered within her in check. The ghostly steed had great doubts as to his ability to face Shade and still maintain that balance. He knew that, by rights, his first and foremost duty was to stop Shade at all costs . . . but that cost would include his benefactress.

Barely more than two or three breaths had passed since his arrival. Seeking to borrow time, he slowly replied to the warlock's initial statement, "You expected me."

"There was nothing planned that did not foresee your eventual success at tracking me down," the faceless figure returned. Shade seemed entirely too much at ease. "Almost everything I have done was merely to maintain your curiosity and stubbornness until our final meeting."

That caused Darkhorse to laugh. "There are few with the audacity to seek an audience with me—and you are foremost among them, my former friend and current nemesis!"

"That's because I have nothing more to fear from you, eternal—*Eternal!*" Shade might have smiled; it was truly impossible to say. Watching him, Darkhorse actually pitied the warlock. To have come so close to escaping his endless curse . . . "I am one with you now, Child of the Void! I am *immortal*. I have succeeded *at last*."

"Not yet, Vraad. The key is in the lock, but it has not yet turned."

Shade said nothing, but Darkhorse suddenly became certain that the warlock *did* wear a smile.

A bitter-tasting wind swept through the chamber, so swiftly birthed that it was near tornado proportions before Darkhorse could even acknowledge its existence. If Shade had created it to destroy him, it was a feeble attempt. Formed in a place between chaos and order, such a wind was little more than a breeze to him and, protected by the shadow steed's power, it did not even touch the helpless Erini.

What it *was* doing, however, was tearing the chamber—even the *mountain* under which the cavern lay—to fragments that flew madly into the air, colliding with one another and flying off into a darkness that was not night. Darkhorse found his footing growing unstable and his bond with Erini being stretched to its utmost. It was too late to stop whatever spell Shade—and it could only be the warlock's doing—had cast. The eternal could only shield himself and the princess and wait for the storm to pass. If it would.

As the last of the cavern walls tore free from the earth and vanished, a new land formed around the three. A land that seemed out of sync with reality. Its colors were haphazard, clashing, and the landscape was twisted and dying. The sky was an odd shade of green, much like mold or something dead left too long to decay on its own.

Throughout all of this, Shade stood where he was, seemingly passive. As the wind died down, to be replaced by a stale, sulfurous stench, the warlock spoke one word ever so softly. In the still of this ugly, decrepit land, he might have been shouting, for Darkhorse heard that word all too clearly.

"Nimth."

A single word that spoke volumes. It told Darkhorse where he was. It told him what sort of power Shade must have had to break a barrier that had remained unbroken since the Vraads' escape from their tortured world, Nimth. It told him something of Shade that he had failed to see upon his arrival.

The warlock had moved more quickly than the eternal had guessed. He had *already* claimed his due from the princess by the time Darkhorse had thrown up the protective shield around her.

Darkhorse had *failed*.

"I restore the balance," Shade abruptly whispered. Again, his voice carried as if he had shouted with all his might.

They were once more in the cavernous chamber in which the warlock had performed his experiment. This time, the transfer was immediate. Shade evidently assumed that there was no reason for further theatrics.

The message behind the sudden return to the Dragonrealm was not lost upon the shadow steed. Shade was telling him through actions that there were deeds within his power that stretched even beyond the laws of nature, beyond the rule of reality.

In the midst of mulling over those thoughts—a period which the warlock was apparently magnanimously willing to grant to his ancient comrade—one realization raised itself above all else and made the huge stallion laugh mockingly.

Shade, who would not have been able to appreciate the humor had he understood what it was that Darkhorse laughed at, lost his calm demeanor. Though his expression was lost to

all but himself, his change in stance was message enough.
Darkhorse quieted, knowing he had touched the greatest weakness of his adversary and knowing that his chances of capitaliz-
ing on that weakness were minimal at best. Better to try and
create a friendly peace between the Silver Dragon and King
Melicard.

Tiny whips of controlled energy darted from the spellcaster's
arms and struck the stallion like a thousand accurate shafts
released by master archers. With each blow, Darkhorse felt a
little of his essence fade. He repelled what he could, sending a
few back at their creator, but there were too many and they
continued to come. There was one certain way he knew that
would rid him of the deadly rain, but it would require releasing
Erini to her fate and Darkhorse refused to do that. It did not
escape him that his death would be followed almost immediately by her own, regardless. Only an ever-increasing output of
his own power kept her from being scattered throughout all.
Soon, he would have none left to defend and heal himself.

The last of the wriggling missiles faded before they touched
the shadow steed. Shade seemed to regain control of himself.
His tone was near apologetic. "I was trying to show you what I
am capable of, Darkhorse. I am beyond even you now. It
would be pointless to pursue your death—and it would be *your*
death, not mine."

"You have only succeeded in revealing to me how much I
dare not allow you to escape me."

"Your efforts go beyond the point of futility now. I could
exile you to a place that would make the Void seem a paradise.
I could compact you into a tiny sphere and drop you into the
deepest sea." Shade's voice was almost pleading, as if he truly
did not want to continue this confrontation. "I could do so
much more, but there is no point to it, anymore. I'm willing to
forget our past differences."

Darkhorse met his threats and condescending words with
disdain. "I think it might be a bit difficult to forget our past
differences, considering how they have affected so many. Exile
me and I will find my way back. Seal me up and I will outlive
my prison. *Destroy* me . . . and you will defeat yourself." The
stallion kicked at the floor. "Destroy me and condemn yourself
to your fate, to your selfmade curse."

The warlock straightened, the tension within him visibly
mounting. After so many failures, there still remained anxie-

ties. Had he seen his visage or lack of it . . . "I am free of my past errors. I am whole."

One of the statues, the one nearest to the faceless spellcaster, collapsed. Darkhorse felt a shrill cry that coursed through his mind as that which had lived within perished. The others quivered in sudden anxiety. The floor of the chamber slowly developed cracks.

Darkhorse knew what was happening, though he doubted the other did. "Listen to me—"

Too late. His adversary was beyond listening. Any hope of a peaceful accord between them had been shattered and Darkhorse knew that it was his own fault as well as Shade's.

His mind already a sea of confusion and turmoil, Shade saw the destruction around him as an attack and the shadow steed's words as a ploy to gain time. A hint of sadness touched him. *That Darkhorse would act so!* That there might be another cause did not occur to him. He, after all, was himself again— and the warlock was not about to give up so quickly what he had sought for so long. Even if it meant killing the one closest to him.

The air around Darkhorse grew oppressively thick. So thick, in fact, that it began to squeeze him. Had he been an actual horse, he would have been crushed in the first seconds. Instead, the eternal found himself being compressed smaller and smaller. The warlock was making good his threat. If Darkhorse failed to resist, Shade would reduce him to the size of a pebble and throw him somewhere where no one would be likely to find him. The hooded spellcaster might even choose to keep him as a memento.

He resisted instantly, of course, but with only a portion of the strength normally available to him. Erini's life was demanding almost as much of his energy as his own rescue. It took him far too much time to finally free himself. The next assault took him even before the last vestiges of the first had faded away. A tear in reality sought to draw him inside, pulling at his form with such persistence that he almost succumbed before he was able to fashion a defense. Darkhorse sealed the rip and let it vanish. It lasted long enough, however, to give him a glimpse of where Shade had intended on sending him.

The festering sore that the Vraads had once called home. Nimth.

He had not wanted to do it this way, but Shade was leaving

him no options. Unless Darkhorse struck back with the one weapon he knew would be effective, the warlock would take him with his next attack—and success or not, this ploy would likely drive the final wedge between them.

The unsavory deed was done even as Darkhorse pictured it. Shade, sensing something materializing before him, struck at its heart. His target shattered into dozens of glittering fragments, which immediately expanded into exact copies of the original. As one, they focused on their attacker, who could not help but look up at them. Darkhorse, watching, could not help but flinch.

Shade stared, possibly openmouthed, at repetition after repetition of his own blurred, featureless visage. They were everywhere and each told him the one thing he could not face. The truth of his condition.

He screamed denial even as his pent-up power caused each mirror to melt like a single snowflake on a raging campfire. Darkhorse himself was buffeted to the ground by the wild forces unleashed. He barely maintained his bond with Erini. Other than the energy utilized to keep her from dissipating like a wisp of smoke, the shadow steed had little more to call upon. What remained he needed just to survive this latest and most horrid onslaught. It was all he could do just to keep his mind coherent.

"Nonononononononononooooo!" Shade was screaming. Rocking back and forth, he *clawed* at his own face, trying to remove what could not be removed. Portions of the chamber ceiling collapsed, but none so much as struck within two yards of the warlock. Somehow, his own defenses were still intact.

He cannot contain the power and the more he releases, the more destruction! It was worse than Darkhorse had feared. Vraad sorcery had destroyed one world already. It tore at the laws of nature rather than worked with them. As with the sorcery of the Dragonrealm, it was ofttimes an almost unconscious, automatic thing and the more it was used, the more chaos it caused. Shade, trapped in his own horror, was allowing it to run rampant. Darkhorse wondered if there might have been *some* other way.

The warlock was on his knees and facing the ground, unmindful of what havoc he was unleashing. Darkhorse had wondered what this new spell would do; the answer seemed to be *create more destruction*. It was as if the intensity of the original curse had been doubled in scope.

"Shade!" he called out, his voice booming above all else. "You must listen to me! A part of you must know the chaos you have invited into this world! I know from the past few days that there is, within you, a desire to end this madness peacefully! If you would hear me—"

Surprisingly, the warlock *did* look up. There was a tenseness in his movements. He had heard Darkhorse's voice, but not the shadow steed's warning. A fierce presence rose about the warlock as his tortured mind mixed facts and suppositions until they no longer had any true meaning. From that came one final, insane conclusion.

"*You!*" Shade rose, all fury. His mind, the stallion noted, was shifting from one extreme emotion to another—and with this particular emotion, he needed a focal point. "You *did* this to me!"

It would have been one of the most absurd things that Darkhorse had ever heard, save that he could have predicted it would be so. Shade could not accept that the grand spell had failed again or that he had not even recovered from the first attempt. He needed a scapegoat in order to preserve what little remained of his sanity—if there *was* anything left. The warlock needed something to lash out at.

What he does next could level settled areas, the eternal realized. *And being in the Tybers, one of those places might be Talak!* How ironic it would be if the Dragon King captured Melicard's kingdom, only to have it sink beneath the earth or simply cease to be.

That image in mind, Darkhorse vanished—

—and reentered the world in the desolate, blistering cold of the Northern Wastes.

Before him, almost as if he had known where the shadow steed had intended fleeing, was Shade. Despite the wind, his cloak remained still, covering him like a shroud. Darkhorse had wondered what death would look like when it finally claimed him. He now knew. There would be no escaping Shade, then. Whatever it took, the warlock would track him down, laying waste to whatever happened to cross his path in the meantime. Perhaps, letting the axe fall here would at least save the Dragonrealm, thought Darkhorse somewhat fatalistically, though he suspected that the tortured figure before him would not completely spend his madness here.

"For our friendship," the spectral figure said, his calm words more chilling than his angered ones, "I would have left you in peace. I would have. Then, you did *this* to me! Now, I have only—"

"Shade, if you would just listen to me!"

"—one question to ask of you before I treat you as you've chosen to treat me. Why do it? Tell me that."

There was no correct response and Darkhorse knew that. The best he could do was give no answer at all. Shade's twisted thought had condemned him already.

"Goodbye, then, my comrade of old."

Despite the distance now separating them, Darkhorse still maintained the shell protecting the helpless Erini, although it sapped almost all of what remained of his strength. He prepared himself now for the worst. Death or, at the very least, the absence of life. Having never died, he could not say what awaited him, if anything. Certainly, he did not fall within the realms of human afterlife.

Scattered thoughts touched him. Curiosity concerning the eventual fate of Talak. Questions as to where the Bedlams had gone. He wondered what their children would grow up to be like. Most of all, Darkhorse wondered what fate awaited the world of the Dragonrealm, with or without the interference and chaos created by its new, blur-visaged demigod.

He would protect Erini with the last vestiges of his power. When Shade finally took him, the shadow steed would give his essence to her. Perhaps it would buy her time enough for Cabe to find her. Likely not.

I have erred every step of the way, Darkhorse decided. *Most of all, I erred in thinking of this one as still human—when all he truly was, was a Vraad!*

Shade moved, but slowly, as if unwell. Darkhorse saw little of consequence in that at the moment, instead concerned with bracing himself against what would surely be the warlock's final blow. His own nature would protect him briefly, but hardly long enough to matter. He only hoped, a foolish hope, that the warlock would feel regret afterward. It might stave off some of the coming devastation.

If only there was some way to take from the warlock the powers he had usurped . . .

There *was*. There *WAS*.

The answer came to him too late. Something darted around Darkhorse like a mad horsefly, something that grew as it circled him. He tried fending it off, but his power was too weak. It expanded as it moved, rapidly wrapping him within a shell whose very presence chilled his form, froze lifelessly his very essence. Given time, it would make of him a monument to his own futility. Given time, there would be nothing more than a shell shaped like a huge, writhing steed.

Given a little more time, there would not even be that.

Darkhorse struggled to maintain his senses. The key was his. He had controlled it all this time, but his own foolish sense of "noble sacrifice" had left him blind to the potential before him. Now, it might be too late.

Entangled in the warlock's death trap, Darkhorse tumbled into the snow and ice. The link with Erini, the one that still kept her alive, was his only chance. Summoning up his will and foregoing his own defense, he called out to her in his mind. *Erini!*

If he was wrong, it hardly mattered. Neither he nor she had more than a few minutes left either way.

A dim shadow fell over him. Through partially obscured vision, he saw a spectral Shade loom over him, likely come to gloat over his throes. To the eternal's confusion, the hooded figure sighed and reached out to touch his foe on the head. Briefly, Darkhorse entertained the thought of absorbing his adversary and trapping him within the emptiness that was his inner self, but he knew that the power of Shade was more than capable of withstanding even that. True enough, the Vraad's hand pulsated with energy.

The fiendish thing—did it live?—had sealed his mouth and Darkhorse found himself unable to form another. He lay there, silent and nearly mummified, as the warlock continued to move his hand along the shadow steed's neck and to his head.

For the first time, he felt the probe of Shade's mind. It was the final defeat. Darkhorse no longer even had the will with which to combat his longtime nemesis and companion.

"Soooo, that's why you fell so easily," the shadow lurking above him whispered. He had discovered the stallion's refusal to abandon Erini. Darkhorse shook, but was no longer able to do anything else . . . unless . . .

The shadow steed opened his mind completely and let his

captor see *everything*, but, most especially, what he knew about Shade's *condition*.

The warlock shook and pulled his hand away as if touching something unclean. He remained stooped over his defeated adversary for some time, muttering things that Darkhorse could not make out save that Shade seemed to be arguing with *himself* adamantly. Finally, however, he came to some fateful decision and wrapped himself in his cloak, staring at the point somewhere beyond Darkhorse's limited range of vision.

"I'll need the girl again," he whispered to himself as he rose to a standing position. With an almost careless dismissal of the muffled figure at his feet, Shade stepped over Darkhorse and vanished into the tundra.

The eternal cursed himself. Of course Shade's first thought would be to recapture Erini! Darkhorse had let him see what was happening: instead of becoming a near-perfect demigod, the warlock was threatened with an existence even less real than in his prior incarnations. As powerful as he had become, Shade was still at the mercy of his self-made curse. The shadow steed had hoped that, knowing this, Shade might come to his senses.

Forgive me, Erini! Oddly, Darkhorse's error gave him the glimmer of hope. He had been abandoned and the deadly spell that had almost ended his existence had stopped, apparently dormant without its master's guidance. Given time, he would be able to free himself.

At that moment, he felt the link between himself and the princess break. Shade had reclaimed her for his dire purposes. *A dangerous error on your part, my dear, deadly friend!*

No longer forced to divide his strength between his own defense and the protection of the fading Erini, the eternal's might returned much more rapidly. He had still nearly burned himself out, but now he had at least the ghost of an opportunity. Shade would be vulnerable now, mentally if not magically, and Darkhorse was already devising a way to increase that vulnerability. He no longer felt much remorse about what he plotted to do; Shade's apparent denial of his own condition had made it clear that the spellcaster was beyond aid. It was either defeat Shade or watch as the Dragonrealm and the rest of this world suffered the same fate as long-forgotten Nimth.

A storm was brewing, one that threatened to become a fullscale blizzard. There was a touch of sorcery about it and

Darkhorse knew then that there was no time to waste. Shade had already begun whatever new experiment he planned. If there was a time to catch him with his guard down, it was before the plan reached fruition. The shadow steed had failed at that once. This time, though, the tale would end differently.

Darkhorse rose quickly, tearing and snapping the bonds that had ensnared him. Where they had sought to leech from him, he now returned the favor, causing them to dissipate in mere seconds. Things of sorcery, they left no remains. The only regrets Darkhorse had was the vile taste of them; they were filled with the taint of Vraad sorcery.

In the distance, he witnessed a vast aurora and knew immediately that there was where he needed to go. There, he would finally have Shade where he wanted him.

A portal offered too much risk. Darkhorse raced across the empty land, feeling somewhat at sympathy with it for all it had been through. Once, there had been trees here, life. Now, nothing but emptiness. The land looked much the way the eternal felt.

It was, he thought, a fitting place for what would be coming next.

Erini was the first to come within sight. She stood much the way she had in the chamber, save that her eyes were open and she seemed to be saying something. Darkhorse slowed. Something seemed wrong. When a rise brought Shade into view, the shadow steed *knew* that the scene before him was not as it should have been, that something was amiss.

The warlock was seated before his captive, his head low and his arms outstretched as if *he* were the one giving of himself.

Darkhorse sped across the remaining tundra and began casting his first—and likely last—spell. Entranced as he seemed to be, Shade would not notice until it struck. From the corner of his eyes, Darkhorse noted Erini's gaze turning toward him. Her mouth opened as if she intended to say something, but the ebony stallion ignored her. For the moment, it was only Shade that mattered.

When the attack caught him unaware, the shadow steed's first angry thought was how the warlock had tricked him again, laying some trap that he *knew* Darkhorse would be unable to resist. Then, as the world turned upside-down, he realized that it was not his ancient adversary who had caught him by surprise, but *Erini*. Erini had attacked *him*, as if she actually wanted her captor's spell completed.

Before he could rise and demand explanations, Shade's voice suddenly rose above the howling wind. "No, princess. It's all right. He doesn't understand—and, besides, it's taking its own course now. He won't be able to touch me; no one will."

"I can only try!" Darkhorse roared, standing. The snow fell from his huge form as if glad to abandon his fearsome presence. "Stand away, Erini! You shall be compelled no further!"

"Darkhorse!"

He ignored her shout, supposing her to be under the warlock's influence. "The female is under my protection, Shade! You will release her will and face me!"

Shade lifted his head toward Darkhorse. It was pale and drawn, but *distinct*. The stallion's first thought was that he had failed *again*. Cursing, he kicked at the snow and readied himself to perish fighting. The warlock, however, rose on surprisingly unsteady feet and shook his head at the leviathan ready to charge him.

"I'll face you, Darkhorse, but only to say goodbye."

"You will not leave me behind again!"

Shade smiled without malice. His face was as pale as the snow—or *was* that the snow Darkhorse saw? The warlock stepped toward him, leaving no trail. His movements were slow and he seemed to *ripple* with the wind. The warlock paused just out of arm's length from his adversary.

"You can't follow me where I'm going."

Darkhorse lashed out with his hooves, hoping to take Shade by surprise with a physical attack. To his dismay, he struck only air. Behind him, the massive stallion heard Erini gasp.

Wrapped in his cloak, the warlock stepped back so that he now faced both Darkhorse and Erini. Turning to the latter, he said politely, "You have what you wanted in return, sorceress. May it please you."

Erini would not respond, but her face grew almost as deathlike as the warlock's. She suddenly shook her head and sat in the snow, shivering from something other than the cold. The princess buried her face in her hands.

"What we gain is never quite what we originally wanted, is it, Darkhorse?" It was impossible to deny anymore; Shade *was* little more than a ghost in form, a memory more than a man.

"What have you done now, warlock? What have you demanded of Erini that leaves her in such pain?"

"She cries at the vast extent of her reward, Darkhorse. I leave that for her to explain. As for me, I have taken the only path left to me. A *final* path, you might say."

"Final—!" Darkhorse probed the figure before him—and found nothing but a dying emanation of power. Nothing physical stood there; what remained was of magic. Magic that was fleeing even now to where it belonged. The farthest stretches of the Dragonrealm and a crippled, tortured place called Nimth.

Shade had made Erini *reverse* his earlier spell, drawing forth not only his newly accumulated powers, but those forces within him that had originally cursed him to what had once seemed an endless chain of phantom incarnations, personalities that existed, but did not truly *live*.

Sorcery was all that truly remained of the original spellcaster and, when the last of it had dissipated, there would be nothing. No Shade. Not even the ever-present cloak. *All* of him was magic, nothing more.

"All that power, all that glory, was not worth facing—facing?—a continuation of that damned, horrible mockery of immortality, of life." There was little left of the warlock now. He looked like a reflection in a piece of glass, wavering in the wind. The storm that had threatened seemed to be dying with the man who had likely been its cause, but the wind, oddly, was picking up in intensity.

Or *was* that so odd? Darkhorse gaze locked with Shade's. The warlock smiled again and nodded ever so slightly.

"I had another name, once," he started, as if seeking to take both of their minds off of the truth. "It was . . ."

Words and warlock drifted away with the wind.

His name. He wanted to say his name to me. The black steed stared at the place where his adversary, his other half, had last stood. There were no tracks, of course. The last tracks were those where Shade had stood and given himself to Erini. Where he had finally, absolutely, ended his curse in the only way left to him.

"Darkhorse?"

Erini. He had forgotten her presence.

"I will never know love as you do, princess," he rumbled without removing his gaze from Shade's last stand. "But I know that I have lost one who could be considered a brother to me despite the evils he caused.''

The sorceress was silent. Darkhorse, urged by a feeling he barely understood, trotted forward and kicked snow across the warlock's remaining tracks, not pausing until they were buried. Gruffly, he turned to his companion. For the first time, the stallion seemed to see her. Though her abilities protected her from the elements, she had suffered as few others had. Twice Shade had used her, forced her to touch something of a world that was little more than a sick parody of this one. He hoped she would recover once they returned to—

His ice-blue eyes widened as he recalled what was occurring in their absence. ''Talak! Lords of the Dead, Erini! You should have said something!''

The human was drawn and weaker than he would have suspected, considering the power she had absorbed. Darkhorse sensed also a loss to the aura, the presence, about her. She was worn to the bone, too, but none of that was why she now sat in the snow, gazing at the emptiness without truly seeing it.

''There's no need to hurry,'' she stated quietly, finally responding to his words.

''No need to hurry? With Talak under siege by the drakes?'' Had her ordeal at last overtaken her mind, too?

''Shade said that I had been rewarded.'' Erini laughed bitterly. ''It seemed so perfect. They didn't deserve to survive. I keep telling myself that they would have killed Melicard and all the rest if I hadn't agreed.'' Her voice caught. ''Yet, for some unfathomable reason, I can't help crying at the suffering they must have gone through, the shock when they realized what was happening.''

''You make no sense, mortal!'' She did, but Darkhorse had trouble believing what he was imagining.

She looked up, so pale he almost expected her to dissipate in the wind as Shade had done. ''I want nothing to do with sorcery, Darkhorse. It seemed the best way to rid us of them, but . . . so many lives!''

''The drake host?'' he finally asked with some misgivings.

She nodded, putting her head in her hands again. ''All of them. Swallowed up without damage to anything or anyone else—save Mal Quorin, I suppose. I even pity him, if you can believe it. Shade killed them all with my permission.

Now it was Darkhorse who could say nothing. He wondered

at the carnage they would see when they returned. In some ways, it had been necessary, but *the scope of what the warlock had been capable of . . .*

Erini looked up again, tears for her enemies in her eyes. "Take me back to Talak, Darkhorse. I—I can't do it myself. I might—might appear in the middle of—I want Melicard!"

The eternal let her cry some of the pain away as he slowly formed a sphere around them. A variation on the portal, it would allow them to travel without forcing the princess to act herself. When they arrived in Talak, he would see to speaking to Melicard privately about her immediate needs.

He welcomed her sorrow and her need for his aid. Her trials would give him purpose and allow him another chance to learn. Some day, he might yet understand the mortal creatures he had chosen to make his own. Some day, he might understand their path through life and, because of that, the definition of life itself. Perhaps then, the shadow steed might one day come to understand what could have created the man who had become known in legend and face as simply Shade.

Perhaps then, he might also make sense of the continuous, wrenching feeling that had begun within him when he realized that the warlock had surrendered his life.

XXIII

Cabe Bedlam found the eternal overlooking the northern lands from one of the palace balconies. A vast, well-cultivated field, half wheat and half oat, covered nearly every inch of the level plain before them. Upon first glance, there seemed nothing out of the ordinary, aside from the fact that this was hardly the time of year for such a mature crop. What made the sight stunning, however, was the fact that it was out there where the army of the Dragon King had once stood. It was out there that settlements, wooded areas, and roads had existed prior to this day.

It was there that the drake host had perished down to the least of the minor drakes.

"I'll never forget the sight," Cabe said quietly, eyes fixed on the innocent-looking field. "We had barely arrived here ourselves, and then only thanks to the Dragon King Green, who arrived at the Manor and broke the spell Shade had cast over us." He had already relayed that story earlier, telling how, in response to word from the Lady Bedlam, the master of Dagora Forest had gained entrance and found the two, victims of Shade's attempt to kidnap their son Aurim. Neither the Bedlams nor their Dragon King ally, Green, could explain why the warlock had abandoned his plan after successfully dealing with the only two standing in his way.

Darkhorse thought he knew, but did not say so to Cabe. It would only make what had happened to the ancient warlock more difficult to accept.

Cabe moved on to the shocking fate that had befallen the charging drakes. "Even with our sorcery, we were only keeping them in check. Some of their number got through from time to time and wreaked havoc until each was killed or driven off. Some of their spells succeeded as well." The sorcerer shivered, remembering some of the more dire ones. "Word reached us at one point that the expedition to the Hell Plains *had* turned around, apparently because of some message etched into the ground by a spell of Drayfitt's just before his death——" Cabe did not notice Darkhorse flinch. *That* explained the final words he had not heard, the ones the elderly sorcerer had spoken before expiring! To the end, Drayfitt had served Talak with the utmost efficiency. "Though the reinforcements were on their way, the fighting was becoming so fierce that we suspected the drakes would be through Talak's defenses before they arrived. It was just after that when the ground to the north began to split *open.*"

What had happened next had driven even stone-hearted Melicard to pity the deaths of his enemies. Great gaps and ravines opened in the earth, but only in and around the moving host. Some estimated that nearly half of the drakes perished in the first minute, as the warriors tried frantically and uselessly to control the sudden panic of their lesser cousins. Warriors and mounts fell screaming into the gaps, which closed up instantly, only to be replaced by others. Many of those who managed to find stable footing during the first onslaught fell easy prey when that ground beneath *them* suddenly yawned wide.

"Did none of them fly away?"

"Seems logical, doesn't it?" Cabe wore a grim smile. "They tried it. The sky over the area was literally filled with them—until the winds began to buffet them *back* to the earth!"

"Winds?"

"Winds followed by lightning followed by a downpour that would have crushed in the roof of the palace had the storms touched the city—which they did not with amazing accuracy! Everything was confined to the area where Silver's horde was trapped."

Quakes, wind, lightning, and rain. Earth, air, fire, and water. Darkhorse had to admire Shade's work. *How extravagantly traditional.*

No one had seen the Dragon King himself perish nor, for that matter, Mal Quorin's fate, either. It was safe to assume, however, that they had fallen with the rest. The entire horrible sight had lasted perhaps five minutes. When the last drake had perished, the wounds in the earth healed themselves and the storms dwindled to nothing. No one could really say when exactly the field had risen up, though everyone swore it was there only moments later.

Voices within informed him that the one he had been waiting for had finally recovered enough to join the rest. Darkhorse excused himself from Cabe.

"I'll not forget the good he did, Darkhorse," Cabe called after him.

"Do not forget the evil, either." He trotted into the vast room.

Her face lit up as she noticed him.

"Princess Erini!" He dipped his head in her honor. "Glad I am to see you better! Cherish this woman, King Melicard, for there are few as worthy as she!"

The king had one arm securely wrapped around his betrothed. The love he bore for her was spread equally across *both* sides of his face. The elfwood arm, the one that held Erini, looked as supple and lifelike as the real thing.

It is the spirit of the wearer that makes of the elfwood what it will be. With love comes life, it seems!

"Darkhorse." Erini separated herself from Melicard, walked

up to the shadow steed, and hugged him by the neck. Off to the side, the Lady Bedlam smiled sourly. "Thank you for giving me my life again!" the princess added.

"It is I who should thank you! Are you truly better?"

"It will take me some time to learn not to shiver each time my eyes turn north and see the field."

Darkhorse laughed. "Think of the field as the first heralds of peace! What Shade did was horrendous, but did not cowardly Silver bring it upon himself?"

"I suppose." The princess looked down, as if remembering. Then, she looked back up, staring into his glittering eyes. "What happens to you now?"

The shadow steed felt as if all eyes in the room were now on him. "I shall roam the Dragonrealm as I always have! For Darkhorse, there is no grand scheme, no destiny! I shall roam and see what there is to see! I—"

It was the Lady Bedlam who spoke the words that he would not. "You shall search the lands to see if, somehow, *he* survived, won't you?"

The room grew silent as he stared first at her and then at Erini. She looked puzzled, having seen Shade freely end his tortured existence. Slowly, he nodded. "Yes, I will search the Dragonrealm for him. There must be *no* doubt. If he *has* survived, he may need help." Darkhorse absently pawed at the floor, leaving scars. "He may also need *destroying* again."

The ebony stallion stepped back from the mortal creatures around him. "It is past the time for me to leave! I am glad you are all well and that most of us have lived to see this peace." He looked specifically at Melicard and the Dragon King Green. There was hope there for some sort of compromise, a lessening of Talak's zeal toward those drakes who sought peace between the races. Erini caught his stare and looked at her betrothed, who nodded noncommittedly. "I now bid you farewell!"

"Come back to Talak when you wish," the princess called.

Darkhorse nodded to her and also to Cabe, who had rejoined his mate. He reared, summoning a portal.

"Come to the Manor sometime," Gwen said, startling both Cabe and the eternal. "You must meet the children. They would love you."

The shadow steed laughed cheerfully, the echoes resounding

through the palace. "This, then, is truly a day of miracles! I shall take you up on that offer soon, Lady Bedlam. Ha!"

He entered the portal still laughing, his destination—and his destiny—unknown even to him.